Praise for the Wild Wicked Highlanders

"High stakes, spirited characters, and off-the-charts chemistry keep the pages turning as Enoch balances humor, heat, and tension. This is Highland romance done right."
—*Publishers Weekly* starred review
on *Scot Under the Covers*

"Enoch delivers another fresh and fun Highlander/English romance with notes of scandal, secrets, cunning escapades, and off-the-charts chemistry."
—*Booklist* starred review on *Scot Under the Covers*

"[An] enticing, enchanting ride."
—*The New York Times* on *Scot Under the Covers*

"A charming and enjoyable tale."
—*Romance Junkies* on *Scot Under the Covers*

"Enoch weaves a tale of love and passion with a little humor thrown in."
—*Fresh Fiction* on *It's Getting Scot in Here*

"An entertaining tale of two people overcoming incredible odds to be together."
—*Romance Junkies* on *It's Getting Scot in Here*

Also by
SUZANNE ENOCH

Hit Me with Your Best Scot

SUZANNE ENOCH

St. Martin's Paperbacks

First published in the United States by St. Martin's Paperbacks, an imprint of St. Martin's Publishing Group.

HIT ME WITH YOUR BEST SCOT

For information, address St. Martin's Publishing Group, 120 Broadway, New York, NY 10271.

www.stmartins.com

ISBN: 978-1-250-29642-9

Our books may be purchased in bulk for promotional, educational, or business use. Please contact your local bookseller or the Macmillan Corporate and Premium Sales Department at 1-800-221-7945, ext. 5442, or by email at MacmillanSpecialMarkets@macmillan.com.

Printed in the United States of America

St. Martin's Paperbacks edition 2021

10 9 8 7 6 5 4 3 2 1

Chapter One

"'Twas a rough night."

MACBETH, *MACBETH* ACT II, SCENE III

I'll find my own damned wife, thank ye very much!"

Coll MacTaggert, Viscount Glendarril, shoved aside the curtains and stomped out of the Oswell-MacTaggert box at the Saint Genesius Theatre. She'd done it *again*. This time his mother, Francesca Oswell-MacTaggert, Countess Aldriss, had thrown *two* lasses at him while he was trying to watch a blasted play.

Two damned women and their families to share Lady Aldriss's private box. Since his two younger brothers firstly weren't present and secondly had already found wives, everyone in the entire damned theater had to know that the lasses were there for him.

"Coll." A low voice came from the curtains, and Matthew Harris stepped into the hallway. "Your mother wants to remind you not to repeat what happened on your first night in London."

That would've been the first time she'd flung a female at him. She'd tried to present him with a pretty wrapped bow of a lass whose family had already agreed to a marriage, and he'd fled into the streets rather than sit through *Romeo and Juliet* beside her. If his mother wanted to delve into the details, Miss Amelia-Rose Hyacinth Baxter *had* ended up married to a MacTaggert—just not to him. But his brother Niall loved her, and she him, so he had nothing else to say about that.

"So, Matthew Harris," he drawled. "I've nae seen ye without my sister by yer side for the past . . . what is it, three days since ye nearly ruined yer family's reputation?"

Immediately Matthew took a half step backward, toward the curtains. "We're all friends here, Coll," he said. "Aden said I still had his blessing to marry your sister."

"My brother Aden is about to wed *yer* sister, so I reckon he has reason to be forgiving of yer previous idiocy. And he's in love, so he sees everything covered with flower petals and cherubs."

"I—"

"He may have proclaimed ye fit to wed our wee sister Eloise, but I havenae done so. And I'm the oldest—and the heir to our father. With him still in the Highlands, I speak for the MacTaggerts here in England."

Matthew took another step back toward the relative safety of Lady Aldriss's very fine theater box. "I made a horrible mistake and lost far more money than I could ever afford to repay," he said, lowering his voice still further. "But you know I was flimflammed—and far from the only man to fall into the trap set by Captain Vale."

"Aye. I do know that. I also ken that ye were about to sell yer sister to Vale to keep yerself from ruin. The only thing that prevented ye from having Miranda marry that vulture was my brother. Aden saved ye both; ye didnae have another plan at all."

The younger man's complexion paled, his generally cheery expression evaporating into glumness. "You're correct. I had no idea what to do. I'm very glad Aden was here in London, and that he cared enough for Miranda to save the two of us. He saved the entire Harris family, actually, and I will forever be in his debt."

"Aden's a good sort, once ye drag him out of the shadows," Coll agreed. "And since he loves yer sister and yer sister's a better woman than either of ye likely deserve, she's forgiven ye as well."

"Yes, she has. I'm very grateful."

"I'm nae yer sister."

"I—oh. I take your meaning. I've sworn off gambling of any kind, you know. And I've surrendered my membership to White's, Boodle's, and the Society. There will be no more clubs and no more wagering. I swear it."

"And that makes ye fit to wed *my* wee sister? I'm supposed to believe that ye willnae get into some sort of trouble again and decide ye need to sell off Eloise to set yerself upright?"

"I would not do any such thing," Matthew said adamantly. Behind them, muffled applause sounded from the theater. The younger man shifted again. "We should get back. Your mother—Lady Aldriss—was quite resolved that you shouldn't open yourself to more gossip by leaving her box yet again."

"I ken who my mother is. Right now I'm talking to ye about how ye keep scrambling away like a door mouse every time I walk into the room."

"Coll—Lord Glendarril—you may say anything you wish to me. I'm certain I deserve it. But I am utterly serious when I say that I would never put dear Eloise in any—"

Flashing out his right fist, Coll caught the younger man flush on the nose. Matthew staggered backward, his hands flying to his face. Blood dripped from between his fingers. Before the young Mr. Harris could regain his footing, Coll stepped forward and grabbed him by the cravat to yank him forward.

"I dunnae put much stock into words," he growled, practically lifting Matthew off his feet. "It's easy to beg forgiveness, and it's easy to swear repentance. I dunnae want to hear either of those from ye again. I am going to be watching ye, Matthew Harris. Eloise loves ye, and my mother says ye've a good heart. That is why ye've earned one—*one*—more chance. The next time ye think to make a wager or a purchase or any wee thing ye might nae be able to afford with what ye have in yer pockets, ye think of how yer face feels right now. And then ye think what the rest of ye will feel like when I drag you up to Scotland and feed ye to my hounds. Do ye reckon I'm serious about that?"

"Yes—yes, I do."

He let go, and the lad staggered backward. To his credit, Matthew didn't immediately retreat into the box, and he didn't swing back—though that would have been a mistake the size of a mountain. Few people had ever been able to stand toe-to-toe with Coll MacTaggert, though more than a handful had certainly tried. They had all reckoned that going through him would be the most expedient way to gain a reputation as a man not to be crossed.

Except none had ever made it through him.

"I understand, Coll," Matthew finally rasped out, his tone nasal with his nose pinched closed. He pulled a kerchief from his pocket, wiped off his face and hands, and pressed it against the bruised middle of his face. "You will never have cause to feed me to your hounds. I swear it."

Coll nodded. "See that I dunnae." He turned on his heel.

"But the play?" Matthew pursued. "This is the closing night for *As You Like It*, and you walked out three lines into the first act. And you have . . . guests."

Facing him again, Coll narrowed his eyes. "I dunnae like it, and they arenae *my* guests. I'll nae be ambushed again just because Francesca reckoned I'd nae get up and leave a second time. Ye can tell her she's wrong about that."

"I'll . . . tell her what you said."

Coll turned his back, then faced Matthew again. "And ye tell her I meant that last bit. I'll find my own wife. If I need her help, I'll ask for it. Now go away before ye rile me up again."

With that, he watched his almost-brother-in-law—twice over, with Matthew Harris marrying Eloise and Aden marrying Miranda Harris—scurry back through the heavy curtains. Then, before Francesca could march out and try to drag him back inside by his ear, Coll headed down the curving hallway toward the long set of stairs at the rear of the Saint Genesius Theatre. As he considered it, he should have realized Lady Aldriss had laid a trap for him; she'd agreed to join him for an evening at the theater far too easily, and without any of her usual clever, tricky conversation. His brother Aden could sort through her nonsense and machinations, but subterfuge simply annoyed Coll.

Being frustrated, though, didn't eliminate his problem. He now had twenty-seven days remaining in which to find a wife, all because when he was eleven years old, his parents had written up an agreement that their sons would wed—and that their brides would be English, damn it all—before their youngest, Eloise, married the man of her choosing. And she'd been engaged for two months, now.

Well, he was fucking tired of listening to reason, tired of trying to find common ground with delicate lasses just out of the schoolroom when he was but a month shy of his thirtieth year. He was tired of wondering if one of those hothouse flowers hovering about the ballroom would swoon, should he ask her to dance. Worse, he was tired of trying to figure out which likely-looking young thing would play pretty and agreeable, and then turn into a cold shrew who had no other goal but to wed a title and rule over the dim giant with the thick Scottish brogue.

As he wandered through the mostly empty hallways and staircases of the Saint Genesius, he considered all the lasses to whom he'd already been introduced. Some were pretty enough, a few had their wits about them, and all of them, of course, had been raised to be proper English ladies who could handily oversee a proper household.

Not a one of them, he imagined, had set foot in the Scottish Highlands. Not a one of them would know how to raise good Scots bairns in a wild and rugged land, where peril waited in the deep, still lochs and the silent, brooding forests and the endless rocky hills. God, he missed the Highlands. The idea that he had to wed to please his mother bit at him like a pack of angry badgers. But damn it all, she had hold of the purse strings.

She'd outfoxed her husband, Angus MacTaggert, Earl Aldriss, and kept all of the considerable Oswell fortune in her name and under her control. And before she'd fled the Highlands, she'd made Lord Aldriss sign that paper. That was why Coll had twenty-seven days to find a bride, or Lady Aldriss would cease funding Aldriss Park.

"Excuse me, sir."

He blinked, swinging around as a petite lass dressed like a peasant of a previous century pranced past him. A stout lad by an unadorned door nodded and stepped aside to let her enter, then took up his guard position once more. "What've ye got there?" Coll asked.

"Nothing for the theater guests," the big man replied. "If you wish to pay your respects to the performers, you can wait at the rear of the theater by the stage door until after the performance."

Coll didn't wish to pay his respects to the performers; he'd seen but a minute of the play. What he did want, though, was a place where he could stay out of the rain and think for a damned minute without being plagued by Lady Aldriss or any more of her messengers.

He dug a coin out of his pocket. "What if I've a mind to take a look through that door anyway?"

The man glanced down at Coll's palm. "Then you'd best have more blunt than that. Night before last, I had eleven gentlemen trying to crowd in behind the stage to see Mrs. Jones, and management don't like that. So the price to get through this door is now two quid."

"Mrs. Jones?" Coll repeated, ignoring the rest of the jabbering and the outrageous bribery sum being sought. "Who the devil is Mrs. Jones that it costs two pounds to set my peepers on her?"

With a snort, the big fellow folded his arms over his chest. "Either you take me for a fool, or you're not from around here."

"I dunnae know if ye're a fool or nae, lad, but as ye might have guessed, I'm nae from around here."

"Then Mrs. Persephone Jones is the actress who's broken half the lordlings' hearts here in London. She's onstage now playing Rosalind, so if you go back to your seat, you can take a gander at her yourself."

Generally, Coll wouldn't even have considered paying two quid for a gander at a lass. But when his mother had dragged him and his two younger brothers down from the Highlands, she'd made it clear as glass that she was the one who controlled the purse strings, that all the blunt in their pockets was thanks to her. That made the money in his pockets tonight hers, and he had no qualms about spending it with the idea of avoiding her talons.

Putting the one coin away and pulling out two different ones, he pitched them to the door warden. "I reckon I'll take a gander from behind the stage."

"Suit yourself, then. But be quiet. If you make any noise in the wings, they will throw you out."

Coll doubted any man could throw him out of a place where he was inclined to be. His brothers didn't refer to him as "the mountain" for no reason. He'd reached four inches past six feet a good time ago, and as far as he was concerned, he had the shoulders and strength to match his height. "I'll be a wee church mouse, then."

The guard pulled open the door. "Be quick about it. If you get caught, I will say I've never seen you before. I've no wish to tussle with you, but neither do I want Mr. Huddle sacking me for letting you in here."

For the briefest of moments, Coll felt a pinch of disappointment that he'd avoided yet another fight. Since he'd arrived in London, he'd fallen into one brawl that hadn't been any of his doing, taken one punch from his brother Niall that he'd deserved, and delivered one solitary jab as a lesson that his soon-to-be brother-in-law had best remember for the remainder of his life. These Englishmen used words as their weapons, and while he'd been attempting to adapt, he still didn't like it. At all. A fist was a weapon. Words, as far as he was concerned, were overrated.

He stepped through the door into semi-darkness. Out in the part of the theater meant for the paying public, the floors were carpeted and the walls a clean white, interspersed with dark red curtains and panels of wallpaper that depicted exotic tableaux of the Far East. Through the door, though, the floor was wooden and plain, the walls bare brick, and up above might have been a lair for giant spiders, it was so crisscrossed with rope and wooden beams and planking.

Everything felt too close to him, so much so that he had to fight the instinct to duck his head. Coll took a hard breath, putting one hand against the brick wall to brace himself. Dim and closed-in, but not to the point where he had the immediate urge to escape. Not yet, anyway. For the moment, this was still better than being gawped at by debutantes too scared to chat with him.

Once his eyes adjusted to the dimness, he moved away from the door, toward the dark curtains bordering the stage and the ring and echo of voices beyond them. Around him, an odd mix of brightly garbed actors and plainly dressed supporting folk scurried about—mice in a maze of painted trees, a stuffed horse fitted with a saddle and bridle, a scattering of thrones and plainer chairs, and giant painted screens depicting a storming ocean, a mountainside, the deck of a ship, and more he couldn't make out.

In some ways it reminded him of a bairn's nursery, with bits of wonder tucked into the corners here and there. The folk around him, though, looked serious-faced and earnest, with the exception of the lass standing beneath a row of hanging sandbags, her attention on the lad playing the role of Orlando onstage. *Hmm.* In the play Orlando didn't win Celia, but he seemed to be doing well enough from this vantage point.

Coll studied her for a moment. She was pretty enough, with black hair and a slender waist, but he couldn't see why it should cost a man two pounds to be closer to her than he could get from his seat in Francesca's box.

"Excuse m—ah, another one," muttered a short, thin man with a roll of blue material under his arm and a row of pins stuck along his lapel. "If you're here for Mrs. Jones, stay out of the way. You can wait over there."

He indicated a small square of space that had a good view of the stage, with only the open curtains blocking him from the view of the audience. That would do, and from there he would likely be able to overhear whatever curses his mother might be flinging at him. "Is that Mrs. Jones?" he whispered, indicating the black-haired lass.

"That? No, that's Mary Benson." The fellow glanced over his shoulder toward the door. "You didn't pay good money to see her, I hope. She's nearly too occupied with ogling Baywich over there to remember her own lines."

"My thanks," Coll returned, but the man had already scurried away.

A trio of men dressed as nobles trotted past him as they

exited the stage. "Stand aside, giant," the one called Bay-wich commanded, his voice lilting and imperious.

Coll ignored it, and they went around him. Half a hundred Sassenachs had referred to him as a giant over the past eight weeks. Aye, he towered over most people and he had done so since somewhere just short of his sixteenth birthday. So the wee Englishmen could have their opinions; he didn't give a damn.

Instead, he tried to reposition himself to see the two lasses arguing onstage, only to be jostled aside again by a quartet of men dragging a forest of potted trees forward, just out of sight of the audience. The foliage looked a bit tame to be the forest of Arden, but they might suffice if the light was dim enough.

A round of applause welled up beyond the curtains, and a heartbeat or two later, a lass pushed through the trees and nearly crashed into him. "Romeo, you seem to be in the wrong play," she quipped with a quick grin that lit her blue eyes before she hurried into an alcove, two women and an armload of costumes hot on her heels.

For a good second or two, he felt like he'd been caught in a gust of wind, bandied about and left unsteady on his feet. Coll took a breath. It was no doubt the way he'd been stuffed into a small corner with crazed Sassenachs tramping around him. He and small spaces had been enemies for as far back as he could remember. That had to be it, because no wee woman could topple him, and not with one damned sentence, clever though it might have been.

He turned to get another look at her, but she'd disappeared into the tangle of scenery and props. Romeo. *Ha.* He had much more in common with Henry the Fifth than the empty-headed boy who'd killed himself over a woman. Henry, at least, knew how to fight a battle.

Still, she seemed to have meant it as a compliment.

Still searching, he finally caught another glimpse of her over a half screen, as one of the other lasses pulled the gown off her while the second one fluffed out a white men's shirt for her to pull on. All he could see was her head, topped by an intricate knot of straight brown hair and a bit of neck and the top of her shoulders, but he was fairly certain she was more or less naked behind that woven cane screen.

"Look away, Romeo," she said with a chuckle as their eyes met again. "I'm Rosalind, not Juliet."

"Aye? Well, I'm nae Romeo," he retorted, and kept staring.

A half dozen people immediately shushed him, and he snapped his jaw closed again. The same quartet of men then walked past him onto the stage to squawk out their lines for the next scene. *As You Like It* had never been one of his favorite plays, probably because he could never believe that any man—much less one who claimed to be in love with a lass—wouldn't know when he was talking with her just because she'd dressed as a man.

The woman in front of him could never pass for a man, anyway, not with her delicate features and slender neck. Not even with her brown hair pinned up and a jaunty hat pulled down over it. She tilted her head, half bending over as one of the other women produced a pair of men's boots. "Scottish," she said in a quiet voice, still grinning. "Highlander. From somewhere near Ullapool. That would make you Macbeth then, I suppose."

Glendarril Park was but two hours' ride from Ullapool. Coll frowned. "Macbeth hailed from Inverness."

She stepped from behind the screen to pull a coat over her slender shoulders. "Near enough for Shakespeare," she retorted, and sauntered past him.

Damn. A woman in trousers, indeed. His fingers flexed;

he had to stop himself from reaching out to take hold of her, to drag her up against him and stop her clever mouth with his. Aye, he'd been without a woman for a time, and aye, she looked a sight in those trousers that hugged her hips and practically forced his attention to her long, slender legs. As he watched her emerge from behind the curtains and onto the middle of the stage, he stopped breathing. Before his eyes, her stride lengthened and loosened, her hips halted their sway, and her shoulders lifted. Her voice when she spoke as Rosalind in the guise of male courtier Ganymede lowered and slowed a touch, in as fair a representation of a young man as he'd ever seen from a woman.

"*That* is Persephone Jones," the tailor from earlier said as he hurried by.

He hadn't needed that information. If any lass could have eleven men panting after her all in one night, it was this one. And for God's sake—no, for *his* sake—he hoped she was a widow.

Her scene finished, and she exited to the other side of the stage. More actors dashed past him to play their roles, but without her out there, it was just a play he'd read and seen performed before. Aye, it had been in Inverness and with a basket-load of Scottish sensibility added to the nonsense, but the words remained the same.

"How much longer does this damned thing go on?" a low voice asked from a few feet behind him.

Coll turned his head. A well-dressed lad in a bright blue jacket stood beneath another set of sandbags, his gaze on his pocket watch. The door guard had made at least four quid tonight, then. Another figure emerged into the dim light at the periphery of the stage, and he mentally corrected himself.

Six pounds, the greedy bastard.

"I say, Brumley," the first one whispered. "I was here first."

"Standing there doesn't make you any more than another man waiting," the Brumley fellow returned. "I'll wager you a hundred pounds I see the inside of her dressing room before you do."

"It's a wager, then. I should tell you, though, that I spoke with Lord Halloway, and he says that Mrs. Jones has a preference for light-haired men."

Brumley snorted. "I don't give a damn what color hair she prefers. Claremont's out of town, and that makes her available. She's a magnificent toy, and I do like to tinker."

"Gentlemen," a short, stout man hissed as he appeared from the depths of the backstage maze, "I must ask you to keep your voices down."

"Don't fret," the not-Brumley man said with a faint smile, "the audience isn't here to hear the play. They're here to see her. And you have to expect there to be *some* disagreement over which gentleman spends the night in her company."

"Which will be me," Brumley responded. "Go away, Waldring. You have a wife to plow."

Waldring made a face. "Only when it's planting season. I prefer more delicate fruit."

It didn't sound as though either of the men meant to ask the lass with whom *she* preferred to spend the night, or what her husband might have to say about it. "The lad asked ye to be quiet," Coll pointed out in his lowest voice, facing them.

"Oh look, Waldring, it's one of the Highlanders," Brumley commented, his eyes narrowing.

"Has no one explained to you, Glendarril, that plays are generally watched from the seats out front?" the second one, Waldring, put in. "I'm certain I saw Lady Aldriss in her box out there earlier. Are you lost?"

"Gentlemen," the stout man repeated, putting his hands together in a prayer. "Please be silent, or you will have to leave."

Out on the stage behind Coll, the lass was speaking again. He wanted to watch her, but he wasn't about to turn his back on these two buffoons. "I'm nae lost. I'm right where I want to be. Now, that wee man there asked ye to be silent. I reckon ye should listen to him."

"You know what I think, Brumley? I think this heathen has his own sights set on Mrs. Jones. The—"

"That's 'my laird heathen' to ye," Coll interrupted, his mouth curving in a grim smile. *Ah, battle.*

The bigger of the two men, Waldring, put a finger in the knot of his cravat to loosen it, a sure sign of a coming brawl. "I'll have you know, sir, that I train at Gentleman Jackson's," he said, coiling his arms and making fists at the ends. "What say you, Brumley? Shall we?"

The dandy hopped from one foot to the other in a prancing half circle while Coll watched, amused. When Waldring finally lunged forward, Coll ducked the flailing swipe easily and flashed out with his own fist, catching the dandy with a solid punch to the jaw. Waldring dropped to the wooden floor with a puff of exhaled air. Cocking his head, Coll turned his attention to the other one. "Ye want the same, Sassenach? If ye do, then step up. If ye dunnae, then get this sack of potatoes out of my sight."

"But—that it is to say—I didn't arrive with Mr. Waldring," Brumley sputtered.

"Well, he cannae stay there on the floor. Someone'll trip over him. So drag him out of here and be glad ye showed more restraint than he did," Coll suggested.

"I . . . yes."

Facing the stage again, Coll folded his arms. The difficulty with using words as weapons was that words couldn't knock a man on his arse. *That* took fists. He would have to point that out to his dialogue-preferring brothers the next chance he got. Of course, who the devil knew when that would be, what with Niall so occupied with bedding his wife, Amy, that the household practically had to remind the two of them to eat, and with Aden gone down to Canterbury for a special license so he could wed his Miranda before the lass found her common sense again and changed her mind.

"That was efficiently—and quietly—done, sir. Thank you." The small man drew even with Coll, his own arms folded over his barrel chest.

"Ye look like ye could have held yer own."

The man grinned briefly. "In my prime, perhaps. But I can't go about punching theater patrons. That makes for very poor attendance and less patronage. So again, thank you."

Coll shrugged. "I've punched two men tonight, and both deserved it. Ye dunnae need to thank me for that."

"Even so, I'm glad this is Persephone's last night playing a romantic lead. We always have more wolves at the door when we perform a romance. After tonight, we'll see ten days relatively wolf-free before we open *Macbeth*. And I daresay most men wouldn't dare even dream of bedding Lady Macbeth. Not if they value their lives."

That seemed peculiar—Persephone Jones was an actress, not the actual murdering lass. But then he'd just seen her transform herself into a boy with but a few shifts in the way she held herself. If she could become Lady Macbeth as efficiently, bedding her *would* seem a mite dangerous. He did like dangerous things, though. And she . . . Well, he could admit to himself that this was the first time he'd found a lad desirable, knowing what lay beneath those trousers as he did.

"Those werenae wolves," he said aloud, just remembering to whisper. "Ferrets, more like, scavenging for an easy meal."

"If they think of Persephone Jones as an easy meal, they're very stupid ferrets." Unfolding his arms, the man stuck out one hand. "Huddle," he whispered. "Charlie Huddle. I manage the madness that is the Saint Genesius."

Coll gripped his hand. "Glendarril. Coll MacTaggert."

"Ah. You're *that* Scotsman."

Lifting an eyebrow, Coll freed his fingers from the firm grip. "Which Scotsman would that be?"

"The one seen a few days ago running naked down Grosvenor Square with a large sword in his hands. Viscount Glendarril."

"Aye. And if I'd caught the bastard who threatened my family, ye'd be telling a different tale about me, I reckon." It had been a close race; even with Captain Robert Vale on horseback, Coll had nearly managed to take an ear off the vulture.

"I'm not one to judge. When you spend as much time around theater folk as I do, naked swordplay doesn't seem all that scandalous. Or unusual."

"Ah, you're still here, Macbeth," a voice came from in front of him in a soft lilt.

He refocused his attention on the lass dressed as a lad standing at the edge of the curtains as Huddle went to chat with his overly exuberant Duke Senior. "I'm still nae Macbeth, lass."

"Duncan, then? Banquo?"

"MacTaggert will do. Or Coll. I'll answer to either of those." He wasn't certain why he didn't add Glendarril, except that the two rutting pigs whose arses he'd just kicked had been aristocracy, and they hadn't shown very well. He wasn't *English* aristocracy, of course, but at this moment pointing out the difference just seemed petty.

"And I answer to Mrs. Jones." She bowed with a flourish. "Or Persephone," she said, her grin deepening as she straightened again. "Now that we're acquainted, MacTaggert, whatever shall we do next?"

Chapter Two

"Give me your favor; my dull brain was wrought
With things forgotten."

MACBETH, MACBETH ACT I, SCENE III

A thing or two they could be doing together came to mind—and they would be naked while they did it. Lasses didn't wear trousers where he came from, Coll reflected, but then he was in a kilt—which had been called scandalous and barbaric by more Sassenachs than he had fingers to count. Given that, he had no complaints at all about her appearance. Not a one.

With her long legs and slender waist, her bosom half-concealed beneath a superfine shirt, waistcoat, and a blue coat that sat just a bit too large across her shoulders, Persephone Jones looked like a well-dressed waif. A very attractive, brown-haired waif with large blue eyes and a grin that made them dance, but a waif nonetheless. "Before I answer that, I have to ask ye where Mr. Jones might be," he said, already better than halfway to hating the man.

She gave a dismissive wave of her hand. "Oh, somewhere about. Why do you ask?"

"Because I'm nae a poacher."

"Ah. A hunter, then. You're assuming, though, that I can be caught."

"I reckon I could make a good go of it."

Her expression speculative, the lass approached him, lifting up on her toes to make herself taller. Even so, the top of her head barely reached his shoulder.

"What sort of hunter are you, MacTaggert? Do you hang your trophy up on the wall for everyone to admire? Or do you eat what you catch?"

Good Lord, she was going to have him poking out from under his kilt in another damned minute. "I've a healthy appetite," he returned.

"Persephone," a female voice whispered from behind him. "Five minutes."

"Ah, excuse me, MacTaggert. I have another costume change, and no more time to chat."

As she passed by Mr. Huddle, the wee man leaned in to whisper something into her ear. At that, she sent another appraising glance at Coll before she vanished into the dim backstage. Coll would have asked what the devil they were gossiping about, but a stone wall rolled in between them, followed by a banquet table, a set of chairs, a giant candelabra, and a throne.

By the time all the furniture had made it onto the stage and the men who'd moved the things had returned to the wings, Charlie Huddle had vanished. More significantly, Mrs. Persephone Jones was nowhere to be seen, either. At least he knew where to find her: on the stage. While the scenery lads marched back and forth, replacing the forest with a fortress, Coll shifted toward the main curtains and parted them with his fingers.

The audience seemed full to the rafters, which made sense now, given both the lass's talent and the fact that this was the final night of her being Rosalind. Shifting a little sideways, he could just make out Lady Aldriss's box. Francesca herself sat there, stone-faced, while his sister Eloise dabbed a handkerchief at her betrothed's nose. The two lasses and their families who'd come to ambush him remained, one of them in tears and the other one's mother weeping.

Christ on the cross. Aye, he needed to find a wife before Eloise's wedding, and that date now loomed but four weeks away. But if a lass could weep over losing him after three minutes of conversation, it wasn't him she was after; it was his damned title. And he wasn't desperate enough yet to agree to his mother's suggestions, anyway.

When he'd first realized there was no getting around his mother's edict, he'd thought to find himself a lass he could wed, bed, and leave behind in London while he returned to Scotland and did as he pleased. While he'd never admit to changing his opinion about *that*, his brothers' success at finding women they loved—and who loved them in return—had turned his head a mite. He could tolerate an English lass if love were involved. If that didn't happen, he could always fall back on his original scheme. Surely even a damned leper with a title could find a bride in four weeks.

In the meantime, he'd found a fine-looking lass to distract him from his bloody conundrum. And even if all he could do was watch her and indulge his imagination, that seemed a much more pleasant way to spend the evening than dodging marriage-minded goslings and the imperious goose in her well-positioned box.

"So, you're the one who sent Waldring scurrying. Thanks for that," a voice came from behind him in a very cultured Sassenach accent. "He tends to charm a lady onto her back before any of the rest of us can say hello. You've rendered him impotent—at least until that bruise heals."

Coll stepped back from the curtains and turned his head. Sounding arrogant wasn't an easy task when a fellow had to keep his voice pitched lower than a mouse's squeak, but the tall, blond man standing in the shadows managed it, regardless. "And who might ye be?" he asked.

"Claremont. James Pierce, the Earl of, to be precise."

Narrowing his eyes a little, Coll took in the gray coat, mauve waistcoat, and black trousers. Well-cut and expensive, he'd wager. The man had even brought a bouquet of red roses. And he was the one about whose absence the other two had been thrilled. "I've nae seen ye about." That had to mean something, because he'd been dragged to nearly every proper event held in London this Season.

"I've been in the south, seeing to my properties. Well, overseeing the construction of a new wing at Claremont Hall, actually." The pretty fellow tilted his head. "From the way you're eyeing a certain attractive lady, I see Waldring isn't the only one to have attempted to move in during my absence."

A stone tumbled into the pit of Coll's stomach. An unnamed disappointment over something he'd scented, but not gotten close enough to taste. "If she's yers, ye've naught to fear from me. If ye're another of the herd of Sassenach roosters preening in hopes that the hen'll look in yer direction, then I reckon ye've a fight on yer hands."

The earl smiled. "Ask her yourself."

As if on cue, Penelope Jones emerged from the gloom, wearing yet another pair of trousers and a green coat. "MacTaggert," she said, with a grin and a nod.

"There you are, my dear," Claremont said, sketching an elegant bow and holding out the posies.

"Claremont!" she exclaimed, dabbing a quick curtsy. "I hadn't expected you back yet." She took the flowers, gave them a quick sniff, and handed them off to a woman walking at her heels. "I've no time to converse, I'm afraid."

"That is what later is for," the earl returned, sending Coll a very pointed look over her head—a look that said he'd proven his claim.

Her mouth had smiled, but her eyes hadn't. Whether that signified anything or not, Coll didn't know. But as he had a wife to find, and as Mrs. Jones had been a momentary, unexpected diversion, he shrugged. "I'm here for the play," he muttered, folding his arms and leaning against a sturdy-looking upright as the lass strolled onto the stage and became a young lad once more.

If the lass was spoken for, that was that. A damned shame or not, in all honesty, he hadn't come down here looking for her. Hell, he'd left Lady Aldriss's box before she'd ever appeared onstage.

That had been a short hunt; more than anything else, it had served to remind him that he'd been reluctantly celibate for the past eight weeks, plus the week before that, as he, Aden, and Niall had meandered south with every bit of luggage they could pile atop their two wagons.

He'd been full of defiance then, ready for the three of them to challenge Francesca Oswell-MacTaggert head-on, tell her that she and her conditions for continuing to fund Aldriss Park could go to hell, and march back to the Highlands. But damn it all, they needed the blunt she provided. That money allowed the MacTaggerts to look after more cotters than any of the other chieftains in the area could manage. It allowed them to supplement a poor harvest, to purchase sheep and cattle when the fall weather made for fewer young ones in spring, and in short, to keep those dependent on them from starving.

And his idea of a united front against their mother—who hadn't bothered to write a letter, much less visit in the seventeen years since she'd left her three sons behind—began to crumble the moment Niall had fallen for Amy. Coll gave a shudder. He liked the lass well enough now, but for God's sake, his mother had meant Amelia-Rose Hyacinth Baxter for *him*. Thank God Amy and Niall had turned out to be perfect for each other and he'd been left out of the equation.

Once the first had fallen, Aden had no doubt seen what

lay ahead, and so when he'd stumbled across Matthew Harris's sister, he'd staked his own claim. Coll sighed. Which left him. As the oldest, he no doubt should have been the first to wed. It was his duty to lead the way into such perils. But every time he thought to make an effort toward wooing a lass, he recalled how badly his father had mangled a marriage with his own Englishwoman. Angus MacTaggert and Francesca Oswell had managed to remain beneath the same roof for twelve years, but none of them had been peaceful. None that he could recall, anyway.

But that was neither here nor there, because tonight all he'd accomplished was an escape from two more prospective brides and a few minutes of imagining that he and Mrs. Persephone Jones might have spent a sweaty, naked night together. So now he could return to Oswell House and make a list of which lasses might serve, or he could stay where he was and watch a rather inspired performance in *As You Like It*.

In the end, the play won out, and while he felt a wee bit cheated that all the lads had found their loves while he stood in the wings without so much as a bridal prospect, he could say one positive thing about English tastes—they were all correct when they raved about Persephone Jones.

All the actors gathered onstage for a standing ovation before they flooded past him to the dressing rooms and the rear door. He waited where he was; no sense making an appearance outside until Lady Aldriss and her weeping maidens were well away.

"We'll be putting out the lights in ten minutes," one of the behind-the-stage men eventually informed him, "and there's nothing darker than a theater."

"Except a lady's heart, mayhap," Coll rejoined, hiding his shudder at the idea of being in this cramped space in complete darkness, and the lad laughed.

Back to Oswell House it was, then, where he'd have

to listen to his mother bellowing about how she was attempting to save the MacTaggert properties by helping him find him a bride, and all he could bellow back was what he'd been saying for eight weeks: he would find his own damned wife. He made his way through the clutter in the direction the rest of the occupants had headed.

"—don't think that's necessary," Persephone Jones's sweet voice came from a cracked-open door, and he slowed.

"What *I* think is necessary is that you stop dancing about and give me what I want," Claremont's voice retorted. "You flutter as if you have some virtue to protect. Do I need to remind you that you are an actress? A pretty one, but that's not enough to see you invited to a soiree. I have purchased gifts for you—several *expensive* gifts, if you'll recall. In recompense, you will give me what I want. And that is what is between your legs, Persephone."

"No." There was just the faintest tremble at the end of the word. "You have forced gifts on me in an attempt to buy what is between my legs. Take them all back. They're here in this box. I never wanted them to begin with. You—"

"You damned whore. I—"

Glass shattered. Before he'd quite settled on what he was doing, Coll slammed open the door and stepped into the room. It was smaller than he'd expected, with bare walls, a table and a chair, and a single full-length mirror, but he only noted that peripherally as he grabbed Claremont by the collar and yanked him backward from where he loomed over the lass, his hands on her shoulders.

He caught a quick glance of Persephone's wide blue eyes and the neck of a broken bottle in her hand before he returned his attention to the sputtering earl. "The lass said nae," he growled, flinging the other man into the near wall.

Claremont went down onto his knees and immediately

struggled to his feet. "This is none of your affair, Highlander. Leave this room before I have you thrown out."

"Well, while ye're searching about for someone who can toss me, I'll go ahead and see ye out myself." Moving quickly, Coll wrapped one arm under the earl's shoulder and cupped the back of his head in the same hand, bending the tall fellow nearly double as Claremont tried to avoid having his arm broken.

"You have no idea who you're dealing with," Claremont sputtered, staggering out of the room as Coll half-dragged him toward the rear of the building. Charlie Huddle and a few of the remaining actors and stagehands stood by the back door, and with a quick intake of air, Huddle pulled it open and stepped aside.

Coll shoved Claremont outside, following that with a hard stomp to the earl's backside with the bottom of his boot. "The next time a lass tells ye nae," he rumbled, "and I imagine that'll happen to ye often, ye'd best listen."

With that, he shut the door and latched it for good measure. When he turned around, the assembled men began clapping.

"I never liked that Lord Claremont," Huddle intoned with a crooked grin. "Glad to see him gone. But he could make some trouble for you, my lord."

With a shrug, Coll straightened his coat. "It's nae the first time for that, and it'll nae be the last."

"Perhaps," a female voice sounded from the shadows, "but now you're going to have to see me home."

Persephone Jones stepped forward as the lights toward the front of the hall began to flicker and go out, leaving her in a halo of candlelight surrounded by murky darkness. She carried a small portmanteau in one hand and wore a deep purple, low-cut silk gown, a silver shawl, and a purple hat decorated with wee white flowers perched at a jaunty angle on her head. Her hair was no longer brown, but rather a long, flowing ivory curled into ringlets about her face, an angel descended from heaven to tease the mortals.

"I reckon I can do that." A lass who turned into a different lass every time he looked around—that could be either very arousing or exceedingly frustrating. But it would damned well be interesting, either way.

Coll MacTaggert, Persephone Jones reflected, could have been mistaken for a mountain, if mountains were made of muscle and bone and were possessed of a very attractive, if severe, face softened by a deep Scottish brogue. Turning her gaze and attention from the towering Highlander, she tucked her shawl a little closer around her shoulders and took a deep breath as Charlie Huddle pulled open the rear stage door. She'd requested the helpful mountain's assistance. It remained to be seen whether he was as efficient at disbursing crowds in public as he was at ousting earls in private.

The second she stepped outside, men young and old pressed in around her, cheering and complimenting and offering flowers or begging for locks of her hair. At least the earlier rain had tapered off.

"If you'll excuse me, good gentlemen," she said as she always did, her own private play performed at the back door every night, "but I've had a very long evening and I'm quite tired."

"Thou art the fairest damsel in the land," one young man shouted above the volume of the others, a bouquet of red roses aimed, weaponlike, at her head, "I should swoon if thee would but give me thy hand."

That caused a round of booing, which she mentally joined. She performed Shakespeare. Why that made some men think they should recite bad poetry written on the back of a betting slip, she had no idea. "Make way, gentlemen, if you please."

"'She walks in beauty, like the night of cloudless sk—'"

"That's Lord Byron. I summon Shakespeare," she interrupted, and some of the vultures laughed at the odd fellow out.

The jostling became worse. Just as she was beginning to consider using her bag as a weapon, a space opened around her miraculously. Persephone glanced over her shoulder, half expecting to see a dragon looming behind her. Rather, it was the Scotsman, his arms outstretched as he shoved would-be suitors away like rag dolls.

"The lass wants ye to make way," he stated. "Dunnae make her ask ye again."

Well. Public acts of heroism it was, then. When Claremont accompanied her, the earl liked having all the hangers-on about, so he could be certain they all saw that she left in his company. She took a half step sideways and wrapped her free hand around one muscular Scottish arm. "Thank you," she said, offering up a smile and silently praying that she wasn't in the process of making a horrible mistake. *Another* horrible mistake, rather. Turning this man away could well take a battalion of elephants, which she didn't happen to have anywhere handy. But she did have friends and admirers about, and she had a good . . . feeling about this Coll MacTaggert. Or it could be as simple as the fact that she'd been enjoying looking at his fine form for most of the evening, but he *had* proven helpful thus far.

He gave her a nod and continued plowing a path through the lingering theatergoers until they reached the corner, where her coach waited. She tugged on his arm, and he stopped. "I have a coachman wait here for me each evening," she said.

Of course, she'd suggested he see her home, but that had been mostly meant as a jest, a small bit of carnal excitement brought about by this wild, kilt-wearing mountain of a man before her, with a little part gratitude added in for someone finally ridding her of Claremont. The earl was more persistent than a mosquito.

This moment would be the test, though. Would he let her leave, or insist on accompanying her? MacTaggert, as he'd named himself—despite Charlie Huddle informing her that he was actually Lord Glendarril—wasn't at all pretty like James Pierce, the Earl of Claremont. Rather, his slash of straight brows, the confident, open expression of his face, unruly dark hair, and amused green eyes spoke of something Claremont had likely never before encountered as a rival—a man. A very handsome, muscular, virile-looking man. One who was either mad, or simply untroubled by the amount of influence Lord Claremont wielded and the trouble he could cause.

"Is that yer way of sending me off to Hades?" he asked in his thick brogue, one of those brows lifting.

She found herself listening to the sound of his voice, studying the inflection of his words, and told herself it was because she was about to begin rehearsals to play Lady Macbeth and that it had nothing to do with the way his deep voice seemed to reverberate into her bones.

"More politely than that, but yes, it is. I do thank y—"

He pulled open the door and shifted to offer his hand to help her inside. "Ye'd best be off before the hounds catch yer scent again, then."

Another surprise. This evening had presented her with basketloads of them. Persephone stepped up, but remained standing in the doorway to gaze at him. "You aren't offended? I mean, I did imply that we might have a more . . . personal connection."

MacTaggert shrugged. "Ye knew ye had a nest of vipers out here waiting for ye, and ye saw me hit Claremont. That's math even a Highlander can do, I reckon." He grinned. "Besides, now I'm a puzzle to ye, and ye'll nae be able to stop thinking about me."

She smiled back, her heart easing as she realized she would not have to do any further clever acting this evening to rid herself of yet another suitor. "You *are* rather memorable, MacTaggert."

"That I am." He closed the door for her as she moved back and seated herself, but he was tall enough to still be able to look in the window. "I'm nae some eunuch or fancy boy, either, and ye are a lass to make a man's heart beat faster. But I fell into being a gentleman tonight, and I'll nae be looked at in the same way ye saw Claremont, so I'll bid ye good evening and sweet dreams. And dunnae be surprised if I come looking for ye tomorrow."

Well. A man who simply stated what he wanted and didn't attempt to purchase her affections or her body. He was also clearly a man who could physically take whatever he wanted, and he hadn't done so. An interesting balance, that, and because she did find it intriguing, she would be wise simply to nod, bid him goodnight, and leave, thankful that she'd escaped unscathed twice tonight. Earls, viscounts, Englishmen, or Scots—they were all trouble.

And though *this* trouble had done her a good turn, he filled at least two of the spaces on her list of people to avoid. Firstly, he was a man, and secondly, he was a man with a title. Even more troubling—she found him attractive. If she hadn't, she would never have begun flirting with him backstage. *Definitely trouble.* "I cannot stop you from looking," she murmured, leaning toward the open window and attempting to ignore the excited goosebumps lifting on her arms, "but finding me is another thing entirely."

He nodded, stepping back. "I reckon I know where to begin. And mayhap when I find ye, ye'll tell me the tale of Mr. Jones."

"Because you're not a poacher?"

"Because if there *is* such a man, and if ye dunnae ken where he is, then he's an idiot."

"Then I shall save poor Mr. Jones the bother of being insulted, and inform you that I, the poor unfortunate, am a widow."

The Highlander grinned again, the sight making her heart give an odd, unexpected thump. Good heavens. He looked like—she didn't even know how to describe it. An angel of God, perhaps. One of the fit warrior angels who slayed demons and dragons. "My condolences, Mrs. Jones," he drawled.

Before she could do something idiotic and admit that there never had been a Mr. Jones at all, the coach thankfully rolled into the street, and she lost sight of him in the darkness. A few of her admirers usually chased the coach for a street or two, but tonight the road behind the vehicle remained empty. Perhaps they weren't willing to risk annoying the Highlander, and she certainly couldn't blame them for that. Her only surprise was that they'd all had that much sense.

"The usual twice around Burton's park?" the coachman asked from up above her head.

Persephone shook herself and leaned toward the window again. "Yes, Gus, thank you. We can't be too careful."

"I'll make certain you get home safe, Persie."

"I don't know what I would do without you, Gus."

"You'd have a bit of a walk. That's for certain."

Laughing, she opened her portmanteau and pulled out a plain blue muslin dress, a matching blue bonnet, and a hairbrush. Then she tugged the coach's curtains closed, musing that Claremont had either not cared that she supposedly had a husband, or he'd deciphered that any actress who wished for a modicum of respectability stuck a Mrs. in front of her name, whether she had a Mr. waiting for her at home or not.

Ah, respectability—that fickle thing—seemed even more foolish once a lady realized how easily it could be purchased, and with such a simple lie. But she had realized it, and she'd also figured out the simplest way to keep all those lusty men at the theater's back entrance from discovering where she lived: a silly wig.

First, she removed her jaunty hat and tossed it into the bag, swiftly followed by her wig of long, silver-blonde hair. Shaking out her own much shorter, honey-colored hair felt marvelous after hours of having the shoulder-length curls pinned tightly against her scalp, and as she brushed it out, she decided to leave it loose.

The risqué purple gown followed the other accessories into the bag, and she wriggled into the far more demure muslin gown before she set the bonnet over her head and tied it beneath her chin. There. Prim and proper once again. Of course, it was just another costume, but this one allowed her to live peacefully in St. John's Wood without gaggles of men disrupting her and her neighbors' lives.

Once she'd settled herself, she opened the curtains again and leaned back in the ill-sprung coach to look out the window toward the grand manor sitting alone in the darkness. Even at this hour, the windows of the Holme blazed, a sight even more striking after its owner, James Burton, had purchased all the bordering dairy farms and demolished the houses and barns, leaving a ruined pastoral mess just north and east of where most of the aristocracy laid their heads. If the rumors were true and he meant to build a park there to honor Prince George, that was all well and good, but in the meantime, half the grounds looked like a war had been fought there.

Gus had circled the Holme twice, which gave her time to change her clothes and him the ability to make certain they weren't being followed. That done, he turned the coach up Charlbert Street to the small house she rented at number four, Charles Lane.

"We're here, Persie, and nary a soul behind us," he announced.

She stood and opened the door, hefting her portmanteau as she stepped down to the dirt road. "Thank you, Gus. Might I see you at half-eight in the morning?"

"That's early for you, ain't it?" the driver asked, leaning over the side of the coach to eye her.

"Yes, but we're beginning rehearsals."

"Then I'll be here at half-eight. I'd rather drive you about than ferry all the housemaids and kitchen help about while they go searching for hair ribbons and pheasant eggs at all hours."

Persephone grinned. "I promise never to ask you to take me to find pheasant eggs."

The rotund coachman doffed his hat. "You keep paying me as generously as you do, and I'd go fetch you those eggs myself."

With a cluck to his team, he and the coach rolled back into the street and turned south, back toward London proper. Sighing, Persephone walked up to the quaint blue door of her quaint gray house, nodding at her neighbor Mr. Beacham as he arrived home from his bakery, and went inside.

"You let that coachman speak to you far too familiarly, Persie," said a female voice from the morning room doorway.

"Considering there are more than a handful of coachmen who won't deign to transport an actress at all, Flora, I have no complaints about his form of address." Persephone handed over the portmanteau and her bonnet to the small, round woman who emerged from the doorway.

Flora Whitney grimaced. "You could hire your own driver. And own your own coach."

"They wouldn't fit in the house. And Mr. Praster wouldn't appreciate horses in his hallways, anyway."

Her maid—and former theater seamstress—waved her free hand. "Mr. Praster has quite a fondness for you. I don't doubt he would tolerate horses in the dining room if you asked his permission."

As far as landlords went, Jacob Praster was a rather tolerant one. After all, it wasn't just an assortment of hired hacks who avoided actresses and other people of questionable repute. Landlords, she'd discovered several years ago, before she'd added a spouse to her list of qualifications, could be even more pompous. "I'm quite satisfied with Gus," she said aloud, heading for the narrow staircase along the right wall of the foyer. "And wherever it is he stables his horses."

"It was only a suggestion. I happened to see today that one of those fine houses along Chesterfield Hill is for sale. Wouldn't that make the blue-blooded set blush, to see you living right there among them?"

It might make them blush, but it made Persephone shudder. "Oh, yes. I can just imagine myself walking through Mayfair while all the good people throw rotten fruit at me. I have no desire to be anywhere other than where I am, Flora. Do leave off."

The maid clucked her tongue, but subsided. They had this conversation at least once a month, but Persephone had long had a hunch that it had more to do with Flora and her dream of living in a castle than it did the location of their current residence. But they all had dreams, and Persephone wasn't about to tell anyone not to pursue them.

"Heavens, I forgot! How was closing night?" the maid blurted. "Did you tell Lord Claremont you've been giving his posies to the church at Charing Cross for their pauper funerals?"

That made Persephone smile. "I didn't have to, as it turns out," she said, nodding as Gregory Norman, her footman and a former stagehand at the Saint Genesius, emerged from her bed chamber. "Gregory."

"Miss Persie. I've put the coal warmer beneath the sheets. Rain's no way to end the run of a play, dash it all."

"If I had an aversion to rain, I would be performing in the Sahara Desert."

"Gregory, don't interrupt," Flora put in. "Persie was telling me she didn't send Claremont packing."

"What? I thought we was tired of his high-handedness."

"We were," Persephone edged into the conversation. "As I was attempting to turn him away—and without any success, I might add—a very large Scotsman happened by and overheard Claremont pawing at me, and the next thing I knew, his lordship had made a close acquaintance with a Scottish boot and the floor of my dressing room—though not necessarily in that order."

"No! Oh, you must tell me all about it! Who was the Scotsman?"

"Do I need to load my blunderbuss and put it by the front door again?" Gregory asked.

With a snort, Persephone strolled into her bedchamber to put her shawl over the back of the chair set before the fireplace. "Not yet. He was actually quite polite for a barbarian Highlander. He's interested, but intends to wait to be invited." She shot a glance over her shoulder at her maid's rapt expression. "Which means, of course, that he expects to be invited."

"Oh, lud, they *all* expect you to swoon at their feet, don't they?" Flora dumped the portmanteau in the seat of the overstuffed chair and began putting the bits and bobs away. "I've yet to meet a man who didn't think he was too handsome and charming to be resisted."

"Excluding me." With a nod at the two of them, Gregory left the room, helpfully pulling her door closed behind him.

As he did so, a small black figure emerged from beneath the stack of pillows on the large green and blue bed and stretched, then lazily picked its way to the edge of the mattress and bowed its head in a clear invitation for her to bestow scratches. "And how are you this evening, Hades?" Persephone murmured, bending to plant a kiss on top of the cat's sleek head.

"That demon jumped at me out of the larder and nearly scared me to death." Flora gave an exaggerated shiver. "Black cats are witchcraft, you know."

"So you keep telling me. The two of you would get along much better if you would only keep in mind that this is *his* house, and he is kindly allowing us in for an extended visit." Offering the cat a quick scratch behind the ears, she sat beside him to pull off her shoes. *Ah, that felt nice.* Gleefully, she scrunched up her toes and straightened them again. Who would have expected that acting would be so hard on her feet? Not her, certainly.

"Well, I think he'd be happy to have you as his only guest. I'm fairly certain he wants to see me dead of fright, and Gregory's told me Hades keeps trying to trip him on the stairs." Wrapping the hem of her skirt around her hand, Flora removed the steaming kettle from where it hung in the small fireplace and toted it behind the screen that sectioned off the far corner of the room. "I've made your bath as hot as I can, but with the chill in the air tonight, that won't last for long."

"Thank you. Off with you then, Flora. I can see myself to bed. But please remember to wake me early; I have to be back at the Saint Genesius at the ungodly hour of nine o'clock."

"Saints preserve us. I'll do my utmost." With that, Flora returned the empty kettle to the hearth, moved the empty portmanteau to the floor to await tomorrow's wardrobe change, picked up Persephone's shoes for brushing off, and shut the door firmly behind her as she left the room.

Persephone shed her plain gown and shift, pinned up her hair in a loose, twisted bun, and, shivering, hurried behind the curtain to the steaming bathtub. She dipped in one toe to find the water pleasantly warm and climbed in to sink down to her chin. *Glorious.* Then she shut her eyes for a moment, just listening to the quiet and feeling the warmth soak into her bones.

Considering that she'd expected to still be fighting off Lord Claremont this evening, and doing so with enough delicacy that he wouldn't attempt to ruin her career, simply being able to sit in the warm water was reward enough for a packed theater every night of the three-week run of *As You Like It.* It wasn't her favorite play, and the entire thing became a bit silly toward the end, but she did enjoy wearing trousers and hearing the corresponding gasps from the wig-wearing set in the audience when she first appeared as a boy onstage. And Rosalind was not only quick-witted, but she had the most lines of any female in Shakespeare's repertoire. Persephone knew that, because she'd counted.

Shocked, those gray-haired, regimented ladies were— shocked that a young lady of any background should wear men's clothes in public. Shocked that she should be upfront with her wits. Shocked that she should kiss a man right up there onstage, inviting people to look.

And while their shock might be genuine, she'd also noted that they all stayed through the final curtain. And on occasion, they came to see a second performance.

The younger set applauded wildly and sent letters addressed both to Rosalind and to her, wanting her—or Rosalind's—friendship, or her—or Rosalind's—love. And Rosalind didn't receive the same quantity of heated correspondence as did Juliet Montague. The number of men—and a few women—who addressed her only as Juliet, who wanted to be her true-life Romeo or her dearest friend, continued to astound her even now.

Lady Macbeth would be a new experience. She imagined there would be those in the audience who would hate her for bringing down Macbeth, for leading him down a thorny path, but hopefully the number of love letters would subside. For heaven's sake, she wasn't certain *she* wanted to make the acquaintance of Lady Macbeth, much less that of a man who would want the horrid woman's love or desire.

Of course, she'd teased the handsome Scotsman about being Macbeth, but that had only been because he was Scottish. Admittedly, at first glance he didn't seem the sort of man to be led about by a woman's ambitions or sexual favors, as had happened with Macbeth the character, but then again, she didn't know if MacTaggert the man had come backstage to meet *her*—or to become acquainted with Rosalind.

Coll MacTaggert, Viscount Glendarril. She read the newspaper's Society page every morning, and she'd seen him mentioned more than once—something about three handsome Scottish brothers coming down to London to find English wives. If that were so, then he was wasting his time hanging about backstage at the Saint Genesius. Titled men did not marry actresses.

Personally, she didn't see why he would still be without a bride after eight or nine weeks in Mayfair. Even without the lure of a title, he was stunningly handsome, a literal larger-than-life presence amid the dandies and gadabouts. And if the fourth-hand whispers she'd heard from seamstresses who'd heard from store clerks who'd heard from maids were true, he had recently been seen running from Oswell House naked and carrying a large sword—and the ladies hadn't noted anything to complain about then, either.

Chuckling, she ducked her face beneath the water and then straightened again. There was something appealing, even refreshing, about a man with enough self-confidence to show his nethers to the world, especially with a large sword to hand for comparison's sake.

Those were just rumors, of course, and by the time any Society news came behind the curtains of the theater, she had no idea of its veracity. Still, she meant to have a second look at the latest Society pages still to hand in the house, this time with Coll MacTaggert in mind. If he did mean to hunt her down, she wanted a bit more ammunition, herself.

As the water cooled and the cloud-obscured moon rose high enough to peep at her through her east-facing window, she stood and dried herself off. Her nights frequently didn't end until sunrise, but for the next ten days she would be observing less nocturnal hours. The theater would go on without its principal players for that time, since Charlie Huddle was bringing in a roving troupe based all the way up in York to perform Aphra Behn's *The Rover, or The Banish'd Cavaliers* while she and her fellows rehearsed the Scottish play. While she liked the part of the determined Florinda from *The Rover*, the play was extremely bawdy, and the admirers who presently lurked backstage and at the rear door of the theater were grabby enough as it was.

Persephone pulled on her night-rail, banked the fire, and climbed under the soft, warm covers of her bed, grateful that Gregory had thought to heat them. A moment later,

Hades leaped up to curl into a midnight ball on the pillow next to her head.

MacTaggert had said that he found her desirable, even if his words had been a bit blunter than that. The viscount was after a wife, though—if those rumors were to be at all believed—so she wondered if he would bother to hunt after her at all. It could have been simple curiosity or boredom that had led him backstage, and a man hunting after a wife wouldn't have time to search her out, anyway. Thanks to him, she'd just rid herself of one "protector," as those men looking to buy her enough things that she would hopefully allow them into her bed called themselves. She wasn't anxious to have to deal with another man looking to buy her with pretty baubles.

Perhaps, though, the Highlander would attempt to woo her with deer carcasses. Then at least she would have some venison in exchange for . . . whatever she chose to grant him. He was, after all, easy on the eyes. And while she certainly wasn't marriageable, she wasn't dead, either.

Chapter Three

"Great business must be wrought ere noon."
HECATE, *MACBETH* ACT III, SCENE V

Coll opened his bedchamber door at just past six o'clock, before the sun had even risen. Back home, beginning the day early came alongside the responsibility of being his father's heir, and barring a previous evening down at the tavern when he'd been younger, and an evening in a lass's bed as he'd gotten older, he was accustomed to starting his day at least an hour before the rest of the house.

Adjusting to London life had been a challenge, with the way the household didn't return home until nearly dawn and then didn't rise until noon, but it did give him most mornings to himself.

Even as he finished that thought, though, a figure topped the stairs in front of him. He had the mornings *nearly* to himself, he amended. "Back from Canterbury, are ye?" he asked, declining to move aside as his younger brother started down the hallway.

Aden patted his coat pocket. "Aye. Seems I'm to be wed on Saturday next. I'd make it today, but Miranda's sent for her aunt to attend."

Silently, Coll took in his brother's loose cravat, half-unbuttoned waistcoat, and disheveled, too-long hair. "And how is Miranda this morning?" he drawled.

"Hush, ye lummox," Aden countered, lowering his voice.

"I need an hour or two of sleep before the MacTaggert lasses take to swooning over the romance of it all." His sly smile touched his gray-green eyes. "And she's well, thank ye for asking."

"I still say ye should elope with her to Scotland, like Niall did with Amy. It's more fitting if ye're wed by a Scotsman, even if the minister is a Lowlander—and a blacksmith to boot."

"Lady Aldriss swears she means to attend this wedding, and I'll nae wait a month for her to pack her bags." Aden cocked his head. "And ye dunnae have the days to waste on traveling. Nae when ye've less than four weeks now to find a bride for yerself." He put a protective hand over his pocket again. "And now that I've got my bride, ye've nae excuse, Coll. Go choose yerself a lass so we dunnae have to fret over Aldriss Park any longer."

"Ye only have a lass because *she* asked ye for yer hand," Coll retorted.

Aden's grin would've made a good number of lasses swoon. "Aye, she did. And I imagine ye could have a lass ask ye today as well, if ye'd stand still long enough for one to catch ye."

News always spread so damn quickly in London, most likely because everyone lived so close together. "So ye heard about the theater last night, did ye?"

"Miranda told me. She heard it from her brother. Who has a broken nose, by the way."

"Good." There were times he found it difficult to believe that Miranda and Matthew Harris were siblings. It was the lass who had most of the common sense, that was for damned certain. And a good share of cleverness, or she'd never have caught the elusive Aden.

Aden narrowed one eye. "I'll admit that he deserved a good thump, but keep in mind that he's nae a Highlander. If ye hit him too hard, ye may break him."

Coll snorted. "I reckon he heard what I had to tell him, and he'll nae be forgetting it." Leaning against the balcony railing, he thumped one fist against the well-polished mahogany. "One of us has to keep our head out of the posies and watch out for the family. Given that ye and Niall cannae see past yer lasses any longer, that falls to me."

"Or," Aden returned, his tone speculative, "ye could decide that while London has its perils, nae a one of us is a fool and we can look after ourselves, and ye could go find a lass to love ye."

"I've been looking, damn it all." Coll scowled. "It was one thing when I wanted to find a lass and leave her here when I go back to Scotland. But with all the Sassenach women knowing that, it seems they're all just as mercenary as me. I'm outnumbered."

"That ye are. And if ye willnae take a look at the women our sister is putting in front of ye, and ye dunnae trust the ones our mother is putting in front of ye, and ye dunnae want Amy or Miranda introducing ye to any of their friends, then ye're on yer own, Coll. And the summer days are getting longer."

"I know that. I'm nae about to put Aldriss in peril. I'm off to Hyde Park this morning to take a gander at the lasses."

With a nod, Aden continued toward his room across the hallway from Coll's. "I hope ye find one, *bràthair*." He paused in his doorway. "Dunnae be so ferocious. Ye're a decent man, when the mood strikes ye."

"I'm trying to be one even when the mood doesnae strike me. If ye see Francesca, tell her I'm doing as I said, and finding my own wife."

"I'm nae telling our mother anything. I dunnae mean to be the first one to see her at all." Aden gave a lopsided grin. "She's fearsome, Coll, but I reckon she didnae reckon on ye."

"Or mayhap she's forgotten that I remember her time in Scotland."

Aden tilted his head. "Have a care, Coll. We've all changed in seventeen years. Except ye, of course. Now dunnae go galloping through the park and trample any of the lasses or their wee dogs. They'd nae wed ye after that."

"I couldnae survive without yer advice, Aden," Coll said dryly, and headed down the stairs.

He paused on the landing to pat Rory the stuffed deer on the rump. Back at Aldriss Park, Rory had stood proud and dignified in a corner of the library, with a suit of armor on either side of him. Now, after being loaded into a pair of wagons with most of their belongings and every other damned thing they could think of to bring to London that might annoy their mother, Rory was adorned with a skirt around his hind quarters, a bonnet with holes cut for his ears, a man's cravat around his neck, earbobs and necklaces hung from the tines of his antlers, and a dancing slipper bound to his one raised hoof.

"Lad, ye arenae as dignified as ye once were," Coll told the stag, "but ye look as though ye've been having more fun than I am."

Breakfast was only partly set out, since the rest of the household wouldn't be awake for hours yet. Coll requested his horse be saddled, then helped himself to a sizeable stack of ham and some fresh, warm biscuits and butter. Together with two cups of strong coffee, the meal left him feeling fortified enough to brave a morning prancing about in Hyde Park.

Of course, he would rather have been riding off to the Saint Genesius for another conversation with Persephone Jones, but with only four weeks remaining to save Aldriss Park, he couldn't risk missing any opportunity to find a bride. He'd already put off marriage for longer than he should have, but with two capable younger brothers, his own duty to provide an heir hadn't seemed as pressing. Lady Aldriss's proclamation, though, hadn't left him any choice.

Outside the Oswell House stables and being given a wide berth by the rest of the servants, Gavin stood holding Nuckelavee's reins in one hand and a handful of carrots in the other. "Yer devil's in a bit of a froth today, m'laird," Gavin said, holding up the carrots for the giant to munch on. "Wouldnae let the Sassenach lads near him, even with a bucket of oats as an offering."

"That's why we brought ye south with us, Gavin," he told the groom. "Ye're the only man that our lad can tolerate, aside from me." Stepping up, Coll rubbed a hand along the stallion's arched neck and received a snort and head toss in return.

Nuckelavee was a giant of a black Friesian, descended from a long line of war horses. He had a fancy black frill of fur about his hooves, a great, curling mane and tail, and a bearing that said the lad knew he'd been bred to carry iron-clad knights into battle. He was, after all, named after a horse-shaped sea demon.

Swinging into the saddle, Coll reached down and relieved the groom of a trio of carrots, which he stuffed into a pocket. Nuckelavee hadn't run off without him yet, but neither of them was particularly fond of London. Having a bribe to hand couldn't hurt.

"Do ye want company this morning?" Gavin asked, stepping back from the front end of the black.

"Nae. If the countess asks after me, ye can tell her I went to Hyde Park to look over some lasses."

The groom snorted, clearly doubting that he meant to do as he said. "Aye."

"You may find some difficulty conversing with any young ladies while you're riding that monster," his mother's cultured voice sounded from behind him.

Damnation. He turned around to see her walking toward him from the direction of the front door of Oswell House. If he rode off now, Francesca Oswell-MacTaggert could rightly call him a coward, but he would be spared the forthcoming verbal brawl. "Lady Aldriss," he said, nodding.

"My friends are going to stop inviting me to luncheon if you keep insulting their daughters," she commented, stopping in front of him.

Lord, she was a wee thing, barely reaching his shoulders, even if she should lift up on her toes, which he doubted she would ever do. Tiptoes were no doubt undignified or some other nonsense. "I'd stop insulting their daughters if ye'd stop flinging them at me," he retorted, circling the restless black about the yard. "I've a good pair of eyes. Show 'em to me from a distance and we'd all be happier."

"Four weeks, Coll," his mother returned. "You have four weeks to find an English lady, woo her, ask for her hand, and marry her."

"Do ye truly expect me to wed one of the hothouse flowers from last night, woman? Violet Hampstead? She's so wee and fragile I'd be afraid I'd break her if I held her hand, much less lay atop her in bed."

The fair skin of his mother's cheeks darkened. "Coll. For—"

"Or the other one, Rebecca Sharpe? I actually danced with her at some soiree or other. Did ye know that? And she spent a good twenty minutes chatting about the weather. Ye ken how many words it takes me to describe London weather? One damned word: mild."

The countess drew in a breath through her nose. "Then perhaps you could give me some indication of what sort of woman interests you, my son. I am only trying to he—"

"Dunnae ye dare say ye're *helping* me," he cut in,

scowling. "I'd nae be here if not for ye getting our da to sign that bloody agreement."

She shut her eyes for just a moment. "All the same, my dear," she went on, opening them again, "seventeen years ago your father and I both signed an agreement that you three boys would wed English ladies before your sister married, or you would lose all of my monetary support of Aldriss. Your brothers have found ladies. And love, I might add. You—"

"First of all, ye didnae say 'ladies' in yer paper."

"I most certainly did."

"Nae. Ye didnae. I've read it a hundred times, *màthair*, and it says, 'Englishwomen.'" As he spoke, he hit on it: the way to confound this confounding woman, at least for long enough for him to find a suitable wife on his own. "And if ye must know, I've found myself an Englishwoman."

Her deep green eyes narrowed just a touch. "You found an English*woman* sometime between the theater last night and breakfast this morning?"

"Aye, I did. I'm off to see her now." He swung Nuckelavee around to face the street.

"And does this mysterious woman have a name, then?" she asked, skepticism in every line of her body.

"She does. Mrs. Persephone Jones. She's a widow. And I'm her protector, until I make her my wife."

Kicking his heels into the black's ribs, he headed into the street at a fast trot. *Ha.* Aden might claim that Coll had a far greater chance of winning an actual brawl over a verbal one, but he didn't have to be a damned debater to know he'd scored a blow just then. *Let her stew on that for a while.*

It only took a few minutes to reach Hyde Park, and he reluctantly bypassed Rotten Row for the more civilized pathways deeper in the park. Nuckelavee pulled hard on the reins, clearly wanting to stretch his legs, but Coll held him back to a staid and hopefully unthreatening walk. As Aden had said, trampling lasses and wee dogs wouldn't win him a bride.

Neither would his continued insistence on wearing a kilt to traverse civilized Mayfair, he imagined, but there were some things a man had to insist on if he wanted to keep that title. And this man wore a damned kilt. If he gave that up, next they'd all be telling him he talked funny.

A barouche approached up the path toward him, and he pulled Nuckelavee to one side. "Good morning, ladies," he said, inclining his head, as he'd decided not to wear a hat.

"My lord," the tall blonde one said, dipping her parasol. What was her name? Petunia or some other flower, as he recalled. Half the women in London seemed to be named after flora, though, so that didn't narrow it down by much.

The smaller one sitting beside her blushed bright red. "Lord Glendarril."

He turned to stay even with the barouche as the driver continued along the path at a walk. "I believe we met at the Gaines ball, did we nae?" he asked.

"Yes. And the Spenfield ball," the wee one returned.

He remembered the Spenfield ball, for damned certain. Half of Mayfair's men had been invited with only a handful of lasses, all so Mrs. Spenfield could find husbands for her five daughters. The desserts had been delicious, but he'd felt like a trapped bull the entire evening. "Aye. The Spenfield ball. I didnae even win the horse they were raffling off."

The tall blonde one gave a wail and collapsed, her head in her hands.

"What the devil did I say?"

The small one ignored him. "Don't fret, Polymnia," she said, putting her arm around the weeping one's shoulder. "You wouldn't want to marry him, anyway."

Polymnia. That was her name. Polymnia Spenfield. *Damn it all.* "I only meant I put my name in the bowl for the horse, and it wasnae drawn," he said, scowling. "I didnae insult her."

"You remembered the drawing rather than Polymnia," the other lass accused. "We must return home, Robert. Good day, Lord Glendarril."

The driver nodded the back of his head, turning the coach toward the boundary of the park. Coll pulled up Nuckelavee and watched them go. "Did ye hear that, Nuckelavee?" he muttered, patting the horse on the neck. "I recalled the drawing but nae the lass, and that's an insult."

The big black tossed his head, just in time for a trio of young ladies strolling past to squeak and dodge out of the way in a tangle of muslin and bonnets.

"Begging yer pardon, lasses. He means ye nae harm."

"He's a monster! You shouldn't be allowed to ride him in the park with civilized persons."

Coll pulled in a breath. "Aye. Ye're correct about that."

Turning the stallion, he headed east. His mother wanted him to wed one of these damned women, when he couldn't even manage two sentences of conversation with any of them without fighting the urge to lift his kilt and show them his Highlander arse. Hothouse flowers. That's what his father had said they would be, and evidently Niall and Aden had found the only decent two in all of London.

Mentally, he went down the list of marriageable ladies to whom he'd been introduced, hoping for a stir of interest—or anything but deep dread. He'd met some fair ones, aye, but not one with whom he cared to awaken every morning for the rest of his life.

He'd arrived in London and insulted Amelia-Rose on his first night here. Even if the other lasses hadn't been aware of the circumstances, they knew that his mother had arranged for him to wed Miss Baxter when he'd never even set eyes on the lass, and that he'd been angry—not at Amy, but at his mother, and at himself. So Amy had gone to Niall, thank God, but *he'd* been left with the reputation for being . . . well, who he was at his worst, he supposed.

It was nothing he didn't deserve, but it made finding a bride even more difficult than it would have been under other circumstances. If he took fondness and affection out of the equation, then any of the lasses would do. But even with the noose tightening around his neck, he wasn't quite ready to close his eyes and point at one of them. Not yet.

"We'd best go back," he said to Nuckelavee, and looked up to find himself in front of the Saint Genesius Theatre. "Damn me," he mused, and swung down to the ground. He would go back to Hyde Park. Later.

"Smythe! Send a footman to my office in five minutes!"

"Yes, my lady. Is something am—"

Francesca Oswell-MacTaggert slammed shut her office door before the butler could finish his query. *An actress.* Oh, this was *not* going to happen. Using a selection of some of the finer profanity she'd learned during her time spent up in the Scottish Highlands, she sat in the chair behind her late father's massive mahogany desk and pulled a sheet of paper from a drawer.

Once she dipped her pen in the inkwell, she brought the fine tip down against the paper . . . and stopped. *Oh, for heaven's sake.* "Smythe!"

The office door opened quickly enough that the butler had to have been standing directly on the other side. "My lady?"

"Which of my sons is home?"

"The two younger ones, my lady. Master Aden arrived not fifteen minutes ago, and Master Niall hasn't yet risen."

Which one did she want? Aden would be more alert, but he was also much less forthcoming and cooperative

than her youngest son. "Fetch me Niall, if you please. And
Eloise."

Sketching a quick bow, the butler practically ran out the
door. She couldn't blame him; as stoic and steady as he'd
been over the dozen years since she'd hired him, the last
eight weeks had been nothing if not unsettling. Her trio of
sons had upended not just Oswell House, but all of Mayfair. And even with the theft of a marquis's coach, his kid-
napping, an elopement to Scotland, a brawl at Boodle's
that had gotten Aden banned from every gentlemen's club
in London, and Coll running naked up Grosvenor Square
in the middle of the morning not four days ago, her oldest
son had just presented her with the most outrageous situation yet.

And to think that, before they'd arrived in London, she'd
believed the infrequent letters from her sons to Eloise had
given her enough information to choose a woman who
would suit Coll. Yes, Amy had suited Niall, so she hadn't
been so very far off the mark, but then again, if Coll had
his mind set on Persephone Jones, then that did a rather
fine job of telling her that she didn't know him at all. And
that troubled her. *More* than troubled her.

"Mama?" Eloise practically skidded into the room. She
still wore her night-rail, her dark hair in a long, loose tail
that made her look even younger than her eighteen years.

"I'm sorry to have awakened you, my dear," Francesca
said, indicating one of the chairs at the front of the desk.
"But we have a disaster to hand."

"If *ye're* announcing a disaster, we're done for," her next
oldest, twenty-four-year-old Niall drawled, appearing in
the doorway.

Bare-chested and barefoot, her mahogany-haired son
was naked but for the kilt knotted about his waist. At least
he'd bothered to put on the kilt; being newly married had
evidently civilized him a touch. "And how is Amy this

morning?" she asked, putting aside her impatience for a moment. This entire enterprise had been about reuniting her with her sons. Whatever Coll's plans, she couldn't afford to ruin what they'd all been working so hard to regain.

"Last I saw her, she was still trembling beneath the bed-sheets, scared by the sight of Smythe bursting into the room while we were both sound asleep. What's amiss? Has Coll disappeared again?"

"No, this time your brother managed to return to Oswell House after fleeing the theater," she returned.

"That's someaught, then. I told ye nae to ambush him with lasses again. At least he didnae insult any of them this time."

Yes, perhaps she'd been overly confident that her oldest—a viscount, for heaven's sake—would have refrained from creating yet more gossip by fleeing her theater box for the second time since the men's arrival in London. "His behavior last night, though reprehensible, is not the issue."

Niall dropped into the chair beside his sister. "Aye? What is it, then? The archbishop didnae deny Aden a special marriage license, did he? Because that wouldnae sit well with Aden."

"Hush, if you please, Niall."

From her son's expression, his maddening line of inquiry hadn't been entirely innocent. They'd begun this visit trying to aggravate her, and given that seventeen years had passed since she'd last set eyes on them, she couldn't blame them for that. But she'd been trying to make amends for lost time. And perhaps eventually, they would realize that there was more to the story than what their father had told them. But for now, she would work with what she had to hand.

She took a breath. "Coll went riding off just now, after he announced that he'd found an Englishwoman to wed."

Niall blinked. "He did?"

Ah, so his brothers weren't even aware. That meant something—and more than likely, it was nothing good. "Yes, he did. This, after an argument over whether my agreement with Angus stated that you three were to wed English ladies or Englishwomen."

"Englishwomen," he responded promptly. "But if he found a lass, then—"

"He's found an *actress*," Francesca stated, the word distasteful on her tongue. "He means to marry her. Of course, he also announced that he's presently serving as her protector, so no doubt by noon everyone in London will know that my oldest son intends to wed a woman he is presently . . . keeping."

Eloise put both hands over her mouth. "He wouldn't," she breathed. "My wedding is in four weeks, Mama!"

"I recall that, my dear. Which is why I am writing your father to make him aware that Coll is on the verge of casting his lineage into the dustbin. Whatever Angus thinks of the Sassenachs in general, he has never been lacking in pride. And Persephone Jones is not going to become a member of the MacTaggert family."

Her daughter lowered her hands, then raised them again. "Persephone Jones? She's . . . Everyone knows who she is. We can't even pretend that Coll didn't know she was an actress."

Niall tilted his head, his nearly colorless green eyes twins to his younger sister's. "Even I ken who Persephone Jones is. She was Juliet at the theater the night Coll stomped off and left Amy to me—and I'll always be grateful to him for that."

Francesca opened her mouth to point out that Coll had made quite a mess that evening at Drury Lane Theatre— and that he'd obviously begun another mess at the Saint Genesius last night—but she stopped herself. For Niall, that night at *Romeo and Juliet* had quite possibly been the most significant in his twenty-four years, because that was where he'd met Amelia-Rose Baxter. In retrospect, Francesca should have realized that introducing Coll to young, eligible ladies at the theater was a blasted mistake—one she'd repeated last night, to disastrous results.

"Perhaps my agreement with your father didn't state that you three were to marry English *ladies*, but that was the intent," she said instead, turning the conversation back to the problem at hand. "I wanted a way to see my sons back in my life. If Coll does as he has threatened and marries someone so far below his station—and not even simply a commoner, but such an unacceptable female—he will be shunned by Society. The MacTaggert name will be whispered and laughed at behind fans. None of us will be welcomed into the homes of our peers."

Niall shrugged. "They're nae *our* peers. They're yours. I dunnae think Coll cares to be welcomed into most Sassenach houses, anyway."

"I do," Eloise said. "And so does Amy. And Miranda. It's not just you three and the Highlands any longer, Niall."

The youngest MacTaggert male's expression slowly shifted from one of amusement to one of concern. "Amy doesnae like people looking askance at her."

"It would be one thing if he loved her," Eloise pursued, "but I've never even heard him mention her name. And with the way he keeps leaving the theater as soon as the play begins, I don't think he's ever seen Persephone Jones in a performance. He's only trying to make trouble."

If this was simply bluster, Coll's last bellow of defiance before he chose someone acceptable—well, that could be managed. But Francesca had overheard several conversations between the brothers, and she knew the original plan for each of them had been to find some empty-headed thing, wed her, bed her, and then leave her behind in England in favor of Scotland. If that remained Coll's plan, then she supposed it wouldn't matter to him who he married, because he wouldn't be in London to face any of the social consequences.

"I hope you and brothers know, Niall," she said slowly, "that I will move heaven and earth to see you happy. At the same time, I am the daughter of the ninth and last Viscount Hornford, a very well-respected man from a very well-respected family. I am a MacTaggert, and a proud one, but I am also an Oswell. This . . . No. It cannot happen." She lifted the pen again. "And that is why I am writing your father to inform him of Coll's intentions."

Eloise gasped. "*You're* writing Father?"

"I must. He is free to enjoy his brawls and drinking and . . . whatever carousing he's been up to. He may choose to continue the pretense that he is presently on his deathbed due to the shock of your engagement, Eloise. But whatever he wishes to pretend, this will not sit well with him."

Niall's expression deepened into a scowl. "Nae, it will-nae. It may even come to blows. But if ye think this'll stir him from the Highlands, *màthair*, I'd suggest ye nae hold yer breath."

"I stopped holding my breath a very long time ago where Angus MacTaggert is concerned, my darling. And I will place more hope in you and Aden being able to reason with Coll than I will in your father doing anything the least bit reasonable and responsible. But as a mother, and an Oswell, and a MacTaggert, I must do whatever I'm able. And that includes writing a letter to Angus."

"Reasoning and Coll arenae close friends when he's got his back up," Niall commented.

Francesca didn't often admit that she didn't know what

to do. This, in fact, might be the first time in seventeen years that she'd done so. If Coll was serious about that woman, she needed more reinforcements than the formidable MacTaggert brothers—the remaining two of them, anyway—could provide. Even if the reinforcements consisted of Angus MacTaggert, Lord Glendarril. Her husband.

Chapter Four

"Such welcome and unwelcome things at once
'Tis hard to reconcile."

MACDUFF, MACBETH ACT IV, SCENE III

B ut when the Scottish play gives his grand soliloquy
about the brief candle, he should be—"

"It's the play that's referred to as 'the Scottish play,'"
Persephone pointed out, lifting her gaze from her well-
marked folio. "Not the character, dear."

Gordon Humphreys scowled at her as the rest of the
assembled cast chuckled behind their pages. "Say what
you will, but when I last performed the Scottish play,
three actors came down with the ague, and our Lady the
Scottish play broke her arm when a coach nearly ran her
down."

"The name is said in the play by Macbeth himself,
Gordon," Charlie Huddle pointed out. "You can't go about
onstage saying 'I am the Scottish play.'"

"At least I'm attempting to avoid ill fortune," their Macbeth retorted. "I heard you last night, Huddle, telling that
big Highlander we were about to begin rehearsals for the
Scottish play, only you didn't call it that. Informing a
Scotsman will likely mean even more peril for the rest of
us daring to pretend to be Scottish."

Everyone had noticed the Highlander, apparently. She'd
barely stopped thinking about him for long enough to fall

asleep herself. Fighting the grin pulling at her lips, Persephone sat forward. "What did Charlie call it, Gordon?"

"He called it by its name, Persie. You can't trick me."

She lifted her folio again. "It's early yet. Give me some time."

"If Gordon won't say 'Macbeth,' I'm happy to take that role," Thomas Baywich announced, as he arrived backstage. "Though I still think my idea to set the play in the Pacific Islands would gain us the raves you've been after this Season, Charlie."

"I am not performing Lady Macbeth bare-breasted, which is all you're after anyway, Baywich," Persephone retorted.

"The play refers to its own setting in Scotland countless times. We cannot ignore that for the sake of seeing Persie's tits," Gordon agreed. "No matter how spectacular they likely are. And *I* am playing the title character. You make for a fine, stout Duncan, Baywich, and I will so enjoy stabbing you every night."

"Offstage," Thomas Baywich countered. "Macbeth stabs Duncan offstage." Taking the seat beside Persephone, he paged through his own folio. "Clive, trade with me. You play Duncan the king, and I'll play Macduff. Macduff gets to cross swords with Macbeth on stage."

Persephone glanced at the tall, red-headed man seated to her right. Clive Montrose had only joined their company this morning, lured to the Saint Genesius by, from what she'd heard from him, a rather generous purse and a promise of the lead role in the next play performed after the Scottish play.

Considering that he generally played at the Covent Garden Theatre and had done so for the past five or six years, she had to surmise that he'd either been asked to move on, or Charlie Huddle *had* offered a great deal of money to bring him over. The former made more sense,

though it was true that acting troupes thrived on fres
blood. It helped them avoid falling into the trap of makin
every performance the same, no matter the play.

Regardless of Clive Montrose's motives for arrivin
at the Saint Genesius, she still couldn't quite figure it—
him—out. He might have contested for the lead in th
Scottish play if he'd wished, but he'd opted for the mor
heroic Macduff, despite that character having many fewe
lines, and the doctor, who had even fewer.

At least as interesting was the fact that he and she ha
never performed in the same play together before. A fe
weeks ago, she'd gone over to Drury Lane Theatre to pla
Juliet while the Saint Genesius had been offering *A Ma
World, My Masters*, and she'd played Juliet the year befor
that at Covent Garden. In her five years of performing i
London, she'd appeared with nearly every other acto
in Town at one point or another. Clive Montrose had bee
the exception—until now.

"I'm content with Macduff," Montrose drawled. "Mac
beth is pleasant enough to act, but I've found it refreshin
to embody a character who's still alive at the end of a play.

"We've been over all this, anyway," Charlie Huddl
stated. "I decide who plays which part. *That* was ou
agreement, to stop you mad people from coming to blow
over it. Now, might we begin?"

"I don't know what you lot are fighting about, anyway,
Jenny Rogers put in. "All the gents will be coming to se
Persie. A rooster could play Macbeth, and they'd stil
come."

"So says Witch Number One," Gordon Humphreys re
torted.

"And Lady Macduff, you old flapdoodle."

"I'll have you know my doodle does not flap, ma'am.
stands proud as a flagpole."

That was the thing about actors, Persephone had found

Each wanted to be the center of attention, and every comment was likely to be followed by a cleverer or funnier one until a given scenario became outrageously silly. She adored it.

Charlie Huddle likely adored it less, but at least he was accustomed to it, and simply sat back, sipping a cup of cooling tea until the laughter died down again. "Opening scene," he said, once they subsided. "We'll need lots of thunder and lightning for this one, Harry."

The head stagehand nodded, jotting down notes in the margins of his folio. "I'll pull out the heavy metal sheets and the miner's lights."

"Enter three witches," Charlie Huddle went on, and Jenny, Rose, and Sally stood to recite their lines.

As they did so, a large shadow to one corner of the rehearsal room shifted. For a handful of seconds, Persephone imagined the curse of the Scottish play had come to life after all, because the figure forming as it neared the light both wore a kilt and loomed several inches above six feet. In the next heartbeat, its face emerged from the shadows, and her heart stilled before it resumed again. Perhaps he wasn't Macbeth, but Coll MacTaggert might have been some perfect, pagan god of the old Highlands, lit by yellow lamplight and chiseled to stunning perfection by some unknown hand. *Trouble*, her heart beat in a fast tattoo. *Trouble*.

"Good Lord," Gordon gasped, crossing himself. "We've summoned the Scottish play himself."

"You're the one who set Claremont on his arse last night, aren't you?" someone else asked.

"Aye," Coll returned, his gaze settling on Persephone's face and remaining there.

Trouble, her mind shouted at her, as if her heart hadn't sounded the alarm loudly enough. "Good morning, MacTaggert. You've found us rehearsing."

"I didnae come to see a rehearsal," he returned in that deep, resonating brogue. "I came to see ye, lass."

"Oh, someone fetch me my salts," Jenny breathed. "I'm going to faint all over him."

"I say, my good man," Gordon put in, "what would you charge to assist me with an authentic Scots accent? That could be just the thing to wow the critics with my Scottish play."

"With yer what?"

"He won't say the name of the play or the character," Persephone offered.

"Are ye soft-headed, then?"

Thomas Baywich snorted. "That is up for debate."

"Is it true the Scots eat the babes of their rival clans?" Lawrence Valense, chimed in with the faux Scottish accent he'd assumed from the moment they'd arrived this morning.

"The lot of you heathens leave MacTaggert be," Persephone said, before a brawl could erupt. The Highlander would lay waste to her entire troupe without breaking a sweat, she imagined, and then none of them would be fit to appear onstage for weeks.

"I can hold my own, I reckon," the viscount—who didn't realize she knew him to be a viscount—returned. "I'm nae here to deliver lessons to Sassenachs on how to sound like a Highlander, and I've nae snacked on any bairns, but if ye go back far enough, I've some blood I share with Banquo. Which of ye plays him?"

"That would be me," Lawrence Valense said through his thick beard, grown, he claimed, especially for the part. Personally, Persephone thought it pure laziness, since Valense typically went after whichever bearded part happened to be available.

"Och," the Highlander exclaimed, blinking. "Ye look more like the father of Christmas than the father of kings."

A laugh burst from Persephone's lips before she could stifle it. Valense's face—the part they could see above the beard—turned beet red as the rest of the troupe joined in the laughter. "I'll have you know, sir, that according to my research, Banquo wore a beard."

"Aye, a wee one, it's said. Ye'll nae find a fighting man with a great beard like that. Ye'd make it too easy for yer opponent to grab onto yer head and lop it off. Yer head, I mean—nae the beard."

"That's a fine enough explanation for me," Charlie put in. "Valense, a wee beard only. No one cares about your weak chin but you."

"It's not—"

"Perhaps I could show MacTaggert about the theater," Persephone suggested, rising. "And perhaps I can convince him to give us all a few pointers in sounding Scottish."

"Yes, do that, Persie. You don't have any lines until scene five, anyway," Charlie Huddle said. "I owe you for disposing of Claremont, Highlander, but please make this brief. You're disrupting rehearsal."

"Oh, let him stay," Jenny protested, shrugging her shoulder to lower the already sagging sleeve of her bohemian-style gown. "I could convince him to teach us all his accent."

Persephone put a hand on the giant's arm. "Come, Mac-Taggert, before the three witches begin ripping off your clothes."

He nodded amid the general laughter and followed her toward the front of the stage. She loved the day the preparations for a new play began, with the arrival of additional workmen and new actors, the smell of sawdust and paint, the hammering and sawing and costume fittings, and the snippets of dialogue as the actors tried on their characters for the first time.

"It wasnae my intention to walk into the middle of all

that," the giant rumbled from behind her. "I'd rather have had a word or two with ye and be gone, but I was waylaid by the carpenters trying to stand a forest upright, and ye'd nae arrived yet."

She faced him once they'd moved far enough away from the rehearsal to chat without being overheard. "You've been helping assemble a forest?"

"Aye. Birnham Wood, I reckon. I helped 'em put it up on some wee wheels so they wouldnae have to carry it about."

Wheels on the forest. A rather brilliant idea, really—and one that might stop the stagehands from tripping all over each other during what was meant to be a thrilling scene. "The wheels were your idea, then?"

"Aye. That set of trees last night nearly killed me backstage, so I reckoned to—"

"You're very charming."

"Nae." He shook his shaggy head. Wild, he looked. Untamed. It was quite enticing. And arousing. "My youngest brother, Niall, is the charming one. I'm the MacTaggert who generally speaks my mind. For example, I'm meant to be in Hyde Park this morning, but my mount carried me here instead. I reckon I've nae complaints about that. Do ye?"

Was he just another one, then? Another powerful man who would do her a favor or purchase her a bauble, and expect something in return? Was he only negotiating her price right now? If he'd been just Coll MacTaggert, she would know better where she stood. A title, though, complicated everything, and he had one. "Is that who you're playing, then?" she asked a little sharply.

He tilted his head, a lock of his unruly, umber-colored hair straying over one of his green eyes. "I beg yer pardon?"

"Your act," Persephone clarified. "You're the affable,

slightly dim lad from yonder Highlands, blundering about with what seems to be simple good luck and yet arriving exactly where and when you mean to be without making a point of it, putting everyone at ease because it suits you to do so, though with a hint that you could be much more formidable if you wished."

Both pretty emerald-colored eyes narrowed just a touch. "Have I done someaught to offend ye, Mrs. Jones?"

"You lied to me. You're not just Coll MacTaggert. Viscount Glendarril, is it not?"

He sighed. "I'm Glendarril. But I chose nae to throw that about. I dunnae need it hanging about my neck to make a lass notice me. So, I didnae lie. I just didnae add any decorations." The viscount studied her for a brief moment. "And what color is yer hair, *Mrs.* Persephone Jones? I reckon I'm nae the only one playing a role."

Well, that shot went very close by her heart. But he was only striking out because she'd hit first, she reminded herself. "I value my privacy," she said aloud, shrugging. "I dislike being hounded as I go about my day. And I prefer lodgings where I'm not likely to be propositioned while I'm pruning my roses."

"I could keep ye from being hounded." Leaning back against the wall, he folded his arms across his chest.

In response to his coiled, predator's ease, slow lightning coursed across her scalp, down her spine, and between her thighs. "And who will keep *you* from hounding me?" she managed to say levelly.

"Do ye want me gone, then? Say the word, lass. I'm nae about to force myself on an unwilling woman."

Oh no, she didn't want him gone. "Then I suppose there is a difference between you and certain other titled gentlemen of my acquaintance. But I've heard that you're here in London to find yourself a wife, my lord. Are you certain you wish to waste your time pursuing me?" Even if she felt tempted. Even if being in his embrace would feel . . . safe. And very arousing.

He gave a quick grin. "Truth be told, it's my mother, Lady Aldriss, who wants me wed. She and my da signed an agreement back before she fled the Highlands. If my brothers and I dunnae wed before my sister, there'll be consequences we cannae afford. And Eloise is to wed in a wee bit less than four weeks."

"Then why the devil are you here bantering with me?"

"I told ye I was in Hyde Park. But then I offended a lass without meaning to, and I rode off to wait for a different set of lasses to come by. Then I ended up here. I'll go back eventually, because I've a duty to do so. This morning, though, I'm here."

"I understand your objections to being forced to marry, but consequences are consequences."

"That they are. My mother, Lady Aldriss, flung two lasses at me last night. That's how I ended up backstage to meet ye. She willnae stop meddling, so I told her before I rode off this morning that I mean to wed *ye*. That should send her into a twirl for a bit and give me time to find my own woman."

The floor dropped out from beneath Persephone's feet, a yawning, endless blackness opening below. Stretching out, she grabbed for the steadiest thing within her reach—the viscount's arm.

"Whoa there, lass," he muttered, putting his other arm around her and guiding her to one of the half dozen thrones sitting about backstage.

She sat heavily, lowering her head until her vision cleared again. "Gentlemen do not marry actresses," she stated, unable to hold back the tremor at the end of the sentence. "Lady Aldriss must have been mortified."

"She did look like she'd swallowed a bug when I told

her. I have to marry; I know that. While she's fretting over ye and me, and doing whatever she can to put a ball through my plans, I'll have a damned minute to find my own woman. But I'm nae wed yet, Mrs. Jones. And neither are ye."

As she listened, the blood began to return to Persephone's fingers and toes and to heat other, more private areas. He'd only been stirring up a distraction for himself by saying he meant to marry her, then. He hadn't actually meant what he'd told the countess. Thank goodness. Firstly, that meant he wasn't a madman, and secondly, it wouldn't bring her the trouble and disruption she tried very hard to avoid. Living on the fringes of respectability was no easy thing under the best of circumstances. Going about as the betrothed of a viscount headed for an earldom, or even having that rumor hanging about her, would have been . . . horrible.

"And here I was debating whether it was Rosalind or Juliet or Beatrice you were expecting to find behind the stage, and which one it was you were lusting after. Instead, you just needed my name to shock your mother. And for a bit of bedchamber fun, of course."

"More than a bit, I hope. Ye ken that standing in the wings last night was the first time I've seen ye perform. It's nae one of those other lasses I'm after. I'll admit, though, that ye prancing about in those trousers definitely caught my attention."

She stifled a grin. "If it's Ganymede you found attractive, my lord, I think you may be looking for something I cannot provide."

Glendarril's eyebrows joined together as he scowled. "It wasnae Ganymede, woman. Christ almighty."

"Even so, you—"

"Claremont said he was yer protector. Last night I reckoned that meant he kept the other lads away from ye and saw ye away from here safely. Since then, I've heard the word flung about a few times, and now I'm thinking it doesnae mean what I thought it meant. Or that it means more than I reckoned."

Her cheeks warmed. "He called himself my protector, yes. That doesn't mean he ever saw the inside of my bedchamber. That is the general . . . assumption that accompanies the word, though. It was certainly what he wanted, whether I agreed to it or not."

"He was disagreeing with ye over the bedchamber bits when I set him on his arse." Keener eyes than she expected studied her face for a long moment. "I'll be yer protector. Lord knows ye need one, if ye have men panting after ye like I saw last night. As for the rest, I've told ye what I want. Ye answer me however ye choose. I need ye to put a fright into my mother. I want ye because ye've gone and caught my interest."

She returned his gaze. He wasn't the only one whose interest had been caught. "You are a conundrum, my lord. If it is a lady like Rosalind you wanted, though, you will be disappointed. I am Lady Macbeth now."

The viscount shook his head. "Ye're both, and ye're neither. I'm nae as thick-headed as ye think I'm pretending to be." He glanced over her throne at the gathered actors rehearsing just out of their hearing. "Now tell me where ye live, and I'll nae trouble ye here."

"No."

One straight eyebrow lifted. "Ye're a conundrum yerself, Persephone Jones." He leaned over her, putting a hand on either arm of the throne. "At least tell me the truth about Mr. Jones."

He was quite possibly the first man to ask her that. What it meant, though, she didn't suppose she cared. She didn't need anyone else's money, and while having someone keeping all the other men away from her was pleasant, she *could* fend for herself. This was fast becoming a question of what she wanted, and *that* was becoming more complicated by the moment. It did occur to her that complications were the last thing she needed. They never led anywhere the least bit pleasant.

"I am in a scandalous profession, Lord Glendarril," she said aloud. "Being a wife—or a widow—gives me a semblance of respectability. It doesn't keep proper women from turning their backs on me in a milliner's, but it allows them to come to the theater to see my plays. It allows me to find respectable lodgings. No, there is no Mr. Jones. He does serve me well in absentia, though."

"Ye dunnae need to defend having a made-up spouse, Persephone Jones. I'd invent one myself, if it would satisfy the solicitors."

She could sink into that lush green gaze. Persephone shook herself. Evidently, she still carried more than a hint of lovestruck young Rosalind about with her. "One of your brothers recently married, did he not?"

"Aye. Niall. And my other brother, Aden, is to wed a week from Saturday." His expression folded into one of attractive annoyance. "Damn all Sassenach women and their underhanded ways, anyway." Coll MacTaggert sat on the throne perched beside hers. King John's, as she recalled. "I'd thought to ask ye to come to Aden's wedding with me to keep my *màthair* off-balance for a wee bit longer, but since when I mentioned marrying ye just now ye nearly fell to the floor, that might be a poor idea."

Despite his words, he continued to eye her. Persephone considered whether he actually understood the enormity of what he'd asked her. She knew Lady Aldriss solely by reputation and rather liked the idea of putting a shock into the aristocracy, but the fact that the countess had kept a prime box at the Saint Genesius for at least the past six years made her loathe to offend the woman. Lady Aldriss had a powerful voice among the *haut ton.* "Yes, I think it would be a poor idea," she said aloud.

"I'm beginning to think ye dunnae like me." The giant stood again and held out a hand to help her up with surprising gentleness. "Let me take ye to luncheon, at least."

Inwardly, she sighed. Not at the gross overconfidence from which most men suffered, the belief that they were irresistible to any and every woman, but at the idea of simply going out and sitting down for luncheon with a very handsome and rather interesting man because he'd asked, and not demanded. Because he hadn't begun this expecting her to comply because he'd done her one good turn. "I don't—"

He held up one hand. "Wait. Let's try one thing, and then ye answer me."

When she nodded, curious, he grimaced, tilting his head again as he gazed at her. Then, before she could ask which one thing he thought might convince her, he took a long step forward, lowered his head, and kissed her.

His lips met hers, warm and self-assured as he placed his hands on either side of her face and tilted her chin up. Hints, promises, and things unspoken but deeply felt all rattled through her at once, leaving her heart pounding, her lungs aching for air, and her eyes shut as she tried to take everything in.

Slowly, he lifted his head again. "Will ye join me for luncheon, Persephone Jones?"

Good heavens. Summoning an answer took far more effort than it should have, likely because the answer she needed to give wasn't the one she wanted to give. "You kiss well," she managed, blinking and trying to call her wits back into her mind. "'By the book,' as Juliet would say."

"And what do *ye* say, then?"

"I say no. I don't need a protector, and you need to find

a bride. So, thank you, but you are more trouble than I need, Lord Glendarril."

He straightened. "I reckon ye'd be more trouble than I need as well, lass. If ye change yer mind, though, I might be willing to see my way past that." With a slight, brief grin that didn't quite touch his eyes, he inclined his head, then turned and walked away.

Persephone sighed. A bit of fun, indeed. Coll MacTaggert was the sort of man to turn a woman's head. It was a shame she didn't wish her head turned. Or rather, she did, but she didn't want—*need*—the trouble that would come with him.

"Persie, Huddle is reading your lines," Gordon Humphreys bellowed from the rear corner of the theater. "For God's sake, come and save us!"

She stood up from her borrowed throne. Yes, Coll MacTaggert was a distraction, and one she didn't need. As she stepped forward, a quartet of sandbags crashed down onto the throne she'd just vacated, smashing it into bits of wood. Something flew against her cheek as she spun around, and she lifted her hand to her face. Her finger came away with a bit of blood on it. *Good heavens.*

More noise erupted around her, queries over what the noise had been, and queries over her safety from those who'd been close enough to see. "Persie! Are you injured?" Charlie Huddle barked as he reached her side. "Good God."

"It's the Scottish play," Gordon said, his complexion ashen as he took in the sight of the smashed throne. "I've sat in that throne!" He half collapsed against a convenient upright beam.

"Harry!" Charlie called, turning around to look for the head stagehand. "For God's sake, do not be hanging sandbags while the actors are wandering about! If we lost Persephone, we might as well close our doors."

"No one was up on the catwalks, as far as I know," the brawny man in rolled-up shirtsleeves returned, crouching to lift up the end of the rope. "It's dusty and frayed, but that seems to me like a clean cut there."

"Nonsense," Charlie said. "You've been shaking the foundations all morning with that hammering."

Beth Frost, Flora's daughter and the company's current head seamstress, dabbed at Persephone's cheek, making her jump. "It looks like a splinter caught you," she said, peering more closely. "I think Charlotte can cover it with powder so no one will ever know."

"I'm fine," Persephone said to the crowd in general. "It's not the first time I've nearly been knocked down by a sandbag."

"I don't suppose anyone has seen Claremont since last night?" Charlie muttered under his breath, leaning in to examine her cheek.

Ice abruptly tipped her fingers. "He wouldn't do such a thing. It was an accident."

"Hmm. I hope so. All the same, you might want to keep that Scotsman about for a few days."

The Scotsman she'd just sent away. The one who had four weeks to find a bride and had teased his mother with *her* name. The one who'd set Claremont on his arse, quite possibly making the earl angry enough to . . . attempt to kill her? No, that made no sense. Even so, Coll had offered to be her protector with no expectation of her granting him any kind of personal favor. "I'll be back in just a moment," she said, turning on her heel, hiking up her skirts, and running for the rear door of the theater.

"Now Persie's gone mad," Lawrence Valense lamented. "And it's only the first day of rehearsals. We're doomed."

She barely noted that bit as she stepped outside, blinking in the sunlight. Someone whistled at her, but she ignored it as she spied the Highlander half a street away and mounted on a great black devil of a horse.

"MacTaggert!" she called, hurrying after him and ignoring the stares and commentary of the passersby around her.

He reined in the horse and turned the beast around, dismounting as she reached him. "Did I forget someaught?" he rumbled.

"We'll be finishing here at one o'clock today," she said a bit breathlessly. "I'll meet you by the rear door then."

"I thought ye didnae need the trouble I bring with . . . What the devil happened to ye, lass?" Without asking, he reached out and gently brushed his fingers along her injured cheek.

"An accident. I have a business proposition to discuss with you, if you would care to take me to luncheon after all. Perhaps we could help each other."

His green gaze lifted to meet hers. "It wasnae business I had in mind with ye, Persephone Jones, but as I said, ye've gone and made me interested. I'll meet ye here at one o'clock."

Relief—and something else she couldn't quite name— ran down her spine. "Thank you, my lord."

That infectious grin of his appeared again, curving his very capable mouth and reminding her that he knew how to kiss. "I told ye to call me Coll."

"Coll, then."

"That's better. Now ye go be Lady Macbeth, and I'll see if I can find a phaeton or barouche or one of those other fancy carriages ye lasses favor."

With that, he mounted his great stallion again and trotted away. Persephone leaned back against the side of a wagon stopped to unload timber for the Saint Genesius. If she'd just been spooked and Lord Claremont wasn't out to injure her, then this would be a one-sided agreement. On the other hand, MacTaggert—Coll—had been extremely useful in keeping her other admirers at bay. *Trouble, trouble*. Boil and bubble.

Chapter Five

"And thence it is
That I to your assistance do make love,
Masking the business from the common eye
For sundry weighty reasons."

MACBETH, *MACBETH* ACT III, SCENE I

Nae, ye cannae drive the barouche yerself, m'laird,"
Gavin grunted as he bent down to fasten the harness around the belly of the left-hand bay—one of a pair Lady Aldriss had purchased, evidently, because they were pretty.

"But I can drive the phaeton myself." Coll led the second bay to its place and held it steady while the groom finished harnessing the pair.

"Aye, but then ye cannae climb down and walk anywhere, because there's nae a groom to hold the team for ye."

"Is that why Eloise and Matthew tooled off in his phaeton earlier with nae a maid for a chaperone? Because he cannae take his hands off the reins?"

"That's the idea, I reckon."

"Whoever thought that doesnae know how to drive a carriage, I reckon."

Gavin snorted, straightening to pat the closest bay on the withers. "I heard it was ye who gave the pretty lad that fine pair of black eyes. Well done, m'laird. I was beginning to think I would have to do it myself, and then her majesty would sack me."

"She didnae hire ye, Gavin, so she cannae sack ye. But if the day ever comes when I cannae defend my own sister's honor, then I reckon I'll be needing to sack myself." Coll scowled at the barouche. What an odd vehicle—good for naught but being driven about so all the bystanders could have a good look at the occupants. A Sassenach coach for silly Sassenach ways. "Can ye drive it, then?"

"Aye. Dunnae ask me to dress up in that fancy Oswell livery, though."

"If ye're leaving," Aden's voice came from behind them, "ye should go now. *Màthair*'s on her way down to forbid ye from taking any carriage with the Oswell coat of arms onto the street if ye mean to have an actress aboard with ye."

"*Tapadh leat*," Coll replied, thanking his younger brother.

Of course, Aden would know by now that Coll had declared his intent to pursue Mrs. Persephone Jones; no doubt the entire household knew, and Aden had never been lax about listening for rumors, anyway. As Coll brushed hay from his proper coat and not-so-proper kilt, he sent his keen-eyed brother another glance to find himself being eyed in return. "What?"

"What what?" Aden returned, leaning back against the exterior stable wall. "Ye ken the price of failing to wed. Whatever ye're about, I reckon ye have enough sense to use Lady Aldriss's panic to yer advantage. And I have to give ye my respect—we tried for eight weeks to set her back on her heels, and ye did it in one conversation."

Grinning, Coll stepped into the open barouche and closed the low, useless door behind him. "I'd nae have thought she'd tolerate a stuffed deer on her landing better than she would the idea of me courting an actress."

"Aye, but the deer is *inside* the house, where nae a soul can see it without her giving them leave to enter. The actress will be in a barouche in Hyde Park with the Oswell coat of arms on the door." He pushed upright and moved to put both hands over the lip of the carriage door. "Ye're a straightforward man, Coll. But an actress isnae a straightforward creature. She spins lies for her livelihood. Dunnae lose sight of that."

"I'm nae twelve, Aden. But I ken I've been wrong-footed since I arrived in London. It shouldnae have taken me this long to figure out how to use that to my advantage."

Nodding, his brother slapped the door and stepped back again. "I'll admit I'm looking forward to the chaos. Have at it, *bràthair.*"

Gavin practically leaped onto the driver's perch. "Her majesty's coming, all right, and she's got three of those Sassenach footmen with her. I reckon we're in for a brawl."

As tempting as it would be to flatten some of the Oswell-MacTaggert stuffy servants and demonstrate to his mother that attempting to thwart him was a fool's errand, fighting wouldn't get him to the Saint Genesius by one o'clock to find out what Persephone Jones meant by a business proposition. "Go. Now."

"Aye," the groom said, and nodded at the stable boy, who released his hold on the team and stepped back. With a flick of the reins, Gavin sent the horses into a quick trot.

Coll finally turned to look, catching a glimpse of his grim-faced mother as the barouche turned up Grosvenor Square. That was one angry woman, one who was unaccustomed to having her wishes, much less her *orders*, ignored.

He could have some sympathy; after all, she'd helped both Niall and Aden when his brothers had needed her rather substantial influence in London. One was married and one about to be, and while she hadn't chosen their damned brides for them, Lady Aldriss had helped clear their paths toward matrimony.

On the other side of the equation, she'd taken then-one-year-old Eloise with her and fled the Highlands when he'd been a lad of but twelve years. He'd written her a handful of letters begging her to return, and she'd never bothered to answer him. At least he'd learned that lesson; fists were much more effective at getting a point across than any amount of flowery language.

She wouldn't chase after him now because that wouldn't look well. *Ha.* As far as he was concerned, the Sassenachs could frown as much as they pleased. He was taking a pretty lass to luncheon. After that, perhaps he'd drive up and down Hyde Park like the other dandies and see which marriageable lass might catch his attention.

Or, if Persephone was after something more personal, he'd revisit Hyde Park tomorrow. Because while he didn't mind a bit of distraction—and even looked forward to it, where the actress was concerned—he still had a duty to find a wife.

Coll leaned forward, checking that the lid on the picnic basket he'd had Mrs. Gordon prepare remained tied down. Now that they were moving, he could admit that he liked the barouche a wee bit more. Anything open to the sky had his approval; the devil knew closed coaches gave him the shivers under the best conditions.

Stretching both arms out along the top of the rear seat, he sank back. Being a man with no responsibilities would bore him in a day, but being driven about beneath the sun with the wind in his face and an interesting lass to meet had its attractions. As an additional benefit, being driven about made it easier for him to view the passersby as Gavin guided them through the heart of Mayfair. A number of lasses attempted to catch his eye, and Coll made a mental note of each one. By now, they'd all begun to swirl about in his head in a blur of skirts and fans and bonnets, but there had to be one—one *more*, since Niall had found Amy, and Aden had won Miranda—acceptable female in London.

He knew most of the available lasses' names by now and had at least figured out which ones he wanted nothing to do with under any circumstance, the ones who pretended to be empty-headed in the hope that he would do as he'd originally planned—wed and bed one of them and then leave her behind with the title of Lady Glendarril while he returned to Scotland alone. Whether he wanted that any longer or not, if it came down to marrying without love, at least he wanted the assurance that his wife would make a good matron for Aldriss Park.

If it did come down to logic rather than sentiment, then pursuing Persephone Jones on the side for a heated tryst or two and some witty conversation might be the most fun he had while he remained in London.

Whatever it was about her—her changing hair color, her quick wit, or even her stated horror at the idea of marrying above her station—she'd sparked his interest. Aye, he might have surprised her with that kiss, but *he'd* definitely felt it deep in his chest, where it rattled around like rocks in a metal bucket and made him . . . not uneasy, but more aware. A first scent of rain on a sunny day.

"Shall I wait out here, then?" Gavin said over his shoulder as the groom stopped the barouche on one side of the narrow street.

"Aye. If they hear another Highlander in there, they might kidnap ye and force ye to teach them yer accent."

The groom frowned. "What accent?"

"Never ye mind, Gavin. I'll be but a moment."

Though he could have simply stepped over the coach's low door, he very properly opened it up and disembarked like a gentleman. One of the carpenters he'd worked with earlier caught sight of him and doffed his hat, which meant that everyone inside knew now that he was a viscount.

Generally, he didn't care one way or the other who knew what or thought what about him, but the English were so blasted conscious of where and with whom they belonged that pretending to be common had felt . . . almost freeing. After all, he'd been a viscount since the day of his birth. He'd never not had it hung about his neck. And while others looked at him with envy, to Coll the title had been both a responsibility and a tool; it gave him cotters and villagers and herdsmen and farmers to look after, and it gave him the means and power to do so.

He found Persephone inside the theater, looking over her folio with Charlie Huddle. With her head bowed, the delicate curve of her neck seemed to beg for a kiss. Coll clenched his hands. No Highlander worth being called such would go about kissing a lass without her damned permission.

Then she lifted her head and caught his gaze, and his breath stilled. Aye, she was a woman worth being distracted over, even with only four weeks left to save the funding for Aldriss Park. If her yellow muslin had been a bit less low-cut, if the sleeves hadn't been quite so short or the sides of the skirt gathered to show glimpses of her ankles, she might have passed for a proper lass. But then he wouldn't be looking at her ankles or admiring the swell of her bosom or imagining his fingers brushing the bare skin of her shoulders.

Nine weeks without sharing a bed with a lass. That was how long he'd been celibate, and he didn't like it one damned bit. Aden had treated Mayfair like his very own breakfast sideboard until he'd met Miranda Harris, but not Coll. No, he'd shouted that every woman should lay a trap for him on his first day in London, and he'd spent the next two months doing everything he could to avoid being caught.

But then last night, he'd run across Persephone Jones, who didn't *want* to marry him. Coll grinned. "I hope ye dunnae mind, but I've brought us a picnic luncheon. It's a fine day, and I'm nae in the mood to dine indoors."

She nodded, handing the folio to the theater manager. "I haven't been on a picnic in ages. After the gloom of Lady Macbeth, the sunshine is welcome."

"Grand, then. Hyde Park?"

Her fingers hesitated before they wrapped about his forearm. It was a tiny gesture, but then noticing the smallest of details had, on occasion, saved his life. "Ye worried all the men who see ye willnae leave ye be?" he asked. "I'll nae let 'em pester ye."

"While you're occupied with flinging men about, we won't be able to discuss business," she returned, favoring him with a teasing smile that didn't touch her eyes. "The area being designed for Regent's Park is lovely. And much closer by."

So being interrupted wasn't what concerned her. Well, he'd made a mess at home over this luncheon, so he might as well enjoy it—wherever it was she wanted to dine. "Just tell my driver where to head, then," he said.

As they left the theater, a handful of men who'd been loitering by the rear entrance broke away from viewing the chaos of scenery-building to head toward them. *Good.* He might not be able to figure out this lass, but he could damned well fend off these hounds.

Ushering her into the barouche, Coll turned around to face them. "Take a gander at this fist," he grunted, coiling his right hand and lifting it. "If any of ye want a closer acquaintance, then ye keep walking this way."

"I only wanted to tell Mrs. Jones how very much I

admire her," the largest of them offered, though not a one of them took another step closer.

"And now ye have. Go away."

"I say, you can't—"

"Let's be off, shall we, Coll?" Her voice came from behind him.

That was all the invitation he required. Without waiting to see how indignant the onlookers might be and if any one of them might care to challenge him, Coll climbed into the barouche and seated himself beside her. "Aye. Off, Gavin. Wherever she tells ye."

"Aye, m'laird."

"North and east, if you please."

They rolled away at a fast trot. The speed was likely contrary to the gentlemanly rules of street travel, but of more concern was the realization that Persephone really could go nowhere without being pursued. "It's like that all the time for ye, is it?" he asked, turning to face her.

"It's worse when I play a romantic heroine," she said, glancing over her shoulder before she sat back against the well-stuffed blue cushions. "But their interest means they will purchase seats, which is what keeps us all employed." Light blue eyes met his. "I'd like to discuss our business now, so you can decide whether you wish to be seen lunching with me or not."

"I'm all ears, Persephone Jones."

She cleared her throat, folding her hands primly in her lap. "A trio of sandbags nearly crushed me this morning."

That caught his attention, and not at all in the way he'd anticipated. The rock in his gut jolted, as if he'd nearly lost something vital without even knowing it was in danger. "That's why ye have a scratch on yer cheek, isnae? Ye werenae hurt elsewhere, were ye?" he asked, reaching over to brush the offending scratch.

"No. It was a near thing, but I was only hit by a splinter when one of the thrones was smashed."

Coll took a breath. He was accustomed to stepping in the moment he sensed trouble. Being informed after the fact left him frustrated. "Ye reckon it wasnae an accident?"

"I don't know. It might have been; I've nearly been knocked down by sandbags before. All of us have had things fall while we've been rehearsing or onstage."

"Ye do realize if they'd hit ye in the head, they wouldnae have just knocked ye down, lass."

Her mouth tightened a little. "Yes. I saw that happen once, a few years ago. Poor man broke his neck. But they didn't hit me or anyone else, and as I said, it *is* a hazard of my profession."

"And it should've been looked after before it could happen."

She nodded. "Yes, it should have. Poor Harry Drew was mortified. I imagine at this moment he's personally checking all the ropes and knots in the entire theater."

Coll eyed her. Whether she meant to make light of the accident or not, it definitely remained on her mind, and it had definitely caught the attention of the theater workers. "Ye reckon it could be Claremont."

Persephone blinked. "I have no idea if it was him or not." A smile curved her mouth. "I thought I might have to work harder to get you to come up with that assumption."

"Och, so ye reckon I'm some muttonheaded idiot because I'm nae English? Ye want me to go murder him, do ye?"

"Not at all! Good heavens. I thought I was perhaps jumping to conclusions, myself. The fact that you went there directly is rather mollifying. But I don't want you to kill anyone, for goodness' sake."

That felt less insulting, at least. "Ye have a way with fancy words, lass."

Her smile thinned. "Speaking fancy words is my occupation, my lord."

She didn't like that he'd pointed out her uncommon vocabulary, then. Coll made a mental note of it, then nodded and sat back against the seat. "I'd wager ye *are* worried Claremont means to make trouble, so now the idea of having me as yer protector sits a bit better with ye. Do I have the right of it?"

"Yes, you do."

He wanted to do it; having an excuse to stay close by her and regularly visit her bedchamber appealed to him immensely. If this had been a voluntary visit to London, he would have agreed to it already. "I've a wife to find, ye ken. Th—"

"What if I were to instruct you in how to be a proper gentleman?" she cut in. "A suitor who could determine whether a woman was after him for his title or for himself?"

That was her offer? He'd figured out women in general a long time ago. The only difficulty here was choosing one to last him a lifetime. But if she happened to be looking for an excuse to have him about, he'd be an idiot not to take her up on it. "I'm listening."

"Begging yer pardon, m'laird, but where are we supposed to be headed now?" Gavin asked from the driver's perch. "If I keep us driving north and east, we're bound to run into the sea."

"Turn up Marylebone Road and head east," the lass said, before he could ask where it was they were building Regent's Park, anyway. "You'll see it on your left. Just drive until you find a spot for a picnic."

"Should I do that, *m'laird*?" the groom asked, clearly displeased at being ordered about by a Sassenach female.

"Aye. As she says."

"As she says," Gavin muttered under his breath, but made the turn as instructed.

With the exception of a handful of maids and cooks, Aldriss Park had been a household without lasses for seventeen years. A lass with authority was something none of them were accustomed to. It was, however, something that was going to change by the time their stay in London was over. Amy and Miranda were ladies, and Eloise would be visiting as well, because he wasn't about to allow another seventeen years to pass without setting eyes on his sister. As for his own lass, well, whether he liked her or not, she would be Lady Aldriss one day, with duties of her own to perform.

"Yer proposal, then," he said aloud, "is that I escort ye about and see that sandbags dunnae dare drop in yer presence, and in exchange ye'll help me figure out how to chat with a lass and nae cause her to faint or run away or scowl like I have fleas or someaught."

"And I will aid you in figuring out which lass wants you, and which one only wants to be a viscountess."

Something occurred to him, and he frowned. "I'm nae some virginal bairn, ye ken. I've had lasses aplenty. And nae a complaint from any of 'em."

The soft-looking skin of her cheeks darkened. "If you were a virginal bairn, my lord, we would be having a different conversation."

"Coll."

"Coll," she repeated. "I've acted a lady more times than I can count, and I've watched silly boors become proper gentlemen during the course of a two-hour play before they resort to themselves again. I can help you catch the lass you want. And if it turns out the sandbags *were* an accident and not a parting gift from Claremont, then I suppose you will have gotten the better part of the deal." She twisted in the seat to face him. "*If* we have a deal. Do we?"

"I keep lads away from ye, and ye show me how to entice proper lasses. Aye. I'll agree to that. Saint Andrew knows I've nae had much luck on my own, and I'll be damned if I let my own mother choose me a wife."

He stuck out his hand. When she proffered hers, he shook it, declining to ask about any more . . . personal aspects of this agreement. He'd had enough rules for his life written out. This one, he'd manage all on his own. And this lass *would* end up naked in his arms, because he'd been imagining it since the first moment he'd set eyes on her.

"These were farms here?" Coll asked.

"Yes, dairy and hay, mostly. And some small houses and shops. James Burton purchased them all."

"And that's his grand house there?" He gestured toward the Holme.

"Yes."

"The man likes attention."

Persephone chuckled. "I cannot argue with that. But it will be lovely, I think. They say John Nash is overseeing the design."

"M'laird, I've set out yer luncheon," Gavin said, a half-eaten biscuit in one hand as he approached to check on the horses.

"And ye've sampled it as well, I see."

"The biscuit fell out of the basket, I swear it."

A few people walked and rode across the half-finished terraces and trails, most of them likely on their way to or from their places of employment. Once the park was finished, no doubt the parades of the finely dressed would begin and she would have to find another place for riding and walking, but for now, Persephone rather liked its busy, unfinished chaos.

She seated herself on the blanket, legs curled to one side

as she settled her yellow muslin skirts around her. Goodness, she couldn't remember the last time she'd been on a picnic. Even if she'd been in a position to be courted, at eight-and-twenty she was well on the shelf. That, added to her profession and social status, limited her opportunities for al fresco dining to nearly nil.

"I like it here," Coll announced, sitting opposite her and folding his knees, adjusting his kilt to keep it covering his nethers with an unconscious ease that told her firstly he wore a kilt frequently, and secondly that he *had* been on picnics before. "It's nae as crowded as Hyde Park, and a lad can walk about without worrying whether he's about to trample someone's wee dog."

She grinned. "You are not like any other viscount I've ever met."

"I'll take that as a compliment." His deep green eyes danced as he held out a bowl of strawberries to her. "My da warned me that all Mayfair lasses were hothouse flowers, wee and delicate and fainting, and that a man had to take a ridiculous amount of care with them or they'd wilt."

"That sounds fairly accurate, actually," she noted, trying not to groan as she bit into the sweet, sugared strawberry. Ladies weren't the only things that lived in hothouses here in London.

When she looked up, his gaze was on her mouth, which made her exaggerate the bite—just because it was nice to be admired in such a voracious manner. She'd been pursued before and had even dined out with a man on occasion, but she generally set out rules beforehand to avoid any unpleasantness later. This time, she could tell herself it was purely business, a trade of specialties for mutual benefit, but they both knew it was more than that.

Last night, when she'd strolled offstage to see him standing there, her breath had actually caught. He'd seemed not so much from another play as another realm, a place where gods walked the earth and flirted with actresses who'd spent so much time playing romantic heroines that sometimes they couldn't recall who they were outside the theater. His appearance had been . . . thrilling. And while she wouldn't have invented an excuse to keep him about, she wasn't above using a possible accident to do so.

Physically, he was a lion, a maned predator who brooked no rivals and had never been defeated in battle. At the same time, he'd clearly at least read the Scottish play and seemed familiar with *As You Like It*. He'd figured out her motives for approaching him, and actually seemed to approve of the logic behind it. At the same time, he had already announced that he wanted her, and he'd done so without first plying her with food and gifts and making her feel obligated.

So muscular, intelligent, and insightful. A formidable trio under the best of circumstances. The Earl of Claremont had come in full of charm and gifts, which had been appealing because once she chose a protector, the wolves might not stop circling, but they would stop biting at her heels. Most of their conversations had involved his wealth and power and her beauty, and she'd tolerated it because it was easy. She lied for a living, after all.

Coll MacTaggert was far more direct than the earl, though, and she would have been willing to wager that his wits were keener, too, even if he lacked a great deal of Claremont's refinement. She liked that this arrangement was actually mutual; she imagined he might take advice from her when he wouldn't from Lady Aldriss. And if Claremont did mean trouble, this man seemed more than a match for him.

The only downside, if it was one, was that she *did* find Coll attractive. Damnably so. If they spent a moment or two in each other's company, well, that might be tolerable. More than tolerable. Hopefully once they'd indulged that . . . interest they shared in each other, that would pass, because he needed to find a wife, and she was the farthest thing from marriageable that she could imagine.

"Where do ye hail from?" he asked around a mouthful of sandwich.

Persephone blinked herself back to the present. "Derbyshire. The less said about my childhood, the better. And you're from near Ullapool, by your accent."

"But two hours from it. I thought all we Scotsmen sounded alike to ye English."

"Only to the ones not paying attention," she quipped, picking up her glass of Madeira and sipping at it. "Why don't we pretend I'm a proper young lady you've just seen walking through Hyde Park, and you'd like to chat with me?"

He scowled, the frown drawing his eyebrows together. "I'd rather chat with ye as yerself."

Had anyone ever said that to her before? She doubted it. "I'm trying to prove that I'm not simply taking advantage of your . . . carnal desires. I *can* be helpful to you. This isn't a waste of your time."

"I nae said it was a waste. Chatting with ye is a damned sight more interesting than trying to think of more ways to describe the weather."

"Even so. Here I am, let's say, just paused in the shade for a moment. What do you do?"

For a moment, she thought he might balk. He seemed a very proud man, after all, and most men hesitated to show their weaknesses anyway. But then he lowered his shoulders, drawing in a hard breath. "Punching things is easier."

"Yes, but you cannot punch your way to love."

"I'm nae obligated to fall in love in four weeks. I'm obligated to get married in four weeks."

Persephone eyed him. "You don't wish to love your wife?"

"I reckon my brothers fell for their lasses the first time they set eyes on them. Neither of them were expecting it. I dunnae think ye can go about with the idea of finding love. I dunnae ken how I could do that. All I can do is look for a woman I can tolerate and respect." He shrugged. "One who'd make a good Lady Glendarril, and a Lady Aldriss who'd nae flee the Highlands and who could genuinely care for the cotters and fishermen and their families."

Was that last comment aimed at his mother? Persephone didn't comment on it, but she did file it away for later review. As far as she knew, Lady Aldriss hadn't set foot in the Highlands since she'd left them behind for London. "Well, then you want to find a lady who has compassion, and intelligence, and has some of the same interests you do. So, what do you like to do, Coll MacTaggert? Other than punching people."

That earned her a swift grin. "I dunnae seek that out. It just seems to happen. But I like to be out-of-doors. I like to ride. I like helping lads build cottages and repair leaking roofs and find lost cattle."

And she liked listening to the lift and fall of his voice, the deep brogue and the genuine truth in his tone. Persephone stifled a sigh. "In simpler terms, then, you enjoy helping people. Perhaps, then, you would be compatible with a lady who does charity work. Someone who reads to the elderly, or who brings food to the poor."

"Aye, that's someaught I hadnae considered," he said after a moment, lowering his gaze to his sandwich as he finished it off and chose another one. Abruptly, his dark green eyes snapped to hers again. "I noticed ye turning the conversation away from yerself, by the way. I'll get back to ye when ye're feeling less skittish."

Her breath hitched. "I'm not some mysterious treasure,

whatever you wish of me. I'm a common girl from Derbyshire who likes to pretend to be other people and get paid for it."

"As I said, I can be patient," he returned, holding her gaze for another dozen hard beats of her heart before he looked away again. "I didnae know if ye'd prefer apples or oranges, so I have both in here, unless Gavin got to them first."

"An apple would be lovely. And you could be as patient as a stone and you would still hear the same story. It's the only one I have to tell."

His expression didn't change, but he dug into the basket and retrieved a shiny red apple, which he put into her outstretched hand. "I'd wager that a common lass who reads and writes, who can tell where a lad grew up by the sound of his speech, and who wears the borrowed robes of other people well enough that she's the toast of London, isnae all that common at all," he said quietly, lowering his hand again.

She forced a smile, making certain it crinkled the corners of her eyes, so it looked genuine. "Thank you for saying so. Now stop stalling and show me how you would attempt to engage me in a conversation. We're in Hyde Park; I'm standing in the shade. Begin."

"Relentless, ye are." He shook out his arms and put a teeth-showing smile on his handsome face. "Good morning, lass." Coll leaned forward, then asked under his breath, "Is it morning?"

"Yes, it's morning."

"Good, then." He straightened again, resuming his broad smile. "Good morning, lass. As warm as it is today—ye see, ye said ye were standing in the shade, so I'm thinking it's warm—it's more fit for riding than walking, dunnae ye think?"

Persephone lowered her head to look at him from

beneath her lashes. "But I am on foot, sir, and am content to remain so."

His smile tightened just a touch. "I'm on foot, myself. Might I walk beside ye?"

"You are too bold, sir. My maid sees me home. Good day."

"What the bloody hell did I do wrong, then?" he burst out.

"You didn't introduce yourself, firstly," Persephone returned smoothly, trying very hard not to grin at his obvious exasperation. "And you asked me—her—to make an immediate decision about whether I want to be seen in your company. You might ask if I'm attending the . . . I believe the Runescroft ball is later this week, is it not?"

He tilted his head. "So I'm nae to speak with her until she has a chance to decide if she wants to dance with me at the next soiree?"

"Precisely. She'll wish to go home and consult with her mother or sponsor, discover your reputation and income, and then decide whether to give you a quadrille, a country dance, or a waltz. If she grants you a waltz, then you can be fairly assured she's amenable to making a match. A country dance would signify that she's being polite but isn't interested. A quadrille or a cotillion, I imagine, could go either way for you."

"What about a Scotch reel?"

"As you're a Highlander, if she grants you a Scotch reel, then she's a fortune hunter and you should claim a bad knee and run the other way."

Coll snorted. "Too bold, then?"

"Definitely."

"Let's try this again, then. But on my feet, nae with a sandwich in my damn hand."

He stood, the motion quick and graceful, and held a hand down to her. "Ah, a dress rehearsal, then," she muttered with feigned reluctance, and allowed him to help her to her feet.

"Aye. I'm a tall man with a wide pair of shoulders, and that factors into how I approach a lass, and how she views me."

That made sense. "Do you prefer tall or petite women, then?"

"Yer size is about right, I reckon."

"Ah, it is, is it?" she returned, hoping the heat running beneath her skin didn't show on her face. He'd been trouble from the moment she'd first spied him, and that wasn't likely to change. She needed to use her head, not her . . . other parts, where he was concerned, because he could also be very useful.

"Aye. Now ye stand there in the shade, and I'll come make yer acquaintance."

Persephone straightened her bonnet and pulled a fan from her reticule. A retiring young lady, pampered and just out of the schoolroom, she decided. Yes, that particular young lass would be his largest challenge, no doubt. "Gavin, you must come over here and be my maid," she told the groom.

"I will nae," the large Highlander returned, crossing his arms over his barrel chest.

"Gavin. Be a maid," Coll instructed. "It's for the good of Aldriss Park."

Muttering under his breath, the groom seemed to collapse into himself. Shoulders slumped in utter defeat, he stomped over to stand beside her. "I dunnae ken how to be a lady's maid," he grumbled.

"Just be protective of my reputation, and far too aware of etiquette and propriety for anyone to be able to tolerate," she suggested.

One of his eyes twitched. "Just remember, m'laird," he called out. "Ye ordered me to do this."

"Shut it. Ye're a maid."

Coll strode away, pacing back and forth in the clearing for a moment as if rehearsing lines in his head, then bent, picked a lone white daisy from the grass, and strolled in her direction.

Good heavens, he was magnificent, his hair ruffling in the wind, his kilt brushing the top of the tall grass, and the proper coat and cravat only accentuating the wildness of the rest of him.

Pushing those thoughts out of the way so she could be useful rather than flinging herself on him, Persephone half turned away. "I'm thinking perhaps I should wear my blue satin gown to the Runescroft soiree, Mary. Do I still have those silver hair ribbons?"

The groom shifted. "Oh, miss, I do think pearls woven through your hair will be magnificent," he uttered in a high-pitched voice, his London accent horrible and barely understandable. At least he was trying, though.

"Yes, pearls might be just the thing. Well-done, Mary."

Gavin curtsied in his kilt. "I live to serve ye, miss."

A great shadow crossed over her, a deeper shade beneath the leafy trees. She looked up, lifting her fan to cover all of her face but her eyes. "My goodness."

"Good morning to ye, lass," Coll rumbled. "I'm Glendarril. I saw this wee flower and admired it, but now I reckon it pales in comparison to ye. Tell me yer name, if ye will."

Oh, that was nice. "Charlotte," she decided. "Miss Charlotte Rumpole."

"That's enough, big man," Gavin stated, stepping between them. "Miss Charlotte, your mama will be expecting ye."

"Will ye be attending the Runescroft ball this week, Miss Charlotte?" Coll persisted, sparing a glare for his groom. "I reckon I'd like to have a dance with ye there."

She curtsied. "I might be, my lord."

"Good. Then save me a waltz or a quadrille."

Persephone fluttered her fan at him. "Oh, I couldn't promise such a thing, my lord."

"Well, I dunnae want a country dance. All that jumping about. Everyone looks like chickens fleeing foxes."

"I cannot say which dances will be offered, my lord. Last week, Lady Albert had but one quadrille, and six country dances. Everyone was so exhausted, two ladies fell asleep in their chairs." She looked up toward the sky. "It's such a fine day, and I must be going. Good day, my lord."

"I'd still like to dance with ye, lass."

Turning her back, Persephone put her hand around Gavin's arm. "I think I see my mother over there. Excuse me."

Behind her, she swore she could hear a low growl. "Now what?" Coll demanded, continuing to swear under his breath.

"You tried to trap me into accepting you."

"I dunnae care for a country dance. I've always said so. Ask anyone."

She faced him again. "Simply because you don't care for something doesn't mean it isn't a necessary tool for someone else. If you'd accept a waltz, you must be ready to accept a country dance."

"If ye'd just tell me ye'd only give me a country dance, then I could be on my way to find a different lass."

She could see the problem; he was direct, and thus he disliked the games played in courting. "You have to be patient. Give a woman more than the space of a few words to decide her entire future." She smiled at his annoyed look. "The part with the daisy was very nice. You should use that." Persephone clapped her hands together. "Let's do it again, shall we?"

His lips thinned. "Aye. Once more."

This time, when he picked a daisy, he wrenched it out of

the ground, root and all. "Good day, lass," he said, holding it out to her. "I'm Glendarril. Ye're a fairer flower than this posy. Will ye dance with me at the Runescroft soiree?"

"I'm afraid I'm not attending that ball, my lord," she cooed, shying away from the dirt-dripping flower.

Coll frowned. "Then at which one might I dance with ye?"

"My father doesn't approve of dancing at all, I'm afraid. I will be playing the harp at a musical recital on Thursday. Might you come and see me there?"

"If I go to yer recital, I willnae be able to attend the Runescroft ball."

"But if you go to the Runescroft ball, I will not be able to accept your courtship. I'm—"

Coll stepped forward, lifted her up by the waist, and tossed her onto his shoulder. Her fan went flying as she grabbed onto his arm to keep from falling. "I reckon ye'll come with me now."

"Coll! Put me down!"

"Nae. I'm taking ye to church right now and marrying ye," he announced.

The groom picked up her fan and smacked Coll with it across the chest. "Put Miss Charlotte down, ye fiend!" he shrieked.

"Ye flail at me again, Gavin, and ye and I are going to have a tussle."

The groom dropped the fan. "Aye, m'laird."

For a heart-stopping moment, Persephone wasn't certain whether he was jesting or not. He *had* threatened to marry her to spite his mother, after all. "Is this how you court in the Highlands?" she asked, lifting her head and hoping Flora had secured her light blonde wig well enough that being upside down wouldn't unseat it.

"Aye. I've four weeks, Persephone. If I wait for every lass to confer with her mama before she gives me a country dance four days later, I'll lose all funding to Aldriss Park. And I cannae do that. I've run out of time to be patient."

"Then we'll find something that *does* work for you."

At that, he shifted her, slowly lowering her in his arms until they were face-to-face. "Ye're very good at being a proper lass, Persephone."

"Well, I'm not a proper lass." She took his face in her hands and kissed him.

She tasted his surprise, swiftly followed by something more heated and heady. A low sound rising from her chest, she opened to his teasing tongue. *Good glory.* If he led all his conversations with a kiss like this, he would have had fifty brides knocking at his door by now. And there she was, her feet literally not touching the ground.

But they needed to find the floor again—at once—because she could not afford flights of fancy. Not now, and not ever.

Chapter Six

"Why do you dress me in borrowed robes?"

MACBETH, *MACBETH* ACT I, SCENE III

The lass's fan slapped Coll across the shoulders. He ignored it, too involved with kissing Persephone Jones and the things the embrace was doing to his nether regions to pay any attention. Another slap, this one harder, across the back of the skull.

He lifted his head to see Gavin cocking his arm back for another blow. "That's enough, ye heathen," he grumbled.

"If any of the lasses ye mean to wed were to see ye here now," the groom muttered, "I dunnae think they'd look on ye kindly."

Nearly empty or not, they were in the middle of a park where anyone could take a stroll. Reluctantly, Coll set Persephone down onto her feet before he took a step backward. "Ye're making me think I'd prefer a marriage to an improper lass over a proper one," he quipped.

She cleared her throat and smoothed her skirt before gracefully seating herself again while Gavin retreated to the safety of the barouche. "Be that as it may, you've told me that you require a lady."

Strictly speaking, it was his mother who demanded he wed a proper female, but he did know what the repercussions would be if he went and married someone who didn't travel in the same prestigious circles as the Oswells and MacTaggerts. He was looking for a lass to help him lead a part of Clan Ross, after all.

"Aye. But as I said, I cannae wait for a week while every lass decides if I've earned a dance or nae."

"There's a risk in putting all your eggs in one basket." With dainty fingers, she gripped her glass of Madeira again and downed it all. "You might try several strategies at once."

He poured her another glass, ignoring his own. Even if he still drank, it wouldn't be Madeira. But Mrs. Gordon, the cook, had said that ladies liked Madeira, so he'd deferred to her knowledge. She'd had the right of it, evidently. "Ask lasses if they'll dance with me at the next ball or two and what else, then?"

"You said you enjoy riding. Go riding in the morning, when ladies who also enjoy being on horseback might be found in Hyde Park. Ask them about their mounts, where the best riding trails are, if they like to hunt, that sort of thing. You could suggest you'll be at Hyde Park at eight o'clock the next morning, if they'd care to try their paces in your company."

"So—asking a lass to ride is safer than suggesting a dance? That doesnae make any damned sense."

"A lady on horseback may escape. Or not make an appearance at all."

She may have accused him of playing a part, of behaving like a thick-headed, countrified squire to set people at ease, but she'd gone along easily enough with that narrative. It was the one that made him the most comfortable, even if he did have some idea what he was about. It was his anger that had gotten in the way of his logic when he'd first arrived in London, and so if it took a bit more patience than he would've liked to smooth over his reputation again, he would put up with it.

Aside from that, he'd just learned a few more things about the intriguing Persephone Jones. She avoided Hyde Park and all the places proper ladies frequented, which wasn't so odd, he supposed, but she seemed almost . . . calculating about it. She knew what time of day the aristocracy went riding, which dances signified which level of matrimonial interest, and actress or not, she'd played the most perfect, dainty English lass he could have imagined.

Of course, she *was* an actress. A fine one, according to all of London. And perhaps she was curious about the blue bloods of Mayfair and read the Society pages and listened to the gossip and stories. Perhaps she was jealous of them, though that didn't come across at all, even when she pretended to be one of them for a few minutes.

"Have ye ever been to a Society fete?" he asked. "Surely ye've been invited."

"Certainly, I've been invited," she echoed, choosing another strawberry. "I'm a curiosity. But no, I've never attended a Society party. My status rests on the ladies enjoying my performances as much as it does the gentlemen doing so. I don't wish to anger, threaten, or annoy either sex."

"But ye just kissed me out here in the middle of a park."

"No, I kissed you out here in the middle of nowhere. Just as I'm picnicking with you in the middle of nowhere. The odds of anyone who could ruin me by seeing us right now are almost nil." She smiled at him. "Not to disappoint you, but you aren't my first protector."

"About that. Ye balked at allowing Claremont into yer bedchamber, shall we say."

"Ah." This time, she downed half her glass of Madeira. "I didn't like Claremont. He was pretty enough and served to keep the rest of the interested aristocrats away from me, but he was supremely condescending in that very polite way the elite tend to have."

"Did he kiss ye?"

She lifted her chin a little. "Yes."

"Did ye kiss him?"

"You mean the way I just kissed you? No. There's no need to be jealous."

And there she went again, turning the conversation back to him, no doubt thinking he would feel the need to protest that he wasn't jealous, and she could then turn the talk to wherever she next chose. "Are ye going to tell me where ye reside? Ye'd be safer if I met ye there and drove ye to the theater in the morning."

"I'll make my own way to the Saint Genesius. If you could return me there by way of Pall Mall, that should inform the gents that I'm not fair game."

And there went his theory that she was avoiding the aristocracy. This was becoming exceedingly complicated, and even more interesting. "But nae by way of Hyde Park?"

"The gentlemen's clubs—or enough of them, anyway—are along Pall Mall. That is a street. I'm permitted to drive down a street on my way to somewhere else. Hyde Park is a destination in itself."

"A minute ago, ye were worried over *my* reputation," he countered, eyeing her Madeira and beginning to wonder if one wee drink would be so horrible. "Explain to me why a lass would be offended at seeing us eating or kissing, but nae driving about in a barouche together."

"It's all in the difference between rumor and proof, my lord. Th—"

"Coll."

Her face dove into an amused grimace. "Coll. If someone sees us driving together on the street, I may be your mistress, you may be my protector, you may be kissing me, you may be taking me to a picnic. You may also be simply driving me to the theater."

"So, if a lass asks what I'm up to with ye in my barouche, I can claim that the most innocent story is the truth."

"Yes."

"And it's nae a lie, because I *would* be driving ye to the theater."

"You see, this isn't so difficult," she said, with a grin that made him want to kiss her again.

What he saw—or was beginning to see—was that Persephone Jones had a very keen mind. No wonder she hadn't liked Claremont despite his pretty looks and his surface politeness; she'd seen right through all of it, probably from the moment the earl had introduced himself. She'd put up with it until James Pierce became too insistent with his cock because she'd found him useful, as she'd just admitted, for keeping the rest of the drooling horde of males away from her. *Hmm.*

"What I see," he said aloud, "is that ye seem to put a man through his paces until he wants to collect what he reckons he's owed, at which point ye find some kilt-wearing lummox to step in and rescue ye so ye can begin dancing yer circles about the new fellow until it all goes round again."

She set her glass down on the blanket. "Have I been at all useful to you today?" she asked, meeting his gaze.

Pretty eyes, he thought, *blue as the noontime sky*, then shoved that nonsense out of his skull. If he meant to keep up with her, he was going to have to toss his general take-on-all-challengers-with-his-fists mentality aside and use his mind. "Ye told me what the dances mean, which I didnae know. And ye made me realize I cannae stomp about Hyde Park like a bear looking for a sow if I want to find anything other than a sow. So aye, ye've been useful. Ye've told me nae to be myself."

"That's not . . . that's not precisely what I meant. Be a more patient, cultured version of yourself. It's still you—just more polished."

It didn't feel that way. Trying to act English felt like wearing another man's coat, which would of course be too small and confining. His reluctance most have shown on his face, because her smile softened. "You are a likeable man. Just shorten your stride."

That made it all sound a bit more palatable, even if he doubted all he required was patience. "What of ye, then? Ye said yerself, the sandbags were likely an accident. Ye may have partnered up with me for nae reason at all."

"That's not so. You've been—or will be—useful to me, when you drive me back via Pall Mall. A fair exchange, I'd call it."

"And yet I dunnae ken where ye live, or if ye have any intention of going with me where yer kisses tease that ye will."

"You are a confounding man."

"I'm an open book," he countered. "Ye're the one who willnae even let me read yer title. For a simple theater lass, ye've nae common, leatherbound cover. Ye're protected by a steel one, I reckon. That sort of thing piques a man's interest. It piques *my* interest." *There. Let her think on that for a minute.* Because she'd been correct about him, as well. Aye, he liked to talk with his fists. But he could also read Latin.

Folding her hands in her lap, she sat up straighter, letting the silence between them stretch out for a good half a minute. He waited, trying on the too-tight patience coat, as she'd suggested. "Number four Charles Lane, in St. John's Wood, the blue house third in from Charlbert Street," she finally said. "But if you come to my home, you'd best be prepared to charm Flora, Gregory, and

Hades. If they don't accept you, don't expect that I will. There. Challenge met."

"Hades?" he repeated, lifting an eyebrow.

"Yes. In mythology, Hades and Persephone were quite close, you know."

Yes, he knew that. More intriguing was that he'd pushed, and she'd given ground. "So ye do like me, then."

She held his gaze. "Yes, I do. I don't encounter many open books in my life."

"And I dunnae scare ye even a bit, do I?" After all, he'd been called intimidating and threatening, and wee lasses trembled when he asked them to dance. A handful had even gotten wobbly on their feet. On first sight, however, Persephone had grinned and called him Romeo—and had made her attraction to him clear as glass.

"I don't know you well, Coll," she said slowly, seeming to choose her words carefully, "but no, you don't frighten me."

"What I want of ye doesnae have a damned thing to do with any agreement." And it wasn't just the agreement between them to which he was referring. Aye, he needed to wed. But now, at this moment, he wasn't thinking about a bride or about Aldriss Park. No, he was thinking about the elegant curve of her neck and the sway of her hips and how kissing her wasn't even close to what he wanted to be doing with her.

"Trouble," she muttered beneath her breath.

"Beg pardon?"

"Nothing." Shifting, she began putting cutlery and plates back into the picnic basket. "You. Gavin. Please come take this."

"Are we leavin'?" the groom asked, shoving the remains of a sandwich into his mouth and rising from the comfortable rear-facing seat of the barouche.

"You are," she said smoothly.

"I—"

"Ye heard her, Gavin," Coll echoed, standing up and lifting the basket to shove it into the groom's arms as heat dove down his spine. "Deliver this back to Oswell House and then ye come back here and get us."

"But I . . ." The groom looked from one to the other. "Oh. Och. That'll take me near thirty minutes, I reckon."

"It'll take ye near an hour."

"Aye."

Grumbling and stealing looks at Persephone as she leaned back against the nearest oak trunk, the groom set the basket in the carriage and climbed up to the driver's perch. Then, still muttering, he turned the team back toward the road and vanished behind the shrubbery.

Coll faced Persephone. "It's quiet here, but nae private enough for my peace of mind."

She bent to pick up the blanket, folding it over her arm. "This way."

Pushing out of his mind the idea that she knew a private place because she'd made use of it before, Coll fell in beside her, taking the blanket from her. He wanted to hold her hand, to touch her—she was one book he damned well wanted to read. But he *was* a big man, and learning to be more patient would do him good, whether he liked it or not.

But if being inside her lay at the end of this path, he'd manage.

She ducked beneath a tangle of low-hanging branches and then descended to a tiny stream that cut through one corner of the land. An old hay cart with a missing wheel tipped into the water and halfway up the far bank, and she made for the broken back end, where it dug into the hillside.

"How'd ye find this?" he asked, keeping his voice pitched low and noting the patches of wild heather growing around the wagon's rear wheels. Now if that wasn't a sign of approval, he didn't know what was.

"I followed a rabbit in here once. It's a good place for thinking," she returned, climbing up to the bed of the wagon and holding her hand out for the blanket. "And I've yet to spy anyone else here."

"They'd have to be following rabbits to find it," he agreed, noting the hanging trees and wild bushes that had overgrown both banks and left the wagon shrouded from every angle but the one she'd found. Her own private bower, it was.

"I hadn't thought to use it for this, but I'm never going to be able to concentrate at rehearsal this afternoon if I don't put my hands on you."

It crossed his mind that she could be acting, playing the part of a wanton young woman overcome with desire for her protector, but as he climbed up onto the wagon bed with her, he didn't give a damn. She was an itch, and if he didn't scratch it, he would never be able to go find himself a wife. Devil take it, he wouldn't even be able to stand up straight.

She sank to her knees, taking his hand to pull him down in front of her, then wrapped her arms around his shoulders and leaned in to kiss him. God, her lips were soft, and warm, telling stories only of mutual arousal.

Mindful of the old wood planks just beneath the blanket, Coll took her by the shoulders, pulling her closer against him. When he brushed a hand across her hair, moving to remove the pins that held it up in its fashionable tangle, she broke the kiss.

"Do not ruin my hair. I have a rehearsal this afternoon that I'm already going to be late for."

"Then I'll nae ruin yer hair," he returned, slipping a finger beneath the shoulder of her yellow muslin gown and tugging it down her arm. "I cannae say that about the rest of ye."

"Mmm," she murmured. "Spare my clothes, but ruin me then, Coll MacTaggert."

Spare her blasted clothes, when he wanted to tear them off her body. If he'd had a sewing kit in his pocket, he might have been tempted, regardless of her warning. But then she reached around her back to unbutton her own gown, and as she stripped her arms of it, he pulled the material down to her waist, revealing a pair of plump, pert breasts that looked as if they would perfectly fit his big hands. He wasted no time testing that theory.

At the same time, she reached one hand beneath his kilt, encircling him with her fingers and stroking a thumb boldly down the length of him. "Oh, my," she whispered, her voice not quite steady.

Coll chuckled, a bit breathless himself. "I know how to use it, too."

"I don't doubt that." She moaned as he dipped his head, taking a nipple in his mouth and flicking across it with his tongue. "Your mouth . . . is rather skilled . . . as well."

Well, no one had ever said that to him before, but then she was probably the first person for whom he hadn't troubled with pretending to be a giant lummox, probably because she'd seen through his act the moment he'd attempted it on her. Aye, his brothers knew he could hold his own, but he'd never had cause to dissemble in front of them. Even so, in public they called him an ox and a giant, just because they all found it amusing. He did as well. Generally.

Freeing one hand and keeping his mouth teasing at her breasts, he unbuckled his kilt and shrugged it off. His coat and cravat followed, before he put a hand around her back and eased her down flat. "Damn me," he murmured, lowering himself over her to take her mouth again.

"'Do not swear at all,'" she breathed, looking up at him. "'Or, if thou wilt, swear by thy gracious self, which is the god of my idolatry, and I'll believe thee.'"

Coll frowned. "Ye dunnae need to be Juliet to please me, Persephone. I dunnae want an imaginary phantom. I want ye. Blood and bone and soft, soft skin."

She shivered a little in his arms, goose bumps raising on her bare skin. "You truly aren't some silly man looking for his Juliet. I don't know what to make of you."

"Likewise, lass. But I reckon I'll take my time figuring ye out." He lowered himself along her body to take one of her breasts in his mouth again, meanwhile occupying his hands with tugging her gown down her hips, over her knees, and onto the blanket beside them.

God's sake, she was glorious. Tall but slender, narrow-hipped but buxom, a lass made for loving. His already engorged cock jumped. Straightening, he pulled his shirt over his head and dropped it on her gown. His boots would have to stay on, because he wasn't taking the time to remove them. Not when someone could stray by the old wagon at any moment. Not when that might prevent him from having her.

Persephone ran her palms up his chest, her fingers tracing the lines of muscle there. "You are a fit man," she commented, her gaze lowering further.

"I dunnae sit on my arse and have servants feed me."

"No, I don't imagine you do. Kiss me again. I do like your mouth."

Coll grinned. "If that's so, there are other things my mouth can do." Shifting backward on his knees, he took her legs, stroking his hands down her thighs to her knees, and set them on either side of his shoulders. Then he bent down and tasted her.

She was wet for him. This wasn't all some elaborate act. That thought—and her responding moan—nearly undid him right then. Through sheer willpower, he fought back against the urge and settled himself again. Parting her folds with his fingers, he licked again, then slid his forefinger inside her slowly as he continued his ministrations.

"Good . . . heavens," she breathed, her fingers clutching at his shaggy hair.

A flurry of Gaelic came to mind, but he wasn't going to begin spouting poetry just because he'd been without a woman for a handful of weeks. She'd have good reason to think him simple-minded if he did such a thing. Shifting his kisses to her inner thighs, he worked his way down one leg and up the other until he arrived at his starting spot again.

"Do stop teasing me," she rasped, tugging on his hair.

Coll moved up over her body, caressing her with his mouth and his hands. Pinching her nipples lightly made her gasp, and when he did it in time with his finger inside her, she bucked, wide-eyed. "There ye go," he murmured.

"I'm . . . beginning to think you . . . a very naughty man," she managed.

When he reached her mouth again, she was panting, and he claimed her in a hot, openmouthed kiss. A few moments later, he had her writhing beneath him, her quiet mewling sounds driving him mad.

When she wrapped her legs around his hips, he gave in to the lust that had pounded at him almost from the moment he'd first set eyes on her. Slowly, he entered her, hot and tight and slick, until he'd buried himself completely. In the very back corner of his mind that still possessed logical thought, he noted that she wasn't a virgin, but he hadn't expected her to be one. This heat between them wouldn't have been possible if she were some blushing debutante.

Persephone threw back her head, groaning, and he licked her throat. Sliding out of her only so he could enter her again, he moaned. He'd been right about her size; she fit him perfectly, and as he rocked into her again and again, the sounds of ecstasy and arousal she made were for him as well.

Just then, her fingers dug into his shoulders and her back arched, and abruptly she began pulsing around his cock, urging him on, deeper, faster, harder. He felt electrified, every inch of him alive and aware of the eager woman in his arms. And he wanted to prolong the moment, but this time, his body refused to listen.

With a grunt, he came, holding himself hard against her. More Gaelic went through the edge of his thoughts, older words that had gone out of fashion a century or two ago. Coll kept his gaze on her, on her blue eyes looking directly back at him.

Finally spent, he put an arm around her and turned the two of them so they lay face-to-face on the blanket. A strand of honey-blonde hair peeked out from beneath the coiffed ash-blonde mass, and he silently reached out and tucked it back in.

At that, she frowned, sitting up to fiddle with her hair. "Don't do that."

"I dunnae care what color yer hair is, Persephone. Ye said nae to ruin it, so I fixed it for ye."

"Yes, thank you. As I said, it's . . . easier to walk about the shops and streets if no one knows precisely what I look like." Smoothing her expression, she lay back on her side again and brushed a strand of his hair out of his face. "There. We don't want you looking disheveled, either."

"Lass, I've been disheveled since I arrived in London. Ask anyone."

"Well, I shall have to make you look like a gentleman,

then. For your own good. No lady who wishes to land a title wants her lord to look like anything but a knight in shining armor."

"The only lasses chasing after me are the ones who want naught but a title." He shuddered. "'Oh, m'laird, ye're so big and strong, and I'm so wee and helpless'," he mimicked in his highest-pitched tone.

Persephone laughed. "That was horribly done, but I believe I know what you mean. You played your part too well."

"The idiot giant, ye mean? I played it once, and the gossips took it from there. I just dunnae care for the opinions of all these soft Sassenachs."

"Yes, but you might use those same gossips to show everyone that you're not who they think you are."

"Am I nae?" He put an elbow beneath his head. "I help shear sheep, I pull stray cows from bogs, I argue with my fists, and I've been told I have someaught of an accent. And a temper."

"You also knew I quoted Juliet earlier, and you seem to have a fair knowledge of the Scottish play."

"Aye, I can read and write, if that's what ye're implying."

"Stop being so self-deprecating. There are people—women—out there who will appreciate your intelligence. And those who think they can lead you about with a smile will take themselves elsewhere."

"Ye do make it sound promising." He looked at her for a moment. "A shame ye think we'd nae suit."

"I don't *think* we wouldn't suit. I *know* we wouldn't suit." Reaching over, she slid her palm along his hip, then past him to dump his shirt and retrieve her gown. "I have another rehearsal this afternoon, for which I will be late, and then we have to be out before four o'clock, when the rovers come in."

He sat up beside her to pull on his shirt. Whatever

poetry had wandered through his soul, she didn't seem to be reading the same book any longer. "The rovers?"

"Charlie never lets the theater close. He's worried we'll lose all our business to Covent Garden and Drury Lane. When we're in between plays, he brings in other troupes to perform. This time, it's a roving troop from York here for the next nine days, while we ready the Scottish play."

"Then yer evening is free?" Even as he spoke, he scowled at London and all its ridiculousness, all the obligations it pulled out of everyone. "Dunnae answer that. I've a dinner tonight at Lord and Lady Crenshaw's."

"Good. You can practice not slinging young ladies over your shoulder if they don't agree to waltz with you," she returned, grinning in a way that lit up her blue eyes all over again. "Or ravishing one of them, however much she might wish you would, because then you will be obligated to marry her. *I* shall be making notes on Lady the Scottish play."

That made him grin in return. "Ye're very matter-of-fact about all this."

With a shrug, she found her shoes and then climbed down from the wagon to pull them on. "I found . . . find you very attractive. I wanted you. And I believe you've already told me something similar."

Buckling his kilt and checking to make certain his *sgian dubh* remained tucked into his boot, he jumped down beside her. "Aye. I'm nae adverse to doing it again, either." Actually, he wanted her again already—repeatedly.

"Well, as I said, I have re—"

"Aye. For the Scottish play. As ye're Lady the Scottish play." He shook his head, determined not to push for something more after they'd both made it clear there was nothing more to be had. He needed a wife, and an actress couldn't be the wife of a viscount. "That fellow—

yer Macbeth who willnae say Macbeth—is a lunatic, ye ken."

"Gordon? Yes, he is. He's a very good actor, though, which is why we put up with his nonsense. If you're about long enough, you'll find that every one of us at the Saint Genesius is more than a little mad, I'm afraid."

"And what do ye reckon all of Mayfair thinks of *me*, Mrs. Persephone Jones?"

One blue eye narrowed just a fraction. "My friends call me Persie. We're not so much friends as we are partners in a mutually helpful agreement, but I'll allow it."

Partners who had sex, but he understood where she was trying to place him. A wee bit of distance so she could think. He felt the same need himself. "Persie? Nae. Ye're more out of the ordinary than that. Persephone suits ye better."

Being about Persephone Jones felt a wee bit like listening to a pretty piece by Mozart, but having the orchestra stop just before the last note. He'd spent a fine afternoon, had laughed and enjoyed keeping up with her conversation, had appreciated that she didn't attempt to simplify her speech like he was some half-witted lummox, and he'd definitely enjoyed the intimacy, but as she descended from the carriage after him at the rear of the Saint Genesius, he definitely wanted more.

"Thank you for escorting me," she said with a smile, lifting on her toes to kiss him on the lips once they were inside. "I need to be here tomorrow at nine o'clock. Shall I make my own arrangements, as you should be in the park asking for dances?"

"Nae. I'll be by yer home at half eight. I reckon I can chat with a few lasses before that."

"Very well. Thank you, Coll, for a lovely and very satisfying afternoon." With a flick of her skirts, she headed for the back room, where they'd all been rehearsing earlier.

Coll watched her go, then went looking for Charlie Huddle. He found the barrel-shaped theater manager in a wee coffin of a room, occupied only by a small desk, chair, and a cabinet that looked to be full of papers. No one of any size could work in such a tiny space, and with an uneasy roll of his shoulders, Coll stopped in the doorway. "Huddle."

Charlie looked up. "Ah, Lord Glendarril. I hope you realize Baywich and Humphreys were jesting. I cannot afford to hire you as a dialect instructor."

"Who's in charge of checking to see that the sandbags are hung securely, so that the heavy things arenae going to kill anyone below?" he asked, ignoring the first bit of conversation.

"Ah. That. Our head stagehand is Harry Drew. After the incident this morning, I saw him personally walk every catwalk and check the riggings. He was beside himself; aside from being our main reason for success, Persie is well-loved here. No one wants to see her injured."

"Do ye reckon it could have been Claremont's doing?"

The manager shrugged. "I suppose it's possible, but he wasn't much liked here. If anyone had seen him, we'd all know about it."

That didn't eliminate the possibility of the earl paying someone to cut a rope, but as that theory also made everyone who walked backstage a possible saboteur, Coll kept it to himself. It might have been an accident. But the idea that it wasn't had troubled Persephone enough that she'd sought him out and suggested a business agreement, which was in itself enough to make him want to have a look at the all the rigging himself. Even if it was up in the dark rafters, and even if the spaces were tight and cramped.

"Ye dunnae mind if I have a look for myself, do ye?"

"Not at all. Just don't knock anything else down while

they're rigging for tonight's performance. I already have Gordon Humphreys refusing to say 'Macbeth.' I don't need any more ill luck before we open."

Coll backed out of the office and looked up. The stage-hands had moved from making props to setting up the stage for that evening's performance of *The Rover*, and the rafters were full of man-sized spiders calling out and tossing ropes up and down as they attached bits of scenery and checked curtains. He scowled. If anything had been done purposely, he'd never find a sign of it now.

In a way, it was a relief that he wouldn't have to go up there, but that didn't mean he wouldn't be watching. Or asking some questions. He would uphold his end of this business agreement, if that was what she chose to call it.

"Let me guess," one of the actresses playing a witch commented, coming around the edge of a curtain toward him. "Persie told you about the sandbags, and now she has you playing her white knight and casting about for dragons to slay."

"Ye think she doesnae have reason to worry?" he countered.

The tall woman shrugged in her low-cut gown. "Claremont wasn't her first beau. Admittedly, I don't think any of the others were knocked to the floor, but men like you don't take women like us as wives. We know we're not permanent, and so do you."

That made sense. Persephone had outright said that Claremont wasn't her first protector. And her part of this agreement was to help him snare a wife. "So ye think she's using it as an excuse to keep me about?"

"I certainly would, if I were her. I mean you're gorgeous, my lord." She gave an elaborate curtsy that showed off a good portion of her bosom. "Jenny Rogers, at your service."

"Glendarril," he returned, inclining his head.

"If you want to know the truth about Persie Jones, you just ask me," she continued in a sultry purr. "She has drawers full of expensive trinkets, and she gets the lead in every play we stage. I'm not saying she's mercenary, but she would make a fine puppeteer." She mimed moving strings with her fingers.

He rather liked the idea of Persephone both knowing how to look after herself and possibly inventing a peril as an excuse to keep him near. He liked being near her, in spite of the fact that it seemed . . . dishonest to go looking for a wife while he was after a different woman entirely. "She said she lives with someone named Hades. Who might that be?"

"Her cat. He hates everyone, especially men. She thought she was being clever, I suppose, naming him Hades, since in Greek mythology Persephone was Hades' wife. She's oh-so-clever, don't you know."

A cat. *Hmm.* "And Flora and Gregory?"

Jenny waved her hand. "Oh, them. Flora Whitney used to be the head seamstress here. She's Beth Frost's mama. Beth is a miracle with a needle and thread. And Gregory Norman used to be a stagehand here, until a wall fell on him during our production of *Henry V*, and he broke his shoulder. Persie's so kind that she hired them both to work for her. And to keep her secrets, I'd wager."

"Well. Thank ye for that. Ye've given me someaught to consider."

Leaning forward, she put a hand on his sleeve. "She's wearing a wig right now, you know. She always wears one. I think she may be bald." Jenny stepped closer, wrapping her arms around his shoulders and lifting up along his body. "I provide exceptional commiseration, my lord."

Normally, he would have been tempted. Not that he particularly liked a lass—or anyone else—who wagged their tongue about their companions, but with her brown hair and buxom build, she was a lass a man could take hold of.

But this afternoon had altered his thinking. And his foremost thought was of how to be rid of her without turning her against him, or more importantly, against Persephone. "I—"

"Jenny," Persephone's smooth voice came from beyond him, "Beth needs to do a fitting for your handmaiden attire."

"Oh, fiddle," the actress murmured, straightening again and lowering her arms. "I'll be about, my lord."

She lifted her chin as she waltzed past Persephone and further into the depths of the theater. In return, Persephone merely lifted an eyebrow.

"That lass seems a wee bit jealous of ye," Coll commented.

"She read for Lady Macbeth," Persephone answered, walking closer. "As did I. Charlie and his investors thought she was too . . . How did they put it? 'Hysterically desperate,' I think it was. They said she would frighten away the audience."

"She scared me just now." He found himself looking at her all over again. She'd been with him, and yet looked as composed as any woman could be, back to jesting and ready to rehearse being a murderess. Lasses. Just when he thought he had one figured out, she surprised him again.

"If you're worried over me," she said, stopping in front of him, "I've arranged for my usual driver to take me home before dark. I will remain there until you come to retrieve me in the morning."

"Does Claremont ken where ye live?"

Persephone shook her head. "I daresay St. John's Wood is far too low for him to have ever wished to set foot." Reaching up, she cupped his cheek. "You have a dinner to attend and a wife to find, Coll. I will see you in the morning."

"When I'm to charm yer household or nae darken yer door again."

"That isn't precisely what I said, but it does seem a fairly accurate representation." She grinned. "Remember, don't attempt to trap a lady into an engagement. We appreciate being left an avenue of graceful escape."

Just like the one he seemed to be leaving her. "Aye. Nae flinging anyone over my shoulder."

"Correct. I might have enjoyed it just a bit, but another young lady might faint at such physical prowess."

Another lady might have, but she hadn't. "I'll keep that in mind," he said aloud. "And tomorrow I'd like ye to write out a list of all yer former protectors or whatever ye're calling 'em. If someaught else happens, I'd like to know where to begin looking."

Coll slid his hands around her slender waist. Just the idea of someone wanting to harm her was enough to make deep fury boil his blood, despite knowing she was likely using him and his attraction to her for her own ends. But then perhaps he was using her, as well. He leaned down and took her soft mouth in a hot, deep kiss.

"Pers—oh." Gordon Humphreys stopped, flushing as he came around the corner. "We're beginning act two, Persie," he finished.

Lifting his head, Coll released her. "I'll see ye in the morning, lass," he murmured, noting that her gaze focused on his mouth. That was good; he'd never yet received a complaint about his kisses, or anything else he did with a lass in private.

She cleared her throat. "Yes. Of course. Thank you, Coll." Blinking, she faced Humphreys. "We're beginning act two of what, Gordon?"

The Saint Genesius's Macbeth scowled. "Of the Scottish play, of course. I told you, I won't be tricked."

"Not yet." Putting her arm around the actor's, she headed back toward the rehearsal room with him.

Watching after her, Coll wiped a hand across his mouth. Whatever the hell this was going on between them, he liked it, even though it left him frustrated. He was a hunter, after all. And the greatest challenge for a hunter was prey that knew he was coming.

Chapter Seven

"Art thou afeard
To be the same in thine own act and valor
As thou art in desire?"

LADY MACBETH, *MACBETH* ACT I, SCENE VII

"Why in the world would you decide to marry Mrs. Persephone Jones?" a familiar female voice hissed in Coll's ear.

He looked over as Eloise plunked herself down onto the couch beside him. Whatever it was he'd been about to say to Miss Eliza Green on his other side flew out of his mind as his sister's words conjured sky blue eyes and a musical laugh akin to angels singing. "Why did ye decide to wed Matthew Harris, and why didnae ye change yer mind after the . . . incident last week?" he retorted, barely remembering that they weren't to discuss any of the details of that disaster in public, even in the hushed, conspiratorial voices they were presently using.

"Because he's a good man who was fooled. And if you're truly betrothed to that woman, I could say the same thing about you." Leaning around him, she patted Eliza's arm. "Excuse us for a minute, won't you?" she asked in her normal speaking voice, standing and attempting to haul Coll to his feet.

She might as well have tried to shift a coach and four, but as all he'd gotten out of Eliza Green was a sentence about the weather and a simper when he'd asked if she liked to dance, he gave in and stood. "Has Persephone done ye wrong, then? Did she murder yer kitten or some-aught?"

"No. Of course not. I'm certain she's a lovely . . . woman. But she's *an actress*, Coll, and she's not . . . She's common. She works for a living. Onstage. Where she stands, barely dressed, in front of strangers. For money. Th—"

"If yer mother didnae have more money than Midas," he broke in, not because any of what Eloise said was un-true but because Persephone Jones carried on a better conversation than any other lass he'd ever met, "and if ye hadnae been born a lady, how would ye live?"

"That's not fair. I'm not saying anything ill about any-one's situation, and I do recognize how fortunate I am. She's just . . . You're a *viscount*. Whoever you wed will one day be the next Lady Aldriss. Our English and Scottish ancestors, our lineage—doesn't that mean anything to you?"

Coll narrowed his eyes. "I reckon ye're nae worried about what our dusty ancestors have to say. Ye're fret-ting because ye receive invitations to every party and every house in Mayfair, but if I wed a commoner who works for a living, ye may nae be so welcome every-where."

Growling under her breath, she pulled him around the doorway at Beasley House, Lord and Lady Crenshaw's London residence. Once they were out of sight of the twenty or so guests who made up the so-called intimate dinner, she coiled her fist and hit him on the shoulder. "People here have long memories, a great deal of pride, and nothing to do but judge other people," she whispered, scowling. "So yes, I do worry that what you do will reflect on me, because it will. I've spent my life learning how to navigate these halls, just as you spent yours learning how to navigate the lands and people up in the Highlands. Why is your way of life more important than mine?" Wincing, she shook out her fingers.

He looked at her for a minute. "Every time I forget ye've just as much MacTaggert blood running through yer veins as I do, ye say someaught like that and remind me, *piuthar*."

Her frown collapsed into a grimace. "I'm sorry. I don't mean to—"

"Nae." Coll held up one hand. "Ye keep doing that, Eloise." He took her arm, leading her down the hallway and through a door to what looked like a study. Shutting them in, he released her. "I'll tell ye someaught. It's to stay between ye and me, and I'm only telling ye because ye're less than four weeks from marrying and we've made enough trouble for ye since we arrived."

"But I've loved having you here. Please don't think I want you gone." A tear ran down one cheek. "You're my brothers, and we've been apart for so long. I don't—"

"Hush. I didnae think any such thing. Ye do have to admit, we've upended things a bit, though."

"Yes, you have." She wiped her cheek. "I haven't minded it at all until now."

"Well, between us, and us only, I'm nae marrying Persephone Jones. I only said that so our *màthair* would occupy herself with spinning about instead of throwing lasses at me. I'll find my own bride."

The relief on her face was almost comical—or it would have been, if he hadn't been the one to upset her so. "Oh, Coll. Thank you." She sighed, sinking into a chair. "I wonder what Mrs. Jones would say if she knew you were telling your family you were marrying her? Good heavens."

"She looked horrified and told me I was mad."

Eloise blinked. "You talked to her? But she's famous!"

Hell, he'd done more than talk to her. The taste of her mouth on his lingered still, but he pushed away the thought before something embarrassing happened. In a room with his sister, of all people. "Aye, we talked. I took her on a picnic today."

"Mama said you were her protector." She tilted her head. "I know what that means, but do you? Or are you literally just . . . protecting her?"

"I comprehend the meaning," he returned dryly. Even his bairn of a sister thought him a muttonhead. "The rest isnae any of yer affair."

She blushed. "Oh, of course not. I just—I'd love to meet her, if we can do so somewhere no one would be able to gossip about it." Eloise put a hand over her mouth. "And nowhere Mother could ever find out. She would have an apoplexy."

Coll grinned. "That riled up, is she? I did notice she barely spoke a word to me this evening. And Gavin swore she ran after us in the barouche for half a mile earlier today."

"She's . . ." Eloise trailed off. "You've definitely set her spinning. My goodness. I haven't seen her so agitated since the morning before you three arrived here."

Francesca Oswell-MacTaggert had been agitated about their arrival? Well, that was interesting. He'd begun to think she was carved of stone, until he'd mentioned marriage and Persephone in the same sentence. "A bit of agitation in exchange for me finding a lass I might care for. That's all I'm asking, Eloise."

She nodded, rising to throw her arms around his chest. "Very well. Some good may come of this, anyway." Stepping backward, her color still high, she turned for the door. "You finding your own bride, I mean. The rest of us have been able to wed for love—or will be able to. You should be, as well."

"Thank ye for that."

"You know, my friend Li—"

"Nae. I dunnae want Lady Aldriss in the middle of this, and I dunnae want ye there, either. By now ye've dragged all yer most marriageable friends past me, and whoever ye think of now, I reckon, wouldnae be anyone I wish to marry."

With a sigh, she wrapped her hand around his arm. "I can't argue with that. It's just that I'm running out of friends, and you're nearly out of time. I want you to find someone you can *love*, Coll. I know you'll marry, because it's what you need to do."

And that was the damned rub. He didn't *need* to marry. Not with two fit heirs in his brothers and both of them well on the way to making heirs of their own. A piece of paper written up and signed when he'd been twelve because his mother hadn't wanted to live in Scotland but *had* wanted to keep a hold over her sons—that was what everyone needed him to obey.

He patted her hand. "Once more unto the breach, then," he said, leading her back into the drawing room. He noted to himself that after a morning of listening to the Scottish play, he'd just quoted the wrong Shakespearean work, but no one else would care. According to Persephone Jones, he was Macbeth, and he could only hope his own quest didn't end in a similar tragedy.

He found everyone divided into twos and threes, chatting about the weather and fashion and whatever else the Sassenachs discussed endlessly whenever they were together. For a moment, he looked at them, all apparently content with the world and their places in it.

Even Persephone seemed to be happy where she was, but she also approached her work—and her life—with a passion he admired and had shared before circumstances had forced him south of Hadrian's Wall.

"Excuse me, Lord Glendarril?"

He turned around to see the lass with whom he'd been chatting earlier, Eliza Green, behind him. Her hands clasped at her waist and wearing a pink chiffon gown with sleeves of white lace, she looked like a black-haired angel of virtue. "Aye?"

"You said you liked to go riding. I was wondering if you might be about Hyde Park tomorrow morning at nine o'clock? My mare, Pepper, and I are there most mornings. She's a bit spirited, but then that makes her more fun to ride."

This was one of those things he was supposed to do—one of the very things Persephone had advised him about—and now Miss Green had actually walked into the clearing to nibble at the sweet grass he'd planted. A pretty lass, and one who liked to ride. And there he was, gazing at her and thinking of another lass entirely—and not just because he'd given his word that he would be at the other lass's home in the morning to escort her to the theater.

"I've an obligation tomorrow morning," he said. "Thank ye for asking me, though."

"Oh. Of course." Shifting her hands to fold them behind her back, she made an awkward, bobbing curtsy and hurried away.

"What the devil's wrong with ye?" Niall hissed from his shoulder. "That lass actually walked up and spoke to ye. About a horse. Ye should have been down on one knee, proposing."

Coll turned around, changing his retort as he remembered that he'd told everyone but Eloise that he had a bride in mind, already. "As I told *màthair*, I have a lass I'm to wed," he returned.

"Then why have ye been talking to all the unmarried young ladies here this evening?"

"Habit."

His youngest brother narrowed his eyes. "What are ye about, giant? If ye dunnae marry, all Aden and I have done is for naught."

"'All ye've done?'" Coll repeated, scowling. "Ye found lasses ye loved and married them. Or rather ye've married, and Aden will in a week. What sacrifice are ye referring to?"

"Ye ken what I mean. We all came down here to honor our parents' agreement. Ye're n—"

"Just a damned minute, ye flea," he cut in, using his old nickname for Niall despite the fact that the twenty-four-year-old now stood three inches above six feet. "We came down here to throw that agreement back in Lady Aldriss's face and march back to Scotland. And then ye took the lass she chose for me for yerself." When Niall opened his mouth to respond, Coll held up a hand. "Aye. I ken I walked out on Amy. I was there. My point being, the only thing ye and Aden have sacrificed is spending yer nights alone. So leave off. I'll wed before Eloise does." He put a slight grin on his face. "Ye and yer proper wives may nae like who I choose, but I'll damn well marry."

"Coll, dunnae t—"

"*Leave off.*"

Niall subsided at his tone, as Coll had known he would. Aye, he could quote Shakespeare and had a finer education than most folk realized, but his brothers knew better than anyone that pushing him could well mean a fight, and he tended not to lose.

They were correct, of course, because he *hadn't* yet found a bride. Even so, he'd given his word that he would escort Persephone to the theater in the morning. And he could acknowledge to himself that he would have been at the Saint Genesius tomorrow whether he'd made an agreement with her or not.

* * *

"You gave him your address?" Flora pulled a green muslin gown with elbow-length sleeves from the wardrobe and held it up.

"I did. No, not that one. Try the blue and white one."

"The one with the little red roses on it?"

"Yes, that one." As she spoke, Persephone pulled her night-rail off and left it crumpled on the quilted bedspread. She'd overslept, which wasn't unusual; being in the theater meant her days could end at dawn and not begin until well after noon, but she'd actually gone to bed before midnight last night.

No, it wasn't the hours; it was the man. A very wicked, sharp-witted Highlander, to be precise. She stretched, lifting her arms skyward. A very, very wicked Scotsman, indeed.

"What in heaven's . . . How did you get that bruise on your bottom, Persie? Did another sandbag fall?"

Damnation. "No. I was . . . at sea with a Scottish fisherman."

Flora's eyes widened. "You let that Lord Glendarril below deck? Persie, you barely know him!"

"I don't need a lecture, Flora; I'm eight-and-twenty, earn my own keep, and rent my own house. Th—"

"I know all that, for heaven's sake. I'm just baffled. You got rid of Claremont because he wanted . . . below deck, and now, after one day of acquaintance, you give in to the Scotsman?"

"I didn't give in. It was my idea." Retrieving her shift from the wardrobe, she pulled it on. "As it turns out, he's a good fisherman. A very good fisherman." Hugging herself, she grinned. "Delicious."

Fanning herself with the skirt of the blue and white gown, Flora chuckled. "Oh, my. I won't warn you to be cautious, because I know you always are. I *will* say that you shouldn't lose your heart to a man you've promised to help find a wife."

"Don't worry about me, my dear," Persephone returned, turning and lifting her arms again so Flora could help her with the muslin. "I've been playing this game for more than seven years now." She snorted. "I did tell him that he won't be allowed in the house if he can't charm you, Gregory, *and* Hades."

"Ha. *I* haven't been able to charm Hades, and I've known him for six years."

"Precisely."

As if on cue, the black cat emerged from beneath the bed to stretch, digging his claws into the expensive Persian rug that covered the polished wooden floor. Flicking his tail upward, he hissed in Flora's direction before he wound himself around Persephone's ankles and then padded for the cracked-open bedchamber door.

"I had Gregory chat with Lady Greaves's maid when he ran across her at the market this morning," Flora went on, buttoning the trio of fastenings going up Persephone's back before moving on to tie the blue ribbon about the high waist of the gown. "Milly says no one's seen Claremont at any soiree for the past few days."

"I hope he's gone home," Persephone commented feelingly, sitting at the dressing table to brushing out her shoulder-length hair. Her hair was her one vanity, she supposed; with the number of wigs she wore, keeping it cropped would be much easier. But she couldn't do it. "He has business there with his renovations, and none here with me. What do you say to that scandalous ginger wig this morning?"

"My, you *are* feeling daring." Clucking her tongue, Flora fetched the bright ginger bob while Persephone began pinning up her own hair.

She wouldn't say she felt daring as much as she felt *awake*. Energized. Ready to push for her interpretation of Lady Macbeth's desperate fear of being ordinary, rather than Charlie's insistence that the lady was simply an ambitious witch.

And this feeling was, of course, merely a result of her finding her way to the character. It had nothing to do with the Highlander who'd given her excited shivers yesterday, and who'd reminded her that being touched could be very pleasurable, indeed.

"Gregory paid four pence for eggs and bread this morning, and he's made something of them that had my mouth watering earlier, I don't mind telling you," Flora said, kneeling to help Persephone step into her pretty blue walking shoes.

"You might have said that earlier. I am famished."

"I would have, but I was too busy hearing about you going fishing. Now go on with you; I'll finish tidying up here."

Persephone regarded herself for a moment in the dressing table mirror. Short, curling red hair, blue eyes, a pert nose, a slightly wide mouth that made it easier for her to show her faux emotions onstage, a few laugh lines around her eyes that would soon make the idea of her playing a character as young as Juliet Capulet ridiculous. For now, she could still manage it, and she did look several years younger than her twenty-eight years.

Soon, though, she would be playing mothers and hags and grandmothers, maids or nannies—whatever Charlie saw fit to put in front of her. She sighed, standing. Hopefully by then she would have enough money saved that she could gracefully retire and purchase a small cottage out in Dover or somewhere and spend the remainder of her days gardening.

Men—a husband—didn't enter into the equation, of course, because she wouldn't be marrying. Not to a lord, and not to a baker or a butcher or a candlestick maker. She would give of her body when and where she chose, and keep her independence for herself. God knew she'd paid enough for it.

She made her way downstairs, guided by the scent of toast and eggs. A bit of dallying here and there probably wasn't wise, especially with someone as compelling as Coll MacTaggert, but for goodness' sake it had been enjoyable. She meant to enjoy him again, if the opportunity arose.

A more intelligent woman probably wouldn't have given him her address, but he'd made a good point about being unable to carry out his end of their bargain if he didn't even know where to find her. In addition, part of her liked the idea of a gentleman coming to call at her front door. Even if he'd never make it past the foyer, because even if he somehow managed to charm Gregory and Flora, Hades would be her clawed conscience and boot him out again.

Halfway through breakfast, the knocker banged at her front door. In a sudden flutter of nerves, she dropped her fork and had to work to keep herself from hurrying into the hallway. Perhaps she'd been celibate for too long. "I assume that will be Lord Glendarril," she said aloud to Gregory. "If a large Scotsman is indeed at the door, please allow him in, but keep him in the foyer. I give you leave to be annoyed by him, if you choose. Charming you is one of the tasks I put to him."

"Most people annoy me, Miss Persie. It comes natural to them," he returned with a faint grin, and clicked his heels together before he left the dining room.

As she listened for any raised voices, she deliberately finished her breakfast and her morning cup of tea. Whatever might be roiling about in her mind, she had a long day of rehearsals ahead of her, and that needed to be her first priority. Her only priority, really. Lord Glendarril—Coll—was a distraction. A pleasant one, but a distraction nonetheless.

The dining room door opened. "You must come see

this," Flora said in a hushed voice, motioning for Persephone to join her. "I can scarcely believe my own eyes."

"Hades hasn't killed Lord Glendarril, has he?" she said, setting aside her napkin and standing, resisting the urge to smooth her dress. She'd had lovers before, after all, and while she didn't make a habit of inviting any of them to her home, Coll MacTaggert had offered a benefit in addition to his masculine charms. What she didn't do was lose her head over any of them.

Flora reached the foyer before her and stepped aside. Persephone continued for another step, then froze. *What the devil?*

Hades stood between the Highlander's booted feet, and wound himself around and around the well-shined Hessians, a black, purring figure eight. It was . . . remarkable. In addition to that, Gregory stood chatting with the viscount as if they'd been friends for years, her footman holding what looked to be a very good-quality hammer, a wooden crate with still more tools at his feet.

Once she noticed that, she looked over at Flora. Her maid and former seamstress held a basket over one arm, and when Persephone leaned over to look inside, she saw lovely folds of purple silk, some silver-edged lace, silver scissors, thread—all things an ex-theater seamstress would value and more than likely treasure.

"Bribery, then?" she asked, lifting her gaze to find Coll looking at her, an easy smile on his lean face. Her heart did a quick somersault, which she put to eating too quickly and decided to leave at that—for now, anyway.

His dark green eyes danced. "Ye're a redhead today. I like it. Dunnae yer neighbors question why ye leave the house as a different lass every day?"

"I've encouraged the belief that I own a wig shop," she returned. "Don't change the subject. You've bribed my employees."

His damned sexy mouth curved in a grin. "Ye said to try to charm them. Ye didnae say I couldnae bring gifts."

She set aside her questions of how he'd managed to discover what Gregory and Flora might find interesting. No doubt he'd asked someone at the Saint Genesius, and theater folk did love telling tales. Of more immediate interest was her famously hostile cat, now sitting on Coll's left boot and rubbing his face against it. "What did you do to my cat, then?"

"Hades? Och, the devil and I are old friends. Surely ye've heard that about me."

"Truthfully, Hades isn't much for conversation." She grinned, completely baffled and rather flattered. Whatever else he'd done, he'd obviously made an effort to charm her household staff and her cat, and that had been her one requirement for allowing him into the house. No one could deny that he'd succeeded.

Nor could she deny that a good part of her was pleased that he'd passed her test. Having him about for a while longer could be quite . . . invigorating, in spite of the mayhem that seemed to surround him and his brothers.

"Well," he said, "I reckon we should be going, Persephone, unless ye can conjure someaught else ye wish to be doing."

She felt sudden damp between her thighs. While she was performing, her days were generally free. Meeting Coll back then would have made for some very interesting times. But now she had an obligation in the mornings. "Yes, we should be off. Flora, my shawl, if you please."

"Hmm? Oh, yes, of course." Setting her basket aside, Flora retrieved the blue shawl and set it over Persephone's shoulders. "Do tell my Beth that I've a lovely roast in mind for Friday."

"I'll remind her."

Gregory pulled open the front door, but with Hades

still seated on Coll's boot, it didn't seem like any of them would be leaving the house. Blowing out her breath, Persephone crouched to gather the black cat up in her arms and set him in Gregory's. "We'll be back later, Hades," she said, scratching between his ears.

The cat ignored her, his gaze on Coll, his chest rumbling with an uncharacteristic purr. Furrowing her brow, she took the Highlander's arm and headed outside to the waiting barouche. The second the front door closed, she was certain she heard a muffled, masculine yelp; no doubt whatever spell Coll had cast had worn off, and Hades was back to himself again.

He handed her up and sat beside her on the front-facing seat, and Gavin clucked at the team of bays, sending them into the street. "It's a lovely morning, lass. Are ye certain ye wish to spend it in that dark theater speaking lines from a dark tale?"

She gazed at him. "What did you do to my cat?"

Coll put a hand to his chest and lifted an eyebrow. "Yer cat is a fine beastie. We understand each other, I reckon."

"Mm-hmm." Bending down, she ran a finger along the side of his boot.

"Ye said I needed to get past 'em," Coll went on. "Ye didnae say h—"

"I know. I didn't say how you should or shouldn't do it." Lifting her finger to her nose, she sniffed. "Coll MacTaggert, why does your boot smell of fish?"

"I reckon that's because I rubbed a fish on it."

Persephone burst out laughing. Of all the ingenious, unexpected things in the world, this Highlander had managed in a day what some of her friends hadn't accomplished in six years. "Well-done, then. I concede."

"Then I'm to be allowed into the house?"

"You may come for dinner on Friday, if you wish. Flora is having her daughter, Beth, and Beth's husband and babies over, and no doubt Gregory will ask his brother to join us, as well."

"I'll be there."

"Good." She met his green-eyed gaze, then shook herself before she could wrap her arms around his shoulders and kiss him in front of London. The man was seeking a wife, after all. "Did you attempt to speak to anyone in Hyde Park this morning?"

"Nae. I'll go this afternoon."

"You won't find riders after noon," she countered. "Only ladies in carriages, trying to be seen by as many of their fellows as possible."

With an exaggerated shudder, he folded his arms over his chest. "Mayhap I should just don a blindfold and point at one of them."

She grinned at his obvious disgust. "That might get you a wife, but the odds that she's someone you could like— or love—would be horribly long, I'm afraid."

"Are ye certain ye're nae secretly a princess or someaught? That would do to please the family, and I reckon ye'd do for me as ye are."

The laugh she forced out sounded fairly convincing, or so she hoped. "I've played a secret princess or two, and I'm presently rehearsing to play the queen of Scotland. I don't come any nearer than that, I'm afraid."

Nodding, he settled deeper into the seat. "Do your neighbors truly think ye a shopkeeper?"

"Well, I haven't come out and lied about my profession, but I have hinted a few times that that's why I change my appearance so often."

"And nae a one of them has recognized ye? My sister says everyone kens who ye are. Even she wants to meet ye, if she can do it without her mother finding out."

"Her mother is your mother as well, is she not?"

"Aye." He frowned. "Damned interfering woman. If she

meant to leave us behind, she should have done so. What kind of lass walks away from her bairns and then makes an agreement that they have to do as she says seventeen years later?"

Was that what had happened? "She walked away from you?"

He shifted a little. "It's a long time done, but aye. She and my da had had enough of each other, I reckon, and when her next bairn was a lass, she decided she couldnae raise the wee one in such a barbaric place as Scotland."

"And she left you—her three sons—behind? I can't imagine doing that." To leave children behind . . . She could understand hating a life and needing to flee it, but her own babies? Lady Aldriss had either been unimaginably desperate, or completely heartless.

Coll made a dismissive sound. "It's done. Now I'm left with the consequences of a thing I had no say over in the first place. But I'll do it, because I dunnae wish to see Aldriss Park and those who rely on the MacTaggerts doomed to poverty. I'm still of half a mind to wed ye, though, just to see the look on Francesca's face."

"I'm not certain how I feel about you using me as a jest." Actually, she did know how she felt; she didn't like it. How she felt about him, though . . . That was becoming much more complicated. He'd rubbed a fish on his boots to ingratiate himself to her cat, for heaven's sake. Who did that? No one else she could imagine. Not *after* they'd been together.

"I dunnae mean to slight ye, Persephone. It's her who needs to be taught a lesson." He shifted again, facing her more squarely, and reached out to take her fingers in his. "Do ye give me leave to use yer name in vain in an attempt to aggravate my mother?"

His fingers were warm and large and calloused, no doubt from flinging sheep about. Well-bred men didn't have callouses on their hands, or anywhere else. It was possible he didn't know how to be a proper gentleman, but it seemed more likely that he simply didn't care what other aristocrats did or didn't do.

As for her name being bandied about in connection with his, Persephone Jones had been linked with other powerful men, and it had only served to bring more people to the Saint Genesius. "My name has no objection to being used in vain, or any other way." She closed her fingers around his. "But please do not ruin your own chances at finding someone to love because you're too occupied with driving me about and annoying your family."

"Och, lass, we've a mutual agreement. Ye show me how to be a gentleman, and I'll keep sandbags from falling on ye."

"And keep the hounds at bay." After all, she didn't want him to think she'd simply made up a potential peril to keep him near, whether she might have unintentionally done so or not. But Claremont had given up far more easily than she'd expected, and that did bother her a little.

"Does that make me a wolf?"

"More a lion, I think."

This time his smile had her thinking about picnics and abandoned wagons—not that thoughts of being with him again had left her for more than a minute since yesterday's luncheon. If she had any thoughts of marrying these days, all of his offhand proposals would have had her heart flitting about like a butterfly in a stiff breeze. As it was, she had to wonder if every other unmarried woman in London was mad. She didn't know how to otherwise explain why a dozen ladies hadn't fallen for him the first night they'd set eyes on him.

"You might consider," she said aloud, "escorting your sister about the park. Her friends would then have an excuse to approach, and you—"

"Nae," he cut her off. "Eloise is but eighteen. I dunnae want a bairn eleven years younger than me for a wife. I couldnae love a lass who'd nae give me a good argument now and again."

"Not everything is a fight, you know."

"Says ye, woman. I beg to differ."

They rolled to a stop at the rear of the Saint Genesius Theatre, and Coll unlatched the low door and stepped down, offering her his hand. Persephone stifled a sigh. She'd expected yet another protector who wanted her to pretend to be Juliet or shrewish Kate needing to be tamed, or any of the other dozens of females she'd portrayed. This man seemed to like *her*, and she found that both disquieting and amazingly arousing all at the same time.

"Please see me inside, then, my lord, and then go off and find yourself a bride."

"What time are ye finished here?"

"Parliament has a long session today, so there won't be a performance tonight. We'll probably finish around eight o'clock. I'll make my own way home. I'm sure you have plans for the evening."

"I'll be here at eight o'clock. Dunnae ye venture outside. I'll come in and fetch ye."

"Coll, I seem to be getting far more from this agreement than you are. That doesn't—"

"Wait for me here, Gavin," he broke in, offering Persephone his muscular forearm again. "I'll be but a few minutes."

"Aye, m'laird."

When she put her hand around his arm, he drew her a breath closer. "If ye havenae realized by now, Persephone Jones, I keep my word. And I honor my agreements. So, if ye dunnae want me about, ye'd best lie to me well enough that I believe ye dunnae want me or need me any longer."

Eventually, probably sooner than she liked, she would

do that. She would tell him that she'd grown tired of him, and that she wanted someone who had better manners or who would create less of a spectacle by virtue of his mere existence. And because she was good at what she did, he would believe her. That, though, wasn't today.

Chapter Eight

"By the pricking of my thumbs,
Something wicked this way comes.
Open, locks,
Whoever knocks!"

SECOND WITCH, MACBETH ACT IV, SCENE I

Stagehands rolling a good portion of Birnham Wood outside for painting exited through the door as they entered, greeting the two of them with a chorus of "Persies" and "my lords." Coll nodded, holding the door open for the conundrum of a woman walking by his side.

Of course, he'd encountered women who spoke their minds, lasses who didn't brook any nonsense. Up to this point, he'd thought they all lived in the Highlands, but clearly he'd been wrong. This one, Persephone Jones, did as she pleased.

Aye, she knew the rules, and aye, she did follow some of them, but she also lay with a man simply because she wanted him, rode about in open carriages with a man and without a chaperone, and encouraged men to address her by her first name. If she declined to be seen with him in Hyde Park, it was because she didn't want ladies staying away from the theater in protest, not because she feared their censure for herself.

She earned her own way in the world and was successful enough to be able to rent a house and employ two servants, even if she chose to call them employees. A damned remarkable woman, taken altogether. Her independence and her defiance appealed to him, even if from time to time, he got the sense that some of it was a deliberate response to . . . something.

A ginger cat hopped down from a wooden crate to lick his boots, and with an amused grunt he squatted to shoo it away. Rubbing fish on his boots had been one of his best ideas, if he said so himself.

Movement suddenly caught his eye, and he straightened as a metal bucket swung directly at them, hard and fast. *Christ.*

Pivoting, he grabbed Persephone around the waist and dropped with her to the floor.

The bucket continued its swing above them before slamming into a post with a resounding crack and splintering the heavy timber. As it rebounded toward them again, Coll rolled to his feet, grabbed a ladder, and slammed it down in front of the missile, using his weight to hold it firm. The metal container hit the ladder violently, broke two of the steps, and lurched away in a slow, drunken spin.

Grabbing hold of it, Coll pulled the knife from his boot and sliced through the rope. The bucket hit the floor and overturned, a handful of bricks tumbling out of it.

With the knife still gripped in his hand, he looked up. Three stagehands were up in the rigging, none of them near where the bucket had begun its swing.

Gradually, he became aware of the loud, shouting chaos erupting around him, and he turned again to see Charlie Huddle helping Persephone to her feet. Half the cast and most of the stagehands had gathered around them, all of them ashen, shaken, and babbling.

Coll shoved the knife back into his boot and moved people aside until he reached Persephone. Only when he had hold of her arm did he let out his breath. "Are ye injured?" he asked, turning her to face him. "Did I hurt ye?"

"No," she returned immediately, her movements jerky and abrupt rather than her usual graceful glide. "I'm fine. You—that—my goodness."

"That's two things coming down at ye from the dark." His jaw clenched, his heart beginning to pound at the thought of what had almost happened. "One's an accident. Two is someone trying to kill ye."

"That can't be," Huddle said, wiping a handkerchief across his forehead. "I've seen actors attempting to take out the competition to get a role they wanted, but that's bruises or a broken arm."

Whipping around, Coll retrieved the bricks, picked up the bucket, and dropped it again at the stage manager's feet. The resounding thud made the smaller man jump. "That weighs four stone at the least," he said, hearing Persephone's intake of breath at his statement and attempting to keep his attention on Huddle. "That's nae a broken arm. That's a broken skull." It might have been worse than that—a broken neck or even a decapitation—and from his expression, the stage manager, at least, seemed to realize that.

Over to his right, Jenny Rogers fainted into Banquo's—Lawrence Valense's—arms. There were too many damned people around, and it could have been any of them. Not the lasses, more than likely; none of them looked capable of hauling a bucket that heavy up to the theater's catwalk. Two dozen men remained, though, and that was without counting the other workers moving in and out all day.

"Coll, a word, if you please," Persephone said, wrapping both hands around his forearm. "My dressing room, perhaps?"

"Aye." He kept himself half a step in front of her and pushed open the dressing room door before he allowed her inside. The last thing she needed was to have another heavy thing swinging at her from the rafters. "In with ye, lass."

She followed him into the small room, which was dominated by its full-length mirror, but also, he noticed now, mounds of costumes, wigs, hats, and books. Coll shut the door behind them, half expecting Persephone to throw herself into his arms. Instead, she walked up to the mirror and stood there staring at her reflection for a good minute.

"Where is Claremont's house in Town?" he asked. "I've a mind to pay him a visit."

"It's Pierce House on Farm Street," she returned, unmoving. "I don't know the number. Do you think it was him?"

"He didnae do it himself, but he may have paid someone to murder ye."

Her fingers clenched and opened again. "I hope it was him," she muttered, giving her reflection a last glare before she turned to sit at her dressing table.

"Ye reckon it could be someone else?" Coll lifted an eyebrow. For a lass so easy on the eyes and so good-humored, she seemed to have rather more enemies than he'd suspected.

"No. No, of course not. I just prefer a definitive answer to questions—I don't like unanswered questions. And I certainly don't like heavy things swinging at my head from out of the dark."

"I dunnae like that myself."

She looked up at him. "You saved my life. I didn't even know it was coming, and then you flung me to the floor. I should be dead right now."

That thought stabbed at him as well, painful and deep. Whatever Persephone Jones was to him, it seemed he cared a great deal that she remained unharmed. Of course, he didn't like the idea of anyone innocent being injured, but this felt more . . . personal than that. More vital. "Ye're nae harmed. Keep yer thoughts on that, Persephone."

Nodding, she rolled her shoulders. "Yes, you're correct. I can't act while I'm shaking with fear."

"I'm going to have Gavin stay here while I'm gone," Coll decided. "Ye're nae to be out of his sight for a single moment, ye ken?"

He'd thought she might protest, but she nodded again. "And if it is Claremont? What will you do?"

"I'll solve the problem," he said flatly.

"Coll, he's an earl."

"And I'm a MacTaggert." He went to the door and opened it. "Huddle! Ye stay here in this doorway until my man comes to take yer place."

"I . . . yes, of course. Thank you, my lord." The stage manager hurried up to the dressing room door, a hammer clutched in one hand. "This madness must stop. Persie, if we lose you, we—"

"Ye're nae losing Persephone," Coll cut in. "Ye're making certain she stays safe."

He wanted to stay. He wanted to be the one watching over her. But he couldn't be in two places at once, damn it all. Turning on his heel, shoving aside the sensation that he was already in far deeper water than he'd realized, Coll strode toward the theater's back door. Gavin and the barouche waited on the far side of the alley, the groom standing in front of the pair of bays and feeding them treats from his pockets.

"Ye ready to head to Hyde Park, m'laird?" he asked, parting with a last carrot. "I've a good feeling ye might find yer bride today."

"Someone just tried to kill Persephone," Coll said flatly. "I want ye in there, and I dunnae want ye to take yer peepers off her until I get back."

"What?" Gavin blinked. "The lass?"

"Aye, the lass. I'm going to sort things out." Hopping up to the driver's perch of the barouche, Coll freed the reins.

"For Saint Andrew's sake, fetch one of yer brothers first," the groom called after him as he sent the team into the street at a fast trot.

Coll ignored the advice. He could fight his own battles. Aside from that, his brothers were undoubtedly occupied with whatever shite accompanied being newly married or nearly married. As the oldest, he generally watched over them. It wasn't their duty to watch over him.

At the same time, he knew better than anyone that this was London—Mayfair—not the Highlands. A lad couldn't settle a disagreement the same way here as he might do there. And he wasn't entirely certain Claremont was the one to blame for these two so-called accidents, anyway.

Cursing, he turned up Bond Street. The earl's house was but two or three streets south of Oswell House, and the proximity felt . . . significant. He'd met enough of his so-called peers to understand that while a good handful of them did have morals and at least some care for the less-fortunate folk, there were likely even more who didn't give a damn about anything but their own wealth and power and comfort.

Perhaps if he'd been raised in London among the peerage instead of in a place where he went out daily to meet with those who depended on MacTaggert protection, and worked side-by-side with men simply trying to earn enough to put food into their larders, he might see it all differently.

But he had grown up in the Highlands. He'd been born but eight years after the repeal of the Act of Proscription, before which kilts, bagpipes, and firearms were all made illegal in the Highlands by British Parliament. Aye, he'd been born into a privileged house, but he'd grown up alongside fishermen, farmers, and peat cutters. All of that had given him a certain contempt for Sassenach lords who only ventured to their country homes to throw parties or oversee in expensive renovations of their drawing rooms.

"Farthing, saddle Nuckelavee for me," he said as he stopped the barouche in front of the Oswell House stable.

His mother's head groom collected the team, but gave Coll a grimace. "Wouldn't Gavin be better suited to—"

"Gavin's nae here. Which of my brothers is inside?"

"Both, my lord. Sh—"

"Saddle Loki as well, then," he decided, naming Aden's chestnut Thoroughbred. The middle MacTaggert brother could convince a bee to part with its honey, and cunning seemed a better match in confronting Claremont than Niall's famous charm.

"I would prefer not to work with Nu—"

"Nuckelavee!" Coll bellowed, and the stallion whinnied from inside his stall. "Behave yer damned self!" As a responding nicker sounded, he nodded at the groom. "He'll stand for ye."

"Thank you, my lord."

He rarely ordered the black to behave his damned self, but that was the phrase he and Gavin had used when training him, and the one Nuckelavee would obey beyond all others. Without waiting to see whether his mother's groom had realized that or not, Coll strode up to the house, entering through the kitchen and snatching up an apple from the table as he passed. The sight of his mother and Eloise in the hallway just outside the library made him frown. Something was afoot, but whatever it was, he didn't have time for it.

"Where's Aden?" he asked.

"In there," Eloise said, pointing at the closed door.

"Thank ye."

"Don't you dare—" his mother began, but by then he'd already pushed down on the handle and was inside the room.

Aden sat in a chair, Miranda Harris beside him and holding his hand, while opposite them, a large, jolly-looking man in priest's robes sat with an open Bible on his lap. *Bloody hell.* Coll stopped short as his brother turned to look at him.

"What is it?" Aden asked.

"I need yer assistance," Coll muttered, cursing under his breath. Instead of warning him not to vex her, his mother might have considered beginning her conversation with "Aden and Miranda are being counseled by a priest before their wedding, so stay out," for the devil's sake.

Aden slid his gaze to Miranda, who quirked her face in an amused smile. "Go," she murmured. "I'll manage this."

"Marriage is a lifetime commitment," the priest said, his round cheeks darkening. "It is not something to be *managed*."

Miranda reached out, taking hold of the priest's hand. "As an English-born woman about to venture into the Scottish Highlands," she said smoothly, "I did wonder if you had any advice for me." She glanced at Aden over her shoulder, subtly urging him to leave. "Advice that you perhaps couldn't give me with my rather uncivilized betrothed present."

That seemed to smooth the man's ruffled feathers, but Coll didn't have time to imagine what advice a Sassenach who'd never been to Scotland could have for a lass marrying a MacTaggert. No priestly advice had helped Francesca Oswell-MacTaggert, that was for bloody certain.

"I owe ye, Coll," Aden said under his breath, leaving the door ajar as they passed Eloise and Francesca again and went on toward the kitchen. "I was on the verge of feigning an apoplexy to escape."

"What the devil was he trying to tell ye?"

"How to be a husband. He's nae married, incidentally." Shaking his head, Aden came to a stop just inside the kitchen door. "But as my Miranda's here and ye seem to be leading me elsewhere, I'm going to ask ye again what's afoot."

"Yesterday a pair of sandbags nearly fell on Persephone. I put it to an accident. This morning a bucket full of bricks came flying out of the rafters and nearly broke her neck. I'm nae putting either of them to an accident any longer."

Aden's faintly amused expression immediately sharpened. "I heard that Lord Claremont's been escorting her about, and that ye set him on his arse the other night. Are ye putting it to him?"

"Aye. He's the only suspect I have in mind at this moment."

"Are ye certain those accidents were meant for her, though?"

Coll hadn't considered that, and now he was doubly thankful to Gavin for suggesting he involve his brothers. "Whether they were or nae, I'm going to suggest Claremont put a stop to them before she gets hurt. I thought ye should come with me on the chance I lose my temper."

"Aye. I can do that. I will suggest to *ye* that ye dunnae kill him until after ye're certain he's the one causing trouble."

"Ye see? Already ye're proving useful to have about."

Both horses waited as he and Aden reached the stable, Farthing looking both baffled and relieved as he held a perfectly still Nuckelavee's bridle. "Do you require an escort?" the groom asked.

"Nae. We'll manage."

With Aden and long-legged Loki beside him, Coll kept Nuckelavee to a barely restrained trot south and east toward Farm Street. If Aden had any further thoughts about Claremont's guilt or innocence, he kept them to himself, but Coll didn't care to hear them, anyway.

"I've a question," Aden said into the silence, and Coll took back the silent praise with which he'd been greeting his brother's characteristic reticence.

"What is it?"

"Do ye actually mean to wed this Persephone Jones, or are ye using her name to put Francesca back on her heels while ye find yer own wife?"

Of course Aden had figured it out; the middle MacTaggert brother had an uncanny ability to see past a man's words and into his meaning. "Does it matter which it is?" Coll retorted.

"I reckon it does. And I reckon ye ken why it matters."

"Is yer Miranda fluttering her fan over the idea of an actress marrying into the family or someaught? Are ye worried she'll change her mind about marrying ye?"

"My Miranda wouldnae care if ye wed a circus bear, Coll. *My* concern is if ye're so intent on getting some kind of revenge against our *màthair* that ye'd sacrifice the MacTaggert pride to do it. The lass ye wed is to be the Countess Aldriss one day, to speak for yer cotters and yer fishwives and yer farmers' daughters when nae anyone else can do it, to stand by ye when the crops fail and when the moors flood. Is that Persephone Jones?"

Coll clenched his jaw. "If ye've already figured out the answer, then dunnae trouble me with the question."

Aden shifted in the saddle. "Then why the devil are we about to go threaten an earl when ye have something else ye need to be doing?"

"Because the lass doesnae have anyone else to go threaten an earl," Coll snapped. "Because I dunnae like it when a man cannae step past his own pride far enough to admit that mayhap he's a fool and should settle for being grateful that all he earned was a punch, and when the thing that makes the most sense to him is trying to murder a lass for nae liking him."

"And now it makes sense to me," Aden returned in a mild tone. "Ye might have said 'chivalry,' though, and nae use up all yer words for the day."

"Shut yer yap, Aden."

They tied their horses in front of Claremont's shiny white house, and Coll topped the steps to slam the brass boar's head knocker against the door. A skeletal butler in red and black livery pulled it open, staring at them with sunken cadaver eyes.

"Yes?"

"Viscount Glendarril is here for a word with Lord Claremont," Aden supplied. "Would the earl be home today?"

The butler's left eye twitched. "I shall inquire," he said. "Wait here." With that, he shut the door on them.

"Ye shouldnae have been so polite," Coll muttered, flexing his fingers.

"If ye'd so much as tapped him, he might well have crumbled into dust. Be patient, giant. It's more than just ye and Niall and me that ye're representing now."

That was the damned truth. There was Francesca— Lady Aldriss—for one, though causing her some consternation had been part of the plan from the beginning. But the things he did also reflected on Eloise, Amy, Miranda, and their families as well. The MacTaggert part of Clan Ross had more than doubled in size over the past eight weeks, it seemed. And it had quadrupled in civility, which was a shame.

The door opened again. Lord Claremont himself stood there, blond and handsome but for a scabbing scratch over his left temple, no doubt the result of being flung into the wall of Persephone's dressing room. "Glendarril," he said smoothly. "If you're here to challenge me to a duel, I decline."

"I may nae give ye that option," Coll countered.

"Excuse me," Aden said, taking a half step forward between Coll and Claremont, "but my brother has a query, and we hoped ye might be able to answer the question. Might we come in? Unless ye care to have him bellowing at ye from the street, that is."

The earl eyed the two of them, then stepped back into his foyer. "This way, gentlemen."

"Ye see?" Aden whispered, motioning for Coll to precede him. "Manners. They're a wee bit like magic here in London."

"Says the man who had a naval captain near shitting himself a week ago," Coll muttered back, following the earl into what he presumed was the house's morning room.

"Very well," Claremont said, strolling over to a liquor tantalus. "I'm on my way back to the House of Lords for our afternoon session, but I have a few minutes. I should offer you a drink, yes?"

He should have recalled that Parliament was in session today, Coll reflected. Persephone had mentioned it as well, not that he expected Claremont to have swung the bucket himself. "Nae for me. I want to kn—"

"Nae, thank ye," Aden interrupted again. "We'd just like to know where ye were earlier today, and yesterday morning."

The earl filled a glass with whisky, from the smell of it, and took a swallow. "I don't believe we've been introduced," he said to Aden. "If you're here to be his second or something equally archaic, you should know I have no intention of battling anyone, much less two of you."

"I'm nae here to protect Coll," Aden said, emphasizing his brother's name.

"Oh. I see. In that case, welcome."

While Claremont and Aden exchanged barbs, Coll watched the earl. Smooth, sophisticated, and eloquent, all the polish of the *haut ton* didn't make him anything but slippery. Even so, he didn't carry himself like an attempted murderer—or Coll's vision of one, anyway. Then again, he'd met more glib-tongued liars here than he'd known in his entire twenty-nine years in the Highlands.

"If the two of ye are finished dancing," he stated, "I want to know why ye've been trying to kill Persephone Jones. And why ye think ye should be allowed to continue breathing after ye've tried to harm the lass."

"I'd heard you stepped in after I stepped back." Claremont lifted his glass in a toast. "May you be more successful than I in touring her garden of delights."

"That sounds magnanimous. Answer my question."

"You didn't precisely ask one, but I do take your meaning. I haven't been attempting to murder anyone. Nor have I asked anyone else to do so, since I surmise no one has seen me anywhere near her in the past three days."

"Prove it."

The earl tilted his head. "I cannot do so." He finished off his glass and set it aside. "I gave her pretty and expensive baubles. Honestly, she never asked for any of them, but I figured I was buying more than her smiles. She—and you—proved me wrong. I made a poor investment. Such is the risk with any woman who doesn't explicitly call herself a whore."

"Careful, Claremont," Coll warned, searching for any sign of a lie and not seeing any, damn it all.

"Of course. As for you, Glendarril, I consider your behavior ungentlemanly, but as I have no wish to be split in two by a claymore, I have no intention of doing anything about either you or Persephone. If that doesn't suffice, then question my servants and ask them if I've sent out any mysterious notes over the past few days. Ask if I've said anything cross—or anything at all, actually—about Mrs. Jones."

Coll kept his gaze on the earl. "Aden, ye're better at digging up liars than I am. What do ye say about this one?"

"In my opinion, *bràthair*, Claremont here has more to lose by appearing hurt over being turned away by an actress than he might gain by killing her. I dunnae think he's yer man."

That was precisely the conclusion Coll had reached, and as much as he wanted to level the man for putting a hand on Persephone, it made sense. An earl behaving like a fool over an actress wouldn't look well, and the way things looked was everything to the Mayfair set. "Then I'm finished here, I reckon."

"Oh, good," Claremont commented. "Best of luck buying your way beneath her skirts, Glendarril, but don't part with anything you value, because you'll likely never see it again. And you may find yourself booted out the back door when she finds someone more stupid than you to protect her when you suggest she owes you something with which she's not willing to part."

Well, that was enough of that. Coll turned around, his fists clenched, only to have Aden step between the two of them. "Ye're after a wife," his brother whispered. "Dunnae make yer reputation with the lasses even worse now by bloodying such a pretty lad."

That made him snort. Reluctantly, Coll turned around again and left Pierce House. "He deserves to have his beak flattened," he grumbled, freeing Nuckelavee's reins and swinging back into the saddle.

"Aye. If ye begin punching every man here who deserves

it, though, ye'll nae have time for anything else." Aden drew Loki up beside him. "Are ye still convinced someone's out to harm the lass?"

"I am. That bucket—if I hadnae been there, it would have killed her. And I'm nae allowing that to happen."

Aden frowned. "Coll, dunnae hit me, but I've another question."

"Ask it, then."

"Are ye certain Claremont's wrong about her? That she'll nae take up yer time and lead ye on when ye have someaught else ye need to be seeing to right now? That ye're nae . . . a hound on the scent, being led about by yer cock?"

"I'm nae a virgin, Aden. And I've already caught the lass. So nae, she's nae leading me anywhere."

He watched as his brother took in that information and mixed it in with the other facts he already had to hand. "If it's nae yer cock leading ye about, then, for God's sake, ask yerself what it is. Because if it's yer damned heart, ye've another set of problems entirely."

His heart? Where had that come from? He was passing the time, sending his mother around in circles while he looked for a suitable bride. That had nothing to do with Persephone Jones, other than the fact that hers was the name that would most annoy Lady Aldriss.

Aye, he enjoyed chatting with the lass, and he liked the way she viewed the world in a combination of bright colors and gaping holes in the pretty fabric, and that it all, palette and pain, interested her. And he liked that she fit him, body to body. But his heart wasn't involved. He wouldn't be and couldn't be in love with a lass he'd known for but three days. Especially when he was on the hunt for a bride, a woman who could stand as his match and a leader to all the folk answerable to the MacTaggerts.

"Dunnae be an idiot, Aden," he said aloud. "I'm done

with ye. Go back to Oswell House and make doe eyes at yer wife-to-be."

"Dunnae mind if I do," his brother returned, clearly not the least bit insulted. "But keep yer eyes on Francesca; someaught's afoot, but I've nae been able to figure out what it is yet."

"If it's another lass for her to ambush me with, I'm nae likely to be happy about it." Coll wheeled the black around to head east and north, to the Saint Genesius. "Thank ye for the warning, though."

"Be safe, Coll. If someone is after the lass, they're nae going to be happy to have ye standing in the way. And ye make for a large target."

"Aye, but this target has teeth." And claws, and a bad temper. And a lass who needed protecting for the sake of honor. Aye, that's what it was. Honor.

Chapter Nine

"Stars, hide your fires;
Let not light see my black and deep desires."

MACBETH, *MACBETH* ACT I, SCENE IV

Persephone wrung her hands, her gaze unfocused. "'I laid their daggers ready,'" she said in a low, musing tone. "'He could not miss 'em. Had he not resembled my father as he slept, I had done't.'"

"Christ, Persie," Thomas Baywich said from a neighboring chair. "You just gave me the shivers."

"That would be the point, wouldn't it?" Charlie Huddle put in, slapping his folio against his knee. "People who get the shivers come to see the play a second time."

"I'm thinking I should be more impatient," Persie commented, looking over the lines again. "More of a 'what's taking him so long?' than a waking nightmare."

"Let's try it that way," Charlie agreed. "Gordon, from your line, if you please?"

"I don't know how the lot of you can concentrate on a play about murder when any of us could be standing beside Persie the next time something falls from the rigging," the actor playing Macbeth snapped. "And that person is likely to be me, since I share the most scenes with her."

That sparked the third argument in twenty minutes.

Persephone sat back in the hard, wooden chair. These people were her family; she'd known some of them since she'd first set foot on a London stage. She couldn't fault them for wanting to keep their distance, but at the same time, a bit more supportive conversation would have been welcome.

A warm breeze seemed to whisper across her skin, lifting the hair on her arms. She glanced over her shoulder at Gavin, the Scottish groom who'd been standing against the nearest wall since Coll had appointed him to watch over her, but he wasn't there.

In his place stood Coll himself, arms folded across his chest and his gaze on the dim rigging at the top of the theater.

She took him in all over again. Several inches over six feet tall, all lean, hard muscle, shoulders broad and strong enough to put Hercules to shame, and a countenance of chiseled, hard perfection . . . Only when he grinned did his face soften enough to give a hint of the good-hearted man who resided within, but even when he was serious, he still looked . . . delicious.

Even more intoxicating, he made her feel safe—and that was taking into account that he'd called her a closed book he couldn't quite read. The way he'd charged into action, saving her from the bricks and bucket and then not even hesitating before going after Claremont—she couldn't conjure an image of anyone else who would have done such a thing for her, or even have been capable of it if they'd wished to step in.

"Persie," came Charlie's voice, and she shook herself.

"Yes?"

"Your lines, dear."

"She's too occupied with ogling the Scotsman," Jenny cooed, sighing. "And so am I."

"Excuse me a minute," Persephone said. "I need to see what he was able to discover."

"By all means, go," Gordon urged. "I need to know if the danger is over with before we continue. The Scottish play is a large enough menace without all of this going on."

When Charlie waved a dismissing hand at her, Persephone stood and walked back into the shadows, where the Highlander stood. He watched her approaching now, and the goosebumps on her arms returned. It was tempting to just walk into his arms and let him enfold her, but that would never do. He was someone to help her pass the time, and to keep buckets of bricks from falling on her—and only for the next three-and-a-half weeks at the most, after which he would be married and she would be well into her nightly performances of Lady Macbeth.

"Lass," he murmured as she stopped in front of him.

"I'm glad to see you unharmed." Persephone curled her fingers to keep from touching him. "Claremont?"

"It wasnae him."

"Damn." From the abrupt tightness in her chest, she'd placed more faith than she'd realized in the idea that it had been the earl out to pay her back for his embarrassment. "Are you certain? Of course you are." She leaned back against the wall beside him.

"Aye. He has nae reason to risk his reputation over ye. Nae offense."

She sighed. "None taken. I know what you mean, and it makes sense. But did you speak to him? How did he react?"

"I did speak to him. Ye said he was nae yer first protector, and I dunnae think ye were his first actress. He said he tried giving ye pretty things but put it to making a bad investment. Between ye and me, I dunnae think he has enough spleen to be angry enough to kill."

That matched her own assessment of Claremont's character fairly well. And yet—she'd wanted it to be James Pierce. She wanted it to be something she and Coll could see finished. If it wasn't Claremont, then she needed to be able to prove at least to herself that these two near-misses had both been accidents. That strained even *her* imagination.

"I wanted it to be him," Coll said aloud, echoing her thoughts. "I wanted to be able to walk in here and tell ye I took care of things for ye."

She turned her head, looking up at him as he gazed down at her. When she'd chased after him the other day, it had been with the idea that he might be helpful. Belatedly, it occurred to her that he knew precisely what she was about, and he'd agreed anyway. And it was more than that; he hadn't just agreed. He'd wanted to help . . . her.

Evidently, she'd been luckier than she deserved. She'd hoped to find a capable man. What she'd found had been an honorable one. "If you're not careful," she said aloud, "I'm going to begin liking you."

His brief smile left her wanting to kiss him all over again. "Ye've already turned my head, lass. But now I have to ask ye who else might nae want to have ye about. Do ye have any ideas?"

Persephone shrugged. Yes, she did have a broad idea or two, but nothing that made sense here and now. "I am rehearsing the Scottish play. Perhaps Gordon has the right of it, and it *is* cursed."

"And mayhap Gordon doesnae like being teased, and he's out to prove the play is cursed by killing Lady Macbeth," Coll suggested.

"Gordon faints when he gets a nosebleed," she retorted. "Just tell me it could have been an accident. Two accidents."

He held onto his silence longer than she liked. "They

could have been accidents," he finally conceded. "But I dunnae think either of them were. So, if ye want my help, ye need to give me a direction to head. Who might wish to harm ye, Persephone?"

She shook her head, pushing upright in the same motion. This was beginning to stray too close to uncomfortable territory. No one trod there, including her. "I cannot think of a soul. I'm an actress. Unless it's one of my critics or rivals or a lunatic admirer, I have no idea. If you press for an answer, I say that both incidents were only accidents. Now, if you'll excuse me, I have a rehearsal to finish. And you have the Runescroft ball to attend."

As soon as she said it, she regretted it, but he only straightened and reached down to take her hand. "If ye think of anything that might help, ye send me word. Gavin will stay here. He or I will see ye home."

"Again, that's not necess—"

"Ye wield yer words like a lass who's accustomed to people doing as she says," he murmured, still holding her hand, still keeping her there beside him. "I dunnae ken who ye are, Persephone Jones, but I dunnae think ye are who ye say ye are. If that's what's putting ye in danger, then I suggest ye decide if ye can trust me or nae." With that, he released her and headed off toward the rear of the theater.

Ice splintered down her spine. "You don't owe me anything, Coll. Go find yourself a wife."

He paused mid-step. "Dunnae fling that at me just when I've decided I like spending time with ye. If ye're scared, it's because ye should be. But I'm nae the one out to harm ye."

She watched until he disappeared behind the growing set of Birnham Woods, trying not to feel as if she'd just run off her only ally. With her friends here, she didn't need allies. The bucket and the sandbags had only been accidents, perhaps brought about by the Scottish play, just as she'd suggested. Coll had been fun and arousing, but as she'd surmised, he was also trouble. And she didn't need more trouble. Any trouble.

Wisps of thoughts she'd kept shoved far to the back of her mind continued pushing at her, trying to come forward, but she shoved back just as hard. She'd just been in the wrong place at the wrong time. Accidents could happen in a large, busy theater, especially with the workers taking down and putting up sets. Thinking anything else was just silly and useless, and it stole away time she needed to spend learning her lines.

The rest of the afternoon, though, was a disaster. Every time she had to wait for someone else to speak their lines, Coll's words rang through her skull, saying that he knew she wasn't who she claimed to be. If he'd come to that conclusion after being acquainted with her for three days, had anyone else done so as well? After all, she had known at least half the cast and backstage workers for more than six years.

What had happened? What mistake had she made? And who wanted to harm her?

"—finished for today," Charlie was saying as she dragged herself back to the present. "I expect everyone—especially you, Persie—to spend the evening going over your lines and then getting a good night's sleep. We'll begin again tomorrow."

Frowning, she reached over to check George's pocket watch. "It's only half five."

"And you've missed every cue this afternoon," Charlie noted. "I don't blame you; I'm feeling scattered myself, and I wasn't almost crushed by bricks. Go home, have a glass of whisky, and tomorrow we'll pretend today never happened. We need you for this play, Persie. You know you're the reason the Saint Genesius fills every night."

She forced a smile. "If you truly believe that, give me the lead in *Hamlet*."

Charlie laughed. "I am your ardent admirer, but I am not a madman. Go home, Persie. Will the Highlander escort you?"

"That one will," she said, gesturing at Gavin, who was presently ogling the three witches.

When she walked up and tapped him on the shoulder, the groom jumped. "Saint Andrew and all the angels," he rasped. "I dunnae ken how ye can stay in a place this dark all day and nae see devils in every shadow."

She'd been doing a bit of that herself, this afternoon. "I'm leaving. I have a driver I generally use, but I thought you should know."

"I'm to go with ye, Miss Persie. Laird Glendarril will have my head on a pike if I dunnae."

Smiling, she wrapped her hand around his arm. "I was actually hoping you would say that. Accidents or not, heavy things flying toward my head do make me a bit nervous."

Holding his arm out rigidly, he puffed out his chest as they walked. "It's my honor to see ye home safe."

His presence, while welcome, would complicate her usual wardrobe change. Perhaps just the wig would do for today; she had dressed rather conservatively, and her blue muslin likely wouldn't shock the neighbors. Once she retrieved her portmanteau and a black wig with a very matronly bun already pinned up at the back of the neck, she headed outside.

Amid the vendors and daringly dressed lightskirts, rather fewer young men than usual lurked. Perhaps word had gotten out that her current protector was a very large Highlander who liked using his fists. However much Coll's prying annoyed her, the space he'd created around her made her grateful. People running at her had never been pleasant; today, she couldn't think of many things that filled her with more dread.

One of the stagehands would have already signaled for Gus—who generally spent the late afternoons snoozing inside his coach around the corner—to come up. She saw him immediately, just beyond the stack of lumber that had been delivered earlier that day.

"That him?" Gavin asked, eyeing the coach and driver suspiciously.

"Yes. Will you be riding up top with him, or inside with me?"

The groom's face turned beet red. "I couldnae ride inside with ye, Miss Persephone. It wouldnae be at all proper!"

Hmm. She'd completely forgotten about that. Pesky propriety—she'd evaded its grip for so long that it generally didn't even occur to her. "Yes, of course. Thank you for looking out for my honor, Gavin."

He clearly didn't know how to take that, so he settled for an awkward nod as he handed her into the coach. She settled into the seat and opened the portmanteau.

"Just once around the Holme this time, Gus," she called up. "And this is Gavin. He's seeing me home."

"For your sake, then, I'll allow him up top, Miss Persie."

The driver clucked to the team, and they rolled off into the street. Perhaps she should have requested they drive around the Holme thrice instead of once; if someone was after her, she certainly didn't want them following her home. Persephone closed her eyes for a moment.

In six years, she'd seen dozens of accidents in the theater, two of them fatal. Odd things did happen. If the sandbag and bucket had been two weeks apart instead of two days, she wouldn't be hesitating to call them accidents now. With Claremont eliminated as a suspect, she would have to settle herself and admit that it was just two odd events close together, and that was all that made them seem suspicious. They were accidents.

She pulled off the red wig and set the simple black one over her head, pinning the edges to keep it secure. There. Perhaps her wig-wearing was silly, but it made her feel like she was doing something to keep her privacy intact. And since no one had successfully followed her home from the theater yet, it seemed to be working.

The coach lurched sideways. With a gasp, she put a hand out to keep from slamming into the far wall. "Gus! What is—"

"Hold tight, Miss Persie!" the driver called, his voice clipped. "Damned wagon dri—"

They rocked again, harder. Persephone lost her grip and slid across the bench. The coach teetered, went back onto all four wheels, then lifted on the left side again. Abruptly everything rolled, and the portmanteau slammed into her hip as she landed first on the right-side door, and then on the roof.

Upside down. The coach was upside down. She flailed upright. It was disorienting, seeing the seats above her head and the broken windows below. Persephone put her hands down to steady herself, and they splashed into water. Good heavens, her whole backside was wet. Her feet tangled into her skirts as she tried to stand, and she went down hard on her knees.

The nearest door wrenched open, coming off one hinge. "Give me yer hand, lass," Gavin said, reaching in for her.

He had blood on one side of his face, his hair wild, but she grabbed onto him and held tight as he pulled her free of the coach.

They'd gone over into a ditch, she realized as she scrambled to her feet outside. At the front of the coach, one of the horses lay in a tangle of reins and harnesses, whinnying, while the other stood a few feet away, its head down and blood dripping down one leg. "Where's Gus?" she gasped, falling back against the side of the carriage.

"Seeing to the horse," the groom said. "Ye stay here. Dunnae move, lass. I'll lend him a hand."

When she nodded, Gavin hurried back to the fallen animal, pulling a knife from his boot and sawing at the harness. Gus did the same on the far side, and a moment later, the horse lurched to its feet.

Staggering, her dress ripped up one side and the hem tangling beneath her shoe, Persephone made her way up the short, steep bank of the ditch. "Are they all right?" she asked. "Are the two of you all right?"

"Aye," Gavin answered, taking hold of the first horse's harness and leading it up and down a few feet while he eyed its gait. "Just some scratches and a banged head. Ye'll have to put a compress on the right rear hock here."

"That damned wagon driver," Gus muttered, climbing out of the ditch with the other horse. "Excuse my language, Persie. He saw us there, plain as day, and he still turned right into our path."

Persephone's heart lurched. "It was deliberate, then?"

"If I could think of a reason why a man would want to murder any of us, I'd say yes," her driver returned. "It's a warm afternoon, and him all kitted up in a hooded cloak and all. He wanted us off the road, and that's for damned certain. Excuse my language again."

She and Gavin exchanged a glance, and she could read his thoughts clearly in his expression. It hadn't been an accident. And that meant nothing over the past few days had been an accident. Someone *was* trying to kill her. And not only had they very nearly been successful, they hadn't cared about murdering two horses, a driver, and a groom, either.

"Gus, I'm so sorry," she said, tears rising in her eyes.

"What for?" the driver retorted. "It's that clod with the wagon who owes me a new coach, da—blast him."

"This wouldn't have happened to you if you hadn't been my driver," she said. "I will of course pay for any repairs, or for a new coach if it's not fixable."

"That's kind of you, Persie," Gus said, freeing one hand from his grip on the horse's harness to pat her shoulder. "But I can't ask you to do that."

"Nonsense," she retorted, swiping a hand across her eyes. "You do what you need to, and you have the bill sent to me. Is that clear?" Perhaps it was a small thing in the greater scheme of things, but helping Gus was something she wanted to do, and it was definitely something she could afford. And a large, nagging part of her knew the damage was her fault, anyway.

Somewhere, somehow, she'd made a mistake.

"Are ye up to seeing to yer team, lad?" Gavin asked, giving Gus's gray mare another critical look.

"I'm more angry than anything else. Yes, Mary, Jane, and I are fine."

The groom nodded. "Good. I'm going to see the lass home."

When Gus agreed, Gavin skidded down the slope and reached into the coach, pulling out her portmanteau. Ignoring the gathering crowd of curious onlookers, he returned to her side and offered her an arm.

"Let's get away from here a bit, and I'll hail us a hack. Too many people for me to keep my peepers on right now."

She'd been thinking much the same thing. Any one of these people could be the wagon driver, or whoever it was who'd hired the wagon driver to run Gus's coach off the road. Wincing at a wrenched knee and bruised hip but doing her best not to limp, she headed toward Albany Street with Gavin.

Every vehicle that drove up from behind them made her flinch. What if the wagon had merely circled around and was now headed back to finish her off? What if someone on the street had a knife or a pistol and they were only waiting for her to turn her back?

"I wish Laird Glendarril had been here," Gavin muttered as they walked. "He'd have jumped into the wagon and yanked that damned villain out of his seat. And there I was, doing naught but hanging on with my fingernails and trying nae to fall into the street."

She could imagine Coll doing just that, leaping from one vehicle to another, kilt flying, and then wrestling the wagon's horses to a halt with one hand while he held the driver aloft with the other. The image made her smile, despite the scratches and bruises.

"What's got ye so amused, then?" the groom asked, frowning.

"My apologies. Does Coll—Lord Glendarril—often leap to the rescue and fling people about?"

"Oh, aye. Far more often than ye'd think a man would need to do such a thing. Once he waded into a bog to rescue a wee lamb and ended up finding the bairn's twin and his dam already near-drowned in the mud, and he hauled 'em all out."

"What about the rumor that he went running down Grosvenor Square naked but for a sword?"

Gavin squinted one eye. "Well, ye see, that's part of a long tale that I'm nae to spread about. I will tell ye that he was after a villain who nearly shot his brother, Master Aden, and that that villain may have a claymore-shaped puncture now in his arse."

"Truly? You're not bamming me?"

"Me? Nae. Aden stared the man down and then let him go, but Glendarril reckoned he needed more of a lesson to remember the MacTaggerts by. The bastard regrets going against us every time he sits down, I'd wager."

She hadn't met any of the other MacTaggerts, though if they were half as impressive as Coll, they were likely formidable, indeed. Tales of their handsome appearances and barbaric ways had certainly reached backstage at the Saint Genesius. "This tale you're not to tell, is it in order to protect the MacTaggert reputation?"

"Nae. It's to protect a lass who's to become a MacTaggert by the end of the week. And that's all I'll say on the matter."

Aden MacTaggert would be marrying Miss Miranda Harris on Saturday, she knew, because the Society page had been filled with opinions on whether such a prominent marriage should be allowed to proceed so swiftly, which she interpreted to mean that some members of the *ton* were upset not to be invited to the ensuing party. The youngest brother, Niall, had arranged an elopement with his bride-to-be, Amelia-Rose Baxter, all the way up in Gretna Green. Well, the official word was that it had been planned. Rumor said otherwise.

Why any of that mattered, she had no idea. As she'd told Coll, titled men did not marry actresses. And she didn't intend to wed anyone, regardless. In a sense, though, hearing all of this felt . . . comforting. Clearly the women who'd trusted the MacTaggerts had found themselves cared-for and protected. And at this moment, that sounded very tempting.

When Gavin whistled for a passing hack to stop, the sound made her jump. How was she supposed to continue like this? For heaven's sake, she would be onstage in a week, in front of hundreds of people—any of whom could secretly wish her dead. For years, she'd preferred to let her parts define her, allowed herself to be seen as

Juliet or Cleopatra or Katherine or Rosalind, rather than as . . . herself. For goodness' sake, she lived a quiet life on a quiet street with neighbors who thought she owned a wig shop.

That actually made her potential list of enemies fairly small. And the answer she kept coming up with made her insides cold and shaky with a dread she couldn't even put into words. If her suspicions were correct, she needed help. But that would mean trusting someone—trusting Coll, because she couldn't conjure anyone else on whom she might call. And since she'd told him earlier to mind his own business, she didn't know if help would be forthcoming, even if she screwed up the courage to ask for it.

Gavin walked her to her front door and didn't move until Gregory pulled it open. "Ye're the man here, aye?" the groom asked.

Gregory lifted a thin eyebrow. "I suppose I am. You're one of the Highlanders."

"That I am. Ye see Miss Persie inside, ye lock the door behind her, and ye make certain all the other doors and windows in the house are secured. And ye dunnae open them until Laird Glendarril arrives. Do ye ken?"

The footman frowned. "I ken, sir, but we do not, in this household, make a habit of following other people's orders. Do you ken that?"

Persephone stepped past him into the foyer. "Do as he says, Gregory. Please."

"Th—of course."

Only when Gavin was gone and she heard the front door lock did Persephone let out her breath. And then she collapsed onto the foyer floor.

Coll looked over at the wee woman holding his fingers. A stiff breeze would likely send her flying, but her father was a duke's nephew, and that made her acceptable as a wife to a viscount. They reached the end of the line of dancers and he bowed to her, letting her fingers go as she curtsied. Then, one on either side, they pranced up the double lines of dancers and met again at the far end.

"I've heard that every clan has a motto," she said airily. "What would yours be?"

"*Spem Successus Alit.* Success nourishes hope."

"Latin, yes? It's quite lovely. Clan MacTaggert seems very civilized."

"There's nae clan MacTaggert. We're part of Clan Ross. That's Ross's motto."

"Oh. You don't have one, then? A motto?"

"We've a family crest. A dragon standing atop a lion. And the words '*Dèan sabaid airson fuireach.*' That's nae Latin. It's Scots Gaelic."

She blinked. "And what does it . . . mean?" she asked, her voice noticeably subdued.

Grand. He was frightening her. "Fight to Live," he translated. "Some in the family say it's more properly 'Fight to Stay,' but ye cannae stay if ye arenae alive, so I prefer the first version."

The lass, Elizabeth Munroe, finished off the fancy set of dance steps alongside him before they began hopping forward again. For Christ's sake, he hated country dances. They lasted forever and a day, and he wasn't a man who enjoyed hopping and preening like a rabbit.

As they reached the head of the line again, he stifled a sigh. He'd managed to find a partner for every damned dance tonight, because according to Persephone, that was how a man could judge whether a woman thought him marriageable or not. The present country dance supposedly meant that he wouldn't ever be walking into a church with Miss Munroe, but Lady Runescroft seemed to adore the things and had far too many of them scheduled for anyone to avoid them all. And at least this lass was talking to him, which was more than he could say of the previous two.

After what felt like an hour, the dance ended. Winded, he escorted Miss Munroe back to her mother, made a bow, and went to find an open window. Most of the side rooms around the ballroom were packed with guests, but he found some open space and an unlatched window in the library, and with a deep breath, Coll leaned both hands on the sill and looked out over the torchlit garden.

Behind him, a young couple seated on a couch murmured quietly to each other, the lady's maid hovering nearby, but he paid them no further attention than to note their presence. This fete nonsense was the main reason he detested London, he was discovering. Unless a man was a member of the House of Lords—which, as the holder of an honorary title, he was not—days were to be spent in clubs or driving about the parks, hoping to be seen. Evenings were for endless parties or more clubs, and for drinking or gaming or whoring.

He didn't drink; with the exception of his first night here in London, he hadn't consumed any spirits since his twenty-third birthday. As Niall had put it, Coll joined up with liquor didn't make for anything pleasant. That left whoring or gaming or dancing, and while he had no objection to spending his evenings in a lass's bed, he preferred to leave the gaming to Aden and the dancing to Niall.

Of course, now that he was thinking about sex, the image of Persephone Jones floated into his thoughts again—not that she'd been far from them since the first moment he'd set eyes on her. He'd thought it had been Claremont after her, that the viscount had been angry she'd moved on to someone else. But that had been based on the assumption that Claremont had cared for her in the first place. Clearly, she'd been a prize to the earl, someone to be flaunted as evidence of his own virility or some such thing.

Claremont didn't care enough about her to go to the effort and expense of seeing her hurt or killed. And since she had nothing else to offer him in the way of suspects, he had to conclude that those two mishaps had been accidents. That didn't feel right, and neither could he shake the feeling that she wasn't quite who she said she was, but he had neither the time nor the information he needed to figure it all out.

As for the woman herself, she intrigued him and aggravated him in equal parts. Subterfuge, lies, complications— those were all things he avoided. He preferred straight answers, honesty, and troubles he could solve with his fists. She was none of those things. At the same time, he enjoyed the time he spent in her company, and he damned well enjoyed her enthusiasm during sex. He liked chatting with her, and he liked never knowing what she might say next. An exceedingly intelligent and opinionated woman was quite possibly the last person he ever expected to find so . . . compelling, but there it was. There she was.

And damn it all, he liked her. A great deal. A lass with whom he could converse and be his generally good-humored self without worrying that his hard reputation would be damaged or that he'd made a fool of himself. When it came down to it, he could imagine himself married to her, and that hadn't been anything he could conjure in his wildest dreams with any other lass he'd met so far—in London or in Scotland.

"For a betrothed man, you're doing a great deal of dancing tonight," came the cultured voice of his mother from somewhere behind him.

Coll didn't budge. The muttering couple on the couch was gone; Francesca had probably pointed a finger at them and they'd fled. "I'm at a grand ball. I reckon dancing is what I'm supposed to do."

"So it is. I happen to know, however, that you dislike country dances, and yet there you were with Miss Elizabeth Munroe. A very eligible young lady of marked beauty."

"What do ye want, *màthair*? Ye ordered me to wed a lass. I found a lass to wed. The only problem I see is yer pride."

Her soft, measured footsteps moved closer. "Not just *my* pride, Coll. Do not let *your* pride and *your* stubbornness lead you into a mistake. Do not let your anger with me lead you into a life you won't be able to tolerate."

At that, he turned to face her. "Are ye speaking from experience, then? Ye and da used to have some spectacular arguments, as I recall. I suppose if Persephone and I dunnae match well, I could always do what ye did and walk away. Pretend I dunnae have three other bairns aside from the one I take with me. I could even write up an agreement with her when I go that says nae matter how long I ignore them, the bairns will have to do what I say when they're grown."

"Oh, that is enough of that," she muttered, her hands clenched together in front of her hips, her gaze down at the floor. With a visible sigh, she looked up again. "Your father is an impossible man. I asked for six months in the Highlands and six months here. He refused. I asked for three months here and nine months in the Highlands. He refused. I asked for an English tutor for the three of you, so you would be able to live in both worlds. He refused."

She stopped beside him, standing straight and stiff, her voice more animated than he'd heard since their arrival on her doorstep.

"So ye left," he finished for her. "I dunnae doubt ye had yer reasons. I just dunnae understand why they were more important to ye than we were. Ye didnae even write."

"I *did* write," she snapped. "Letter after letter after letter. None of you ever answered me, but I kept writing. For years. It was only after Eloise was old enough to compose a letter that we had any response at all. Nothing from me was ever replied to. So yes, I left. But I did not abandon you. You abandoned me."

Coll frowned. "Ye say whatever ye wish, Lady Aldriss. I nae received a single letter from ye. I wrote a handful of them *to* ye, and nae heard back. I reckoned ye'd washed yer hands of us. And I was but twelve years old, if ye'll recall."

"I recall everything—every birthday I missed. You are my children. My sons. I would never . . . Damn that man. I thought he was keeping my letters from you, but I never thought he would be keeping your letters to me." A tear ran down her ivory cheek. "You wrote to me," she whispered.

"Aye, when I was a bairn. When I might have wanted ye about. But I'll be thirty years old next month. And there ye stand after seventeen years away, demanding that I wed some English lass so ye'll be able to tell yer proper friends that ye have three civilized sons, and so ye have a better chance of seeing us down here in England again. Dunnae expect me to smile and cooperate, woman."

"Oh, for God's sake, Coll. I'm trying to make am—"

"Excuse us," came Niall's voice from the doorway.

Coll looked up to see not just Niall, but Gavin, standing there and looking exceedingly uncomfortable. Worry stabbed through him. "What the devil are ye doing here? Ye were to stay at the Saint Genesius and watch over Persephone."

"Aye, m'laird." The groom shot an uneasy glance at Francesca. "Excuse me, yer majesty."

"Gavin!" Coll demanded.

"The lass left early and took her usual hack. I hopped

up with the driver, a pleasant lad named Gus. Then a wagon ran us off the road and overturned the coach into a ditch. Th—"

"*What?*" Coll rasped, striding toward the groom and the door beyond him. "Is she hurt?"

"Nae. A few bumps and bruises." Gavin took a half step backward. "It wasnae an accident, ye ken. The driver wore a hood so we couldnae see his face. And he rammed into us thrice, then drove off without stopping."

"And you left her?" Coll could barely spit out the words. His heart pounded; he'd guessed wrong and she might have been . . . she might have been killed.

"I saw her home and had that skinny lad secure the house. I told him to nae open the front door until ye arrived. I had to come fetch ye, m'laird, or I wouldnae have le—"

"How did ye get here?" Coll broke in, striding for the door and dragging the groom with him.

"I stopped by Oswell House for a horse. And I brought Nuckelavee with me. The pretty-dressed lads out front are holding him for ye, hopefully."

"Good." Brushing passed a surprised-looking footman, Coll shoved open the front door and trotted down the trio of steps. Nuckelavee whinnied when the stallion saw him, pulling free of the clearly terrified groom and charging to the foot of the steps. "Come with me, Gavin. I may need more help."

"Aye."

Swinging into the saddle, Coll reined in the black long enough for Gavin to mount the gelding he'd brought along. "Ye did well, Gavin. I'm grateful."

The groom gave a solemn nod. "The lass's first question when I pulled her out of the coach was whether the driver and I were injured. She offered to purchase the lad a new coach or pay for the repair of the mangled one. She's a *bean-ghaisgeil*."

Aye, she was a brave woman. And he'd been a damned fool to leave her safety to someone else, even a man he trusted as much as he did Gavin Corbat. As soon as they cleared the crush of waiting coaches, he kicked Nuckelavee in the ribs. The big war horse snorted, accelerating into a smooth, effortless gallop.

Someone had tried to kill the lass. And this time, they'd nearly succeeded.

If he'd needed an additional sign to tell him how he truly felt about her, the black fury and fear that boiled his blood made it plain enough. Persephone Jones was the lass he wanted. Damn all propriety and tradition that said he couldn't have her. And damn anyone who tried to stop him.

Chapter Ten

"False face must hide what the false heart doth know."

MACBETH, *MACBETH* ACT I, SCENE VII

Persephone paced from her bed to her door and back again. The heavy lilac curtains in her bed chamber stood closed, but she stayed clear of them anyway. No sense in tempting fate if someone happened to be lurking outside, waiting with a rifle in hand for a likely silhouette. *Good Lord, had it truly come to that?*

Returning to her door, she faced the bed. Her portmanteau sat there, open, waiting to be filled. That was what she should be doing. A few gowns, a few wigs, some shoes, a shawl, and all the money she had to hand. Everything else she needed, she could send for when she found somewhere safe, or she could simply purchase anew. Yes, that would be wiser.

Still, though, she hesitated. Gregory would likely come with her if she asked; he had only his brother nearby. Flora wouldn't leave London, not with her daughter Beth still employed at the Saint Genesius and her grandbabies living in Charing Cross. And the theater—they could move Jenny over to play Lady Macbeth, but Charlie already had leaflets printed and advertisements paid for. She had a contract through next Season, and breaking it would break her heart.

Even with all that, it wasn't those things that had her portmanteau still empty. For that, she could blame a mountain of a Highlander with deep green eyes, a hearty laugh, and a face over which even Michelangelo would weep with envy. For heaven's sake, she'd only known Coll MacTaggert a few days. To pin any hopes and dreams on him at all was the height of foolishness. To think of trusting him . . . It had to be desperation.

A trio of knocks at the front door thudded so hard they rattled the windows upstairs. Persephone jumped, her hand going to her heart as the muscle nearly leaped out of her chest. It had to be Coll. But if it wasn't . . .

Taking a quick breath, she ran to her nightstand, opened the bottom drawer, and pulled out the small, cloth-wrapped bundle she kept there: a small flintlock pistol, more suited for hiding in a man's coat as protection against highwaymen than for stopping a killer, but she freed the Queen Anne pistol, cocked it, and aimed it at her door anyway.

The latch rattled, swiftly followed by a hard thump. "Persephone," Coll called in his low brogue. "It's me, lass."

"Oh, thank heavens." Lowering the pistol, she ran forward and unlocked her door.

Coll stood there, dressed in a fine black coat, a very fashionable cravat, blue trousers stuffed into Hessian boots, and a black waistcoat embroidered with purple thistles. Barely taking the time to note how odd it was to see him not in a kilt, she wrapped her arms around his solid chest and tucked her face into his shoulder.

"Thank you for coming," she whispered, trying to stop the sudden tears from filling her eyes.

"Of course, I came," he returned, pulling the pistol from her fingers and pocketing it. "Gavin said yer coach rolled over. Are ye injured?"

She shook her head, digging her hands tighter into his coat. "Just bruises and scrapes."

"Have ye eaten?"

Persephone lifted her head to look up at his face. "Food?"

"I dunnae know about ye, lass, but I've been dancing and leaping about all evening. I could eat an entire heifer."

Gasping, she pushed away from him. "The Runescroft ball! I forgot it was tonight. Oh, you shouldn't have left for me." Helping him find a wife at the ball had very nearly been her entire side of their bargain. And now he'd left it midway through to come see to her. "Coll, you have to go back."

He shook his head. "I'll do nae such thing. Ye—Flora, is it? Find us someaught to eat, will ye?"

Flora squeaked in annoyance from the hallway behind him. "I do not take orders from you."

"Please, Flora," Persephone seconded. "We should all eat something. You and Gregory, as well."

"Very well, Miss Persie. But you shouldn't be in there alone with a man. I could—"

With a low snort, Coll stepped forward and closed the door on the maid's complaint. "Ye should keep that lass about. She looks after ye," he murmured, leaning down to kiss her.

She kissed him back, twining her hands into the lapels of his black coat. Her worries and fears faded into mist when he wrapped his arms around her and held her close. No one could possibly be foolish enough to attempt harming her while Coll MacTaggert was by her side.

That, though, was a path to more trouble. Firstly, he couldn't be by her side at every moment. Secondly, he had his own worries without shouldering hers as well. Persephone frowned. She wanted to confide in him. Doing so, though, would only mean more hurt when he walked away.

When she lifted her hands to shove against his chest, he let her go, and she crossed the room to the bed again. "Thank you for coming," she said, utilizing her years of acting experience to keep her voice low and even. "As you can see, though, I'm relatively unhurt."

His gaze moved from her to the portmanteau on the bed and back to her again. "Ye going somewhere, Persephone?"

"I'm considering it," she admitted, though she wasn't about to confess that she'd been halfway to France in her mind. "A few days in the country while I sort some things out in my head."

"And ye reckon a few days away will see ye safe again? That whoever's trying to harm ye will forget and flit off to go murder someone else in yer stead?"

Of course he wouldn't believe that she meant to take a holiday. Persephone drew in a breath. "Very well, perhaps I won't return. Evidently my critics have spoken, and I'm no longer London's darling. Cornwall has a well-respected acting troupe. Th—"

"Ye ken who's after ye, dunnae?" he broke in, closing the distance between them. "Why'd ye let me go threaten Claremont if ye knew it wasnae him?"

"I thought it *was* him," she retorted. Or at least, she'd *hoped* it was him. The alternative . . . A chill went down her spine. The alternative now seemed to be the most likely explanation. She didn't want to consider it—didn't even want to think about it. At the back of her mind, though, the truth kept pushing at her thoughts; her preferences didn't matter. What mattered was whether she meant to run or stay. And if she stayed, she would need help. That, though, meant relying on someone else—relying on Coll

MacTaggert. The man who'd only just been dancing with a field of prospective brides.

Her breath caught. "You should go," she made herself say. "As I said, I'm not injured, and you have other concerns."

His jaw clenched. Beneath his breath, he muttered something that sounded like "stubborn," then turned on his heel and dropped into the reading chair by the small hearth. "I dunnae like wee spaces," he said abruptly, the very image of a proper gentleman in everything but his size and accent and unruly hair.

"I—what does that have to do with anything?"

"When I was but a bairn, my brother Aden and I played hide-and-seek. I closed myself in a wardrobe, and it locked. I was in there in the dark for what felt like days before someone found me. Since then, wee places and I dunnae deal well together." He blew out his breath. "I dunnae drink, either. I say things I shouldnae, and I break things, and I hit people." Coll shrugged his broad shoulders. "I do the same thing when I'm sober, but at least then I know what I'm about and I remember it after."

"It's admirable to see a man who will admit to his flaws," she said slowly, "but forgive me if I've missed whatever point you're attempting to make." If he was one of those men whose own dilemmas were required to be more significant than whatever anyone else faced, then he'd answered several of her unspoken questions. She could *not* confide anything to him.

"Aye. I'm nae saying it well. My point, lass, is that I can avoid wee spaces, and I can avoid drink. How do ye mean to avoid someone who's trying to kill ye? If ye make one mistake . . . Well, ye cannae. So, for God's sake, let me help ye."

"Why?" she burst out. "Why on earth do you want to spend your time helping *me*? You've wasted weeks and weeks here in London, intentionally making a muck of things, and now you have less than a month to find a bride. And you need to find a wife, because otherwise you will lose the funding to your family's estate. So give me a reason why you would risk all that for an actress. And it had best be a very good reason, because believe me, I've heard them all. Twice."

He looked at her for a long moment. "How many lasses do ye reckon I've chatted with since I arrived here?" he finally asked.

"Dozens, I would imagine."

"Aye. Hundreds, maybe. Some of them are bold, ready to lift their skirts to gain a title. Others are deeply offended by me being Scottish. Another handful are actually scared of me, though more than that feign it because they think it's amusing to pretend the big Highlands brute might squash 'em or someaught." He shook his shaggy head. "I like to argue with my fists, but I do have some wits about me. Enough to ken that nae a one of them would do me for a wife. But then I met ye, Persephone."

Heat flooded her face. "Oh, no, you don't," she snapped, holding her palm out in his direction. Good heavens. He had no idea. None. "Perhaps you fell for Rosalind, or for Juliet, or perhaps you like the idea of my fame. But you are not—"

"I'm nae proposing, woman," he interrupted, scowling. "I'm telling ye that I like ye. That I enjoy spending time with ye, and it would pain me nae to have ye in my life. And that whether or nae ye and my own mother agree that I cannae marry ye, mayhap I'm willing to push her as far as she'll go to release me from that agreement so I dunnae have to find someone else."

That was . . . nothing she'd expected. "You would forego marriage to spend your time with an actress?"

"Aye. I reckon I would."

"What about children? Heirs?"

"I've two brothers and a sister. Any of them, or their bairns, would do for the next Lord Aldriss after me."

"And what about Aldriss Park? It's very far from here, and here is where the Saint Genesius is."

"Ye dunnae put on plays while the aristocracy's nae in Town, do ye? Then ye dunnae need to be in London all year 'round. But that's a different conversation, one we can have after I know nae a soul's after ye."

"I'm not your responsibility, damn it all." She clapped her hands together. "Is it that we were . . . together? That you've been celibate since you got here and finally found a woman who'll sleep with you?" Striding over, she patted the bed. "Then come along, Coll. Let's be together again, and then you can go find your bride."

"I'd nae found a woman here I cared to be with, until I met ye. I'll admit that. And I've damned well nae met another lass here who'll stand toe-to-toe with me and argue. I need an argument now and then, or I tend to stomp all over people."

Persephone put her hands over her ears. "I am not listening to this any longer. Stop saying nice things."

"I will, if ye'll tell me what's truly afoot here. Because I have noticed a few things about ye, lass. Ye've an education, for one thing. A good one. Even better than mine, I'd guess. And ye ken what's proper for a lady, even if ye choose nae to follow the rules yerself. Ye know how to run a household, and how to manage servants. Ye're kinder to them than most blue-blooded folk would be, but ye know that, too." He narrowed his eyes a little, giving her an assessing look. "In fact, I'm going so far as to say that ye're a lady. A true lady."

She opened and closed her mouth again as the walls came closing in around her, the sensation making her feel light-headed. Swiftly, she forced a laugh. "Or it could be that I'm an *actress*, you clod. A good one. Good enough to fool you into thinking I'm something more than I am."

"A clod, am I?" he said softly, rising to his feet with a surprising grace. "And ye're fooling me, are ye?"

"That is what I said. How in the world do you think I get men to pay for my pretty things? By saying what they want to hear. I had you figured out the moment I set eyes on you."

Her door opened and Gregory started in with a tray of sandwiches. His gaze never leaving hers, Coll stepped aside, took the tray out of her footman's hands, shoved the man gently backward, and shut the door again. This time, he locked it. "Did ye now?" he returned, as if they'd never been interrupted.

"Is that your strategy? To ask if I said what I just said and did what I clearly did?" Good God, he was stubborn. If she'd spoken that way to Claremont or any of her three previous so-called protectors, they would have walked out in tears by now. Or one of them would have hit her, though she had no worry at all that Coll would do any such thing. He was far more a gentleman than anyone else she'd ever met carrying that title.

Coll took a sandwich off the platter and held the silver tray out to her. "Nae," he said, taking a huge bite. "My strategy is to wait until ye've finished yelling at me and then ask ye again what I might do to help ye. I'm here, and I'm willing. Ye just need to trust me a little."

"Well, that's a stupid strategy." Harrumphing, she grabbed a sandwich and plunked herself down on the bed to eat it.

"So is thinking ye can pack a bag and run."

"Ha. It worked before."

"Until now, I reckon." Finishing off one sandwich, he picked up a second one. "Ye did run, then. From what,

Persephone? What would send ye away from one life to start another one?"

It was on the tip of her tongue to tell him. The names would likely mean nothing to a man who'd never set foot in London until this Season. To have someone else who knew, someone who might actually help her—but then she'd done just fine on her own for the past eight years. Until now, of course.

She took a deep breath. "It was a man, if you must know. One I didn't wish to marry."

Setting aside the tray, he and his third sandwich sat down on the bed beside her. "If there was ever a tale with which I could sympathize, it's that one."

"No doubt. He was far older than I was, but exceedingly well-connected. He was also . . . cruel. Not directly, but all of his little suggestions for my behavior gave me a very good idea that married life with him would be far worse than the engagement." She shuddered. "'My dear, surely you can make a cup of tea as well as did my first wife. Do try again,'" she imitated. "Or 'you do know that I prefer you not wear green,' or 'that sound you make when you're eating, is that meant to be charming?'"

"Sounds like a man I'd like to meet," Coll said darkly.

"No, you wouldn't. When my family wouldn't listen to me, even after I begged them not to make me marry him and told them he only wanted the family fortune because he'd said as much to my face, I . . . left."

"Is it him trying to harm ye, then?"

She shook her head. "I doubt it. He married some other heiress six months later. Someone even younger than I was."

The fingers of his free hand closed over hers—not tightly, but enough to make her feel safe. Protected. And wanted. "Ye nae went home after that, though. Why?"

"Because I wasn't going to give my family another

chance to auction me off," she said, the anger and disgust of it all still choking her a little. "And because I'd found something I enjoyed, that I could never do as—as I was."

His third sandwich finished, he reached over to brush hair off her cheek. "Ye made yer way in the world alone, and now ye're the toast of London. That's damned admirable."

She'd never thought to have that description attached to her. "Thank you for saying so," she returned, leaning into his hand. The warm presence of him was simply intoxicating. And it wasn't just because he made her feel safe.

It had never been that, she realized.

"Will ye tell me yer true name, lass?" he whispered.

Persephone twisted on the bed to face him, bringing up her hands to cup his lean face. "I don't want to talk anymore." Leaning up, she kissed him, feeling the immediate response of his mouth against hers, the heat of him against her chest, the strength of the arms that swept around her.

"If ye're trying to distract me, ye're doing a damned fine job of it," Coll murmured against her mouth, nibbling her bottom lip with his teeth.

"Shh," she breathed, kissing him again.

If this was merely a distraction, it was meant for her, rather than him. Thinking about the mess her life had been—all the things that had nearly been forced on her because her family sought more power and influence—made her sad and angry all over again. And the idea that one of them had found her and decided the most expedient way to be certain she didn't inherit anything was to murder her. In a sense, it didn't even surprise her.

Hades appeared from beneath the bed to begin grazing on the tray of sandwiches Coll had set aside as Coll untied his cravat and tossed it to the floor. "I dunnae care what name ye go by, lass," he said, untying the ribbon beneath her breasts, and then shedding his coat and waistcoat. "Juliet, Persephone, Mabel, or Sally. It's the woman beneath the pretending that I like, and that's the woman I want."

That was perhaps the nicest thing any man had ever said to her. And she believed it, because he'd said it before, when he hadn't known her to be anything more than a common-born actress. Persephone pulled the shirt from his trousers to run her palms up his hard, muscular chest. If she did have to flee to Spain or Prussia, she at least wanted one night spent in his arms, one night of feeling wanted and desirable for who she truly was, one night of feeling safe and protected from whatever lay beyond her front door and was trying to kill her.

Coll gathered her gown up in his big hands and pulled it over her head. Her shift followed, and then his mouth was on her breasts and she couldn't breathe. She groaned, tangling her fingers in his hair as he nipped and licked. No, he wasn't her first, but back then she'd felt like losing her virginity was simply inevitable, and so she'd chosen the least offensive man in her circle to relieve her of it.

Lord Albert Pruitz, her first "protector," had had the imagination and wit of a potato, but he'd been handsome and gentle, thank goodness. Afterward, she'd decided that sex was definitely not at all what Shakespeare and most other people made it out to be, and the two gentlemen since then had done nothing to alter her opinion—until she'd flung caution to the wind in the park with Lord Glendarril the other day, and realized that not only was Lord Albert not the expert he'd claimed to be, but that she was supposed to climax, as well.

"Damned trousers," Coll growled, standing up to kick off his boots and unbutton the offending article of clothing.

"They're not so bad," she countered, knocking his

hands away to finish opening the trio of buttons. That done, she dipped her hand in to curl it around his engorged member. "I like to think of them like opening a gift at Christmastime."

"Well, this gift is definitely happy to see ye," he said, taking her upturned face in his hands and kissing her with a thoroughness that left her panting.

Persephone put her hands around the waist of his trousers and drew them down past his hips and knees until he stepped out of them and joined her again on the bed. Mouths fused, tongues tangling, they stretched out with her beneath him.

"Ye've such soft skin," he murmured, trailing his fingers down her breastbone, along her stomach, and around her hip to cup her bottom. His mouth followed the trail but continued straight south. When he parted her legs and dipped lower to taste her, she clenched her fingers into the sheets and moaned.

As she threw back her head, her back arching, she realized she still wore her stupid, prim black wig. Trying to keep her fingers steady as he licked and teased at her, she unpinned it and threw it aside. Now they were both truly naked, and she was as close to being herself as she could ever be. And it—he—felt glorious.

When one of his long fingers slipped inside her, curling as his free hand lightly pinched one breast, she came in a delighted spasm of breathless, shivery wonder. Even if there had been nothing else between them, nothing else that drew her to him, Coll MacTaggert would have the very fondest of places in her heart.

As her muscles relaxed, Coll made his leisurely way back up her body, a man enjoying a sensual, erotic holiday, investigating her most sensitive places. Persephone grinned; she couldn't help herself.

"That's the smile of a satisfied woman, I reckon," he

noted with a breath-stealing grin of his own. Another thing at which Lord Albert Pruitz had failed: showing her that sex could be . . . fun. A delight.

"So I am," she sighed, stretching her arms out on either side of her. "And yet I am not."

"Good. Because I'm nae finished yet."

"Yes, I have noticed that. Do come closer, Coll."

Pulling her legs around his hips, his hands on either side of her shoulders, he pushed forward, entering her. The warm, filling sensation, paired with the weight of him on her hips, sent heated shivers from her spine down to where they were joined. "How's that, lass?"

"Oh, much . . . Yes, much better."

He rocked into her again, holding himself deep inside her. "I like yer hair," he murmured, shifting his weight onto one arm and pulling out a hair pin with his other. Slowly he withdrew, then entered her again, freeing more of her hair until he could draw his fingers through the honey-colored mass. "Aye, that is much better."

"Coll," she gasped, shivering in delighted goosebumps.

Her hair a wild mane around her head, she slid her hands over his shoulders and pulled him closer. With a deep kiss he pushed inside her again, taking up a hard, fast rhythm, burying himself in her over and over, pausing only to kiss her open-mouthed or to suck on her breasts. The muscles of her abdomen and thighs tightened again, drawing her closer around him. The low, panting moans coming from her chest in time with his thrusts hardly sounded like her, but she didn't think she could have stopped making them even if she'd tried. This felt . . . glorious.

Abruptly, she came again.

With a low growl, Coll joined her, burying his seed deep inside her, his gaze holding hers, both of them breathing hard, sweat slicking their skin. She watched him come, the carnal satisfaction on his face. This man. She still didn't quite know what to make of him, what motivated him. Duty, yes, and honor—even before he'd figured out that she wasn't precisely who she claimed, he'd promised to protect her. He'd saved her life at least once, had left a grand ball and his best chance to find a wife to be certain she wasn't injured. No, she didn't quite know how to classify him, but she did know one thing. She trusted him.

Persephone drew her fingers through his damp, disheveled mahogany hair, pulling his face down for another slow, sensual kiss. "Temperance Hartwood," she murmured, the words sounding familiar yet foreign on her lips. "That's my name. Lady Temperance Hartwood."

Chapter Eleven

"Whither should I fly?
I have done no harm. But I remember now
I am in this earthly world—where to do harm
Is often laudable, to do good sometime
Accounted dangerous folly. Why then, alas,
Do I put up that womanly defense,
To say I have done no harm?"

LADY MACDUFF, MACBETH ACT IV, SCENE II

Coll looked down into Temperance Hartwood's pret
blue eyes, their bodies still intertwined, his heart st
pounding, and his mind still very far from logical thin
ing. "Pleased to make yer acquaintance, my lady."

Temperance Hartwood. He'd heard the name som
where, and recently. Where the devil had it been? Aft
weeks of speaking to lasses who knew how to discuss t
weather, fashion, and the most innocent bits of gossip,
had so many pieces of information battering about in l
brain that he could scarcely remember his own name.

With a short laugh that sounded bitter at the end, s
put one hand over her eyes. "I shouldn't have told you. I'
managed for years to keep it to myself, and then you lo
at me with those . . . eyes of yours, and I begin blabbi
like a baby."

"These eyes of mine happen to like lookin' at ye,"
returned, shifting off of her to turn on his back beside h
The lass needed some room to think; as a man with an a

preciation for open spaces, he understood that. "And I'm nae a fool. I told ye that ye could trust me."

"Yes, I know that, but I've done this on my own until now. I've been rather proud of that fact, actually."

With her name still rolling about in his brain, he abruptly remembered where he'd heard it spoken. "My sister mentioned ye the other day," he said slowly, attempting to piece together what had been a rather silly and inane conversation, a complaint about his harsh treatment of Matthew Harris's beak. "Ye're an heiress. There's a wager in the book at White's over whether ye're deceased, or ye've run off to America, or ye're somewhere in the countryside and wed to a butcher with a half dozen pudgy bairns."

"I've heard that one myself," she commented, her expression easing a little. "It's rather flattering that no one has come close to guessing what I've actually done with my life."

"Aye, but someone has, I reckon." Bending an arm behind his head, he reached out with the other one to tug her up over his chest. "Are ye certain it's nae the man ye ran from? Mayhap he saw ye at the theater and recognized ye. Some men would rather murder than be revealed to be a fool."

Persephone—Temperance—lay her cheek over his heart, her fingers idly stroking his chest. "I'm still trying to decide whether I'd rather flee than find out who it might be," she muttered.

"How many people want ye dead, lass?"

Snorting, she lifted her head briefly to look at him. "It's not funny, truly, but at the same time it's just so horrid that I'd rather laugh than cry."

"I'm all for lying here with ye all night and giving ye all the comfort I can manage," he responded, twining a mid-length, honey-colored strand of her hair around his finger, "but ye ken I'm a fighter. Give me names—point me at someone I can battle."

What he didn't say was that he wasn't going to allow her to leave London. He wanted her there, with him. Not just to protect her, though that made for a damned fine excuse. He simply wasn't prepared to part from her. This connection between them felt stronger than iron, but at the same time, as delicate as a butterfly's wings. No, she wasn't going anywhere. Not until . . . Well, just not.

The thing that he'd begun to pull out of this conversation, beyond the way it confirmed what he already knew—that she was a brave, bright, independent woman—was that while his mother might have made a sliver of sense in not wanting him to wed a commoner, at least for the sake of his sister and new sisters-in-law, Temperance Hartwood wasn't a commoner. She even had "Lady" in front of her name, for the devil's sake.

"I haven't done anything wrong, have I?" she muttered, half to herself. "My parents would say I did, and I suppose I've shirked my obligation to improve the family lineage by marrying into an impressive title, but I've spent eight years away, six of them here in one small part of London, simply living my life."

"Ye protected yerself," he stated, whether her question had been rhetorical or not. "And ye've done well at it all. If disappointing a parent were grounds for murder, there'd be a lot fewer children in the world, I reckon. So right or wrong, ye dunnae deserve having someone trying to hurt ye."

"Of course you'd say that; you make sense, Coll. You approve of anyone who stands on their own two feet."

"Nae only do I make sense, lass, I've an affinity for sorting out things that dunnae make sense." Coaxing information out of her would likely give him an apoplexy before he'd managed it, but clearly fists didn't apply here.

He needed to be someone she could trust and prove to her that her secrets were safe with him.

But there was also someone after her. He didn't have all the time in the world to be patient—not that he'd ever much favored patience.

"I don't want you entangled in this. I just . . . I wish we could go back to the night we first met, and just leave things as they were then." She kissed his nipple, nearly sending his eyes rolling back in his head.

"I already knew what I wanted, the first time I set eyes on ye. And I mean to help ye, Temperance. If ye fear that obligates ye to me, it doesnae. I like ye, and I dunnae want ye hurt. There arenae enough people I truly like in the world, and I'm nae willing to lose one of them. So ye tell me who ye reckon is after ye."

"Coll, th—"

"Nae," he interrupted. "Tell me."

She lay there with her cheek on his chest, one arm across his shoulder and the other tucked into his side, for so long that he began to worry he'd finally found someone more stubborn than he was. Finally, though, she sighed. "I'm not certain. I don't have any reason to think my parents would want me harmed; as far as I know, they haven't even disowned me." Temperance snorted. "Disowning me would ruin any value I would have to the family, and they made quite the investment in my education. I'm very nearly a prodigy at the pianoforte, don't you know."

"I believe that," he said, admiring the fact that she could jest even with all the weight on her shoulders. "Who are they, though? If ye'll recall, I'm nae from England."

"I'm surprised you didn't read about my disappearance up in Scotland, even. My parents are Michael and Georgiana Hartwood, the Marquis and Marchioness of Bayton. Bayton Hall is in the middle of Cumbria."

"Cumbria. That's the Lake District, aye? Wild country." He frowned. "Wild for England, that is."

"Yes, it is. Bayton Hall overlooks Lake Windermere. It's quite lovely. Or it was, the last time I saw it."

"Yer da's a marquis, and that's still nae enough for them? Who'd they want ye to wed, Prince George himself?"

"If they thought they could manage that, I'm certain they would have. Prinny was no doubt on their list, at least. No, the man they found for me was Martin Vance, the Duke of Dunhurst."

Coll propped up his head on one arm to look at her. "Tall man, bald but for two white tufts of hair over his ears? Looks like a walking scarecrow with nae enough skin pulled over his skull?"

He felt her shiver against him. "Yes, that's him. You've met, I take it?"

"I dunnae recall that we've been introduced, but I've seen him about with his two granddaughters."

"One granddaughter. Maria Vance-Hayden. She came out this year. The other one is his wife, Penelope Vance, the Duchess of Dunhurst. She came out two years after I did."

Dunhurst had to be seventy years old, at the least. The idea of that severe, harsh man wed to the lively, bold lass presently in his arms—and that her parents had welcomed the match—left Coll feeling pinched and ill. It had been bad enough when Amelia-Rose Baxter's mother and Francesca had conspired to have her engaged to him before they'd ever met, but they'd at least been born in the same decade.

"As I recall," he said aloud, grasping for memories for which he hadn't had much use over the years, "my mother kept her maiden name when she married my da because it was her family who had the money. Da would-nae wear Oswell at all and went to hurling things at the walls if Francesca ever referred to his bairns as Oswell-MacTaggerts, but letting her keep it was part of the agreement for allowing the marriage."

She nodded. "Yes. Maria Vance-Hayden has a wealthy mother, who married Dunhurst's hideous son Donald for *his* title. That's why Dunhurst wanted me; the Hartwoods—my parents—are quite well-to-do."

It was quite a round of names to sort out, but most of them wouldn't have a reason to want any harm to come to Temperance Hartwood. Perhaps some scandal and ruination, but not a broken neck. "I'll be making Dunhurst's acquaintance, then," he said, "and we'll see what sort of man he is."

"Other than the cruel, cold sort," she returned. "In my experience, vengeance takes effort and patience. He wasn't proficient at either one."

"Were ye engaged, or was it an understanding?"

"I fled a week before the wedding," she said, scowling. "I shouldn't have waited that long, but I kept hoping . . . I don't know, that something would happen to intervene."

"Then if he came to the Saint Genesius and saw ye onstage, he might reckon killing ye would be better than ye being discovered. A lass who became an actress to avoid marrying him—that would be damned embarrassing."

"I was wearing trousers and a black wig. Aside from that, Dunhurst spent all of his time in my company scrutinizing my bosom. I doubt he knows what color my eyes are."

"Blue, lass," Coll said, lowering his head onto his crooked arm again. "Blue as Loch an Daimh at noon beneath a cloudless sky."

Silence. "For a man who claims to prefer speaking with his fists," she said very quietly, "you do have a way with words."

"Ye should see me fling a tree trunk about."

He felt her body shake with a silent laugh, and he grinned at the ceiling. In the short time he'd known her, he'd probably said more words to her than he had to every other female in London combined. She'd taxed his wits but not his patience, because she was harder to keep up with than a fox on marshy ground.

"Have yer parents been to London since ye've been at the Saint Genesius?"

"I'm certain they have been. Neither of them ever particularly enjoyed the theater, though. There are fewer people to impress with their wealth in the dark." She hesitated. "I never saw them, if they did make an appearance."

"Are they in London now?"

Her spine stiffened beneath his palm. "You are not going to call on my parents, Coll MacTaggert."

"I didnae say I was. I asked if they were here. Ye seem fairly aware of all of Society's to-dos, so I expect ye know one way or the other. If ye dunnae, I can find out easily enough. My *màthair* practically keeps a list."

"No," she snapped, slapping him on the chest. "No one else can know about me."

"I'm nae going to tell her anything," he protested, her body shifting against his making him stir again.

"You are not a subtle man, Lord Glendarril."

"Ye'd be surprised, lass. I generally dunnae have cause to be subtle." Shifting his arm from behind his head, he lifted her squarely on top of him. "For instance, do ye notice anything about me now?"

The smile that curved her mouth very nearly stopped his heart. "Well, now that you mention it," she murmured, lifting up on all fours and sliding down the length of him.

Perhaps she meant to distract him from asking questions. She'd spent over seven years keeping her secrets to herself, after all. As her mouth closed over his cock, Coll decided that questions could wait until tomorrow. He had a lass to pleasure and a future to consider. One that included her, whether she'd realized it or not.

Coll awoke in the morning to a black cat sitting squarely on his chest and staring at him. "I ken who ye are, Hades," he muttered, staring right back at the wee animal. "And *ye* ken that I'm nae going anywhere. I reckon we'd best ally ourselves if we mean to save our lass."

The cat lifted one paw, flexed it to show his claws, then set it down again.

"Well-played," Coll commented, ignoring the light pricks. The cat could've done a great deal more damage if he had wanted to. "I'm glad we understand each other."

With a sniff, Hades stood up and padded off the bed. Coll watched him glide across the room and disappear beneath the oak wardrobe. Then he turned to find Pers— Temperance—watching him from the dressing table, a pink and yellow silk dressing robe over her shoulders and knotted at the waist.

"Impressive," she said with a smile, "considering you don't smell like fish at all."

Sitting up, he stretched his arms over his head. "Did Hades eat all the sandwiches? I'm half starved."

"I've already asked Flora to make us something for breakfast." She tilted her head, still gazing at him. "I expected—well, more of a reaction to you finding out my identity. It's horribly scandalous, after all, for a marquis's only daughter to become an actress."

His main reaction had been the realization that he'd previously bedded her without knowing who she was, not that he'd now spent the night in the naked company of a marquis's daughter. That generally meant a marriage was in the offing, even in the Highlands. This was all a wee bit more complicated than he'd planned for, but it had also become a great deal more interesting than he'd expected.

If he knew one thing, though, it was that pointing out that he'd ruined a lady and now had an obligation to marry her wouldn't go over well. She'd run away rather than be forced into a match she didn't favor, and he wasn't about to attempt to force her into anything now.

"Ye're a fine actress. It'd be another thing altogether, I suppose, if ye didnae have any talent for it." He climbed out of the soft bed, looking for his kilt before remembering he'd been wearing Sassenach trousers. "I dunnae scandalize easily, Temperance, if ye've nae noticed. I'm more troubled that we cannae narrow down who might be trying to harm ye."

"I don't want to leave, you know," she said, gesturing at the portmanteau they'd knocked to the floor last night. "I like my life here. I like the . . . friends I've found here. If I could narrow down the list of suspects, I would certainly do so." She shed her robe, naked and glorious in the dim light from the edges of the curtains, then wrapped her arms around herself. "I haven't seen anyone I know from my life before. And the idea that someone might have seen me without me noticing is unsettling, to say the least."

Coll walked around the edge of the bed and wrapped her in his arms. "I dunnae mean to widen our search, but could it be someone who's admired ye on the stage? Some lunatic who cannae accept that Rosalind paired off with Orlando or someaught?"

"Oh, good heavens, I hadn't thought of that. Yes, I suppose it could be. I receive some *very* interesting letters sometimes."

"Letters? I'd like to see them, if ye dunnae mind. Anything over the past fortnight or so, unless ye recall something untoward nearly happening to ye before that."

"They're downstairs. But Coll, while I'm exceedingly

relieved you came to see me last night, you have other obligations. I don't want you to lose your inheritance because I didn't hide well enough."

He looked down at her upturned face. Coll reflected that he owed Niall and Aden both an apology for making fun of their claims that they'd just "known" when they'd found their lasses and hadn't been able to explain it any other way. "Dunnae ye worry about me finding a wife," he said with a slight smile. "I've someone in mind already."

"Good." Abruptly, she shrugged out of his grip and went to retrieve her prim black wig. "I hope my suggestions helped."

"Aye, they did. I still havenae kept up my end of the agreement, though. I'm yer protector, and I mean to protect ye. If ye've paper about, I need to send Gavin over to Oswell House with a note for a couple of lads to help me keep watch here."

"Gavin's here?"

"Aye. I left him outside last night, watching the house." He bent to pick up a hairpin and set it on the table next to her. "And dunnae fret about him. He's been asked to do far worse."

"We should still have him come in for breakfast. But I'm not staying here all day, hiding under the bed. I have rehearsals."

"Temperance, ye—"

"I'm not trying to be foolish," she broke in. "I told you that I want to stay. I have an obligation to Charlie and the Saint Genesius. At the least, I need to tell Charlie that I may be putting the rest of the troupe in danger and give him the opportunity to find someone else to play Lady Macbeth."

That made sense. If she stopped appearing at the Saint Genesius, whoever wanted to harm her would have a more difficult time tracking her down. Keeping her safe mattered far more than a part in a play. "Ye should stay here. After I set some men on watch, I'll go talk to Huddle."

She shook her head, pausing to settle a pretty green and brown muslin gown over her shoulders. "I owe a great deal to Charlie. I will speak with him myself."

"Temp—"

"Persephone, for heaven's sake," she broke in. "Temperance Hartwood was a long time ago, from a life I don't want."

"But I like knowing who ye are beneath everything else."

"I'm the same woman I was before you knew I had another name, Coll. I don't want you forgetting and calling me . . . that other name in front of people."

She didn't have an objection to being seen with him, then. That, of course, wasn't at all the point of her argument, but it felt significant. "I'll nae forget." Stepping forward, he fastened the quartet of buttons running up her back, then closed his hand around her shoulder, turned her around, and kissed her.

Her arms crept up to grasp his shoulders as she returned the embrace, sinking along his chest. "What I've told you doesn't change anything, you know," she whispered against his mouth.

"It changes everything," he countered. It changed the entire architecture of his world, but only as far as she would allow it. Any final decision rested with her. After what she'd been through, he wouldn't have it any other way. Thankfully, he could be far more persuasive than people generally realized. "Have it as ye will, though," he went on, to avoid another round of arguments. "Paper. I need paper."

He pulled his shirt over his head and followed her out of the bedchamber. As soon as they trotted down the steep, narrow stairs to the wee dining room, he wrote a note to Aden, requesting a handful of the Highlanders they'd brought south with them. The rest of the staff of Oswell House could likely be trusted, but they owed their loyalty to Francesca, not to him.

Flora the maid wasn't a grand cook like Mrs. Gordon at Oswell House, but with a small household like this one, he had to admire her skill. She'd made the dress Temperance currently wore, and several of the others in which he'd seen the lass. And though the bread and ham with gravy wasn't anything fancy, it felt closer to a true Highlands breakfast than anything he'd eaten since he'd left home.

"Is there something I need to know, Miss Persie?" Gregory asked, stacking dishes to return to the kitchen. "That Gavin last night with all his talk of locking the door and finding a weapon had me awake sitting in the front room with my musket across my knees until dawn."

Flora appeared in the dining room doorway on the tail of that comment. "And I nearly threw a pot at the milkman when he knocked at the back door. Miss Persie, I know something's wrong. Please let us help."

"It's nothing," Temperance said, sipping at a cup of tea Coll knew had long ago gone cold. "A bit of trouble with an old beau." She sent a glance at Coll. "Isn't that right?"

Damn it all; he didn't like lying. But in a sense, she was correct, since as far as they knew, this *was* about her previous life—though it could just as easily have been about some madman disapproving of her performance as Juliet Capulet. "We think so, aye. I reckon I'll get it sorted today."

"Good," Flora said, fanning at her face with a cloth. "My nerves haven't been so rattled since that banker tried to follow you home for three nights in a row after you played Ophelia."

Temperance grimaced at Coll's sideways glance. "He was quite mad, I'm afraid, and was convinced that *I* should be placed in Bedlam for my own good."

"Well, that's nae at all worrying," he muttered, mentally moving his low ranking for enraptured onlookers several rungs higher on his ladder of suspects.

"That sort of thing doesn't happen often. Usually it's men enamored of the character I'm playing and wanting to romance me."

He liked that even less. How many men had attempted to woo, buy, or charm her since she'd begun acting? And how many of them had succeeded, if only for a night or two? Was he being an idiot for refusing to count himself in that number? Was it only because, by chance, he'd seen her first as herself backstage?

He'd never been foolish with women. Aye, he'd bedded his share, but he'd never given one enough of his heart to feel regret when they parted company. There had always been a more important obligation—to Clan Ross, to the MacTaggerts, and to Aldriss Park. Now, though, just the idea of her in another man's arms was enough to make his jaw clench and his muscles bellow for battle. What it all meant, he didn't know—or rather, he thought he *did* know, but given the lass's reaction to the idea of forevers, he meant to keep it to himself. For now.

"I need ye to make me a list," he said quietly, when the footman and maid returned to the kitchen. "All yer family, everyone ye've been . . . close to, anyone with whom ye've had an argument."

"That's quite a bit of my personal life, sir," she stated, her cheeks growing pink. "I'm not certain I wish you to know all of that."

"I ken, Persephone," he commented, using her faux name deliberately, to remind her that he could be trusted. "Ye've done this on yer own until now. I can do more looking about than ye can, and me blundering my way through Society will cause less of a stir than if ye attempted it."

"I don't like that, Coll. You blundering, I mean. I have the feeling that if you truly wished to, you could have half a hundred women ready to wed you by now."

"Aye?" He snorted. "Why have I nae, then? I could certainly use a bride."

"Because you are as stubborn as the rain, and because I don't think you generally do *anything* you've been ordered to do."

That sounded fairly accurate, actually. "I'm nae a man to follow other people, I'll admit. I'll also admit that until a week or so ago, I wasnae hoping to find anyone with whom I'd care to spend my life. But then Aden went and agreed to wed Miranda, and my chances of getting that agreement changed went from fair to miserable."

"'Agreed to wed?'" she repeated, furrowing her brow. "Was it arranged, then?"

"Nae. She proposed to him." He grinned. "Aden doesnae think he's very honorable, but he got himself wrapped up in being proper toward her and then couldnae see a way out. Miranda solved it for him."

She played with her fork for a bit. "You seem happy for him."

Coll sighed. "Aye. I am. And for Niall. It's just nae the way I'd planned any of this, and now I'm the one who's stuck." Clearing his throat, he downed the rest of his luke-warm tea. "That doesnae signify now, though. I made an agreement with ye, and I need those names if I'm to hold up my end of the bargain."

"I'm only agreeing because I don't want to leave London, and I would have to do so if I were on my own." Pushing back from the table, she rose gracefully. "I have two hours before I need to be at the Saint Genesius. I'll be in the morning room writing out a list if you need me."

"Keep the curtains closed."

"Ah, yes. We don't want anyone shooting at me, do we?" With a smile that looked entirely forced, she glided out of the room.

Coll sat back in his chair. She lived in a modest house but employed two servants, had an abundance of nice clothes and wigs aplenty, and from the look of it, didn't lack for food or money. And she'd done all that on her own. He meant to ask her why a proper lass with a proper education had decided to make her way in the world as an actress, but he imagined it had to do with her wanting literally to disappear—to become someone else, which she'd done onstage and off.

And she was good at it. The toast of London, famous and successful enough that his own younger sister had been near giddy with excitement at the idea of meeting her, and Eloise had made the acquaintance of Prince George and Queen Caroline in her short time being out.

All morning, he'd wracked his brain, trying to recall if he'd met Lord and Lady Bayton. He didn't think so, since they hadn't flung a marriageable daughter at him, but then he had to wonder how he would have reacted to a proper introduction to one Lady Temperance Hartwood. At eight-and-twenty she would have been considered on the shelf, her parents no doubt desperate to find her a husband and a title—and he likely would have run in the opposite direction.

If he and she managed a word or two before his flight, though, he preferred to think that she would have caught his attention—and his interest. The sound of her voice, the way she used words . . . Was that because of her training on the stage, or was that something she'd come by naturally that made her so well-suited to acting? Whatever it was, he found it mesmerizing.

He found *her* mesmerizing. And only the fact that he

was loathe to leave her this morning kept him from pounding on every door in London until he'd discovered who it was trying to take her away from him. Even though it had been seventeen years since he'd last experienced being abandoned, it wasn't anything he wanted touching him again. At least with his mother, hope had lingered for a time that she might return, that he might see her again. If he lost Temperance to someone else's scheming, though, it wouldn't be anything temporary.

Cursing, he went back upstairs and pulled on his waistcoat and coat, not bothering to button either of them. The cravat went into a pocket, and then he headed downstairs to wait for help to arrive—and to make a plan to save his lass, even though he didn't know who might be after her.

Chapter Twelve

"But screw your courage to the sticking-place,
And we'll not fail."

LADY MACBETH, *MACBETH* ACT I, SCENE VII

"Ye shouldnae have let him ride off alone, Niall."

At the sound of Aden's hard voice, Francesca Oswell-MacTaggert gripped her morning newspaper more firmly and kept her gaze trained on whatever it was that someone had written about. It hadn't taken long for her to realize that she had a much better chance of figuring out what was going on if she occupied herself with overhearing bits and pieces, rather than asking direct questions.

Her sons weren't accustomed to being second-guessed or explaining their actions. Their father had allowed them to run wild from the moment she'd left Aldriss Park. And while under calmer circumstances she could admit that they'd become confident, competent, resourceful young men, there hadn't been much calm since they'd arrived in London.

"I sent Gavin off with him," her youngest son protested.

"And Gavin would jump off a roof for him, if Coll asked. Ye should've joined them. Ye do recall what happened last time Coll stomped off on his own."

"Aye, I recall. I found a wife."

"And he spent a day drunk in a fighting pit while I rode all over London looking for him. Sweet Saint Andrew,

Niall. At least tell me ye ken where he went. I'm getting married in four days. I cannae be chasing Coll through the Midlands."

"I recall. And nae, he didnae stop long enough to tell me. I reckon Gavin knows, but that doesnae help us."

"Damn it all. I'll give him another hour to get his arse back here. If he doesnae, I reckon we begin looking at the Saint Genesius. If the lass is there, Coll will be as well."

Their voices faded as they headed toward the kitchen and the stable beyond. Francesca sat back and lowered her newspaper. After her initial panic, she'd figured her oldest son had been lying about making plans to wed Mrs. Persephone Jones. It had been too close to the very opposite of her expectations for it to be a coincidence. If someone had asked her to name the very last person in London she wanted for one of her sons, the least respectable name she knew was that of the actress.

Of course, there were lightskirts about, and beggars and thieves, but he'd chosen a name that every Londoner knew. It made sense that he'd done it with the express purpose of hurting her—she'd been the one who demanded he marry, after all.

But she'd been looking at his face last night, when Niall and the groom had interrupted her attempt at reasoning with him. All the blood had fled his face when Gavin had told him about the carriage overturning. Yes, the MacTaggerts looked after their own, and if he'd involved the actress in something dangerous, he would have felt some responsibility toward her safety. But even if he had made some sort of agreement with Mrs. Jones to induce her to go along with the marriage nonsense, Francesca didn't think his reaction would have been so extreme.

His brothers expected to find them together. That meant he'd either lied to them about his intentions and completely fooled them, or none of it had been fake. She put a hand to her chest. Her oldest son, Viscount Glendarril, after an actress. But not just in pursuit.

He cared about her. And that changed several things.

Picking up the newspaper again, she turned to the Society page. Currently, the Saint Genesius was hosting a traveling troupe for one of those bawdy plays that actors loved to perform. In just a few days, though, the renowned actors of the Saint Genesius Theatre would be performing . . . Ah, there it was. *Macbeth*. With Mrs. Persephone Jones playing the part of Lady Macbeth.

Hmm. She'd always been partial to the Scottish play. "Smythe," she said, turning her head to the butler.

"Yes, my lady?"

"I'll be in my rooms. The moment Lord Glendarril returns, have my coach readied and inform me. Discreetly."

He nodded. "I'll see to it, my lady. More trouble?"

"I imagine so." She picked up her cup of tea, but before she could lift it to her mouth, a rustle of voices sounded from the direction of the kitchen. "Go," she said, and Smythe left the room. Another footman took his place.

Several hurried sets of footsteps thudded up and down the hallway for a moment. She wanted to rise and demand that she be informed of what was causing the chaos beneath her roof. But as forceful as she knew she could be, and as wild and willful as her sons were, demands would only be met with sarcasm and evasion. So she remained seated, trying not to grip her tea cup tightly enough to break the delicate handle.

The door opened again. Jane Bansil, Amy's cousin and former companion, gave a polite nod before heading for the sideboard and the generous selections waiting there for anyone in the growing household wanting breakfast.

"Good morning, my lady," she said, picking out a slice of toast and a fresh orange and seating herself at the foot of the table.

"Jane, you're a guest here. You may sit wherever you wish."

The rail-straight young lady cringed. "Yes, I know, and I thank you again for your generosity. The—"

"Nonsense. Come up here and sit beside me. I require a distraction."

Her black hair in its ever-present and excruciatingly tight bun, Jane jumped to her feet again, picked up her plate, and hurried up the table. When she sat again, the plate clanked onto the smooth, polished mahogany, and she flinched again.

"I'm sorry."

"Don't be. If this house is one thing, it's not quiet."

"It is very . . . lively," Miss Bansil offered.

"What do you see ahead for yourself, my dear?" Francesca pursued. "I haven't had time to ask."

"Oh, I'm—I—certainly I won't impose on you much longer. I've put out several inquiries, and I believe I may find a position by the end of the month."

"Is that what you want?" The woman had been let go from her previous employment—her own aunt—for allowing Amy to elope to Scotland with Niall. "I don't recall you or Amy enjoying the Baxter household overly much."

"I'm a woman without means, my lady. I must find employment, or I shall starve. Somewhere that provides me a roof over my head and meals would be . . . a relief, I suppose."

"Even if you could stay here as long as you wish?"

"I'm not cursed with ambition, I know, and I'm . . . well, I bumble a great deal looking for the correct words, but I would like to have some task before me. A reason for getting up in the morning, as it were."

Francesca sipped her tea. "Ah. You don't wish to be a woman of leisure like myself, then."

Jane's cheeks turned bright red. "Oh, dear. No! Not . . .

That's not what I meant. You are a mother and you have charities, and you are rarely at leisure, from what I can see."

"Well, thank you for that. If you wish to find a position, then do so. It does occur to me that my daughter will be married shortly, and I have no doubt my sons will be returning to Scotland as soon as they can manage it. What would you think of remaining here with me? Officially? As my companion, or my secretary, or whatever we decide to term the position?"

"Oh, my goodness. I hadn't—oh, my."

The door opened again. Smythe glided into the breakfast room with a note between his fingers. "Consider it, Jane. I imagine I'll want your answer after Eloise's wedding." She motioned, and the butler walked to the table and handed over the paper.

Francesca opened it. Coll's surprisingly elegant scrawl took only two lines, giving an address and a request to Niall or Aden to send four trustworthy lads there immediately. By trustworthy, she assumed he meant Scottish.

"Niall and Aden have seen it?" she asked.

"Yes, my lady. Master Niall and four of their fellows rode off just a moment ago."

She folded the missive and put it in her pocket. "Who delivered it?"

"That groom."

Ah, that would be Gavin. Rising, she went to the hallway door. "Have him sent to me in my study. Now. I don't want to give him time to think up a story."

She knew Mrs. Jones's address now, and her place of employment. What she didn't know—and what she needed to know—was who this woman was, other than an exceptional actress. If Persephone Jones was simply playing the part of a damsel in distress and had thereby caught Coll's

attention, this nonsense needed to end. If there was something more to it all, Francesca meant to discover that too.

Lady Macbeth frequently had a flock of female attendants
about her. She had been the queen of Scotland after all,
if only for a very short time. Temperance stepped down
from the Oswell-MacTaggert coach, Coll on her heels, and
looked up to see a pair of broad backs in Clan Ross kilts
in front of her, and another two walking up to take the
rear guard. With Coll's brother, Niall, exiting the coach as
well, that made six. Six very large, very capable-looking
Highlanders, all there for one purpose: to keep her safe.

She wanted to tell Coll all this might be a bit much,
but for the moment, she was glad to have them there. If
Coll hadn't been in London, if they hadn't met, she would
likely be dead from that brick-filled bucket, or she would
have had to hire someone to protect her. She had no idea
how one even went about finding that sort of person.

If perhaps all this had been simply a coincidental string
of bad luck, and no one had deliberately run her off the
road yesterday, then all of this and the list she'd written
out for Coll would be for nothing. A very small part of her
clung to that idea, because the idea that someone out in
the world wanted to see her dead chilled her to her bones.

"Persephone," Charlie said, walking up from the depths
of the theater as she entered the Saint Genesius with her en-
tourage. "You're late for your fitting with Beth. Don't . . .
What's all this? We're not taking outside auditions for
Scotsmen."

"We're nae playing Scotsmen," Niall commented, narrowing one eye. "We *are* Scotsmen."

"Why are there a half dozen Scotsmen backstage,
then?" The manager went on, eyeing the lot of them as if
they'd risen from the witches' cauldron to torment him.

"I need to speak to you about that, Charlie," Persephone returned, releasing her hold on Coll's arm and putting a hand around Mr. Huddle's. "In your office, perhaps?"

"Oh, God, you're not with child, are you?" he asked, putting his free hand over his face. "We have our roster of plays made up for the next year. I coordinated them with Covent Garden and Drury Lane. If you—"

"I'm not with child," she cut in, her jaw clenching. For heaven's sake, she was careful about such things. And yes, she and Coll had been intimate several times now, but she could read a calendar. If they remained together, which she hoped they would, in the next week or so he would have to begin wearing a French condom. Her lips quirked. How would he react to that, she wondered?

"Ye want me in there, lass?" Coll asked on the tail of that thought.

Pushing away her abrupt amusement, she shook her head. It felt so odd to racket between terror and fond amusement all in the same few beats of her heart. If not for him—if he hadn't arrived last night with a healthy dose of logic and caring and arousal—she might well have been on her way to Dover by now, seeking passage to the Continent. She would have surrendered without ever knowing who or why someone was after her.

As she and Charlie headed for his office, Coll barked out orders to his men behind her, stationing them about the theater. All around her, actors and stage crew exchanged curious looks, loudly speculating about why the Highlanders might be in attendance and what it had to do with the play.

"Out with it, then," Charlie said, freeing his arm to cram himself behind his tiny desk.

"Someone ran my coach off the road last evening." She pulled her left sleeve up to her elbow, revealing scratches and a bruise.

His face lost its ruddy coloring. "What? On purpose?"

"They rammed us three times, so I'd have to say it was on purpose." She sank into the flimsy chair opposite him. "Coll is convinced that someone is trying to murder me."

"It bloody well sounds like it," Charlie exploded. "Good God." He pounded his fist on the desk, taking several deep breaths. "I'm actually a little relieved. When I saw you walk in here with those giants, I thought you meant to demand an increase in pay. This is worse, of course, but if I had to offer you more salary, Thomas and Jenny and Gordon would have been right on your heels."

"I'm glad this is only your second worst nightmare, then," she said dryly. "But I have to ask you—do you want me to remain here? Honestly, if you please. The next time someone flings a bucket of bricks at me, it might hit someone else."

The stout theater manager looked at her for a long moment. "Before you came along, Persie, the Saint Genesius did a fair business. But since you've been here, there hasn't been a seat to spare in the entire house. I have the luxury of bringing in traveling troupes while we design sets and costumes the like of which have never been seen before, because I know the seats will be filled when we perform the next play." He sat back, waving a pencil at her. "That, my sweet, is because of you."

The chill in her bones began to recede again. "I don't want to put anyone else in danger, Charlie."

"Do you know who's doing this? Did you hop into bed with someone's husband?"

"No, and no. I have no idea." She closed her eyes for a moment. "That's not entirely true. It might have something to do with my time before I came to London."

"Before you became Persephone Jones, you mean?"

She blinked. "I beg your pardon?"

He offered her a slight smile. "My dear, I've been here

for twenty years. I know the name of every actor in every theater and troupe across England. Someone as skilled as Persephone Jones doesn't just *appear*—unless she literally sprang out of thin air, fully formed."

This day was turning out to be full of surprises, and she definitely didn't appreciate some as much as others. "All this time you suspected, and you never said anything?"

"I don't know who you were, and frankly, I don't care. Yes, I want you to stay, even if it means two dozen Highlanders prowling about the theater. Hell, perhaps we can use them as decoration."

"Thank you, Charlie," she said feelingly. "Not just for this, but for the past six years. The Saint Genesius has done at least as much for me as you say I've done for it."

She'd brought trouble to his doorstep, and yet he'd invited her to stay, anyway. If she'd known she would meet and befriend people who valued her for herself and her contributions without caring about the importance of her birth or how much money she stood to inherit, running away from Bayton Hall wouldn't have been nearly as terrifying as it had been eight years ago.

"Your Highlander doesn't seem the type to wait about for someone else to try to hurt you," Charlie commented. "Does he have a plan?"

Her Highlander. Was he? Or was he simply the next man, the one who would keep her bed warm until they grew tired of each other? When he looked at her, when he touched her, it didn't feel that way. But he needed to marry, and clearly, she needed to remain hidden. Better hidden, even. Those two things simply didn't go together.

"I gave him a few names to look into," she said when Charlie lifted an eyebrow at her. "I'm frankly hoping, however, that it's some rabid Rosalind admirer who disliked my portrayal."

"We could do something with that," he mused. "'Per-

formances so fantastical, they drive men mad.' Hmm."
Swiftly pulling out a piece of paper, he wrote a note to
himself.

And there was Charlie Huddle, trying to turn every mis-
hap into an opportunity. "If you do that, you'll have every
ladies' group carrying signs to protect their husbands."

"Eh. You do make a point." Scowling, he crossed the
line of writing out again. "As for you, Persie, I want to
know when you're to be here every morning, and when
you're leaving every evening. I'll escort you home myself,
if need be."

"It won't be," she returned. "Coll has declared that I'm
not to venture anywhere without at least two of his men
accompanying me." That had actually been a compromise,
after she'd refused to allow him to be the one at her side.
He had a stupid wife to find, and three weeks in which to
do it. If that venture failed, she did not want to be the one
responsible for it even if she preferred that he remain just
as he was.

Charlie glanced toward the open doorway. "This Lord
Glendarril. You're generally more cautious, Persie. Are
you certain he's not the one making you look vulnerable,
so he can . . . do as he's done?"

"I'm not worth that much trouble," she countered. If
there was one thing about which she could be certain, it
was that Coll MacTaggert wouldn't spend his time trying
to frighten or harm a woman. Or anyone else, for that
matter. If someone angered him, he told them so. If he
wanted someone, he told them so. "Even if I was, he's very
likely the most honorable man I've ever met."

"Well. That's a statement I've never heard you make before."

"It is, isn't it?" She sighed. "Someone is going to end
up with a broken heart, and I have more than a sneaking
suspicion that it's going to be me." With that, she rose

again. "I'm off to see Beth for my fitting. I'll leave it to you to tell the rest of the troupe whatever you choose. Gordon will likely blame it all on the Scottish play, regardless."

"I can hear it now. 'The ghosts of Banquo's descendants come to curse him for daring to play King the Scottish Play.'"

Temperance snorted. "You've known us for too long."

"Definitely."

When she left the office, the first person she spied was Coll, head bent over her list with his youngest brother, Niall. The gossip pages had spent weeks drooling over the MacTaggert brothers' handsome appearance, and for once those chin-wags hadn't been exaggerating. If the third brother, Aden, measured up to the other two, then the MacTaggert parents had managed to produce the three most attractive males she'd ever seen.

The two men spoke quietly, the words a mix of English and Scots Gaelic, Coll's lower-pitched voice mesmerizing in its ebb and flow. She could tell herself she found the sound so attractive because voice and speech in general always caught her attention, but she could admit that it had more to do with the fact that she found the man himself fascinating. Unexpected. Delectable. Addictive.

So addictive that for the next two days he managed to keep her completely distracted from everything but the play and his hard, lean body. Whatever plans of his own he'd had to cancel to stay with her overnight, she had no idea, because he refused to tell her. He missed at least one additional soiree, she knew, but she didn't argue against it, because she wanted him there with her.

Whether that made her selfish or simply frightened of the outside world, she didn't know, but then lately she'd almost felt as if she'd begun to split into two separate people: the daring Persephone Jones, who enjoyed her skilled lover every night, and the terrified Temperance Hartwood, who jumped at every shadow and couldn't sleep without Coll's strong arms around her.

With him as an added distraction, the usual speed with which the Saint Genesius racketed between plays seemed even more ridiculously swift this time. The sets were nearly finished, lines had been memorized almost to perfection, and all but one of her costumes waited for her already in her dressing room. She sighed, setting aside her folio to see Gordon Humphreys strutting by in his Macbeth finery, gesticulating wildly to be certain the seams would hold.

In truth she'd always been both women, Temperance and Persephone. The only difference now was that someone else knew it. Oh, from the moment she'd seen Coll standing in the wings she'd known that he would be trouble to her equilibrium, and now to her heart. No, not . . . troublesome, precisely. Disruptive, perhaps. He had definitely upended her thoughts. She couldn't blame him for the attempts on her life, though they'd begun shortly after she met him.

Or had they? Now that she thought about it, there had been a few other odd things recently—a horse pulling a carriage, spooked by a bottle thrown as she left the theater late one night. That horrible garlic-smelling brandy someone had left on her dressing table ten or so days ago.

Those things might have been coincidences. One of the stagehands might have drunk the brandy and replaced it with a cheaper liquor. Drunks did fling bottles from time to time, especially in the small hours of the morning. Oh, it was enough to drive her mad.

"That's quite a frown ye're wearing, lass," Coll said, and she looked up to find him just a few feet away, gazing at her.

"It just occurred to me that the sandbags might not have

been my first near miss," she said. "Unless . . . How am I to know if something was an accident, a coincidence, or something malevolent?"

"Ye cannae. What did ye recall?"

She told him about the brandy and spooked horse, watching his generally level expression darken as she spoke. That told her what he thought about them, whether she was convinced or not. "What did ye do with the brandy?" he asked when she'd finished.

"I threw it away. The moment I opened the bottle, it smelled so pungent I nearly cast up my accounts."

"Would ye recognize the smell again?"

"I think so. But—"

"This evening, we'll go by an apothecary's shop."

"I'm hosting a dinner tonight. I'm not about to disappoint Flora."

He frowned. "Lass, it's nae a good idea to have people about yer house—about *ye*—right now."

"I've known these people much longer than I've known you, Coll, and you've been . . ." She glanced around them at the busy backstage. "You've been sharing my *bed*. You're welcome to join us, and I'm not trying to be stubborn, but you and I both have lives. I will not stop mine and save someone else the trouble of doing so."

"Stubborn," he muttered under his breath. "I'll join ye, then. We'll go by the apothecary in the morning."

"You have a wedding to attend in the morning. And now, if you'll excuse me, I have a final fitting."

"Aye. I've a few things to see to today. My men will be about. If ye need anything, feel a cool breeze ye dunnae like, ye tell one of 'em."

"I will." She wanted to ask where he might be headed, if he meant to look further into Dunhurst's finances, or if this place he needed to go was to a young lady's house to speak with her parents about a marriage. She didn't want him to do either, but she couldn't argue against the first one, and she'd actually encouraged the second one.

He put his forefinger beneath her chin, tilted her head up, and kissed her. "I dunnae like leaving yer side, lass," he murmured, then bent and pulled the knife from his boot. "Ye keep this with ye."

"Macbeth is the one who sees the floating dagger," she said, attempting to find some humor again.

"Promise me," Coll pushed, his expression unchanged.

Blowing out her breath, she took the dagger. "I don't know what I'm to do with it while I'm being fitted for Lady Macbeth's gown."

"Ye've a seamstress here. Find some cloth and strap it to yer leg." Squatting, he ran his palm from her hip down one thigh, to just below her knee. "Hereabouts, so ye can reach it beneath yer skirts."

Now he'd stirred up all kinds of naughty thoughts, and she was going to have a devil of a time remembering her lines. "I would still prefer to discover that no one is after me at all, you know."

Straightening again, he took her hand. "Sorry to tell ye, lass, but ye've got one man after ye, regardless."

With a final swift kiss, he released her hand, turned on his heel, and disappeared into the gloomy backstage. Temperance sat on the nearest stool. He thought knowing her background changed everything. He'd been tasked with finding a proper wife, and while Persephone Jones certainly wasn't that, Lady Temperance Hartwood fulfilled all of his and his family's requirements—in his mind, anyway.

Men. She loved her life—she loved acting and being on-stage and hearing the roars of applause. When she'd run initially, it had been only with the thought of escaping a marriage to the Duke of Dunhurst. It had been weeks later, when her pocket money had begun to run out, that she'd made a choice between working in a shop for a man whose leer gave her the shakes, offering her personal wares on some street corner, and answering an advertisement looking for a young lady to assume the role of Maria, Olivia's maid in *Twelfth Night* for a small theater troupe in Cornwall.

It had been a very fortuitous moment; *Twelfth Night* was her favorite play, one she'd nearly memorized while growing up, and it was a chance to don a disguise and become someone else entirely. No one would look for Temperance Hartwood on the stage. That had been the day Temperance had ceased to exist altogether, and she'd become Persephone Jones.

"Persie," said Flora's daughter, Beth, "Mr. Huddle finally agreed that three costume changes for you are enough for us all to manage. Let me get you in the last one again so I can have them ready in time for dress rehearsal."

"Of course. I'm sorry; I was lost in thought." Temperance stood, falling in behind the seamstress as they hurried over to the table overflowing with cloth, thread, beading, lace, and leather.

"I don't blame you. That Lord Glendarril is rather spectacular."

"Yes, he is," she said. Truer words were never spoken. "He may join us for dinner tonight."

Beth grinned. "A grand lord, condescending to dine with stagehands and seamstresses? I've never heard of such a thing."

Neither had Temperance. Once they'd finished with this mess of possible killers running about, she needed to part ways with him. He didn't fit her life, and she certainly didn't fit his. This just happened to be a perfect little moment in which they could be together. It wouldn't last. It couldn't. No matter how much she'd begun to wish that she hadn't caused Lady Temperance to disappear so thoroughly.

Chapter Thirteen

"Double, double, toil and trouble,
Fire burn, and cauldron bubble."

THE THREE WITCHES, *MACBETH* ACT IV, SCENE I

I don't understand," Eloise said, her tone exasperated. "First you want to know everyone who's going to be attending Lady Fenster's masked ball on Sunday, and then you ask me to describe half of them to you. Why not simply go and see for yourself?"

"They'll be wearing masks." Coll flipped through his notes again. "And I'm trying to find a wife, *piuthar*. I'd like to know with whom I'm entangling myself. Ye ken as well as anyone that a marriage isnae just two people. It's two families."

"You might ask Amy or Miranda; they know as well as I do. And I'm trying to find a hat, for heaven's sake." Sending him another glare, she moved off deeper into the milliner's shop.

Following her, Coll made another note to himself. The half dozen other women in the shop parted before him like sheep before a shepherd, but other than trying to avoid knocking any of them over, he ignored them and their curious stares. "What about this one?" he asked, returning to the list of names that actually interested him. "Maria Vance-Hayden? She's the Duke of Dunhurst's granddaughter, aye?"

Eloise stopped so quickly he nearly ran into her. "Maria Vance-Hayden?" she whispered, sending a glance past him, no doubt to see if anyone might be listening. "She's the one you're . . . *Her*?"

"I dunnae know yet, lass. What's her grandda like?"

She wrinkled her nose. "He's a duke," she commented, as if that explained everything.

"I know he's a duke. Is he pleasant? Serious? What?"

Moving closer, she wrapped a hand around his forearm so she could lift up on her toes and reach his ear. "He's not very nice. I haven't spoken more than two words to him, but he's married to Penelope Vance, who I think is the same age as Maria, and he always has a hand on her. It's not like he's worried she'll run away, but more as if he . . . wants her beneath his heel or something." She lowered herself to the floor again, releasing her grip. "I suppose one can't actually blame him for that. He was supposed to marry Lady Temperance Hartwood, you know."

He lifted an eyebrow. "Who's that?"

"My goodness, you don't know *any* of the good gossip, do you?"

"Apparently. I dunnae." Temperance wasn't on his list, but he wasn't about to pass up a chance to learn more about her. "Speak."

"I only know rumors and such, since I was . . . ten or eleven, I think, when it happened. But she was supposed to marry Dunhurst, and instead she ran away from home in the middle of the night the evening before the wedding."

It had been a week before the wedding, according to Temperance, but he only nodded. "Where did she end up?"

"No one knows. She hasn't been seen since. I heard that she fled to the Americas and married a French trapper and dresses like an Indian."

"How does anyone know that if she's nae been seen since she ran off?"

"Oh, don't be so logical." Eloise grinned at him. "Imagining where she went is half the fun, don't you know."

Fun. Temperance hadn't seen it as anything amusing, but at the same time, the wilder the speculation, the safer she likely was. "Do her parents have any other bairns?"

"No. Just her. I heard another story that she married a butcher up in York and has six fat children."

"She's nae sent word to her mama and da that she's well?"

"I told you, no one's heard anything. You would think that she *would* tell them where she is, because even though her cousin, Robert Hartwood, will get the title, she's still the one who'll get most of the money. After Mr. Hartwood's marriage, though, he'll probably push Lord and Lady Bayton to have Lady Temperance declared dead. I would; if she can't be bothered to claim a hundred thousand pounds or whatever it is, the next marquis should get it."

The tip of Coll's pencil broke. *A hundred thousand pounds?* That much blunt—or half, or even a third of it—made for one hell of a motive to kill a lass. Why hadn't she said anything? He'd been doing his investigating based on someone being embarrassed if she was discovered. "Are ye certain she's worth that much?" he forced out.

"That's the rumor. I think her parents haven't disowned her yet because having that much money still attached to her might encourage her to return, wouldn't you think?"

"Aye, ye'd think so."

Abruptly, Eloise laughed. "If you're thinking of finding her for yourself, Coll, you'd best get a move on—and hope the rumors about the butcher or the French trapper aren't true."

It took every bit of willpower he had to grin back at her.

"That much money does make the lass sound a wee bit more attractive, doesnae?" He clenched his jaw beneath his smile. "Her cousin—what's his name again? Have ye met him?"

"Robert," she repeated. "Robert Hartwood. I've danced with him a time or two. He's very serious. I'm not certain what Caroline Rilence did to get him to propose to her. Maybe she made him laugh, and that addled his brain."

"When are they to wed?"

"At the end of summer, I think. I'm sorry I don't know all the gossip, but I've been planning my own wedding, you know." She took his arm again, squeezing it. "And I need a new hat to wear for Aden and Miranda's wedding. I thought I had one, but it's very like the one Miranda said she's wearing, and I don't want to look like I'm aping her."

"Aden said the wedding was to be a wee affair with nae but family and the pastor."

"And a few of mama's friends. And luncheon afterward. People always talk about weddings, regardless of who they're for, Coll. I don't want anyone to be talking about my poor choice of hat." She put her hands on her hips. "So either help me look for one, or go away."

"A few of mama's friends" could mean anywhere between five and five hundred people. He hoped Aden knew that, though his crafty brother likely did. Which meant Aden had agreed to it, and he and Francesca were well on their way to making amends.

Cursing under his breath, Coll kept pace behind his sister and continued looking through his notes. Aden might have forgiven their mother for fleeing Scotland, but *he* had no reason to do so. The woman hadn't helped him with anything but frightening off lasses at the theater. And as for her claim that she'd sent letters he'd never received and that she'd never received the letters he'd sent her, he didn't believe it. That would mean someone—his da, Angus MacTaggert—had taken hold of them.

He slowed his charge through the milliner's shop. Earl Aldriss, Angus MacTaggert, was a damned stubborn man. He clung to the old ways and had raised his three sons to be wild, independent, and suspicious of anything English. Especially their own mother. Did it make a difference if she'd written? Letters didn't change the fact that she'd left the three of them behind, or that she'd never returned. If any letter contained an explanation for *that*, he wanted to see it, by God.

For the moment, though, returning to the Saint Genesius and having another word with Temperance was more urgent. She'd given him perhaps two dozen names, half of which he'd already crossed off thanks to Eloise and her knowledge of the *ton*. Most of them would have no reason in the world to wish her harm, even if she did have a large inheritance waiting for her. That still left four or five names, though, and with what Eloise had just told him, dear cousin Robert Hartwood sat directly at the top.

Comparing Temperance's list with the one he'd made of the guests attending Lady Fenster's idiotic masked soiree, it looked like six people Temperance had known before her flight would be in attendance—including her parents and, more significantly for her safety, her cousin Robert.

He'd used the list as a way to ask questions of Eloise, but now it looked as if he'd be attending. With every damned guest in a mask, though, he had a flea's chance in the ocean of figuring out who it was he needed to watch.

"—new patron of Persephone Jones," one of the other lasses in the shop was saying to her companion. "Didn't you know? And he's supposedly after a wife."

Coll looked over at her. A petite blonde lass with curling ringlets framing her face and pouting lips she likely practiced in the mirror for hours. "I am after a wife," he said. "Are ye offering?"

The young lady squeaked like a mouse—and fainted to the floor. The other lasses rushed to surround her like a herd of cows protecting a calf, and with a short grin, he turned and left the shop.

The proper set, then, called him Persephone's patron. He wasn't her damned patron. He didn't help her find roles or shop her about to other theaters. He was her damned lover, and her friend. And for the moment, her protector. Whether he wanted any or all of those things to continue indefinitely didn't signify at the moment, because firstly he needed to keep her alive, and to stop whoever was trying to murder her.

The name he'd circled, the one most likely to try to kill her, had to be her cousin. In the Highlands, he'd have ridden to the man's house, called him outside, and either beat him to a bloody pulp or outright ended him. But this was London, where people were civilized and family only tried to stab a relation in the back, not in the front. And so he had to be patient and careful, and figure out how to get himself close enough to Robert Hartwood to determine whether he was a villain—all while he didn't even know what the man looked like.

Putting the list back in his pocket, he swung up on Nuckelavee. Identifying a man at a costume party without letting anyone else, including said man, know he was being tracked—that would be tricky. But he did happen to know one person who could point him out and who wouldn't ask too many sticky questions, because she already knew the secret he'd promised to carry.

Would Temperance attend a ball in Mayfair, though? Even a masked one? If she wouldn't do it for him, perhaps he could convince her to do it for herself. For them, because he damned well wanted to dance with her.

* * *

Temperance took the tray of glasses out of Gregory's hands. "I can manage," she told him, chuckling at a story Flora was telling about her early days working backstage at the Saint Genesius. "You stay and attempt to explain our general insanity to your brother."

"I doubt anyone could do that," her footman returned, but resumed his seat on the long couch.

"They all adore ye," a deep Highlands brogue came from behind her as she entered the quiet kitchen.

"We're family, I suppose. Lord knows everyone else thinks us mad." Setting down the tray, she turned to face him. "Thank you for coming tonight. The little ones are very impressed with your title and accent."

"And my kilt. The littlest bairn, Michael, tried to pull off his trousers and wrap a napkin about his waist."

"Well, it's a very attractive kilt. I can hardly blame him." The kilt was far from the only attractive thing about him, but he'd probably already overheard both Flora and Beth refer to him as a Scottish god enough times tonight.

"Are ye truly worth a hundred thousand pounds?"

She was immediately glad she'd already put down the tray. "And where did you hear such a thing?" she managed, fluttering one hand.

"My sister. Dunnae fret, I wasnae talking about ye. But she said ye were worth a hundred thousand quid, and that yer parents likely havenae cast ye off because they hope the money's enough to convince ye to return."

The pleasant face her parents continued to produce for public use constantly amazed her. Perhaps they were where she'd gotten her talent for acting after all. "I imagine the reason my parents haven't had me declared dead or disowned me is because then my cousin Robert would know he has the title and money coming to him, and he would cease to bow to their every whim. By dangling that money, they keep control." She sighed. "And no, last I knew, it wasn't a hundred thousand pounds. It was closer to fifty thousand."

"That's nae a thing to scoff at, lass. Th—"

"It's how they attempted to control me, as well," she interrupted. "I would have the money under my own name after they died. Until then, I'd best do as they say, or it would all go to Robert."

"Eloise thinks that after Robert weds, he'll press yer parents to have ye declared dead."

"He probably will. I doubt he'll succeed." She picked up a dishcloth, wiped her hands, and tossed it down again. "I don't want the money. And I certainly don't wish to be valued for it, as I was with Dunhurst." Temperance eyed him. Of course she hadn't mentioned the money. It always came down to that. Even with Coll, who needed money to keep Aldriss Park funded. If he had her, he wouldn't need to respect his mother's wishes. And while the idea that he had a legitimate reason to want to marry her had a certain appeal to it, despite what the rest of Society thought of her, she didn't want to drag him into that game. No one ever won, except for her parents.

"Temperance," he began, lowering his voice so no one beyond the kitchen would be able to hear him, "fifty thousand pounds equals fifty thousand reasons for someone to kill ye, if they thought it would give yer parents leave to hand over the money."

She stared at him. "You think . . ." Choking on the words, she fetched the bottle of cooking wine and took a swig from it. "You think *Robert* is trying to kill me?"

"It's the best motive I can see," Coll returned mildly, "unless there's someone else who'd inherit it after him." He shrugged. "Ye know he's betrothed, aye? Set to wed at the end of the summer."

"Yes. To Caroline Rilence. We went to school together."

Temperance grimaced. "I keep up with the Society pages. I like to know who's in Town, who's marrying whom, and whether I'm still alive or not."

"It's a smart thing to do. I'd expect it of ye." Stepping forward, he took the wine from her hand, set the cork back, and returned it to its shelf. "I need to take a look at Robert Hartwood, both in person and on paper. But I also need to be subtle about it."

Her own cousin, trying to murder her over money? Such a thing wasn't unheard of, of course, but for heaven's sake. She'd been gone for nearly eight years. "I've been missing for a long time," she said aloud. "If it's Robert, why now?"

"He's here in London. Mayhap he saw ye onstage and recognized ye. Rather than go to yer parents, he reckoned he'd see to it that ye nae reappeared. And he's to wed, so blunt's likely on his mind."

"No. I can't believe it. We were never close, but he's not some devil."

"The truth doesnae care if ye believe it or nae. It just is. We only need to find it." Approaching her again, he pulled a small vial from his pocket. "Take a whiff of this, lass, but dunnae touch it."

Scowling, she waited while he uncorked it, then leaned in to take a tentative sniff. "Garlic," she said aloud.

"Like that whisky ye didnae drink?"

She sniffed again. "Yes. What is it?"

Corking it again, he returned it to his pocket. "Arsenic." His expression grim, he put his hands on her hips. "That wasnae bad whisky, lass. It was poison."

Good heavens. All those little things she'd wondered about in passing—they weren't simply coincidences or accidents. Someone had been trying to kill her for at least a fortnight.

"Persephone," Coll said, and she blinked.

"Yes. I'm listening."

"I need someone who can point your cousin out to me, who can tell me what he's about without half of London noticing." His grip on her firmed. "There's to be a ball on Sunday, at Lady Fenster's house. A masked ball. If ye—"

Ice shot through her. "No! I will not go there with you!" Making a fist, she pounded against his unyielding chest.

He only drew her closer. "I need ye to help me help ye," he went on in the same even tone. "I'll nae let a thing happen to ye. I swear it on Scotland, on my own family's blood."

"And what if my p-parents are there, and they recognize me?" Blackness edged her vision, surrounding her.

"Then we'll go to the Highlands," he whispered. "Ye and me. Nae a soul would dare come for ye there. Nae with me and all of the MacTaggerts and Clan Ross standing with ye."

Shutting her eyes, she lowered her cheek against his chest. The hard beat of his heart sounded steady but swift—he wasn't nearly as calm as he pretended. That realization actually steadied her a little. She wasn't the only one having difficulty with this plan of his.

"I can't, Coll. I'm sorry. It's . . . Ask me to do anything else."

She felt his sigh. "Dunnae fret, my lass. I'll figure out another way. I'm sorry to upset ye."

"Please don't make any of them suspicious. I don't want them back in my life. Any of them. Promise me, Coll."

His arms enfolded her. "I promise ye, *mo chridhe*."

"Thank you." Whatever he'd called her in Gaelic, it sounded lovely, and she left it at that. The last thing she wanted to know was that he'd called her a fool or an idiot.

"Do ye think Beth or Albert would object if I brought a wee kilt for Michael to the theater tomorrow?"

Albert, Beth's husband, would likely faint at the idea

of a viscount bringing his youngest son a gift. "I think that would be lovely."

"I'll do it first thing; I've Aden's wedding to attend in the afternoon. I reckon I'll leave my men with ye and come back here before dinner."

"Your brother is marrying tomorrow. You need to be there for as long as he wants you about. And I imagine your men will want to be there, as well. You said they came down from Scotland with you."

"Aye, they'd prefer it." His sigh felt warm in her hair. "Ye could come with me to the wedding. It's to be a small ceremony, with just family and the lass's dearest friends."

"I don't seem to fit in either of those categories," she said dryly, deeply surprised at how tempted she was to spend the day with him, despite all the glares and snubs she was likely to receive. In a sense, she even welcomed the insults, because that meant none of them had any idea of her true identity.

"Ye're my friend, I reckon. And I've nae upset the household for days. Hell, I've barely set foot in Oswell House for days. They'll all be thinking I've gone soft. Come with me."

She would be safer in his company. And it would allow him to focus his attention on his brother and the wedding. Yes, it would be quite the magnanimous gesture on her part—or so she could tell herself. "Very well," she muttered. "But only because I've kept you from causing an uproar for days."

He chuckled. "Mostly, anyway."

When she looked up at him, he bent his head and kissed her, soft and slow and achingly gentle. She'd seen him angry, though with her he'd never shown more than frustration. Coll MacTaggert would be a formidable enemy, and she was glad—more than glad—that he'd taken her side in this mess. She could claim it was gratitude she felt toward him, but she'd been grateful on occasion before, and these deep yearnings and longings had never been part of it.

"Just don't expect that your mother will be unexpectedly delighted to see me," she warned, for her sake as much as his. It would be easy to sink into that daydream, where Persephone Jones could marry Lord Glendarril and she could continue acting while he . . . well, in her daydream, she supposed he would decide that he did actually prefer London to the Highlands, and he would have no qualms about her continuing to act while he simply stayed by her side at the theater all day and pleasured her all night. Surely that would be enough to keep a man accustomed to hard work and authority more than occupied.

"This isnae about Lady Aldriss," he replied, kissing Temperance again.

Good heavens. With a last kiss, she pushed at him, and he released her. "I'll come with you tomorrow," she said, forcing her voice to remain steady. "But you still need to find a wife."

Coll tilted his head. "Tem—"

She put a hand over his mouth. "Don't you try to charm me. Go find a damned wife. The sooner, the better. For all of our sakes."

"*Ceannairceach boireannach,*" he murmured, his voice muffled beneath her palm.

"What does that mean?"

"I called ye stubborn and rebellious, because ye are," Coll said, pulling her hand down. "We're a good pair. At least think about that, before ye prance off to the theater again. I know ye dunnae want to hear it, but there it is."

"I am not prancing anywhere," Temperance stated, scowling. "I have an occupation—a job where I work and am paid—and that is how I afford this house, my clothes, and my meals. Simply because you live off your mother's charity and then justify it by turning around and insulting her doesn't give you the right to insult me."

For a long moment, he glared down at her, his green eyes nearly black in the dim light of the kitchen. "I do live off her charity, I reckon," he said, his voice flat. "And I'll continue to do so, because her charity also keeps crops in the fields and thatching over the heads of my cotters. Most other lairds have turned their lands over to sheep-grazing and burned out their own people. The MacTaggerts havenae, and we willnae. Even if it means bowing to the will of a Sassenach countess when she tells me I have to marry." He turned and headed for the door leading to the narrow alleyway and the street beyond. With a yank, he opened it, strode through, and slammed it behind him.

Now she'd done it. She wouldn't have to fret about choosing between him and the Saint Genesius any longer, at least, and she wouldn't have to keep her heart locked inside her chest so tightly it ached whenever he walked into the room. She picked up the tray of glasses, grasping for a heroine she'd once played whose heart had been as wounded—but frowned before slamming it down again. This was not a stupid play.

She'd railed against being everyone's heroine, being some fabled fictional female, and then when she met a man who liked her for herself, she drove him away. Yes, she liked her life, and yes, she'd found a safe place to live and to . . . be. But the most idiotic thing of all was that she *wasn't* safe. All she was now was alone.

The door opened again. "I'll be by for ye at noon," Coll said. "Two of my lads will sleep in yer front room, and the other two will stay on watch. They'll trade off, and ye're nae to leave the house without all four of them. And lock this damned door."

This time the door clicked shut in an almost civilized

fashion. For a moment, Temperance felt frozen on the outside, while her insides caught fire.

He wasn't gone. He hadn't left. Coll, the amazingly stubborn man, had bent. She'd insulted him in probably the worst way anyone could—accused him of choosing to live on an Englishwoman's charity—and he was still taking her to a wedding tomorrow. A wedding where her presence would do nothing but cause him more trouble.

Abruptly, her bones unlocked, and she sagged against the table. She'd known he would be trouble for her, but she hadn't given more than a passing thought to the idea that she could also cause a great deal of trouble for him. That she had been, from the moment he'd mentioned her name, or her faux name, to his family. And still, he remained.

"Miss Pers—goodness, are you all right?" Flora said, hurrying into the room to put a steadying arm around her shoulders.

"I'm fine," Temperance lied. "Just a dizzy spell. Would you lock the kitchen door, if you please?"

"Good heavens, yes. Gregory should have locked it an hour ago. Foolish man. How he manages to keep his head on his shoulders, I'll never know." Releasing her, the maid stepped over to secure the door. "Do you wish for some water? Or something stronger? I do notice the giant man isn't here any longer."

She shook her head. "Give me a moment to catch my breath. Coll is taking me to his brother's wedding tomorrow."

Flora blinked at her. "That would make me tumble to the floor myself. His mother is Lady Aldriss, isn't she? One of the Saint Genesius's patrons? Oh, dear, I hope she doesn't send an angry letter to Mr. Huddle. Not when you already have Scotsmen swarming all over the stage."

Temperance had forgotten that Lady Aldriss not only had a seasonal box at the Saint Genesius, but that she contributed to the theater's annual upkeep, as well. Charlie wouldn't like it at all if one of his troupe made her angry, even if she was his lead actress. The countess wielded a great deal of influence in Mayfair. If she turned her back on the Saint Genesius, others would, as well. "I shall be humble and grateful," she decided. "I'm curious to see an aristocratic wedding."

"I would be curious myself," Flora agreed. "Just don't be too curious, or she'll think you're digging your hooks into Glendarril."

Oh, it was too late for that. She hadn't dug in her claws, but somehow, they'd both gotten tangled up in each other. And she was halfway to hoping that neither of them found a way out.

Chapter Fourteen

"Stands Scotland where it did?"

MACDUFF, *MACBETH* ACT IV, SCENE III

Where the devil are ye off to?" Niall asked, leaning over the balcony railing to peer into the foyer below.

He wore his dress kilt, as Coll did: beneath a black coat and red waistcoat, a black leather sporran with red tassels and an embossed silver cantle across the top, and gillie brogues tied up his calves for once, rather than boots. Aden had dressed the same, and while it felt stiff and formal, the three of them standing together would no doubt put the fear of the devil into any enemies of Clan Ross.

"I'll meet ye at St. George's," Coll shot back, sliding his spare *sgian-dubh* into one stocking, with only the hilt and top of the scabbard showing.

"Coll."

Straightening, he looked up at his youngest brother. "What? I'll nae be late. Ye ken I wouldnae miss Aden's wedding any more than I'd miss yers. And I rode all the way from London to Gretna Green for that one."

Niall's eyebrows dove together. "I only wanted to ask if ye had any news about the lass. It's nae an easy thing, to have someone after ye."

As Niall spoke, his wife, Amy, joined him at the railing. She wore a simple peach muslin dress embroidered with myriad yellow and green flowers and a peach bonnet topped with fresh flowers, and her hands were sheathed in white, wrist-length kid gloves. Coll made note of it all. He had no idea what Sassenach guests wore to a wedding, and he wanted to be sure Temperance had as little to worry over as possible. She hadn't been to a wedding since her own, he'd wager—and she hadn't made it to that one. It had been eight years ago, anyway, and who knew what had altered since then.

"Amy, ye look very fine," he drawled, waiting for Smythe to pull open the front door.

Smiling, she dipped a curtsy. "As do you. Half the women in London will be sighing at the sight of the three of you today."

He scowled. "I preferred yer wedding, lass. Brief, nae crowded, and with a fine, homecooked meal after."

Amy laughed. "And a good price offered for any shoeing we needed done before we turned the horses around for London."

Niall leaned over and kissed her. "I'll wed ye again, more proper this time, if ye like."

Cupping his face in her gloved hands, she kissed him back. "I am utterly content, husband. Don't fret. We'll have plenty of things to celebrate in more proper fashion."

Judging by the glow of her cheeks and the light in her eyes, they'd be celebrating the first something in less than nine months. Coll grinned. "The two of ye are making my teeth ache. I'll see ye at the church."

As Gavin rounded the corner of the house with horse and phaeton in tow, Coll paused. The groom was in his best finery as well, topped with a proper Scottish tam and what looked like an ostrich plume dyed black.

"Gavin, ye're lovely!" he exclaimed.

The groom's cheeks turned a burning red. "I'm to drive

the barouche from the church. I'll nae have any man saying I didnae dress to honor the bride and groom."

"Nae a man would dare." Coll climbed up to the seat and leaned over to take the leads from the groom. "My thanks."

"Just between ye and me, m'laird," Gavin said, stepping up to the front wheel and lowering his voice, "have ye mentioned to yer *bràthair* that ye mean to disrupt his wedding with yer lass?"

"Today is for Aden and Miranda," Coll returned flatly. "I've nae intention of disrupting a thing. I'm bringing the lass to keep her safe from harm and in my sight, and so most of the lads can join us."

Nodding, the groom stepped back again. "As ye say, then, m'laird."

Aye, he did say. He and the lass had an agreement. Whether he wanted her close by him or whether she'd accused him of being soft for acquiescing to his mother's demands, she needed protecting.

As for that accusation, aye, he'd decided to give in, because it wasn't just about his pride being pricked. Francesca Oswell-MacTaggert funded all of Aldriss Park—four thousand acres, three hundred men, women, and bairns, dozens of farms and shops and two fishing villages, peat cutters, seaweed harvesters, and the mansion with all of its servants and gardeners and grooms and cooks. In a good year, they very nearly paid for themselves, but more often than not, the expenses outweighed the profits. If not for the Oswell-MacTaggert money, half the cotters would have had to leave for America, and the land would all be valued for nothing but sheep-grazing.

Temperance had set out on her own at age twenty. She'd left her family and her home and friends and everything familiar, and she'd found a way not just to survive, but to flourish. He admired that a great deal. He admired *her*. But she had only herself to look out for, and that gave her certain freedoms and luxuries that he didn't have.

When he stopped in front of her small house, Gregory pulled open the door and stepped aside. Before Coll could call out a greeting to him, his tongue froze in his mouth, his jaw unhinging itself to hang open.

Two kilted Highlanders ahead of her, watching their surroundings like hawks, Temperance Hartwood walked out the front door. She wore a perfectly proper peach and lavender gown of muslin and lace, a matching lavender shawl over her shoulders, and a bonnet decorated with lavender and yellow flowers over hair redder than a sunset. The combination of propriety and daring simply . . . stunned him. Somewhere deep in his chest, a small stone broke free and vanished. She still wanted to be around him, and he damned well wanted to be around her.

"Good glory," he muttered under his breath, shifting in the seat to offer her a hand up. "Good morning, Persephone."

She inclined her head. "Coll. I half thought you might have changed your mind about me accompanying you today."

Taking her hand, he half lifted her up over the wheel and onto the phaeton's seat beside him. "We had an argument," he said, shrugging as he clucked to the long-legged bay. "I reckon we both made some valid points."

"No, we didn't," she countered, holding onto the seat with one hand as they lurched into motion. "Our circumstances might be similar, but you've stayed for the sake of people who rely on you. That's noble."

Coll cleared his throat. "Ye had a quiet night, I hope. I didnae have any word from my lads about any trouble."

She nodded. "Yes. I'm afraid I didn't sleep well, but no one attempted to murder me."

He hadn't slept well either, and for him that was highly unusual. But then it had been the first night in four that he'd spent in his own bed. "I nearly rode over here twice to check on ye. And I nearly went to find yer cousin and flatten him out of principle."

"We have no proof. We actually have no proof that anything intentional is afoot." Someone on the street shouted her name, and, immediately putting on a smile, she turned and waved. "And Robert? He has no sense of humor, and we were never close, but that doesn't make him a murderer. Or someone who would hire a murderer."

He didn't like that people recognized her. Even her guise of being Persephone Jones wasn't safe any longer. Keeping her safely locked up in her house, though, would kill her just as surely as bullet. Temperance never seemed to be still; physically and mentally she could run circles around most everyone he knew. She might even be able to give Aden a thrashing.

"Until we know who it is, I'll be suspicious of everyone, if ye dunnae mind. It doesnae take any great courage to offer someone else a few quid to drop a sandbag at the right moment." That bothered him even more than the idea of a villain out there—how many people had he paid to make certain Temperance suffered a fatal accident?

She gazed at him for a long moment, which he pretended not to notice as he guided the phaeton toward Hanover Square and St. George's Church. Finally, she cleared her throat, clasping her hands in her lap. "Tell me the names of three women you're considering for marriage."

For a moment, he couldn't conjure another woman's name to save his life. He'd found the one he wanted, for God's sake, and the entire world thought him too good for her. If anything, the truth was just the opposite. "Elizabeth Munroe," he said, not because she would suffice, but because Temperance had asked for names. "Lady Agnes Mays. Polymnia Spenfield."

"Isn't Miss Spenfield one of the Spenfield girls? There are five of them, yes? Their parents auction off a horse every year to try to get men to attend their ball."

"Aye. And I didnae even win the horse, so it must be true love."

Because he looked for it, he saw her jaw clench and her hands tighten their grip on each other. *Good.* She did want him, at least a little—even if she wouldn't admit to it. He didn't know how they'd manage it, either, but he knew who he wanted.

"Good, then," she said a bit quietly. "When will you propose?"

"I was being sarcastic, and ye know it," he snapped, pulling the phaeton to a halt and ignoring the drivers who began protesting behind them.

"Coll, we'll be late."

"Nae, we willnae. I have someaught to say to ye, Temperance Hartwood. I love ye. I ken that that doesnae change a thing, that to the world ye're an actress and I'm the oldest son of an earl, no matter how unfit these Sassenachs think I am to be a lord. I have a duty, and ye have a life ye've made for yerself. But I've looked for nine weeks—and longer than that in the Highlands—to find a woman with whom I'd care to spend my life, and I damned well know when I've found one. It's someaught I'm willing to fight for. But nae if ye dunnae feel the same about me. So, do ye? Either lie or tell me the truth, but ye'd best make certain I believe ye."

Flicking the reins, he sent them off again, his gaze on the bay's ears. If this was something he could solve with brute force, it would have been well settled days ago. But as strong as he was, he couldn't overthrow an entire way of life. Figuring out a way they could remain together would be another kind of battle altogether—and it was one he had no real idea how to fight. If he didn't have her heart, he couldn't win, regardless. And he would be an even greater fool than the Sassenachs currently thought him.

"I'm still—I'm still an actress, Coll. As far as the world knows, and as far as I want anyone else to know, I'm just some common-born girl who prances about onstage in front of strangers. You're Viscount Glendarril. One day, you'll be Earl Aldriss."

"I didnae ask ye who we are, my lass. I asked ye if ye loved me."

She opened her mouth, then shut it again. "Do you have any idea of the scandal that would ensue?"

Shrugging, he slowed the bay as they turned up Regent Street. "I didnae say I had a solution. Nae yet, anyway. I only want to know if ye feel at all for me what I feel for ye."

She sat silently beside him for so long that he began to fear he *had* misjudged every bloody thing between them. If she'd only wanted a protector to keep the other wolves away, if every man at whom she smiled fell in love with her, then he supposed he would go and find himself a wife tomorrow and spend the remainder of his life wondering why the devil he hadn't managed to be more charming, or wield a sharper wit, or simply be more civilized, and how he'd misjudged her so horribly.

"How I feel doesn't matter," she finally muttered. "It doesn't change anything."

"If how ye felt didnae matter, ye'd have married His Grace Dunhurst eight years ago. How ye felt, lass, changed yer entire life. So aye, it matters. And it bloody well matters to me."

Abruptly, she shifted closer, laying her head against his shoulder and wrapping a hand about his arm. "Of *course* I'm in love with you, Coll MacTaggert," she blurted out, her voice shaking a wee bit at the end. "How could I not be? You are mountains and craigs and rocky streams and winter winds and the first breath of springtime. My first taste of springtime."

Well. He believed that. She'd put it much more poetically than he had, of course, but it rang true. His heart stopped beating for a breath, and then resumed again, hard and strong. "Ye do have a way with words, lass."

And if he didn't kiss her right then, he might well catch fire from the heat of wanting her. Reaching for her free hand, he pulled up the bay with the other.

"People will see us."

"Let 'em." While the drivers of the milk and hay wagons behind them began shouting and cursing again, he bent his head and took her mouth. Her soft lips molded against his, warm and wanting. "*Is mise mo chridhe*," he murmured.

She leaned her forehead against his, her bonnet shading them both from the onlooking passersby. "What does that mean?"

"Ye're my heart," Coll translated. He needed to apologize to Niall and Aden for scoffing at their descriptions of being in love. He *had* simply . . . known.

And while she'd been correct that saying the words didn't change anything, didn't make her troubles go away or make his family suddenly accepting of a lass who preferred to be thought of as a commoner, it did give him a reason to fight. And a cause worth fighting for.

"Goodness." Straightening, Temperance cleared her throat. "We should get going before we start a riot."

"Aye." Taking the reins back in both hands, he snapped them and the bay jumped back into a trot.

Today belonged to Aden and Miranda, and he meant to do his utmost not to take away from that. But if anyone wanted to challenge him over his wedding guest, he would take on all comers, and do it with a smile on his face. Temperance Hartwood, or Persephone Jones, or whatever she chose to call herself, loved him. Aye, today he could fight the world and knock it on its arse.

He nearly hadn't said the words, because he knew as well as she did that being in love didn't solve anything. Part of him hadn't wanted to make things harder for her. But the other part, the stubborn part that spoke its mind, had demanded to know that she wanted what he wanted. And knowing now that she did, it *did* change everything.

Temperance had driven past St. George's Church in Hanover Square on two or three occasions, but she'd never strolled between the stern ionic columns or seen the interior of Mayfair's parish church. Actresses didn't receive invitations to aristocratic weddings. Not until today, anyway.

Keeping her hand tight around Coll's black-sleeved arm, her eyes respectfully lowered as she wondered if she would be struck down by lightning for daring to tread upon the stone floor, she walked through the main doors at the rear of the church.

A small group of people stood near the altar, enough red and black and white-patterned kilts among them that she knew it had to be the MacTaggerts. "I'll just sit in the back, Coll," she whispered. "Please don't make a to-do about it."

To her surprise, he inclined his head. "Nae in the back; I want ye away from the doors," he murmured, but paused halfway up the rows of wooden pews. "This should do ye," he said, and handed her onto the bench. "The lads know to keep their eyes open for anyone nae invited, but if ye see someaught that troubles ye, I expect ye to make some noise."

"I'm certain that would go over well," she returned dryly.

"I dunnae care how it goes over, lass. I dunnae want to risk ye being harmed. If ye dunnae agree, I'll forego standing with the groom and sit here with ye."

She knew him well enough to realize he meant every word he said. "I will make a great deal of noise," she muttered. "Go stand with your brother."

He had the bad manners to grin at her before he turned away and strolled the rest of the way up to the front of the church. It was a pretty place, with more white columns inside, dark, polished wood, and a large painting of Christ and his disciples that she thought had to be the work of William Kent behind the altar. Lovely as it was, the people held far more interest for her.

And they'd definitely noticed her, as well. She recognized the youngest brother, Niall, as he said something to the pretty, blonde-haired woman at his side, nodding at her as she turned to look. Beyond them, a slender young lady with black hair and light green eyes bounced up on her toes and whispered at the tall young man beside her. That would be Eloise, she reasoned, the youngest MacTaggert, and the one who'd been raised English, which would make the young man with the fading black eyes her betrothed, Matthew Harris.

On the other side of the stunningly pretty, white-wearing bride and her poetical-looking, kilted husband-to-be, stood an older couple that had to be the bride's parents. The petite woman wearing a gorgeous blue gown sewn with yellow beading, her hair a peppered black and gray beneath an elegant matron's hat, would be Lady Aldriss. Temperance held her breath as the countess turned to look at her, breathing out only when the lady turned away again.

A dozen or so other guests sat in the first two rows of

pews, standing only when the black-and-white clothed pastor stepped forward. Temperance hurriedly climbed to her feet as well, only retaking her seat when he motioned accordingly. She knew most of the words he spoke, because eight years earlier, another pastor in another church had recited them to her as they rehearsed a wedding that would never happen.

Halfway through the ceremony, an older man with generous sideburns and a lean, stern face took a seat one row in front of her and off to the side. Temperance swallowed. Coll had said his men were on the lookout for strangers, and this man had made it past them. Could she assume, then, that he was another friend of the family? If so, why hadn't he joined the group at the front of the pews?

Without knowing whether he was there for the wedding or for her, she wasn't about to make a ruckus, whatever she'd promised Coll. Instead, she kept her attention squarely on his profile. If he turned to look at her, or if she saw a knife or a pistol in his hands, then she would most assuredly make some noise.

When the pastor introduced the couple as man and wife and Aden swept his bride into his arms for a kiss that made even Temperance blush, the rest of the guests stood and crowded forward to congratulate the couple. The older man remained seated, as did she. As he finished pounding his brother on the back, Coll turned to look at her— and froze, his gaze on the late-arriving man.

Her heart leaped into her throat. Did he recognize a threat? He certainly had an instinct for knowing when she might be in danger. When Coll abruptly strode forward, she stood, moving away as quickly as she could.

"*Athair?*" he bellowed. "What the devil are ye doing here?"

The rest of the group turned as well. Persephone saw baffled expressions on the faces of the Harris parents and the other guests, surprise on the two remaining MacTaggert brothers, a delighted grin growing on the face of their sister, and the Countess Aldriss going white as the bride's gown.

"Papa?" Eloise exclaimed, hurrying forward. "Is it you?"

Papa. Angus MacTaggert, Earl Aldriss. Coll's father. Clutching a hand over her heart in relief, Temperance sank onto the pew. *Thank heavens*.

"What am I doin' here?" the earl replied. "I had a letter that said ye'd lost yer mind, Coll. That's what I'm doing here."

Coll immediately stopped, his gaze sliding over to meet hers. "I've nae lost a damned thing," he stated, returning his attention to his father. "Ye've two married sons, though. Come and meet all of yer daughters."

Another kind of worry entirely speared through Temperance as young Eloise flung her arms around her father before his more restrained daughters-in-law added their greetings. She didn't know much about Lord Aldriss, except that he'd claimed to have collapsed onto his deathbed when his sons had been summoned to London, and that he'd encouraged the boys to live rough-and-tumble lives.

The fact that he'd traveled here, and that he'd arrived barely a week after she and Coll had met, told her several things. Whoever had sent him word about Coll's proclamation that he would marry her had spared no expense at getting word to the Highlands, and the earl had spared no time in making his way down to London. Something had upended the patriarch of the MacTaggerts, and she could make a good guess at what that thing had been. Her.

"Let's all return to Oswell House, shall we?" Niall said loudly, over the growing mutters. "The countess has set out a luncheon for everyone in the garden."

"Yes," Lady Aldriss said, visibly squaring her shoulders. "Everyone, my friends and family, please join us there. We have much to celebrate."

Moving toward the rest of the MacTaggerts, the countess touched a finger to the necklace she wore. To most everyone, it was likely an innocent, unconscious gesture, but to Temperance, with her study of moods and emotions, it spoke volumes. Lady Aldriss was *nervous*. Extremely so.

But then she was presently looking at a man—her husband—whom she hadn't seen in seventeen years.

Seventeen years—very nearly their daughter's lifetime. Temperance looked at Coll again, at his wary expression, his coiled fists. A man ready to fight his own family over her.

If she simply shook her head at him, he would know that she'd decided that whatever they had—or might have—wasn't worth fighting for. Everything would go back to the way it had been before they'd met, with the exception, of course, that someone wanted her dead. The idea terrified her, but not as much as the thought of not seeing Coll for seventeen years, or ever again. Of watching him marry some other woman simply because he had a duty to do so. Of watching him leave London without her.

"Husband," Lady Aldriss said, stopping a few feet from the earl.

He looked at her for a moment. "Wife." Slowly, he reached out for her hand and brought it to his lips. "Ye look very fine this afternoon."

She freed her hand. "I look older," she countered. "As do you. I assume your being here means we're in agreement about one thing, finally?"

Blowing out her breath, putting out of her head the thought that this would have to be the most brilliant performance she'd ever given, Temperance stepped forward. "Good morning, Lord and Lady Aldriss. Thank you for allowing me to come; I don't know if Coll has told you, but evidently someone is trying to harm me. He insisted that I would be safe here, and I am exceedingly grateful for the reprieve."

Everyone looked at her now, but two pairs of eyes, one dark green and one gray, concerned her more than the others. "Of course," Lady Aldriss said a moment later, her tone clipped. Once a lady was informed that she'd done a kindness, she couldn't very well turn her back, after all.

"I have no wish to be a point of contention on such a momentous day," Temperance went on, smiling at Aden and Miranda. "This is a time for family and friends, and I don't wish to intrude any further than I already have. I should be going."

"Nae," Coll said on the tail of that. "I gave ye my word to keep ye safe."

"If someone's trying to harm ye, lass," the earl put in, "and we've the means to keep them at bay, then I reckon ye shouldnae be going anywhere but with us to have luncheon."

"I . . ." Lady Aldriss closed her mouth over whatever she'd been about to say. "Of course. Coll, we'll meet you at Oswell House. Don't delay. We have things to discuss."

"Oh, I'll be there for that, dunnae ye fret," her oldest son agreed.

He took Temperance's arm, leading her toward the door. "What was that?" he whispered. "This isnae about me doing ye a good turn. I'll nae have it reduced to that."

"And I won't have the lot of you arguing over my lack of breeding in a church," she returned in the same tone. "Give them a moment to think of me as something other than an upstart after a title, for heaven's sake."

Coll cocked his head. "So ye're a damsel in distress?"

"I am someone who was hopefully able to invoke a little bit of sympathy for a minute or two." She took a breath.

"I want you, Coll. You said you're willing to fight for us. I reckon I am as well."

A slow grin touched his handsome face. "Ye reckon, do ye? Then I reckon that now that ye've gotten yerself invited to the house, I may nae let ye leave."

At the moment, that would suit her just fine.

Chapter Fifteen

"Signs of nobleness, like stars, shall shine
On all deservers."

DUNCAN, *MACBETH* ACT I, SCENE IV

The front entry of Oswell House had been draped with white ribbons and red and white roses. Aden would likely have preferred to vanish somewhere private with Miranda, but even the elusive MacTaggert brother knew better than to avoid the friends and family who had aided him in finding his bride. Coll would have preferred to avoid the luncheon himself, because if there was one thing the MacTaggerts excelled at, it was stating their own damned opinions of everything.

At least with guests present, he might have a few moments of peace with Temperance in the Oswell House garden before he dove into the fray. And peace, he'd begun to discover, had its own attractions. A bit of conversation here, a look or stolen kiss there—things he'd altogether underestimated until he'd met Temperance.

No additional MacTaggert wagons had yet arrived, so Angus had either traveled without luggage, or ahead of it. For a man on his deathbed, his father had made it from the Highlands in impressive time. The earl's horse wasn't his usual gray gelding, coincidentally enough named Banquo, but a fast-looking chestnut wearing Angus's tack. He'd changed horses at least once, then.

It was all a wee bit disconcerting; Angus did things on his own time, and while he growled and bellowed whenever he had the chance, rarely had he ever seemed . . . unsettled. This now, would be an exception.

Avoiding the group of servants gathered in the foyer to give Aden and Miranda their congratulations and good wishes, Coll led Temperance through the depths of the house and out to the stately garden. A dozen tables had been set, and a long table sat to one side, laden with plates of sandwiches and cakes and fresh fruit and puddings and pies. So much for a simple luncheon—but then Francesca never did anything halfway.

"It's lovely," Temperance said, taking a half step away from him as Niall appeared with Amy, Eloise and Matthew on their heels.

"I reckon we should sit with Eloise and her beau," he suggested. "I'd like to get a sandwich or two in me before the battle begins."

"If I might suggest," she commented, "you've said yourself that you have a reputation as a fighter. They'll expect that from you, then."

"Are ye suggesting I bring Francesca posies?"

She sent him a sideways look. "I happen to know you are more than a brawler."

"Aye, but I didnae think I'd be facing Angus in addition to Francesca." As he thought about his last few conversations with members of his family, it seemed likely that Eloise had definitely known they'd sent word to the earl. Niall, as well, though as much as he'd have liked to bellow at them for not warning him, neither of them had any reason to think Angus would actually make an appearance in London. After all, their father had sworn on multiple occasions never to set foot there again.

"I very nearly hit him with my reticule when he sat

down in front of me," she said, lowering her voice still further. "And then when you charged at him, I thought—"

"He's an imposing man on a good day." Coll glanced
over his shoulder as the other guests appeared in the garden, along with the bride and groom. "Give me one moment, will ye?"

"Of course."

Sending Eloise a pointed glance, he left her and walked
over to Aden. "I didnae mean to disrupt things for ye," he
said.

Aden shook his head. "I'm married to my lass. Ye didnae disrupt anything as far as I'm concerned. I did nearly
fall down dead when I caught sight of Da, though."

"Ye and me both."

"Do ye love the lass?" his brother asked, his gray eyes
growing serious. "Or is this ye putting yer great foot in the
middle of Francesca's pretty plans?"

The fact that Aden had asked the question about love
said a great deal about how much the middle MacTaggert brother had changed over the past few weeks, as
did the way he grasped the hand of the dark-haired lass
beside him. "I didnae set out to," Coll returned, "but
aye. I love her."

"And dunnae hit me, but ye're certain she's nae after
blunt and a title?"

"That's one thing I'm damned certain of," he said em-
phatically. She might have had a duke's ring on her finger and an inheritance of fifty thousand pounds, but she'd
turned her back on both for a bit of freedom to shape her
own life. "If I could figure out a way to marry her and nae
hurt the civilized part of the family, I'd nae be here for the
argument."

Miranda put a hand on his arm. "If I could give you one
piece of advice today, it would be to follow your heart."
She smiled, her eyes brimming with unshed tears. "I am

also not thinking very logically because I'm practically giddy with happiness."

Smiling, Coll bent down and kissed her on the cheek. "I've nae seen Aden so content," he murmured. "Seeing ye and him, and Niall and Amy, makes me glad we all came down to London."

Aden snorted. "I'm going to write that down. I nae thought I'd hear any such thing coming out of yer mouth."

"Just wait. I'd wager ye'll have a handful of things to write about before the day is finished."

While his brother contemplated that, Coll returned to find Temperance sitting with Eloise and Matthew. Good. Eloise had caught his meaning, then. He took the seat between the two lasses. "Matthew," he said, eyeing Eloise's fiancé. "How's yer beak?"

The younger man reached up to touch his nose carefully. "Painful. And an effective reminder of my errors in judgment."

"I'm glad ye added that last bit. Have ye met Mrs. Jones? Persephone, Mr. Matthew Harris and my sister, Lady Eloise MacTaggert."

Temperance nodded, putting a charming smile on her face. "I'm pleased to meet you. And I hear good wishes are in order."

Eloise beamed. "Thank you. You are . . . My goodness, you're even prettier up close. Your Rosalind made me wish to stand up and cheer at the end of *As You Like It*. Oh, to be such a brave heroine!"

"Thank you, my lady. That's very kind of you to say."

"Oh, pish." Eloise reached over to put her hand on Temperance's. "You are marvelous! I read the review from Adams; he said that at some point the viewer realizes that Mrs. Jones has ceased acting, and has quite simply *become* Rosalind. That's not an exact quote, but I so agree!"

"And yet here she is," Coll interrupted, before Eloise

could begin picking garden roses to toss at Temperance, "nae Rosalind at all."

Temperance furrowed her brow. "I will never have a complaint about someone complimenting my craft, Coll. I think most young ladies wish they could be as daring as Rosalind. I know I did."

Eloise stuck her tongue out at Coll. "Which role are you playing next?"

"We're rehearsing for the Scottish play now. We open in two days."

"Oh, you're going to be Lady Macbeth!" Eloise abruptly put a hand over her mouth. "Am I allowed to say it?"

With a chuckle, Temperance nodded. "It's an odd tradition. Saying the name of the character is perfectly permissible; it appears in the play several times, after all. It's only saying the name of the play that we're all petrified of."

"Thank heavens." Eloise scooted her chair closer. "Is it true what Coll said? That someone is trying to hurt you?"

"It's either that, or I've been having some very poor luck lately."

Coll didn't like that she kept trying to put it all to coincidence, though he could certainly see why she would wish to do so. "It's nae poor luck," he stated. "It's good luck that so far ye've had but some scratches and bruises."

Footmen approached the tables, trays of sandwiches and sweet treats in their arms. Thank the devil. A man could starve before etiquette permitted him to eat. While the others at the table were offered a choice of sweet wines, Smythe appeared with a wee tray holding a glass of lemonade, which he set down at Coll's elbow.

"Thank ye, Smythe," he grunted. It hadn't taken over a day for all of the Oswell House servants to figure out that he didn't drink liquor. In fact, he could swear that on more than one occasion, a liquor tantalus disappeared shortly before he entered a room. He did have a temper when he drank, but he'd only inflicted that on the house once—and it hadn't been entirely his fault. Aden had been the one to drag him back before he'd sobered up, after all.

"My lord," the butler returned with a nod, disappearing toward the luncheon table again.

As he looked up from the lemonade, he caught Temperance looking at him, a contemplative expression on her face. "What is it?"

"You could make the next few weeks so much easier on yourself," she murmured. "A pleasant young lady, a quiet ceremony, an intimate luncheon in the garden, and a glass of lemonade for the groom."

"If that was all I wanted, I could have had it weeks ago," he countered, reaching beneath the table for her free hand. "I prefer a fight, and fire, and roast venison in gravy with my lemonade. And my woman."

On his left, Eloise cleared her throat. "You told me this was for show," she whispered.

"And ye didnae tell me that the countess had sent for Da," he returned.

"She didn't," his sister protested. "She sent him a letter saying she was worried that you'd gone too far because he hadn't bothered to tell his sons about the agreement until payment was due on it."

"So ye knew there was a letter." He lifted an eyebrow.

"And you didn't think there would be one?" she shot back.

The thought *had* occurred to him. Even so, the idea that his father would travel south to London, especially at his estranged wife's request, had seemed so far-fetched that he could scarcely believe that the earl was actually sitting there beside Niall and Amy. "It was a wee bit more effective than I might have expected," he said finally.

"I know. That's actually my papa." Eloise squeezed Matthew's hand. "We've corresponded for years, but I never thought . . ." A tear ran down one cheek. "We're all here. All the MacTaggerts in the same garden. It's been seventeen years."

The remainder of the guests—Lady Aldriss's and Miranda's friends—seemed to have realized the same thing. The conversation seemed muted for a wedding celebration, and the Sassenachs all clung together like chickens when they thought they'd heard a fox.

"Dunnae put much hope in it lasting, Eloise," he said after a moment. "Ye're too young to remember, but I recall all the squabbles and the cursing."

"Considering that I've spent seventeen years waiting to set eyes on you and Aden and Niall, I will put hope in whatever I choose," his sister retorted. "And don't change the subject. Do you mean to marry Mrs. Jones? Where is Mr. Jones?"

Nails dug into his hand, and he shut his mouth over the retort he'd been about to make. "For some reason," Temperance said, "being a widow is much more acceptable to the world than being unmarried. Mr. Jones is a construct. Without him, I could never have rented a house, and I likely would have never been offered a contract with the Saint Genesius."

"A silent husband," Eloise said, with a sly nod. "I like it."

"Grand," Matthew quipped, grinning. "I haven't a chance now of ever getting a word in, have I?"

"None," his betrothed answered brightly.

"Eloise," Lady Aldriss called from the table she shared with Aden, Miranda, and Miranda and Matthew's parents. "A moment, if you please."

Obediently, Eloise and Matthew rose, and after a word with the countess, they ended up taking seats with Matthew's aunt and her three bairns.

"Did ye see that?" Coll grunted. "She didnae want Eloise landing on our side of an argument."

"I can't blame her," Temperance whispered. "I shouldn't have let you talk me into coming. Then you might have had a happy family reunion."

"Nae, because it would have been all of them against me. With ye by my side, I reckon my odds are much improved."

"Yes, I can fling Shakespearean quotes about with great abandon."

His mouth quirked. "And ye wield sarcasm like a sword. Dunnae forget that. Ye've nearly decapitated me more than once."

"Never. The world would be a poorer place without your handsome face in it."

For God's sake, he adored her. "Aden used to say the only difference between me and me without a head would be my height."

She laughed. "That's horrible," she said, covering her mouth with one hand before she gave up, still chortling.

"Aye, the two of ye would get along, nae doubt about that," Coll snorted.

"It would be lovely to have the opportunity to try," she said, her smile softening. "But please don't ruin what you have with them. With your family. You clearly all adore each other. Don't lose that for my sake. I would never forgive myself."

"What happens between my family and me is up to them. They know where I stand." He didn't want to see that relationship hurt, either; every lesson he'd learned over the years had been about the importance of family, and every brawl he'd ever fought had been done with the knowledge that at least two other people in the world would stand with him.

If today and from now on he stood alone, it would

change some things—drastically. But he wasn't standing up to be left alone. He was standing up to be with Temperance. Even if they would only know her as Persephone.

"Coll, that's not a way to begin an argument."

"It's only an argument if they decide they dunnae agree with me." He bit into his third sandwich. "Look at 'em over there, trying to decide if I can be pushed somewhere I dunnae choose to go."

As he spoke, Wallace, one of the pipers they'd brought with them down from the Highlands—and more importantly, one of the lads he'd left to watch Temperance's house—ran into the garden, found him, and skidded to a halt beside the table.

"M'laird, it's on fire."

Coll shoved to his feet. "What's on fire?"

"The house. We were watching the front and back, but then Charles saw smoke and yelled for me, and by the time I got back around the front, the whole first floor was catching. I—"

"My house?" Temperance gasped. "Flora? And Gregory?"

"I dunnae, m'lady. I came here as soon as—"

"Ye stay here," Coll ordered Temperance. "Smythe! She doesnae leave yer sight!"

At the butler's curt nod, and ignoring the demand for information coming from his family, Coll tore through the house and onto the front drive, where he swung into the saddle of the gelding Wallace had ridden. Kicking it in the ribs, he took off at a gallop up Grosvenor and east toward St. John's Wood.

If someone had been watching her house, they would know she wasn't there. Was this an attempt to draw her out? To have her return in a panic for a waiting gunman? Or had the arsonist missed her departure, and this had been yet another attempt on her life?

Cursing, he cut between a phaeton and a furniture wagon and continued north and east. The gray gelding didn't have Nuckelavee's speed or stamina, but despite the noise and traffic, it kept its ears back and kept running. Coll could see the smoke rising as he turned up Charlbert Street and onto Charles Lane. Lines of residents stretched between local wells and the house, buckets passing back and forth.

The upper floor of the house had begun to burn, while the ground floor looked ready to disintegrate into ash at any moment. Still swearing, he jumped down from the horse. "Flora!" he bellowed. "Gregory!"

"Here, my lord!" Gregory, coatless and with his white shirt turned nearly black with soot, limped forward. "It just started burning," he lamented, tears flowing from his eyes, either from the smoke or from the loss.

"Where's Flora?"

"She's in the shade over there," the footman said, pointing to where a cluster of women had gathered, one of them fanning the air with an apron. "We couldn't find Hades. That damned cat—oh, heavens. Persie will be heartbroken."

Coll looked up toward the master bedchamber's front windows. Pulling off his coat, he handed it to the footman. "Stay back from this," he ordered, and jumped to grab the lower eave in his hands.

From there, he levered himself onto the roof and scrambled around the open, smoldering bits to the windows. They were closed. He pulled off his cravat, wrapped it around one hand, made a fist, turned his face away, and punched.

Glass shattered around him. Clearing it away with his elbow, he hopped into the room. "Hades," he called, noting that the bedchamber door stood open. Smoke wafted through the room, pouring out of the opening he'd just made.

"Hades. Come here, boy." Lowering himself onto his stomach, he peered beneath the bed. A pair of reflective green eyes looked back at him. "There ye are. I thought so."

The floor beneath him felt hot. Another minute or two, and the entire house would be on fire. Edging forward, he extended his wrapped hand. The cat swatted at it, hissing, and backed against the wall until it couldn't retreat any further.

Coll took a breath, waiting for the cat to extend a paw again, then shot his hand forward to grab it by the back of the neck.

Rolling onto his feet, he took another glance at the door. Flames curled up along the doorframe. They wouldn't be leaving that way. With the black cat a coiled ball of claws and teeth and tail, he wouldn't have much luck climbing down outside, either.

He could toss Hades down and the cat would likely land on his feet, but then he would flee, and they'd never set eyes on him again. Clenching his jaw, Coll turned the beastie to face him. "We're getting down now. I'm saving ye, damn it all, so dunnae kill me."

With one hand, he freed the bedsheet from beneath the quilted bedspread. Moving as swiftly as he could, he bundled up the cat and his hand and arm, all the way to the elbow. Then he let go of Hades and yanked his arm free, closing the opening with both hands.

With the sheet writhing in front of him, he knotted it, making a sling that he could put around his head and one arm. Claws poked at him, and the beastie hissed like the devil himself, but it would have to do.

Ducking back outside, he took a trio of steps before his left foot went through the roof. Heat licked at him as he caught himself with his hands and freed his shoe again. He'd picked one hell of a time to wear proper shoes rather than sturdy boots.

"Coll!"

He looked down to see Niall on the ground, along with Gavin, Wallace, and a half dozen other men from Aldriss Park and Oswell House riding up to join him. Unslinging the sheet, he held it up. "Catch the cat!"

With as gentle a toss as he could, he sent Hades over the edge of the roof, toward the ground. Niall caught the bundle in his arms, then yelped as claws caught him. Once he'd set the squirming sheet down and taken a step backward, he nodded. "Get down here!"

With fire licking up over the edge of the roof and pouring up through the growing holes around him, it looked as if he wouldn't be escaping with any more dignity than Hades had. The shingle sagged beneath him.

Taking a breath, he pushed away and jumped.

He hit the ground hard with his right shoulder and rolled, just as the second floor collapsed into the first with a thunderous, spitting roar.

All of Temperance's work—six years of her life—lost. No. Taken from her.

"That was too damned close," Niall said, offering him a hand.

Taking it, Coll climbed to his feet. "I couldnae save anything for her."

"Ye saved her cat. And ye're nae dead, which I reckon is a good thing."

Coll gazed at the burning wreckage. She rented the place, he knew, but that didn't make the loss of all her belongings any less. "It's nae enough," he muttered. "I had two lads here, watching, and someone still managed to burn it down."

"M'laird," panted Charles Pitiloch, Clan Ross piper, coming forward. "I reckon ye need to sack me. I heard someaught around the side of the house, and I went for a look. When I came back, the front window was open and the sitting room was on fire."

Swallowing his own anger and frustration, Coll clapped a hand on the smaller man's shoulder. "The lot of ye keeping watch forced 'em to wait until the lass was away," he said, though he wasn't certain that was true. "Ye did all I could expect of ye."

"It doesnae feel that way," Charles said grimly. "I dunnae like getting outfoxed."

"I dunnae either." Releasing his grip, Coll walked over and gingerly picked up the bedsheet. "Find me a basket with a lid, will ye? I reckon Hades will be through this cloth in less than a minute."

"Aye, m'laird." With a swift nod, the ginger-haired piper trotted off toward the gaggle of neighbors.

"Someone *is* trying to kill that lass, then," Niall said, lowering his voice. "I thought mayhap ye'd made that bit up."

"I wish I had." Coll turned his gaze from the burning house. "Thank ye for coming."

Niall shrugged. "Nae MacTaggert stands alone, whether ye've lost yer mind or nae."

"I may see fit to remind ye of that soon."

"She's a lass in danger, Coll, and ye're a man who likes to fight. Ye were bound to like her. But ye do recollect that she's an actress. Are ye certain all this is real? Might she have had her own house burned, so she'd have nae a place to go and only ye to help her?"

If he hadn't known what he did about Temperance Hartwood, it did almost seem like the plot of some play in which Persephone Jones would play the damsel. But he did know who she was and how she'd come to live in that wee, quaint house outside of Mayfair, and why she never went riding in Hyde Park and wore a different-colored wig every day.

Of course, he couldn't disclose any of that to Niall or the rest of his family, but in the end, it didn't matter. "She didnae have a thing to do with this. I'll swear that on a Bible."

Niall took a breath and let it out again. "Then what are ye going to do with her? She's pretty enough and has a manner that doesnae seem any different to me than any aristocratic lass in Mayfair, but she's nae that English 'lady' ye're to wed. Amy says she'll nae be invited anywhere proper, or be asked to stand for any charity or church. Do ye reckon ye'll be enough for her?"

"I wouldnae be if she was after me for my title," Coll returned, working to keep his voice level. These were the same questions the rest of the family would ask, and Niall was likely being more delicate about it than others would be. "I'm more worried that she'll nae leave the stage long enough for me to show her Scotland."

Niall snorted. "If ye wanted to find a way to put Francesca on *her* deathbed, telling her ye want to marry an actress who willnae leave the stage after ye wed her would likely do it."

A great deal of the facts they knew about Persephone Jones weren't true. That one, though, troubled him even more than the coming brawl with the MacTaggerts, because she loved acting, and he couldn't imagine her giving it up voluntarily. He had no idea if the pull of the stage would be stronger than him and his responsibilities in the Highlands.

Chapter Sixteen

"That is a step
On which I must fall down, or else o'erleap,
For in my way it lies."

MACBETH, *MACBETH* ACT I, SCENE IV

The guests were gone. Well, all but one of them, anyway. Lady Aldriss had gone about it so skillfully that Temperance hadn't even noticed until the parents of the bride disappeared into the grand house and she turned back to see empty tables all around her.

For a moment, it looked to be a standoff, with the Mac-Taggerts and Oswell-MacTaggerts huddled around one table, and her alone at the opposite end of the garden. Their numbers had thinned; Niall had run off on Coll's heels, taking a good share of footmen and grooms with him.

Coll had gone to her house, which was apparently on fire. The thought had stuck in her mind more as words than anything that had meaning. The only sharp bits were the names that kept jabbing at her. Flora and Gregory were her family. And Hades . . . Oh, she hadn't even thought to remind Coll about her fierce little cat.

A figure sat opposite her. Temperance wiped the sudden tears from her eyes and looked up. "My lady," she said, the sound of her own voice small and distant.

"I owe you an apology," the countess said. "I doubted your tale about someone attempting to harm you."

"I keep doubting it myself," Temperance conceded with a faint shrug. "Taken separately, they're just . . . minor things. Sandbags falling where I'd just been sitting, a bucket full of bricks falling from the scaffolding in my direction. But then someone ran my hired hack off the road several days ago and overturned it, and they simply drove away. And now . . ." Another tear ran down her cheek, and she brushed it away.

"You haven't received any odd notes or threats?"

"I receive odd notes almost constantly, my lady. A surprising number of people—mostly men—evidently believe I am the fictional character I portray onstage." She grimaced. "At first, I even thought Coll might have been in pursuit of Rosalind."

"But he wasn't."

She shook her head. "No." A handkerchief was pressed into her hand, and she dabbed at her eyes again. "Thank you. And then he said he'd told you that he meant to marry me, and I was—I was mortified."

"But you're not mortified now?"

Temperance looked up, meeting Lady Aldriss's sharp gaze. She *should* still be mortified; she'd chosen to make her way as a commoner, and Coll remained very much a viscount, courtesy title or not. They weren't equals because she'd intentionally made certain they weren't. And yet . . . And yet.

"Lord Glendarril is very persuasive," she said aloud.

"I would say forceful rather than persuasive, but yes, he can be."

"*You* remain mortified, however, if I'm not mistaken." Taking a breath and reminding herself that he had been ready for this battle before she'd learned that her house was very likely burning down, Temperance attempted to focus her thoughts. Mentally, though, she had to compliment the countess on her timing, if not on her compassion.

"Did he tell you that I've ordered him to wed, and within the next seventeen days?"

"Yes."

"Eloise tells me that despite your choice of address, you have actually never been married."

"That is correct. I never have seen why it makes a difference, but even the illusion of a husband makes a female more acceptable, even if said husband is nowhere to be found."

The countess narrowed her eyes just a little. "You have claws, then, I see. Interesting."

"I may at this moment be losing all of my earthly possessions, my lady. That makes me feel as if I need to protect what I have left, even if that is only my pride." She set down the handkerchief. "I am in love with Coll. I find his forthright nature and fierce spirit to be admirable. I have told him that we shouldn't marry, and I have pointed out the problems it would likely cause for both of us. As you said, you have ordered him to marry. If he is going to spend his life with a woman, I would prefer that it be me."

"He has brothers, you know. Lord Aldriss could well cut him off if he does choose to marry you, and the title will go to Aden."

Temperance grimaced. "That would actually make things easier. It is a threat, however, that only he can answer."

Coll and a simpler life seemed very compatible, actually, but Coll being idle here in London while she trod the boards in the evenings didn't seem very realistic. He liked to use his hands, and he was accustomed to having people about who needed his help. Even if his pride allowed her to earn an income for the two of them, he would never stand for being useless. And all that was aside from the fact that she might well have nowhere to live now.

"What if I could offer you the means to live as comfortably as you chose?" the countess said, on the tail of that thought. "You and the nonexistent Mr. Jones could purchase a house in Knightsbridge, and you wouldn't have to pursue parts on the stage."

"I like acting," Temperance replied promptly. "And I do very well with it, thank you very much."

"Even more, she's good at it," came Coll's voice from the doorway behind them.

Temperance whipped around. His coat was missing, his white shirt soiled and black. Soot was smudged across his face, and his expression made her breath catch.

"It's gone, isn't it?" she asked, unable to keep her voice entirely steady.

"Aye. Flora and Gregory are safe, though." He held up a lidded basket in one hand. "And I fetched Hades for ye."

Her hands went to her chest, relief setting a sob tearing loose. "You saved him!" she stammered, hurrying forward and throwing her arms around Coll's hard chest.

He set the basket down and enfolded her in his arms. Safe. He made her feel safe, protected, and wanted, all at the same time. It was a giddy, heady feeling, even with the bleakness around her. "I'm sorry, lass. I couldnae save anything else."

"You're not hurt?" She pushed away to look up at his face, brushing at the smudges there.

"Nae. A wee bit singed, mayhap. And clawed-at." He lifted one hand to show her a pair of deep scratches across his knuckles. "I think Hades may be part Scottish wildcat."

She chuckled, wiping her eyes again. "I wouldn't be at all surprised."

He lifted his gaze, looking over her head toward the table where she'd been sitting. "Ye couldnae wait until I got back here to start yer fight, eh, *màthair*? Did my lass get in a few jabs, at least?"

"Yes, she did," Lady Aldriss said smoothly. "I would have asked to speak with her alone regardless, but my timing did leave something to be desired. I apologize for that."

"You're defending your family name," Temperance replied, facing the countess again. "I do understand pride." Kneeling, she unfastened the lid of the basket and gingerly opened it a crack. "Hello, Hades," she said soothingly. "My good boy, are you well?"

The cat peered out of the narrow opening, then gave a plaintive *meow*. Holding her breath, Persephone let the lid open wider, and the cat surged onto her lap and then curled into a tight ball of fur. *Oh, thank goodness.* Not everything had been lost. Not the little alley cat on whom she'd taken pity six years earlier. She stroked him gently for a minute, then lifted him into her arms and stood again as Coll put a hand under one arm to steady her.

"Thank you, Coll," she whispered, lowering her face into the black fur. "Thank you."

"Ye should have seen him," another male voice announced, "dancing across the rooftop while fire bit at his feet. He didn't make it three steps on the ground again before the entire house collapsed."

Gasping, Temperance grabbed at Coll again with her free hand. "For God's sake, don't do that again," she hissed, looking up at his face. The idea that he might have been killed made her entire being go cold. "Promise me."

"I dunnae intend for any more houses to burn down, *mo chridhe*." With a slight smile touching his mouth, he leaned down and kissed her. "And Niall, keep yer damned mouth shut."

His brother, still wearing his proper coat but also a bit singed, nodded as he made his way over to his wife. "Ye near scared *me* to death, so I wanted to share."

All the MacTaggerts were together now—even the patriarch newly arrived from Scotland, apparently to put a stop to Coll marrying her. But they were family, and they hadn't all been beneath the same roof in a very long time, from what Coll had told her. "I should go see to Flora and Gregory," she said, setting Hades back in the basket. "We need to find somewhere to stay."

"Ye'll stay here," Coll stated, his voice flat.

"I will not. Today is your brother's wedding. You should be celebrating, not worrying if someone will put a torch to Oswell House."

"I'd like to see someone try," he returned, in a tone that made her shiver. She hadn't seen him truly angry since that first night, when he'd punched Lord Claremont. This, though, was something more. "I've already sent a carriage for Flora and Gregory. Ye'll stay here."

"Yes, of course," Lady Aldriss put in, apparently realizing that she'd lost this argument before it could begin. "You'll be safe here while we discover who is trying to harm you." The countess gestured at her daughter. "Eloise, please show Mrs. Jones to the yellow room. And with the number of young ladies residing here now, I believe we can put together a wardrobe for you until you can arrange to have some of your clothing replaced."

Though she had frequently found it baffling, not to mention maddening, the incessant need for the aristocracy to be polite could occasionally be useful. Temperance curtsied. "Thank you, my lady."

Coll took her fingers in his. "Huddle and the rest will be worried about ye. If ye write 'em a note, I'll see it delivered."

This hadn't been at all how she'd thought today would proceed. But then she generally slept late on Saturdays, and so she likely would have been in bed when her house burned down. Coll MacTaggert had saved her yet again.

With a glance at the rest of his formidable family, she nodded and turned to follow Eloise into the house.

One thing was becoming evident. If she meant to be alive for long enough to see how all this turned out, she was going to have to take a stand and begin saving herself. Being the damsel in distress was one thing, but now Coll had nearly been killed. That could not happen, no matter what. If she lost him, it would be because they simply couldn't work out their differences. Not because he'd been killed trying to keep her safe.

"That lad's in love," Angus said in what passed for his quiet voice. Despite not having heard his smooth brogue for seventeen years, Francesca would have known it anywhere, just as she recognized the man despite the mahogany hair turned steely gray and the lines about his deep gray eyes. And his hands—good heavens, she remembered his big hands.

"But is the woman?" she retorted, setting aside all those roiling thoughts and moving past her husband to inform Smythe that in addition to the actress he would have to find room for an earl and two servants, and that the table this evening would be set for ten, rather than the eight she'd expected.

"Ye're the one who spoke with her. What do ye think?" he pursued, keeping up with her.

"I think that you should be speaking with your daughters-in-law and your own daughter, none of whom have set eyes on you before today."

"Nae a kind word for me, then?"

She stopped in her tracks. "I'll have several words for you in five minutes, after I settle the rest of my family."

When she'd written him, she'd expected some sort of help, some order from him that would stop her oldest son's madness before it could hurt the family. But seeing him standing there at the back of the church, an older but unmistakable version of the man who'd stolen her heart and swept her off her feet in a matter of days, all those years ago—it had stopped her breath.

That wasn't supposed to happen. He was stubborn and short-sighted and arrogant and argumentative, and she'd cursed him enough in seventeen years that he should have dropped dead at least a dozen times by now. Why, then, did she have the damnedest desire to find a mirror and check her hair?

Deliberately slowing her steps, she found Smythe and then headed into the house for her study. Oswell House was hers, thankfully; her father had seen to it that not only did the family's wealth remain in her name, but so did the Oswell property. He and her mother hadn't trusted Angus, especially after a courtship that had lasted but a week, and the result was that Angus had never quite caught the wealth he pursued, which had been difficult for a man of his pride to swallow. Looking back, consulting her before every expenditure or improvement had likely been more difficult than she'd ever realized. She took a seat behind her desk, opened the bottom drawer, and produced a bottle of whisky. After pouring herself a glass, she downed it and returned everything to the drawer.

"Ye've done as ye said ye would, then," Angus said, stopping just past the doorway of the room. "Ye civilized my lads, found them wives, and now ye'll have yer claws in them for the rest of yer days."

"They found their own wives," she retorted. "And I'm still one short."

"Aye. I reckoned Coll would give ye the most trouble. Good lad. Stubborn lad."

"Why did you never give them the letters I wrote? Or send me the letters *they* wrote?"

One gray eye twitched. "Ye took our wee daughter and

left me. Left all yer boys. Did ye leave me a reason to be kind to ye? Because if ye did, I didnae find it."

"It would have been a kindness to them to know that I still cared for them and thought of them."

He made a dismissive gesture. "Ye wrecked 'em all when ye left. All three of 'em, pining after ye. I helped 'em heal, showed 'em how to be strong and to nae rely on anything but each other. It would've softened 'em again, to give 'em yer flowery letters about kisses and hugs and lullabies."

"I'm amazed they turned out so well. I do know it was despite your influence. And at least they understand that love means compromise. I *will* see them all in London again, because they care that their wives have lives and families here. I know damned well that you had nothing to do with teaching them that."

To her surprise, he gave her a short grin before he dropped into the chair opposite her. "Aye. Just as I had naught to do with them learning to dance or read Sassenach poetry or learn French and Latin." He patted the arms of the chair. "I smell whisky. I could use a glass."

With a sigh, she pulled the bottle and glass back out of the drawer and slid them across the desk to him. "Are you trying to tell me, in your usual maddening way, that you raised three refined gentlemen who care about the opinions and feelings of others?"

"Ye tell me, *bean na bainnse mo àlainn.*"

She remembered that phrase. *My beautiful bride.* He could be charming, but she'd thought herself long past falling for his brogue and confident manner. And yet . . . her heart still beat faster when he spoke in Scots Gaelic, when he called her by any of the silly pet names he'd had for her.

Francesca squared her shoulders. "Are you here to talk some sense into Coll, or not?" she finally asked.

"Did ye nae see the same thing I did, lass?"

"Do you *not* see that everything in a marriage would benefit her, and not him?"

"It would secure Aldriss Park's funding. That's someaught. And ye're the one who settled that on his shoulders."

Yes, she had done that to all three of them. And it *had* brought them back into her life, and two of them had no regrets about the results. Aden and Niall had found love, and both were happy—amazingly so. And in that love, they'd found some space for her as well, whether they considered her to have earned it or not.

She couldn't make the same claim where Coll was concerned. At least half of it was his fault; from the beginning, he'd seemed determined not to be ruled by an agreement he hadn't even known about until a week before they'd arrived in London. And equally determined not to allow her to dictate the terms of his life.

Was it enough that she had three of her four children? If she released Coll from the agreement, he wouldn't be obligated to marry. He wouldn't feel obligated to marry Persephone Jones, in other words, and while she might never see him again, he *would* have the opportunity to find a woman he truly loved, rather than one he thought would most offend his mother.

"Ye're wondering if releasing Coll would convince him to turn his lass away," Angus mused, sipping at his whisky. "Ye saw what I saw, Francesca. I reckon ye and I havenae ever agreed on the color of the sky, much less what's best for us and our bairns, but he's nae a bairn. And he's seen what he wants."

"You read my letter, yes?" she retorted. "Admittedly, Mrs. Jones is a highly regarded actress, but she is an *actress*. A commoner. No doubt you find it amusing that I'm nonplussed, but is she truly who *you* want to see as the next Lady Aldriss?"

"I wanted a nice Scottish lass for each of the lads, if ye'll recall." He crossed his ankles, at home, as he'd always been wherever he went. If only he'd chosen to go where she wanted to be—they might still be living beneath the same roof. "Those lasses, though, they're nae who I expected ye to choose."

"You mean they're not the fainting, delicate, hothouse flowers you warned our sons about? No, they aren't. They're women. Strong women, both of them." She sighed. "I suppose the best we could hope for is that if I remove the obligation for Coll to marry, he and Mrs. Jones remain lovers until he eventually tires of London and goes back to the Highlands to find someone more appropriate. That, of course, depends on whether Mrs. Jones will remove her claws from a wedding band and a future earldom."

"Or ye might consider exchanging more than a few barbs with her, open yer eyes, and realize she's nae just a walking scandal." Coll leaned into the doorway, his arms crossed over his chest.

Well. She would have preferred to have a plan in place before beginning an argument, but as the argument had come to them, she would make do. "What is it about her, then, that you find so irresistible?"

"She's nae a child, for one thing," he answered promptly. "She's a woman grown, with a woman's experience and a woman's view on the world. She's at least as clever as Aden, I reckon, and isnae shy about using her wits. And she's damned funny." He tilted his head. "She's nae scared of me, when even my own brothers look for ways to keep my temper tethered. She's a hundred women all in one, *màthair*, and I find her endlessly fascinating. Is that enough of an answer for ye?"

"Will she give up the theater for you?"

"I dunnae. I've nae asked her to."

"So you would have a viscountess whom strangers pay money to see onstage every night?"

"There arenae plays except during the Season," he countered, his tone still mild, but sheathed in steel. "Strangers can look at her if they wish, as long as she comes home to me." To her surprise, he came forward, sinking into the chair beside his father. "I see it this way. Ye can force me to wed, and I'll marry her. Ye can free me from having to wed, and I'll still marry her. Or ye can forbid me to wed and threaten to hold all of Aldriss Park hostage if I do. Ye'd win that one, but I reckon I'd find a way to be with her anyway."

Francesca looked at him. She *could* attempt to force him to do as she wanted. That would give him the choice of either defying her and losing Aldriss Park—or, more likely, he would marry some weak-minded, milquetoast chit and keep Mrs. Jones as his mistress, which would keep him from having a happy life. And it would keep him out of *her* life.

"Coll," Angus said, downing the rest of his whisky, "go fetch yer lass, will ye? Yer ma and I need a minute to converse."

"Aye. I'll give ye five minutes."

Once he'd gone, Angus poured another glass of whisky and slid it toward her. "Drink."

"I've already had one."

He cracked a grin. "Another willnae harm ye. For God's sake, woman, ye're about to have to swallow yer pride and admit ye've been outmaneuvered by love."

Scowling, she took the glass and drank it down. "This isn't the first time I've been outmaneuvered by love, you know."

His smile softened. "I am aware. I owe ye such apologies, Francesca, I hardly ken where to begin."

She snorted. "One whisky's clearly harmed you,

Angus, if you're ready to apologize. And two have clearly harmed me, if I'm even considering listening."

"Are ye?"

"Perhaps."

Damn him, anyway. She could be nearly seething with anger for seventeen years, and the moment he walked through the door, the moment she heard his voice, she could only remember the times he'd made her laugh, the moments he'd made her heart sing.

Francesca took a breath. "She'll cause a scandal, you know. For your daughter, for your daughters-in-law, and for me."

"Ye're the thinker in this family; think of a way to prevent that."

"That's not very helpful." In a sense, though, it was. She had more than her mind here; she had power and influence. With it, she could ruin Persephone Jones and make certain the woman had no further career here in London, if not the rest of the Kingdom. Her reaction to this match would say a great deal. People would watch, and they would listen.

She walked to the window and pushed it open. Aden had wanted Miranda to choose the day for their wedding; she'd picked a lovely one. Sun kissed the roses in the garden, and a light breeze ruffled the leaves of the grand old oak tree in its center. And she, Francesca, had attempted to begin a fight with a young woman waiting to hear if her house had burned down. That woman had not only stood her ground, but drawn blood.

"We're here," Coll said. "What's it to be?"

Francesca turned around. Persephone Jones stood hand-in-hand with Viscount Glendarril, and she had removed her bonnet—and her bright red hair. Honey-colored curls hung halfway down her back and over her shoulders, improper and loose, but rather refreshingly so. Her lavender and peach gown looked expensive in its simplicity, as if she'd worn her very best dress to attend the wedding. Had it been meant to impress Coll's family, or was it a measure of her pride that she wanted to fit in with what had been, after all, an aristocratic ceremony?

"I've seen you onstage perhaps a dozen times," she said, noting out of the corner of her eye that Angus had gotten to his feet. "You've been Rosalind, Juliet, Cordelia, the courtesan in that silly *A Mad World, My Masters,* Recha from *Nathan the Wise,* and a half dozen others I can't remember at the moment." As she recited the list, another question caught at her attention, and she frowned. "Do you have any influence over the plays put on by the Saint Genesius, Mrs. Jones?"

Persephone nodded. "I'm not always listened to, but I do give my opinions."

"It occurs to me that you've played a fair number of strong, clever women."

"Thank you, my lady. I like to think there's a reason I found them interesting."

Hmm. Coll had said she was quite intelligent, and after two brief conversations—or one-and-a-half, rather—Francesca had no reason to dispute that. "To return to my original line of inquiry, you are a very pretty young woman who has portrayed legendary romantic figures, and you have been pursued by more than one wealthy, handsome, and titled gentleman. Why is it that you've set your sights on Coll?"

"I'm nae certain *I* want ye to answer that," her oldest son muttered.

Persephone glanced up at him with a brief smile before she faced Francesca again. "The answer is in your question, I think," she said slowly. "I have played some very romantic heroines, and I have known men in pursuit of those heroines. One even refused to call me anything but

Juliet. Coll ran into me backstage, and I . . . Well, he is very handsome, you know."

"Yes, I know," Francesca returned dryly. "Do go on."

"We spoke and, well, it turned out he had come back there to escape . . . something, and he hadn't seen me onstage at all. He only saw . . . me. Which sounds very silly, I suppose, but I have been a great many people in my life, and he's the first man I've known to value the me underneath them all."

It didn't sound silly. Francesca sent a quick look toward Angus. Either he was being uncharacteristically quiet, or he'd learned a few things in the time they'd been apart. She didn't know which one she found more unsettling.

"Well, then," she said aloud, her voice catching, but hopefully not enough for anyone else to hear. "If the two of you can figure out how in the world you mean to go on together, I—we—have no objections to your union."

"You don't?" Persephone said in a very small voice.

"No. There will be a great deal of gossip, and I cannot say that I approve of your remaining onstage, but I am not marrying you. What I am going to do is make certain everyone knows the two of you have been inseparable from the moment you met. My sons began this Season by upending it, and I see no reason they should conclude it in any other way."

"That means she wishes ye happy, I reckon," Angus put in. "As do I."

Coll swung Persephone into his arms and kissed her. The passion Francesca saw was nearly enough to make her blush, but it did demonstrate to her that she'd made the correct choice. Commoner or not, no one she'd been able to find suited Coll better than this woman. And he'd found her for himself, the discouraging of which had been her mistake to begin with.

A moment later, Persephone batted Coll on the chest,

and he let her loose. "Are you certain, my lady? My lord? The scandal—"

"People will talk. I don't care. I am certain," Francesca stated.

Persephone took a small step forward. "Then I think you should know something."

Behind her, Coll frowned. "Persephone, ye dunnae—"

"Family, yes?" she interrupted. "You trust them."

"Aye, I do."

"Then so shall I." Squaring her shoulders, the actress folded her hands primly in front of her waist. "I am not Persephone Jones," she said quietly. "Or rather, I have only been Persephone Jones for the past seven years. Prior to that, my name was—is—Temperance Hartwood."

Chapter Seventeen

"Let us speak
Our free hearts each to other."

MACBETH, *MACBETH* ACT I, SCENE III

"Och, what a night," Coll said with a groan, turning over in the comfortable bed of the yellow room to see Temperance grinning at him from the pillow next to his. "What's got ye so amused?"

"You barely got to threaten anyone yesterday," she returned, leaning closer to touch her mouth to his. "And yet, here we are."

"Aye, here we are. For now. If ye keep telling everyone about yer true identity, though, I may expire in the next day or two."

"I didn't tell everyone. I told your parents."

"And my two brothers, my three sisters, and one near-brother. For the devil's sake, lass, I'm glad ye trust me and mine, but ye ken I'd have married ye whether yer true name was Persephone Jones or Temperance Hartwood or Mary Dairy."

She laughed. "Mary Dairy? Oh, I'm so glad you weren't about when I was looking for a faux name."

"I amnae. Ye wouldnae have been alone if I'd been there."

Her expression sobering, she reached over to brush his dark hair back from his temple. "My life would have been so different," she breathed. "But given what I've found now, I wouldn't want to change anything."

He understood that, even if he disliked the idea of not being there for eight years to keep her safe and to keep her from being alone. Imagining all of that, though, only made him frustrated and angry. She had the right of it; they were together now, and that was what mattered. "I'm glad for that, then."

"Your sister wants to take me dress shopping today," she went on, "to replace my wardrobe. I could go to the Saint Genesius for some of my costumes, but I'm not certain whether going about in Lady Macbeth's robes would help your mother's quest to stop all the gossip."

Sitting up, he stretched. He'd known her for a week, and had been intimate with her for nearly that amount of time. In the past, he would never have thought himself as domesticated as to enjoy sharing a bed with the same woman every night and waking up beside her in the morning. There he was, though, looking forward to a long lifetime of it.

"Ye ken we've only jumped over one hurdle," he said, catching her hand and bringing it to his lips. "Ye still have someone after ye, and I'll nae tolerate that."

She shivered a little. "I didn't think it possible to be so happy and so frightened all at the same time. How certain are you that my cousin is to blame?"

"I cannae be certain until I get a look at him and we exchange some words, but who else has a damned thing to gain by getting rid of ye? Unless it could possibly be Jenny or one of the others after yer parts—but ye'll nae even tolerate me saying that."

"No, I will not. I've known Jenny and most of the rest of them for years. If she'd wanted me gone, she would have killed me well before now. Rosalind's a much more popular character than Lady Macbeth." She sat up beside him. "Speaking of which, I still need to go to rehearsals."

"Nae."

"We open tomorrow. It's not just about me. The other actors, the stagehands, Charlie—this is our livelihood."

Swearing under his breath, he flung off the bedsheets and stood. "Then I'm going with ye. Seems I dunnae have to spend my time searching for a bride any longer."

What he *did* have was a masked ball to attend that night. At least now that his family knew about Temperance's identity, he could hopefully get Eloise or one of the other lasses to dance with Robert Hartwood and ask him a few pointed questions. He wanted to ask them himself, of course, and he wanted to beat the man senseless. Doing so without proof or an admission of guilt, though, wouldn't go over well with the rest of the aristocracy.

That didn't even matter all that much to him. What continued to trouble him was the thought that perhaps it wasn't Temperance's cousin. If he couldn't find a potential killer, allowing her to go anywhere—much less onstage—made no damned sense, yet he wasn't certain that even he, with his size and his muscles, would be able to stop her.

Something warm rubbed against his ankle. Bending down, he scratched Hades behind the ears. At least the cat was grateful to have his life saved. "Make certain ye close yer cat in here," he said, reaching for his kilt and belting it around his hips. "Aden has a dog with five wee pups, and they've the run of the place."

Once he'd pulled on his shirt, he walked back to the bed, put his hands around Temperance's hips, and kissed her long and slow. "I'll be down in the breakfast room in twenty minutes or so, if ye care to meet me there so I can tell ye good morning."

"If you tell me good morning any more enthusiastically

than you just did," she said with a satisfied smile, "we'll have to be naked again."

"Dunnae tempt me. That'd be one way to keep ye indoors all day, except that I cannae be with ye and find a villain all at the same time."

By the time he'd sorted who would watch over Temperance with him, who would check to see that Robert Hartwood remained on the guest list for Lady Fenster's ball, and whether he could go to Canterbury for a special marriage license if he didn't give the bride's true name—and whether that was the least bit legal or not—most of the family, with the notable exception of Aden and Miranda, had crowded into the breakfast room alongside him.

"Do you need a gown for tonight?" Eloise asked Temperance over her cup of too-sweet tea. "You're taller than I am, but I have several with generous hems we could let out."

"Temperance isnae going," Coll broke in. For God's sake, the lass had been terrified by the idea of attending the party when he'd mentioned it to her, and so he'd promised her he would find another way. If the rest of them wanted to think he was being controlling, let them. "If Hartwood is the one after her, I'm nae giving him a chance at her."

"I've been thinking about that," Temperance said. "Someone else can ask questions, but I'm the one who knows him. Seeing me there might well surprise him into giving himself away." She finished her own tea. "And then I can punch him."

"Are ye certain?" Coll asked. "I thought ye didnae want to risk seeing yer parents there."

He saw her shiver. He'd added two more Sassenachs to his list of people to punch back when she'd told him her story, but even more than her words, her reaction to speaking about them or even hearing they might be in the area truly told him all he needed to know about Lord and Lady Bayton.

Blowing out her breath, she shook her head. "I am willing to risk it. I want to know who's trying to kill me, and I want it stopped."

"Ye and me both, *mo chridhe*."

A tight smile touched her face. "Will someone tell me what that means?"

"'My heart,'" his father said around a mouthful of hard-boiled egg. "I used to call the lads' *màthair* that."

"Och, I dunnae want to hear that." Coll scowled. "What happened to ye being on yer deathbed, anyway, Da?"

"I had a miraculous recovery. Dunnae question my behavior when ye've been seen running about London in naught but a claymore."

"I was after a snake. Nearly took off his ear too," Coll retorted.

"Good."

"Aye."

They managed to get Eloise's favorite dressmaker to the house by half nine, and Temperance had a midnight blue silk and lace gown that fit her like a glove and flowed like water by half ten. Niall volunteered to go speak to the pastor who'd married Aden and Miranda about certain legalities, while Francesca herself summoned her solicitor for a chat about special licenses and names.

Before that fellow arrived, Coll, Temperance, and three capable lads headed for the Saint Genesius and the last dress rehearsal for the Scottish play. Watching her transform into the cold, regal, and viciously ambitious Lady Macbeth continued to stun him, especially in the moments when they stopped and she laughed at something one of her fellow actors said, back to herself again.

"You're marrying her, Persephone says," Charlie Huddle said, coming to a stop beside where Coll sat on a crate of wooden swords.

"Aye."

"She has a contract through next Season to perform at the Saint Genesius, and I—"

"That's nae my affair," Coll interrupted, "unless she doesnae want to be here."

"She'll be Lady Glendarril, though. Doesn't that trouble you?"

"Nae in the least. Think of the publicity for the Saint Genesius, though." Hiding his grin, Coll watched the theater manager absorb that bit of information.

"I . . . am. Now—oh, my. This could be—we could see our most profitable Season ever. I . . ." Huddle strode away, calling over his shoulder, "Excuse me, I need to do some figuring."

People kept telling Coll he should be mortified at the idea of having a wife who acted onstage. If he cared what other people thought, it might have made a difference, but he hoped it wouldn't have. Seeing how good she was at it and knowing how much she enjoyed it, he couldn't imagine even trying to take it away from her. As he'd told his mother, the Season only lasted from mid-spring to late summer. He could spend that in London with her. The rest of the year could be for Scotland.

His father had refused to make that compromise for his mother, and Coll wasn't about to repeat those mistakes. Aside from that, just the idea of seeing Temperance sad or lonely left him angry. If he could prevent that by coming down here among the dandies, he would damned well do so.

Ten minutes later, Temperance strolled up to him, not stopping until she'd slid her arms around his shoulders and kissed him, her soft mouth smiling against his. "I'm nae complaining, lass, but what did I do to deserve that?" he asked, putting his hands on her trim waist.

"You told Charlie that my staying or going wasn't up to you," she murmured.

"And what else would I say?"

"You? Nothing else. I *have* begun to wonder if you're so accustomed to looking after the needs of other people that being selfish simply doesn't occur to you."

"I am being selfish," he returned. "I like seeing ye happy."

"And I like being happy," she whispered back to him. "I've been content with my life until now, I think, but you . . . you make me truly happy."

"M'laird," Gavin called down from his perch in the rigging, "ye said ye wanted to be back to Oswell House by six o'clock. It's nearly that now."

"I shouldnae have given him a pocket watch," Coll muttered, reluctantly releasing Temperance. "Are ye finished here? There willnae be food tonight at the ball, Eloise says, so I plan on having a large dinner."

"Yes, we're finished. Ready as we can be for tomorrow."

She didn't say anything else, but he heard the nerves in her voice. It wasn't only about playing a complicated lass in front of hundreds of people—or more, once the news got around that Persephone Jones was to wed Lord Glendarril. "If I have to personally separate every man in the audience from his pistol before they set foot inside the Saint Genesius, I will do it," he stated. "Ask me if I'm jesting."

"I know you're not. It's all been fairly subtle so far. A pistol is much more direct. I'm still worried about sandbags and falling forests."

"I helped make Birnham Wood. It willnae fall on ye."

He followed as she went into her dressing room to

change out of her rich, dark robes and into the more proper green muslin walking dress Miranda had lent her. She also donned her wig of ivory blonde hair after she pinned her own up.

"What do you think? Passable? Most of the rest of my wigs were at my house, I'm afraid."

"Aye. More than passable. Ye take my breath away."

Halfway out the door, she stopped, pushing him back inside and shutting them in. "You do realize that once whoever this is hears that we're to be married, they may get more desperate. Once I'm wed and my parents can't threaten me with anything, I will have no reason not to go to them and announce my return. No reason other than my general dislike and disgust, that is."

"It's crossed my mind, aye." Of course she'd thought of that; she had a mind like quicksilver. "And whatever Robert thinks, ye go to them if ye want to, and ye stay away if ye prefer. As far as London and the rest are concerned, I'm marrying Persephone Jones. Ye dunnae need to tell anyone otherwise on my account."

"You are a very nice man, Lord Glendarril," she whispered, wiping at her eyes.

"Dunnae be telling anyone else that. I've a reputation, ye ken."

They arrived back at Oswell House in the family's coach, a quartet of outriders accompanying them. The house was packed with armed footmen and a handful of Lord Aldriss's fighters, too, who'd begun to arrive a day behind the earl. The more weapons between Temperance and the outside, the better Coll liked it—especially since he'd potentially brought the fight to Oswell House and his own family.

After dinner, he retreated to his bedchamber to find the gray coat, blue trousers, and yellow waistcoat Oscar, the valet he shared with his brothers, had laid out for him together with his white shirt. It looked far too civilized and yellow seemed a color for dandies, but he had more important worries than fabric.

He'd had Eloise choose a mask for him; he supposed Amy and Miranda had selected those Niall and Aden would be wearing. While Oscar slipped in and attempted to tie his cravat into something that didn't look like a horse had stepped on it, Coll pulled the mask out of the silk bag Eloise had left for him.

"Hmm. A lion," he said aloud, not surprised. He liked the bronze color of it; it went well with the gray and yellow. That thought, though, made him frown; he was marrying soon, for Christ's sake, not becoming a lass. And he damned well had not become civilized.

Carrying the mask with him, he walked down the long hallway to where Temperance was staying, next door to Eloise's bedchamber, and knocked on her door.

"Who is it, please?" Flora's voice called.

"Me," he answered. "Coll."

"Coll who?"

"MacTaggert, ye witch. Laird Glendarril, if that was yer next question."

Flora opened the door. "There haven't been witches in my family for at least one generation," she quipped, and moved aside.

Temperance stood in front of the closed window, her back to him. Slowly, she turned around, her midnight blue skirts swirling about her ankles like azure shadows. A blue-and-pearl peacock mask covered her eyes and nose, the fan of feathers arcing across her forehead into the air. With her bright blue eyes glinting and her now red-colored hair twined through with blue and black ribbons, the effect was . . . magical.

"God's blood, lass," he murmured.

"He likes it," Flora interpreted, clapping.

Coll crossed the room to Temperance. "If I liked it any more," he breathed, "we'd nae be leaving this room."

"I was about to say the same thing about you." Lowering her gaze, she took him in from head to toe and back again. "Is that a lion?"

"Aye." He put it on, immediately disliking the closed-in feeling. At least it left his mouth free so he could pull in some air.

"That . . ." She trailed off. "It suits you," she finally said, and went up on her toes, leaning her hands on his shoulders, to kiss him.

"Ye're going to have to kiss me enough to distract me from wearing a prison on my skull," he said, kissing her back, careful not to disturb her hair or her peacock mask.

"I think I could manage that, if you'll kiss me enough to distract me from remembering that I will be facing my cousin tonight."

"Ye have a deal, lass." He leaned closer, brushing her ear with his mouth. "Does Flora know about ye, or are ye still Persie to her?"

"I told her and Gregory a few minutes ago." She grimaced. "I should have told them ages ago, but I didn't want to risk anyone calling me by the wrong name. That is bound to happen here, so I wanted them to hear the truth from me."

"I understand, Persie," Flora said from her station by the door. "Or my lady, I should be saying now, for heaven's sake."

"No, you shouldn't. Persie is fine. It's a perfectly acceptable shortening of Temperance, anyway."

"It is, isn't it?" The maid smiled. "I always said you had elegance up to the rooftops. Now I know why."

Removing his mask again, Coll offered Temperance his free hand. "We should head downstairs. Ye'll be in the coach with my *màthair*, Da, and Eloise. I'll be right beside ye on Nuckelavee. The second coach will have Aden, Niall, and their lasses."

A few short weeks ago, the MacTaggerts in London had numbered five, and that was including Francesca and Eloise, who both went by Oswell-MacTaggert. Now they were eight, with Temperance for a near-ninth and Matthew Harris ready to make it ten, even if he didn't bear the name. He would still be family, and that made him a part of the MacTaggert clan.

A good portion of them were downstairs in the foyer already, and damn it all, every one of the MacTaggert men was wearing or carrying a lion mask. They were all different, but unmistakable nonetheless. "I think the lasses may be having a bit of fun with us," he commented, lifting his mask in his free hand.

Aden chuckled. "I'd rather be part of a pride of lions than a gaggle of geese or someaught."

The ladies all wore different bird masks, with Temperance as a peacock, Eloise as a swan, Miranda an owl, and Amy a falcon, while Francesca wore a white and ivory gown topped with a feather-and-jewel-encrusted dove mask. They'd all coordinated, obviously, and had included Temperance without hesitation. For that, he would bow to their collective sense of humor and wear a damned lion head over his own.

Outside, he handed off his mask to Niall and swung up on Nuckelavee. Three other outriders joined him; it may have looked ostentatious to the rest of the world, but it wasn't only Temperance he needed to protect now. She'd been taken in by his family, and that put them all in a degree of danger.

Lady Fenster's grand house stood only five minutes

from Oswell House, but that was enough time for him to run his mind through everything that could possibly go wrong tonight. It wouldn't have been proper to drag Robert Hartwood into a corner by his ear and demand some answers, but he preferred that to making Temperance confront someone she'd spent nearly eight years avoiding.

The crowd of vehicles clogging the entire street did little to make him wish to be reasonable again. He gave the black over to Gavin and opened the coach door himself. "I dunnae like this," he said, handing out his mother and then Temperance. "Too many people behind too many masks. We'll manage this another way."

She shook her head at him. "I've managed to screw my courage to the sticking place, Coll. If I turn around now, I don't know that I could do this again."

"Ye wouldnae—"

"A word, Coll," his father broke in, putting a hand on Coll's shoulder.

"Dunnae fret," Aden said smoothly, stepping in to offer his free arm to Temperance. "We willnae go in without ye."

Frowning, Coll followed the earl a few steps away from the others. "What is it?"

"I'd like to think I've learned a few things, even if it's taken me far too long," Lord Aldriss said. "And even though it may be too late for me, it's nae too late for ye. Ye've chosen a strong woman. A strong woman willnae do as ye say, and she'll nae watch her tongue when she disagrees with ye. My advice is to nae expect her to. She told ye she's ready for tonight. Trust her to be."

Coll cocked his head. "What happened to weak-willed, weeping women and hothouse flowers? That's all ye said we'd find here in London."

"I'm a prideful man, lad, as ye know. I didnae want

to lose ye, and I didnae want yer mother to be the one to make that happen." The earl slipped on his lion mask, this one onyx with yellow. "And yet here we all are, together."

Aye, they were all there together, and they made a bloody formidable group. Lions, indeed—and a lovely flock of birds no other men had been able to catch. Coll rolled his shoulders. He wouldn't be the only one watching over Temperance tonight; if he did move against Robert Hartwood, he wouldn't be doing it alone. The MacTaggerts stood together. Always.

Temperance watched father and son. Coll was taller and had broader shoulders, but any of the MacTaggerts could likely put even Gentleman Jackson on his arse. Whatever it was they'd discussed, the smile on Coll's face as he walked up to her warmed her all the way to her bones.

This mountain of a man, whom others underestimated because, for some reason, they thought muscles didn't equate with mental acuity, wanted *her*. This Highland god with his chiseled good looks and his warm laugh and his very capable hands and mouth, who'd been ordered to find a bride and had searched throughout London for weeks for one, had chosen her—even though she hadn't even been on the registry.

"Are ye ready?" he asked, accepting his mask from Niall and slipping it over his dark, unruly hair.

"'Once more unto the breach'," she quoted, as Shakespeare's warriors always made her feel braver.

"I *told* ye I was Henry the Fifth," he said.

"I never doubted it." Putting her hand around his hard forearm, she resisted the urge to lean into him for strength. At this moment, people knew he was her protector, with all the sexual intimacy that went with the term. Some might guess that Persephone Jones had dared enter an aristocratic ballroom uninvited, which would be scandalous, but no one knew yet that they were to be married. *That* scandal would lift the roof off the house.

At the entrance to the ballroom, Lady Aldriss handed the butler the family's invitation. A moment later, they were announced as "Lord and Lady Aldriss, Lord Glendarril, and family," and Persephone stepped inside the room without being pointed at or having anyone turn their backs on her. It was still early, though.

Gold, yellow, and white ribbons hung from the ceiling, reflecting the chandelier light in a thousand different directions. The effect was striking and lovely and exotic all at the same time. Up on the overlooking balcony, a small orchestra played, while directly below them two tables stood laden with punch bowls and sweet treats.

A hundred or more people had already crowded into the house, and while she'd initially been pleased to be able to wear a mask, she quickly saw the disadvantage in everyone else being disguised. If Coll was correct, the person who'd either burned her house down or hired someone else to do it was here, and whoever had cut the rope holding the sandbags or swung the bucket or driven the wagon could well be gazing at her right now. All she would see would be a bear or tiger or parrot.

"Care to take a stroll with me?" Coll suggested.

She nodded, trying to keep her mouth in an amused half smile. The killer might know she was staying with the MacTaggerts, but no one had any reason to believe she would dare make an appearance here—either as Persephone or as herself. She had the advantage, at least for the moment. And she had Coll.

"If ye see anyone ye reckon could be Robert, ye squeeze my arm," he said. "Francesca's making a few discreet inquiries to see if we can discover which mask he's wearing."

"Is it odd that I'm looking forward to frightening the

devil out of all these people tomorrow as Lady Macbeth?" she asked, her gaze flitting from one mask to the next.

"Nae. I'm looking forward to that myself. Ye scared me, and that was just a rehearsal."

"I doubt anything scares you," she retorted.

"The idea of ye being hurt scares me," he returned softly. "The idea of someaught that I cannae fight coming between us scares me."

"The last two days have gone from being a nightmare to a happy dream," she said. "I'm afraid I'll wake up and find none of it to be true." Shakespeare would have adored it—the woman who'd given up on the idea of love and marriage while playing romantic heroines, and the man who'd seen through all the characters to her heart and awakened her again.

"I have upended things for ye, I ken."

"And I love you for that, you know."

The smile beneath his fierce mask made her grin in return. "Aye. And I love ye. Ye upended a few things for me, as well. And I'd nae change any of 'em for gold."

Neither would she. Before she could say that aloud, though, a thin man in a fox mask passed her, and a shiver went down her spine. She tightened her fingers around Coll's arm without even realizing it.

"Is that him?" Coll asked immediately, stopping and turning around. "Yer cousin?"

"No," she whispered, beginning to shake. "That was my father."

"Damn." They reversed course yet again, and he strode in the opposite direction, practically lifting her off her feet as she tried to keep up. "Let's get ye back to Oswell House. Now."

Swallowing, she pulled on his arm. She might as well have been poking at a thundercloud, but he slowed, looking down at her. "This is still our best chance to find Robert," she breathed. "The play opens tomorrow, and I can't—"

"It's too risky, Temperance."

"It is what it is. I'm here. He walked right by me without batting an eye. We have to stay."

From his clenched jaw and aggressive stance, he wasn't at all pleased with her conclusion. Even so, after a moment he nodded. "Dunnae move a step away from me. If it comes down to it, Nuckelavee is outside. I *will* toss ye over the saddle and make off with ye to the Highlands. All I need is a wee excuse."

That was far more tempting than it should have been. "My parents are far more averse to scandal than yours are," she said, doing her best to keep her voice steady and not sound like a scared mouse. "I doubt they'd care to make a scene even if they did recognize me." That made sense, at least, and she clung to the thought. If they recognized her, they might try to approach her in private, but never in public. And tonight, she didn't mean to be caught in private with anyone.

"Aye," he grunted. "Let's tell the others, though. We dunnae need Aden or Niall tackling yer da."

As they found Aden and Miranda and let them know that at least Lord Bayton was in attendance, Lady Aldriss joined them. "Your cousin is here, my dear," she said, "wearing a rooster mask. And don't be alarmed, but your parents are here, as well."

"She saw her da a minute ago and nearly went out the window," Coll provided.

"I did not. He startled me, is all. I'm finished running."

It all sounded very brave, but it felt terrifying. At the same time, she meant it. She'd run eight years ago and had been in hiding ever since, even if her best disguise happened to be hiding in plain sight. Now she had a reason to stay and fight for what she'd found. The only problem was that a fight might actually be involved.

"Then you know your father is a fox. Your mother is a swan, like Eloise."

"She should've been a hen to go with his fox," Aden suggested with a brief grin.

"That's far too whimsical for my parents. Come, Coll, I want to find that rooster and get this over with."

"And I'd like to wring his neck," Coll put in.

Now that they knew which animal to look for, it didn't take long to spy cousin Robert. He stood by the refreshment table, sampling each one of the treats methodically, one after the other. He looked so . . . familiar, as if it had only been a week since she'd last seen him, and not eight years. He had put on a bit of weight around his middle and his chin had doubled, but even with the mask on, it could be no one else.

Beside him stood a blonde duck, and every so often he would hand a treat to her and she would pop it into her mouth. His betrothed, Caroline Rilence. Temperance hadn't been particularly close with her at school, and she doubted she would have recognized Caroline on the street, but she couldn't think of anyone else to whom Robert would be giving sweets.

"That's him?" Coll murmured from close beside her.

"Yes. I'm certain of it."

In response, she felt his muscles tense, a crackle in the air as the tension rose around him. Turning her back on her cousin, she put a hand against Coll's chest. "No hitting. We need to speak with him first."

He took a hard breath, her hand moving as his lungs filled and emptied. "I'll signal Eloise, then." Pulling a button from his pocket, he turned, looked, and flipped it through the air. As she watched, it flew halfway across the room to strike young Matthew Harris on the back of the head. He turned, startled.

"Over here," Coll mouthed.

With a grimace, Matthew took Eloise's arm and led her over, still rubbing the back of his skull.

"You didn't need to hit me," he complained.

"It was a wee button, and ye were supposed to be paying attention. We found him. Eloise, can ye get him to give ye a waltz?"

"Of course I can," she answered, with all the confidence of an eighteen-year-old who'd been the belle of the Season from the moment she came out. "Point him out to me."

Once they'd done so, she fluffed the swan feathers on her mask, sent Matthew a quick, excited grin, and glided away. Temperance had the distinct feeling that Coll would have preferred to be much closer by in case of trouble, but with his height, he could at least see his sister speaking with Robert.

A moment later, Eloise returned, one hand to her chest. "My goodness, that was exhilarating."

"Did it work?" Coll demanded.

"Yes. The first waltz of the evening. Luckily, he didn't know that Matthew has already claimed it from me, but since I won't actually be dancing with him anyway, I suppose it doesn't signify." She patted Matthew's arm, as if comforting him. "The woman with him didn't look very happy, though."

"That's his fiancée," Temperance informed them. "You must have surprised him; Robert was never much of a dancer."

As she spoke, it dawned on her all over again that she would be dancing face-to-face with her cousin in a very few minutes, and she stifled another bout of shivers. Surprising him might well be their most effective weapon, and she was certainly the best choice to do it.

"Ye still dunnae have to do this." Coll moved in front of her, blocking her view of Robert. "We can find another way."

"I can't say I'm looking forward to it," she conceded, meeting his glittering green gaze through the fierce and fitting lion mask, "but I *am* looking forward to being finished with having to be afraid."

Music for a quadrille, the first dance of the evening, began, and Coll held out one hand. "Do ye have a place on yer dance card for me, then?"

"Always." Taking his fingers, she let him lead the way to one side of the ballroom, as far as they could manage from her own family. He danced well, graceful and athletic and very conscious of the people around him, who no doubt feared being trampled.

It had been ages since she'd danced more than a theatrical reel or two, and she was grinning and breathless by the end of the quadrille. Aden claimed her for the country dance, and Niall for the quadrille after that. If nothing else, those three dances were a forceful reminder that her life had changed. She didn't have to stand alone any longer. If she fell, someone would be right there to catch her before she hit the ground—both literally and figuratively. It felt . . . empowering to have these men, this family, at her back. Even as a young girl, she'd rarely dared to stray from the path set out for her, because once a five-year-old heard that if she didn't do as she was told she would be left outside for the gypsies, she tended to believe it.

After a brief respite for the orchestra, Lady Fenster announced the waltz. Temperance's heart jumped, and she grabbed Coll's hand and squeezed it hard. Then, without a backward look, she strolled forward and intercepted the rooster on his way to meet Eloise's swan.

He took a half step backward as she blocked his path. "Excuse me. I have a partner for this dance."

"Yes, the swan. I've traded with her."

"That is not how—"

"Dance with me, cousin Robert," she said deliberately.

Brown eyes widened behind the rooster's beak. "Good . . . good Lord! *Temperance?*"

Chapter Eighteen

"It is a tale told by an idiot."

MACBETH, *MACBETH* ACT V, SCENE V

"Hush," Temperance said, watching every twitch of his face carefully. "You don't wish to cause a scene, do you?"

"I—where? How?"

She'd forgotten cousin Robert's utter lack of imagination. "Dance with me if you want to chat," she said, surprised to find herself more filled with annoyance than fear. If he was feigning his own startlement, he was doing it very well, and she couldn't quite guess why—unless, of course, it was to hide the fact that he'd known who she was for at least a week and had been trying to kill her.

Damn him, anyway. Temperance clapped her hand against his, put her other hand on his shoulder, and practically dragged him into the dance. He continued to gawp, and she stifled a scowl.

"You feign surprise well," she commented, keeping her voice pitched low so the dancers around them couldn't hear their conversation, "but I'm unconvinced. When did you recognize me? Did you go to a performance of *As You Like It*, perchance?"

Beyond his shoulder, Coll swung by, his sister-in-law Amy in his arms. She ignored his inquiring look, though.

This was not the time for her to allow herself to be distracted.

"What are you talking about?" Robert whispered. "Were you at the theater? I thought . . . I thought you'd run off to America or somewhere. I'm sorry, but after all this time you can hardly blame me for not noticing you in the middle of a crowd while I was watching a performance, especially when I thought you to be halfway across the world."

Temperance blinked. Was he saying he thought she'd been watching the same performance he'd attended? "You were at the Saint Genesius, then. I knew you'd recognized me."

"I did not see you at the Saint Genesius, Temp. I would have told your parents if I had, and they would stop holding your idiotic inheritance over my head every time I mentioned wanting to live in Devonshire instead of damned Cumbria. God, I hate it there."

"You're living in Devon?"

"I'm trying to. My mother's brother, my uncle William, had an estate there. It's mine now, but your father keeps telling me that the Bayton title belongs in Cumbria, and if I want him to disown you so I get your blunt, I'd best remain there."

"But you've relocated anyway?" None of this made any blasted sense now.

"A year ago. I'd tell him to his face that I don't want the money if it means living in that drafty old hall, but that inheritance has to go somewhere, doesn't it? After you left, I figured I would end up living there eventually, because they'd make me agree to it—and a million other things, more than likely—before they'd hand over the blunt. Now that you're back, though, they'll stop torturing me with it and I can finally settle where I want to." He frowned. "But what does that have to do with going to the theater?"

"Nothing, apparently." For heaven's sake. But he *had* been there. And someone *was* trying to kill her. "With whom did you attend?"

"Your parents and Carolyn. You know, maybe Carolyn saw you there. She was very quiet afterward, but I thought it was because she was angry with me for not pressing your father about having you declared dead. No offense, of course, but eventually they would have had to realize that Bayton will belong to me whether I live there or not, and the only difference would be that with the blunt to hand I could actually renovate it. If it's so precious to them, you'd think they would at least wish for it to be maintained properly." He sighed. "No hope of that now, unless you did marry a butcher and have a litter of pudgy butcher's children. Did you? You're not dressed like a butcher's wife."

"I'm not married," she said slowly, the exchange swirling about in her head as she tried to make sense of it. To make sense of anything, really.

"That's that, then. If I were you, I'd make them promise me the blunt in writing in exchange for you marrying someone of whom they approve. Though that didn't work out for you before. Why'd you run, anyway? All you had to do was keep Dunhurst happy in his doddering old age."

"Because I didn't want to marry a doddering old man forty years my senior. And he wasn't doddering. He was cruel."

"I don't like him much, I'll admit, but that's no real business of mine."

The music stopped, and so did they. While the other couples separated to applaud, Coll was abruptly there beside her. "Well?" he prompted, his very level gaze on Robert. "Do I get to kill him?"

Robert blanched. "I say, you're that large Scotsman, the

one who's taken Persephone Jones as a lov—" He trailed off, his white face taking on a gray tinge. "Good God, Temperance. You're—"

Grabbing her cousin's hand, she towed him toward the doorway. With Coll falling in behind and shoving Robert from behind, they sped down the hallway and through the first closed door she found. Only then did she release Robert, turning to glare at him. "Keep your voice down," she ordered.

"You're *her*!" he exclaimed in a hushed, husky voice tinged with excitement. "You're Persephone Jones!"

Behind him, Coll lifted an eyebrow. "What the devil?"

She waved her hand. "He's an idiot."

"Who is?" both men said in ragged unison.

"Him." She jabbed a finger at her cousin. "You."

"Why? Because I didn't happen to recognize my cousin, whom I haven't seen in eight years, when she reappeared as a famous actress three hundred miles from her home?" He put a hand over his mouth. "Definitely have your parents put in writing that you're to inherit *before* you tell them what you've been up to."

Temperance wanted to cover her eyes and her ears all at the same time. For Robert's immediate conclusion after not seeing her for eight years to be that she would simply resume her life from the point where she'd left off, as if she'd never had any cause to leave in the first place . . . "I need a moment to think," she said, taking a seat and bending her head over her knees.

"And keep *him* away from you," Robert went on. "If Uncle Michael and Aunt Georgiana realize you've been fucked by a Scotsman, they'll never forgi—"

His voice stopped, followed by a dull thudding sound and something heavy hitting the floor. Temperance lifted her head to see cousin Robert crumpled on the carpet. "Coll!"

He shrugged, uncoiling his fist. "He wouldnae shut up. And he insulted ye."

"He didn't say anything untrue."

"I still didnae like it." Stepping over him, Coll approached to crouch beside her chair. "I'm guessing ye dunnae think cousin Robert is the one who tried to kill ye."

"No. He was surprised to see me, only wants my supposed inheritance because it needs to go to him if it doesn't go to me, and only figured out that I'm Persephone Jones after he saw you."

"I hoped it was him. I've a need to see ye safe, Temperance. And a need to know that now I've found ye, nae a man will be able to take ye from me."

Reaching for his face, she cupped his cheek with its beginnings of evening stubble. "You have no idea how long I've wanted someone who simply valued . . . me," she whispered. "I'd almost forgotten who that person was."

He smiled, kissing her palm. "I'd have known ye anywhere, *mo chridhe*. Now tell me, did he say anything at all of interest?"

"He did see a performance of *As You Like It*, but had no idea it was me onstage." She took a breath, wishing she could simply sink to the floor with Coll and let everything else go away. "My parents and his fiancée were there, as well."

"Ye still reckon yer folks have nae reason to harm ye?"

"I suppose if I was enough of an embarrassment, they might wish me dead, but killing Persephone Jones would more than likely cause the truth about my identity to emerge. They certainly wouldn't want that."

"I agree. It'd make less of a stink if they quietly disowned ye or paid ye a sum in exchange for allowing them to declare ye dead."

"Yes."

"What about Miss Caroline Rilence, then? Ye said ye went to school with her."

She was past being surprised that he'd remembered Caroline's name and where she first made her schoolmate's acquaintance. "Finishing school. I didn't know her well. Just well enough to remember the name, I suppose."

Coll tilted his head a little. "Was she an ambitious lass?"

"I don't really know." She closed her eyes for a moment, attempting to ignore both her cousin crumpled on the floor and Coll's assessing gaze on her. Mrs. Paulton's Finishing School for Ladies of Good Breeding had been twelve years ago. When she summoned Caroline's name, she recalled a thin, blonde girl with a hesitant smile and a tolerable singing voice. "She's just . . . there," she finally said, opening her eyes again. "I certainly don't think we were well-enough acquainted for her to wish me dead."

"And yet she was at the theater. Is she here tonight?" Despite his easy tone, the steel beneath his words reminded her that he was not a man with whom one trifled.

"Yes. She's a duck—a white one with green beading."

He stuck out his hand. "I cannae leave ye here. I'll send Niall back to wake yer cousin and tell him that he hit his head on someaught. And that if he doesnae wish to hit his head again, he'll be keeping his gobber shut about seeing ye tonight."

Coll helped her step over her groaning cousin as they made for the hallway again. "I've nae hit a woman in my life, but if this Caroline Rilence has been trying to harm ye, I mean to make certain she stops. Whatever that takes."

Back in the ballroom, Coll found his brothers and caught them up, sending Niall back to threaten Robert and Aden to watch the front doors for a female duck's departure. He handed Temperance over to Amy and Miranda, who each took a hand to lead her to where Lord and Lady Aldriss stood.

"Caroline Rilence," the older of the two, Miranda, said in a musing tone. "I know her, but only slightly. She always seemed rather timid. Seeing her as a killer . . . It seems so odd."

"We can't be certain it's her," Temperance countered. "Simply because we know she was at the theater doesn't mean anything. A half dozen people I've seen here tonight would know me as Temperance, if they thought to look for me."

But no one other than Robert and the MacTaggerts knew her as Temperance Hartwood tonight. People were beginning to whisper behind their masks at each other, though, sending her glances or outright staring. They'd begun to recognize Persephone Jones. This wouldn't end well—not if she continued trying to be incognito.

As another country dance ended, a plump woman clothed in white and pink marched forward, a unicorn's head with a towering horn perched above her graying black hair, a half dozen other masked ladies behind her. Yes, it was always the women who didn't like seeing her about, as if they all expected her to cast some sort of spell on their husbands.

"Perhaps we should depart," Lady Aldriss murmured, putting a hand on her shoulder.

"Just a moment," Temperance countered. "I think I can be of some help to Coll."

Walking forward to meet their hostess, she sketched an elegant curtsy to Lady Fenster. "My lady," she said grandly, "I thank you for your indulgence. Gentle people, tomorrow the Saint Genesius Theatre will premiere our first ever rendition of the Scottish play, otherwise known as"—she leaned forward a little, cupping a hand to her mouth as she conspiratorially lowered her voice—"Macbeth."

Her name—her faux name—began echoing through the ballroom, and she made a broad, beckoning gesture. "Might I further indulge you, my lady, and your radiant guests? Perhaps a portion of Lady Macbeth's sleepwalking soliloquy? Something to cast a few shadows and make the ladies long for a husband's arm to protect them?"

The exaggerated shivers and muttered approvals from the gathering crowd answered her well enough, but she didn't move until Lady Fenster nodded her approval. Taking a deep breath, Temperance blew out the nearest set of candles and turned her back, then slowly faced forward again. With the mask on, she would have to rely more on her tone than her facial expressions, but she was accustomed to that. The audience in the rear seats of the Saint Genesius could barely see the stage, after all.

Lifting her hands, she slowly rubbed them together as if washing them over a basin.

Out, damned spot! Out, I say!—One: two: why, then, 'tis time to do't.—Hell is murky!—Fie, my lord, fie! a soldier, and afeard? What need we fear who knows it, when none can call our power to account?—Yet who would have thought the old man to have had so much blood in him?

She tilted her head, still staring at her hands, silently reciting the lines that weren't hers, noting the audience surrounding her in a half circle, mesmerized and silent. *Good.* That should make finding Caroline a bit easier on Coll.

The thane of Fife had a wife; where is she now?—What, will these hands ne're be clean?—No more o' that, my lord, no more o' that: you mar all with this starting.

Catching sight of Coll at the rear of the room, she gave
a slight nod, and he motioned at her to continue, his father
and Niall now there with him.

Wash your hands, put on your nightgown;
look not so pale.—I tell you yet again, Banquo's
buried; he cannot come out on's grave.
To bed, to bed! There's knocking at the gate:
come, come, come, come, give me your hand. What's
done cannot be undone.—To bed, to bed, to bed!

With that, she lifted her head and took a quick step
forward, seemingly startled by her surroundings. One
woman toward the front of the crowd shrieked, and several others jumped. Temperance lowered her shoulders, put
on a smile, and gave another deep curtsy.

The roar of applause would have made Charlie Huddle weep. No doubt every performance would be packed
to the rafters now. More importantly, though, Coll approached, his hand around the arm of a young lady in a
duck mask as he half dragged her forward.

"This her?" he asked without preamble.

The hair was blonde, but the duck's beading was simpler, and the feathers not as full. "No," she whispered.
"Let her go before you frighten her to death."

"What is—Lady Aldriss!" The young lady sketched a
nervous curtsy.

"Ah, Lady Agnes," the countess said, taking the hand
Coll released and squeezing it gently. "I'm sorry my
son has no manners. I know you enjoy the theater, and
I thought you might wish to make Mrs. Jones's acquaintance."

"Oh." Lady Agnes began a curtsy, then stopped, evidently remembering that one did not bow to a commoner.

Instead, she inclined her head regally. "Mrs. Jones, that was wonderful. I don't think I shall be able to sleep tonight."

Persephone smiled. "You are very kind, my lady."

Once she'd hurried back to her friends, Lady Aldriss frowned. "Do stop grabbing women, dear," she said to her oldest son. "Whoever they might be, or whatever you think they might have done."

"She was the only bloody duck in the house," Coll responded. "Where's Robert Hartwood?"

"On his way home, I reckon," Niall said. "Poor fellow, knocking his head on a post like that. He'll keep quiet, but nae for more than a day or two, I reckon. He mentioned being out from under his uncle's thumb nae fewer than three times as I dragged him out of the house."

She'd fled, then. Caroline had left Fenster House, and without making an excuse to her betrothed. Cold crept down Temperance's spine again. How could it be her? Someone she barely remembered wanted her dead? Why? Because of the money? That had to be it, but killing someone who only wanted to remain hidden had a cruel, brutal ring to it.

"Robert may nae care whether he gets the blunt meant for ye," Coll said, "but I'd wager money now that his fiancée isnae so happy to see it gone."

"I will discover her address," the countess stated. "The rest of you, we're going home. Then you may call on her, Coll. With your brothers."

Lord Aldriss stepped forward. "I'll be with ye, wife. We dunnae stand alone, ye ken."

Now everyone wanted a word with Temperance as the MacTaggerts headed for the front door, and their exit slowed to a crawl. When a fox and a swan appeared in the line to add their accolades, she reached for Coll's sleeve.

He moved immediately, putting himself between her and the well-wishers. "The lot of ye are suffocating me," he grunted, creating a space for the rest of the MacTaggerts just by virtue of his presence. They filed out the door in pairs, with Coll bringing up the rear.

"Lass, that was sterling," Aden said, taking her hand and shaking it. "If Coll ever gives ye trouble, ye just give that speech. I reckon that'll settle him down."

"'Sterling?'" Miranda repeated, grinning.

"Aye. I've been learning to speak Sassenach, ye ken."

"Well, stop it, for Saint Andrew's sake," Coll muttered, taking Temperance's arm and pulling her close against him. "We know who it is, lass. Now we only need to find her."

"And then what?"

"And then I reckon we'll see just how much power Lady Aldriss can wield with a judge or two. Or I'll put Caroline Rilence in a crate myself and ship her off to America." He lowered his head. "And that's me being as civilized as I can manage."

Strictly legal or not, it sounded definitive enough to settle her a bit. The logical part of her could see why it might have happened—Caroline wanted the money for herself and Robert, and so when she'd seen the person meant to inherit it, she'd taken steps to keep Temperance from claiming it. Perhaps it was because Temperance had walked away from the money without a second thought that the whole idea seemed preposterous—certainly not worth anyone's life.

As she stepped into the coach behind Lady Aldriss, she glanced over her shoulder to see Coll mount Nuckelavee, his monster of a black horse. If they couldn't find Caroline, there remained one way to stop her. Walking up to knock on the front door of Hartwood House was the very last thing she wanted to do, of course. But this wasn't just about her any longer. The MacTaggerts had taken her in, and one of them loved her. She would not allow them to be put in danger because of her.

MacTaggerts, she'd begun to realize, did not stand alone.

Chapter Nineteen

"Leave all the rest to me."

LADY MACBETH, *MACBETH* ACT I, SCENE V

Caroline Rilence wasn't home. According to the butler and her stiff-necked parents, the lass had suddenly taken ill and left for the family's seat in Leeds, though why they would allow an ill woman to take such a long coach trip with but a maid for company, they couldn't say.

It seemed far more likely that she'd made up some tale about troublesome Highlanders and gone to stay with a friend. The trouble was, Coll realized, that none of them knew enough about her to be certain who her damned friends were.

"I need more names," he said, resisting the urge to pound on the breakfast table. He'd already broken two pencils, and that had done nothing but cause Eloise to chastise him for being an "angry mountain," as she'd put it.

"I'm sorry, Coll," Miranda said, twiddling her teacup in her hands. "Caroline is five years ahead of me, and even more than that for Amy and Eloise. I simply don't know her well enough."

"She would have been considered on the shelf, to be unmarried at twenty-seven or twenty-eight," Amy put in. "More likely to attend recitals and book readings than soirees."

"She's had less than a day to vanish," Coll insisted.

"Nae a man or woman can do so that quickly and nae leave some sign behind them for a hunter to track."

"I did it that quickly," Temperance countered, her own cup of tea untouched. "It all depends on what she's willing to leave behind."

"She tried to kill ye for money. She's nae trying to leave anything behind. She's only hiding until we stop looking for her."

In the meantime, the woman could be more desperate than before. The easiest solution would have been to inform Lord and Lady Bayton that their daughter was alive and well, but Temperance didn't want to go anywhere near them—and he couldn't blame her for that.

"Now that you're suspicious of her, perhaps she'll realize it's too risky to attempt anything else." Eloise reached across the table to put her hand over Temperance's. "I wouldn't want us after me."

"The problem is, we dunnae ken where she's gotten to. Temperance, I dunnae want ye going out this door until we find her."

Immediately, she lifted her head, pinning him with her blue gaze. "I have a performance tonight, and every night for the next four weeks."

"But ye—"

"I am *not* missing that play," she said, her voice clipped. "Everyone at the Saint Genesius is relying on me. I don't even have an understudy."

Swearing, he slammed his fist against the tabletop. "I dunnae know how to protect ye, then!" he snapped.

"Just be there. I doubt she would dare make an attempt with all those eyes watching, anyway. Thus far, she—or whoever she's hired—has struck while I was more or less alone."

He didn't know if she was trying to convince him or herself, but he did understand it. Wherever she went, she would be in danger. Even at home, they couldn't guarantee someone wouldn't attempt to burn down Oswell House. Onstage, she would have hundreds of witnesses, at least, and relatively few entrances and exits to watch.

Logically, it was safer than anywhere but in his arms. That didn't mean he liked it. At all. As his father had said, though, the trouble with loving a strong, opinionated woman was that she had strong opinions, and wasn't timid about expressing them. "Fine. Ye perform. I'll be backstage, watching every bloody minute."

"And we'll be in the audience, keeping watch from there," his mother commented, strolling into the room. "This is your life, Temperance, and heaven knows you've earned the right to approach it as you choose. But please keep in mind that whether you decide to be known as Persephone or as Temperance, your last name will be Mac-Taggert."

"And her title will be Lady Glendarril," Coll put in. "Dunnae try yer guilt on her, my lady. Her parents did wrong by her. But she's nae the only one who can make such a statement."

Her lips thinned a little, but Francesca nodded. "That is true enough."

"A bit harsh, wasnae?" Niall asked, as their mother left the room.

"I'm done with agreements that serve someone else's purpose," Coll shot back. "And now I reckon we're off to the theater. I'll see ye there tonight, aye?"

"Aye," Aden said. "I'll bring ye someaught proper to wear."

"And in the meantime, we'll be making a few more inquiries about who might call Caroline Rilence a friend," Niall put in.

He would have to rely on them; he couldn't be everywhere at once, and he needed to be by Temperance's side.

Whether they thought she would be safer onstage or not, he wasn't only thinking about tonight. His mind was on all the other nights, for the rest of their lives. And he damned well wanted her in them.

The next few hours didn't leave him any less worried, though he was impressed that Charlie had taken pains to stage men at every exit who would ask for tickets or for audience members to confirm they were who they claimed to be. Even so, on a performance night, the theater was full of people back and front, actors and their friends or family, stagehands looking to impress a lass or two with an introduction to Gordon Humphreys or Thomas Baywich or Persephone Jones or Clive Montrose, who was far too pretty for Coll's liking.

They ran through the play once more, and for the first time, Humphreys even said the word "Macbeth" before he had to sit down and fan himself with his well-marked folio. It was a good performance—likely the best he'd seen, and he'd attended several throughout the Highlands. If he said so himself, Temperance's Lady Macbeth had never and likely would never be equaled—and that was the damned rehearsal.

A dull muttering that began on the far side of the curtains slowly grew in volume until he couldn't even hear himself think. "Is it always so loud?" he asked Temperance, watching Charlotte, a petite lass, finish pinning up the pitch-black hair Lady Macbeth would be sporting.

"On opening night, yes. Generally, no," she answered, eyeing herself in the dressing mirror before adding a touch more rouge to her cheeks. "Healthy at the beginning, pale at the end," she said aloud, sending him a quick smile.

A gong sounded from nearby. "Five minutes till curtain," rang out. Persephone stood. "Time for a prayer to the theater gods," she quipped, her humor at odds with the severe gray and burgundy gown she wore.

He straightened from where he leaned against the wall. "I'd like to kiss ye," he murmured, catching her hand to place it over his arm, "but I'll nae be blamed for ruining yer healthy bloom."

"You, my dear, are the reason for my healthy bloom. I hardly need the face paint." She twisted, leaning up along his chest, and slid one hand up to cup the nape of his neck. Her ruby-red lips met his, her kiss tasting of tea and desire.

Coll wrapped her in his arms and lifted her off her feet, deepening the kiss. Whoever the devil she dressed as and whatever name she went by, all that mattered was that she belonged to him, and he to her. "I love ye, lass," he murmured.

"I love you, Coll," she returned. "Now put me down."

He did so, though he would much rather have locked her dressing room door and peeled her out of those somber, dark clothes and replaced them with his mouth. She pulled a kerchief from a drawer and carefully wiped his mouth, then fixed her own.

"Good—"

Swiftly, she slapped a hand over his mouth. "Do *not* wish me good luck," she whispered. "That's the worst luck imaginable."

"Ye lot are all mad, ye ken," he whispered back, kissing her palm and transferring her hand to his forearm. "I'll nae wish ye ill."

"Say something in Gaelic that would make me swoon in English," she suggested, her gaze on his mouth.

"*Tha mi airson a bhith còmhla riut an-dràsta.*"

"That makes me want to swoon just hearing it," she said softly. "Tell me what it means after."

"Aye. That's a promise."

Coll left her on the stage with her fellows, while he hung back in the shadows, watching, as Charlie Huddle led them in a combination of prayer and witch's spell for success. That done, the actors went to their opening positions, and he found a place to stand where he could see both Temperance's dressing room and the stage.

The curtains parted to a resounding roar, and the three witches began their lines amid sounds of thunder generated by Harry Drew and his stagehands. As many times as he'd seen it rehearsed, his desire to watch the spectacle anew pulled at him. He sternly resisted. She might well be safer there onstage than anywhere else, but that didn't mean he would stop looking for trouble.

As each of the actors made a first appearance, the audience reacted with applause and cheers, though none so loud as the round awarded to Temperance. He had no idea what the blue bloods would think if they ever discovered they were clapping for one of their own, a lass who dared defy them and their proper ways, and did so with skill and flair.

The play was short for Shakespeare, and they'd decided to forego an intermission—at least for opening night. The three murderers killed Banquo in rather spectacular fashion, causing at least one lass out in the audience to shriek, and then someone apparently fainted when Banquo's ghost arrived at Macbeth's banquet, all dressed in gray strips of muslin and clanking a chain for effect.

"You don't think someone would attempt to do her harm here, do you?" a hushed voice came from beside him.

He turned to look. The pretty lad who Temperance said had been stolen from one of the other theaters, Clive Montrose—which sounded like another made-up name to him. "I'm nae willing to risk it," he said.

"You're a good man, my lord."

"I'm a cautious one."

"Speaking of which," Montrose went on, "I happened to notice someone carrying a heavy-looking sack a moment

ago. I don't recall a sack that heavy being needed for ar
thing, especially up in the scaffolding."

"Where?" Coll hissed, straightening. The damned ri
gings remained dark, though he could see men moving
in them, as they would be for the remainder of the play

"Here," Montrose whispered, and something hea
came down on the back of Coll's head.

A sharp ringing sounded in his ears, as though someo
was clanging a pot incessantly with a spoon. Coll open
his eyes to see . . . nothing. Frowning, he put his han
behind him and pushed—and smacked his head on som
thing before he could sit upright.

Trying to twist, he hit another wall, and another. *Chri*
All around him, walls and blackness. His breath car
in gasps, and he struck out over and over, unable to g
enough force behind the blows to budge anything.

A small space in the dark—his worst damned nigl
mare. And he . . . He was supposed to be doing som
thing. Something important.

Forcing his eyes shut, he stopped moving. The th
ater. *Macbeth*. Temperance. God, he was supposed to
watching over Temperance. Holding his breath, he l
tened. Faintly, he could hear Malcolm delivering the ne
to Macduff that his wife and children had been slain.
had only been a moment, then, that he'd been in here.

Lady Macbeth's final scene, the one she'd performed
the masked ball last night, would be next. Forcing hims
to breathe slowly, he reached out again. Wood. Planks.
crate, then—probably one of the ones they used to hou
the wooden swords, which would all be in the acto
hands now, because those boxes latched shut.

Turning over, he put his hands beneath him and push
himself up. Before his arms entirely straightened, his ba
hit the top of the crate. He gathered his legs beneath hi

crouched on all fours, and then shoved upward with all his strength. The wood cracked, but the crate remained closed.

Cursing but keeping his eyes closed so he wouldn't see how very small the space was, he lowered himself and then pushed again. The third time, the crate lid flew open and then came down again, nearly striking him in the back of the head. Catching it with one arm, he vaulted out of the box.

Montrose had left him in a tangle of unused sets and furniture. By the time he found his feet again, Temperance was onstage, wringing her hands. *Thank God.* He moved forward, wiping the blood dripping from his scalp.

Temperance paused in her speech, and the doctor and then the female attendant began their conversation— except the female attendant didn't sound like Jenny Rogers. Nor did she know her lines. Coll's blood froze.

Abruptly, the doctor stepped aside, and the attendant ran at Temperance. With a roar, Coll charged onto the stage, shoving the doctor—damned Clive Montrose—aside to get to her before she reached Temperance.

"Stop him!" he bellowed, jabbing a finger at Clive Montrose as he reached the black-clothed attendant and bodily lifted her off her feet.

Dimly, he thought he heard Aden answer him, and then blinked as the woman kicked him in the gut, swearing. When she swung a dagger at his face, he dropped her. "Get back, lass!" he ordered Temperance, ducking another swing.

He'd been raised not to strike a woman ever, and while he could have tackled her to the floor, he hesitated. When she turned back with a scream to face Temperance again, though, he grabbed her around the legs, tripping her.

Abruptly, the woman froze, and he looked up to see Temperance. Her severe black and purple skirts hiked on one side, she stood like a goddess of vengeance, the dagger he'd given her clutched in one hand and but an inch away from Caroline Rilence's face.

"You will stop," she commanded. "I am not some petty thing for you to toss aside like refuse in order to suit your own ambitions. I have dreams and desires of my own, and they do not include putting up with your jealousy."

"I'll tell them!" Caroline shrieked. "I'll tell them all!"

Temperance didn't budge. "No, I will tell them," she said coolly. "I am Persephone Jones. I am also Lady Temperance Hartwood, and you are on my stage. Get off. Now."

For an instant, everything became so silent that Coll could swear he heard his own pocket watch ticking. Then—the theater erupted.

In the chaos, Niall appeared beside him, grabbing hold of a squirming Caroline while Coll climbed to his feet.

The stage swarmed with people, some from backstage and still others from the audience. Wincing, Coll strode forward, flinging people aside until he reached Temperance. "Did she hurt ye?" he demanded.

Slowly, she lowered the dagger and handed it to him. "No. She hurt you, though." Reaching up, she touched his head, and her fingers came away bloody. "That's it. I'm killing her." Temperance reached for the dagger again.

He held it away from her. "Ye willnae. It was Clive Montrose who clubbed me over the head. I thought I'd nae get to ye in time. The—"

"Got him!" Aden and their father dragged Montrose onto the stage, his wardrobe torn and his face dirty and bruised.

"What is going on here?" Charlie Huddle demanded, his face white. "Persephone, I—who—what—"

"Get us some Bow Street Runners," Coll broke in, "and we'll tell the lot of ye. But away from this." He gestured toward the crowd behind them, a good third of the audience trying to reach the stage and a second third fleeing, while the last third simply stood and stared. "And one of ye find Jenny Rogers. She's likely in a crate somewhere backstage."

"Yes. Boys, clear the theater!" Huddle yelled, and the stagehands and actors hopped off the stage to begin herding people toward the doors at the theater's front. "Gordon— Lawrence—find Jenny."

"Very effective," Niall noted, eyeing the flood of people leaving the audience.

"We practice this in case of a fire," Huddle muttered, color beginning to return to his face. "I never . . . She tried to *kill* you, Persie."

"So did Clive," Coll added with a growl.

Huddle turned to look at where the actor stood between Aden and Angus with a defiant look on his face. Walking forward, the theater's manager faced him. "I wondered why you asked to join the Saint Genesius and then declined any part other than the most minor one in the play," he said, hands on his hips. Then, abruptly, he jabbed out with his fist, catching Montrose in the jaw. "Traitor."

Once a trio of Runners arrived, Coll and Temperance told her story, with a great deal of dramatic help from the scattering of actors remaining. They had to do it again when a judge walked onto the stage in the company of Lady Aldriss, and by then it had practically taken on a life of its own.

Finally, in the wee hours of the morning, Coll took Temperance's hand in his. "Let's get ye home, my lass."

She leaned against his shoulder. "If my parents weren't here, they'll certainly have heard the tale by morning," she said, her voice thin.

"They were here," Eloise said, taking Temperance's

other hand as they walked toward the rear of the stage. "I saw them. I think they were swept out with the rest of the audience."

"Sleep first. Then we'll settle with them," he said. He disliked seeing her look so fragile.

"Yes. Sleep first."

She fell asleep in the coach before they'd even started moving. Coll carried her upstairs to her bedchamber, locked the door on all offers of assistance, undressed her himself, and covered her in soft blankets before he stripped out of his clothes and joined her. After tonight, he didn't much care who knew what. All that mattered was that he wasn't going to bed or waking up without her by his side ever again.

Chapter Twenty

"O Scotland, Scotland!"

MACDUFF, *MACBETH* ACT IV, SCENE III

We want to see our daughter," Lady Bayton insisted, a handkerchief going to the corner of her eye again. "We haven't set eyes on our darling in eight years, Lady Aldriss."

Francesca glanced at Coll, who nodded. He'd seen enough to assess precisely who the Marquis and Marchioness of Bayton were, and to be perfectly satisfied that Temperance had described them accurately.

"Very well," the countess said. "If you don't mind, Coll?"

He pushed to his feet and walked to the library door. Temperance stood in the hallway, bouncing on the balls of her feet as she did before she began a performance. "I'll still happily throw ye over my shoulder and ride with ye to the Highlands," he suggested quietly.

"No. I made my identity public to make me—and everyone else—safe from any more plotting. This needs to be done. I need to do this."

She nudged him sideways and walked past him into the Oswell House library. Her parents both shot to their feet, coming toward her until she put up a hand.

"Do not," she said calmly. "I only agreed to see you to tell you what I wish I'd had the strength to do eight years

ago. I do not want your money. I do not yearn for a title or a
lord with influence. I do not intend to manipulate any said
lord into gaining more power or influence. What I am going
to do is marry Coll MacTaggert, Lord Glendarril. And I
am going to continue performing onstage for at least the
remainder of this Season and through the next, because I
have a signed contract saying that I will. I do not care if
you're ashamed of me or mortified that your own reputa-
tions will be damaged. I thank you for keeping me fed
and clothed, and for paying for my education. And that is
all I have to say to you."

Her words were measured and calm. Coll was damned
proud of her. When the one hand she held behind her
back waved at him frantically, he took a step forward and
grasped it, squeezing her fingers gently.

"But you are our daughter," her mother countered.
"There are familial obligations, and promises that have
been made, not to mention the . . . upset you have caused
us. Eight years, Temperance! And now we find you on a
stage? Acting? It's enough to overset a saint."

"According to the newspaper," her father took up, "your
home was burned. Certainly, we can help you rebuild, after
which we can speak again about your future. You're no
longer a debutante, after all, but I believe we can do better
than a viscount from Scotland. The—"

"Who the devil are these powdery daisies?" Lord Aldriss demanded, walking into the room. "Did I hear them
insult my son and heir? Do ye ken what we do in Scotland
when a man insults another man in his own house? We
feed him to our dogs! And in Scotland, we have bloody
big dogs—big as sheep, they are. Damn ye, whoever ye
are, and get out of my house before I put a boot in yer
arse!"

"What my husband is saying," Lady Aldriss took up,
"is that your daughter has stated her intention to marry our

son and has quite plainly informed you that she no longer wishes to be part of your lives. I therefore suggest you go, before you do find a Scottish boot in your arse."

Like all Sassenachs, they had a fine talent for words and arguments and contracts and agreements. Threats of physical violence, though, wound them up like tops and sent them reeling. Still stammering their indignation, they allowed Smythe to usher them out the front door.

"Well, that was something," Francesca said faintly. "Dogs as big as sheep?"

"Och," her husband grunted. "They're gone, are they nae?"

"Yes, they are."

"Aye, they are," Coll agreed, tugging on the hand that Temperance still squeezed.

Rather than releasing him, she turned to look up at his face. "They're gone."

"Aye."

"I'm free."

"Aye."

"Did I hear the gong? I believe breakfast is set out," Lady Aldriss said, gesturing none-too-subtly at the earl.

A moment later, Coll and Temperance had the library to themselves. "What are ye thinking?" he asked her. The idea that she was free sounded pleasant, but it also seemed to mean she had no entanglements, and he didn't much like that. *He* was an entanglement, after all.

"I'm thinking you should lock the door," she whispered, cupping his cheek in her hand.

"Ye dunnae need to tell me that more than once."

He locked all three doors that led into the library from various parts of the house, then returned to take her in his arms. Lifting her, he carried Temperance over to the deep couch and settled there with her on his lap.

"Will they expect us for breakfast?" she asked, pulling

his shirt from his kilt and sliding her warm hand up along his chest.

"Aye. Everybody'll be there."

"Then we shouldn't be late. Too late."

"I can see to that, as long as ye dunnae hold it against me later."

Temperance laughed. "Out, out, brief candle."

Coll narrowed his eyes, unable to stop his grin. "Oh, stop that right there."

Shifting, he set her on her knees to lift her pretty borrowed yellow and red muslin up over her hips, then shoved his kilt aside. The sight of her dismissing her parents like a queen had already aroused him, and with her kissing him like that and squirming about on his lap now, he was damned ready for her.

"Come here, lass."

She sank down over him, moaning as she took him in. When she put her hands on his shoulders and began bouncing, Coll grabbed hold of her hips, thrusting up to meet her. This was what mattered: the two of them, together. Not where they lived or whether she spent her nights on a stage for a few months of the year. Hell, he'd go see her every night.

"Coll," she rasped, arching her back, clinging to him as she came.

He let himself go over with her, filling her as he pushed hard inside her. "Temperance Hartwood," he breathed, when he could speak again. "Temperance MacTaggert."

She smiled a bit breathlessly. "I love you, Coll. Just you being with me, it makes me . . . more than I was. I don't know how to say it, but I . . . I never thought I would be this happy."

"That sounded fine to me. *Tha mi airson a bhith còmhla riut an-dràsta*," he said for the second time.

"Now tell me what it means," she breathed, kissing him again.

"It means 'I want to be with ye right now,'" he translated. "*An-còmhnaidh*. That means 'always.'"

"*An-còmhnaidh*," she repeated, her accent startlingly good. "It's what I want, as well."

"M'laird? Breakfast is served," Smythe's voice came, muffled through the door. "Lady Aldriss has requested your presence."

"Of course she has."

"She helped us, Coll. And she accepted me even before she knew I wasn't Persephone Jones."

Aye, she had. And she'd told him some things that bore thinking about—and a few questions he wanted his father to answer. If he'd discovered one thing through falling for Temperance, it was that when two strong people met, one of them had to bend. And bending didn't mean losing. It only meant finding a different path.

"Let's find some food, then," he drawled, helping her to her feet and settling the skirt back around her ankles.

When they reached the breakfast room, though, neither of his parents were inside. The rest of the family, though, stood huddled about the countess's carefully ironed edition of the *London Times*.

"Did you see this?" Eloise asked, shaking the newspaper. "'The audience could only sit, transfixed, while Lady Aldriss's box spewed Scotsmen over the side and another Highlander, Lord Glendarril himself, charged onto the stage, kilt akimbo, to fling actors about like chess pieces.'"

"I barely flung anyone," Coll retorted. "I shoved Montrose aside, mayhap."

"Hush. 'And then the Queen of Scotland revealed herself to be not one Mrs. Persephone Jones, but Lady Temperance Hartwood! This witness was heartily entranced

by the magnificence of it all. The only shame was that
Macbeth was prevented from uttering his famed closing
soliloquy. Perhaps, though, tomorrow.'"

"We were magnificent," Niall echoed with a loose grin.
"I wouldnae say we spewed from the box, but Aden and I
did vault over the side. I nearly landed on Lady Darling-
ton's hat."

"I am so sorry I ever had a single uncharitable thought
about you, Temperance," Eloise said, setting aside the
paper to throw her arms around Coll's betrothed. "My
brothers spent the evening vaulting over things while wearing kilts, and I've already been invited to two additional
parties this morning."

"Just ye keep in mind we're nae going to be so acro-
batic every time we go somewhere," Aden cautioned,
laughing.

"I've been thinking," Coll's sister went on. "You could
marry at the same ceremony with Matthew and me, Coll.
As long as you say your 'I do's' first, the agreement will
have been honored."

He flung some food on a pair of plates and sat beside
his sister, his lass on his other side. "I dunnae—"

"We wouldn't dream of it," Temperance answered before he could. "That is *your* day. And for heaven's sake,
you've had the longest engagement I can remember."

"We had to make it long enough to give my brothers
a chance to find English wives and marry," his sister returned with a cheeky grin. "In return, I've been promised
a grand wedding ball, so I am appeased."

"I'm marrying Temperance as soon as I can ride down
to Canterbury and back," Coll put in. "Tonight, more than
likely."

Lady Aldriss walked into the room. "Weddings are
generally performed on Saturdays."

"Nae mine."

Temperance cleared her throat. "Charlie's put off tonight's performance so he can find someone to learn Clive's lines," she said, her gaze on Coll. "So . . . I'm available."

Lady Aldriss sighed. "I'll send word to Father Thomas, then." She put her hands behind her back, then around to the front, twisting them a bit. Something was biting at her.

"What did ye want to tell us?" he prompted.

"Yes, that." She took another breath. "Forgive the timing, but your father has something to say to all of you."

With a heavy-looking wooden box in his hands, Angus MacTaggert followed her into the breakfast room. "Lads, I did what I did so ye'd grow up strong and independent and nae willing to bow to any lass and her opinions," he said without preamble.

The countess cleared her throat.

"That being said," he went on, "I reckon I overreacted to yer *màthair* leaving us behind. The letters ye wrote her, begging her to return, I didnae send them on to her." Opening the box, he removed a stack of letters bound with twine, and set them on the table.

Coll scowled. She'd said as much, but he hadn't quite believed her. Or rather, he'd preferred to believe the version with which he'd grown up—that she had a cold heart and had happily left them all behind, never to return. "Ye lied to us."

"Aye, I did. For yer own good. Or so I reckoned." The earl drummed his fingers on the lid of the wooden box. "And she sent ye a letter or two, and I didnae pass them on to ye, for the same reasons."

"'A letter or two?'" Lady Aldriss quoted, lifting an eyebrow, her arms folded across her chest.

"Bah." Lifting up the box, he dumped out its contents. Letters fell to the table. A hundred, if not more, covered the surface and spilled to the floor. "There. It was me and my damned pride. Make of it what ye will. I'm nae going to apologize for making ye grow up to be who ye are, three lads of whom any man would be proud." With that, he put the box beneath his arm, turned on his heel, and left the room.

Aden leaned out of his chair to pick up a letter from the floor beside him. "Niall, this one's for ye," he said, flipping it at their youngest brother, who caught it against his chest.

"Those letters don't excuse one thing," Francesca said quietly, lowering her arms again. "I waited for your father to invite me to return, to visit you—or better yet, to announce that he couldn't manage raising the three of you and that he needed me back. I should simply have gone. I should have gone to see my sons, and I didn't, because as proud as Angus is, I am just as guilty." She gestured at the sliding stack of correspondence. "As your father said, make of this what you will. I just wanted you to know that for all those years we were apart, I did—and I do—love you. All four of you, all seven of you, all soon-to-be eight of you."

A tear rolled down Temperance's cheek as the countess slipped out of the room again, closing the door behind her. The servants had all exited as well, no doubt at one of her secret signals. All the lasses, in fact, had begun weeping. Coll pushed back his chair.

"I reckon the lesson at the end of all this," he said slowly, knowing his brothers would follow his lead, "is that all of us have managed to find someone to love us, mad as we are. I'll take that with me, along with the promise that my own bairns willnae grow up with two parents too stubborn to find the center of the argument, that being the fact that they love each other."

Temperance stood up beside him. "You are a good man,

Coll," she said quietly, going up on her toes to kiss him on the cheek. "I am lucky to have found you."

"I reckon he found ye when he was running away from two other lasses," Aden said, not bothering to hide his grin.

"Dunnae step on my moment," Coll retorted, taking Temperance—his stubborn, smart, beautiful lass—around the waist and kissing her.

"Speaking of moments," Niall said, pushing to his feet, "I think I should tell ye that Amy and I are—"

"Nae," Coll interrupted, grinning. "*My* moment. Our moment." Lifting Temperance in the air, he looked up at her as she chuckled breathlessly, her hands on his shoulders for balance. "I love ye, lass."

"*An-còmhnaidh*," she returned, smiling down at him, tears in her sky-blue eyes. "Always."